PROVENANCE

John Delacourt

AOS Publishing 2022

ISBN: 978-1-990496-10-3

Visit AOS Publishing's website:
www.aospublishing.com

1.

Mr. Lorenzo Verzaro,
Director, Art Crimes Unit (Milan)
INTERPOL NCB
October 22nd, 1993

Dear Lorenzo,

Thank you for your patience as I gradually put together this report on the case regarding the recovery of artworks from the estate of Harry Maes. I realize this has been close to two years of work now, and I miss our conversations in person. I hope you come to Rome again soon. I cannot see myself coming to Milan, unfortunately. There is so much to sift through as I try to figure out what is true and what is false from my interviews. But I will send you reports on those in a separate note.

I suppose we both should not be surprised by the complex nature of this effort in recovery and reclamation. I remember one of the first meetings you convened for the art crimes unit, when you told us there would be a lot to investigate after the Berlin Wall came down. It would follow that many works of art would come up for auction that were once thought lost or destroyed. They would be made public as, say, paintings kept in the attic, 'forgotten' treasures bequeathed on the death beds of those who'd made it through the war on the other side. I remember my own skepticism when you remarked that all of us in the unit would be very busy because most of this work would turn out to be art that once belonged to families murdered by the Nazis, not, as one auction house phrased it, 'treasured heirlooms.'

I think my doubts were rooted in my first principles as an investigator, in my belief that, despite the nature of these crimes, it was that much more important to presume innocence. I believed that a suspect doesn't walk into an auction house for an appraisal of a painting that has no documentation of provenance and thinks that she's getting away with something. More often than not she is unsure of the work's value, genuinely curious and hopeful that what she has found or inherited might be worth more than what she originally thought.

And usually you can tell otherwise. We both know most people are terrible liars, compelled to falsify information because difficult circumstances have driven them to deceive. Desperate measures. The fear of sudden destitution, the shame, the loss of dignity. It can be greater than the fear of being arrested for a crime that many would say is victimless, and many could plausibly deny.

As you've said, context remains important. I'm not saying it explains everything, but I'm sure you'd agree it remains helpful in determining motivation. At least from my memories of those first months after Yeltsin took over in Russia, there was more than enough desperation to go around, given how it had all fallen apart on the other side. The appearance of a Silvia Stanciu, Romanian-born, naturalized citizen, in the offices of Phillips auction house in Berlin almost two years ago to this day, could have almost been expected. This is how it all started for me: she had in her possession a painting by Egon Schiele: one of the artist's many self-portraits.

I found out about this particular case because you'll remember we had just begun creating the database for stolen work in our offices here in Rome. I started working closely with the auction houses that had branches in cities like Budapest, Prague and Moscow to take advantage of these markets in what we called 'the newly liberated economies.' It's different now but back then many of the more dubious transactions were taking place in Paris, Amsterdam, Berlin and Rome because this is where the thieves presumed they'd find the highest bidders for stolen work.

The staff at Phillips in Berlin were particularly sharp-eyed. You would think it would only be in their interest to be so, given the damage to any auction house's reputation that trafficking in stolen goods might cause. Yet this is not normally the case, I discovered, to my surprise. We were all so naive at the beginning of this—or maybe I should only speak for myself.

Provenance

So. How it started: word about the Schiele, along with photos of the work, came to me via fax, addressed 'Urgent for Ms. Christina Perretti.' The staff had taken Stanciu's contact information along with the photographs of the Schiele and told her to please return with the painting in a few days once they had done their due diligence, and that they would call her. But she never did return and the phone number she gave them turned out to be false.

And that's all I had to begin with. Suffice to say that after Silvia Stanciu disappeared with her Schiele painting, I got down to work. What I could tell, from the photographs, was a small seal that said 'Reichskulturkammer.' Yet another one of these new finds of ours from the Nazi era: 'raubkunst.'

I began to imagine how this particular story would end. Silvia Stanciu was going to attempt to sell the Schiele somewhere else and we could recover it as stolen property. And we would be able to arrest her, find out more about this case, where she found this work. But then, just four weeks later, she was stabbed on the street, allegedly the result of a confrontation between her and a Romany woman, begging near Zoo Station. Silvia would take her secrets about the painting to the grave, it seemed.

However, through Silvia Stanciu's credit card receipts, we were able to track down where Stanciu sold the Schiele. Moscow, of all places. Why would she travel all that way? What an interesting woman, yes?

There would be no way to reclaim the painting now. Possession nine-tenths of the law, as the Americans say. The Russian police weren't about to co-operate. Whoever Silvia sold the painting to in Moscow had enough power and influence to close such a case.

It was just this summer when the painting showed up again. The new unit, focused on criminal syndicates, shared a file on the assassination of Gennady Popov. This man was a former KGB officer who had become an instant millionaire and had run afoul of the Vory, the Russian mafia. The Schiele was hanging in a well-lit room in his dacha, two hours outside of Moscow. In the photo I saw there were blood stains on the wallpaper but mercifully none on the painting.

But they had more than that file to share. There was a false back to the painting, and once removed, the Russian police unit discovered this tranche of papers, which are ostensibly notes on the provenance for a number of paintings in the former art dealer Harry Maes' possession. He had passed away in Berlin just months before the Wall came down. As I began to read through each section, devoted to a particular painting, I realized he was addressing a son—Nikolaus Maes—whom we are currently making efforts to track down (there are, at last count, eighteen individuals with that name, in locations as varied and far afield as Ostend, Sydney, and Jakarta). Harry Maes had intended to bequeath his estate to him. There was additional mention of Maes' first wife, the daughter of a Benjamin Ostriker. But we're having difficulty finding any record of one Sabine—"Sally" Ostriker, who may have taken on the surname of Cluny. It is thought she may have died just before Berlin was taken by the Allied Forces.

So there was clearly more to all of this that would merit a deeper investigation. I felt Silvia Stanciu would be my way into this story. And she has not disappointed, despite her mysterious journey with the Schiele painting to Moscow and her untimely death. I hope to send you my full report on her soon, along with my leads on where we might find the other paintings Maes mentioned. It seems that at last I am starting to make progress.

In the meantime, as promised, please find, with this fax, a full copy of Harry Maes' notes of provenance, just translated by our German colleagues in Bonn.

Sincerely,
Lt. Christina Perretti
Art Crimes Unit (Rome)
Interpol NCB

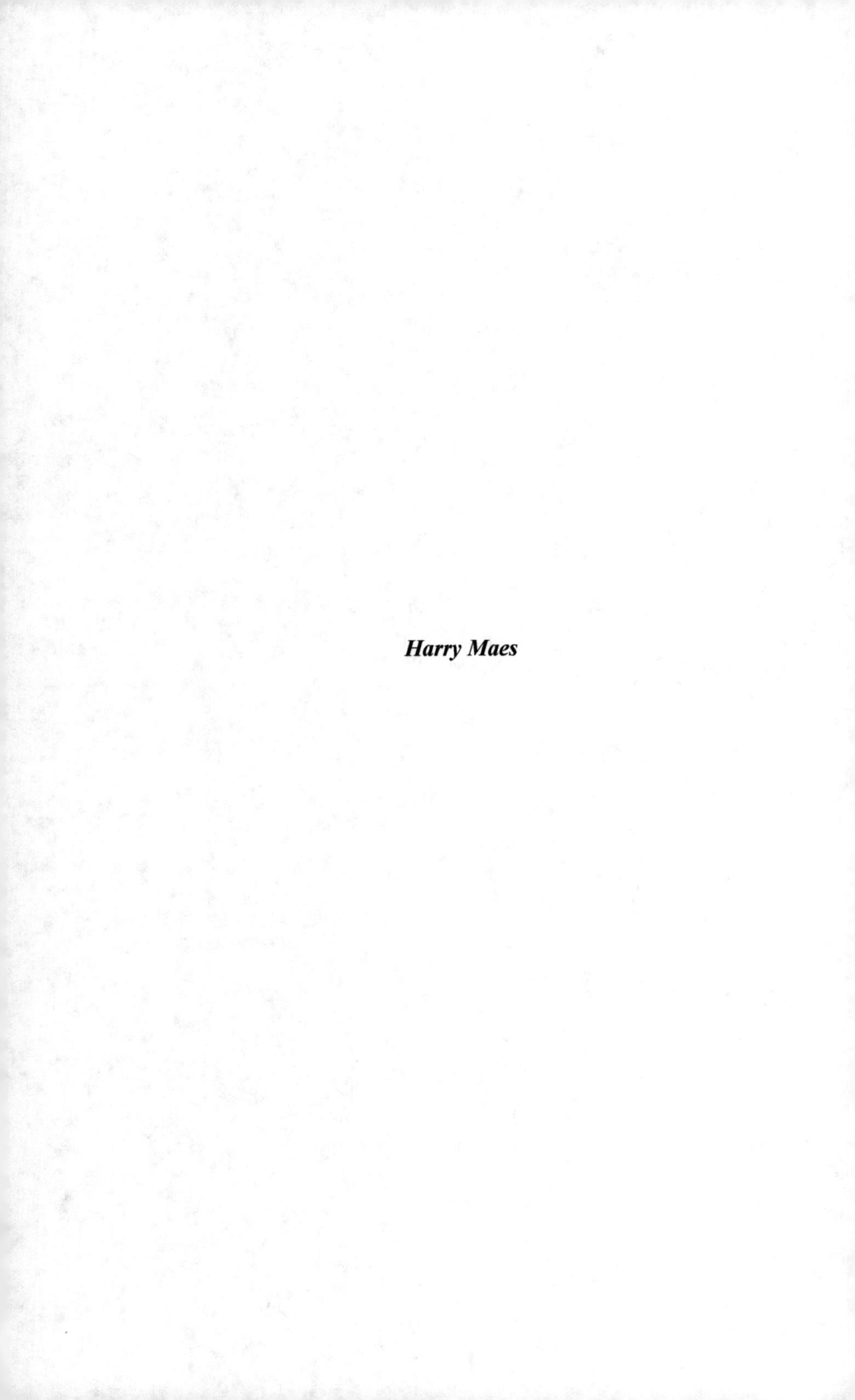

Harry Maes

2.

03 / 22 / 89

Dance of Death Bridge Panels (Kaspar Meglinger, c. 1635)

I write this for you, Nikolaus, the son I haven't spoken to or seen for close to fifty years. I could say I'm writing to a stranger but of course that could never be the case, I'll always feel like a part of me – and a part of you – are still as close as we once were decades ago.

This is not my first effort at writing to you, however. I'm hoping Mr. L., the gentleman who tells me he has all these important contacts on the other side, truly has provided you with my earlier efforts: the birthday notes, the Christmas cards. But who knows? As I think about Mr. L and Mr. K, these new friends of mine, I think to myself can you ever really trust anyone? I hope it's still possible and that you receive that first batch.

These notes before you are for the paintings that came to mean something to me. They "signified," as we used to say, back in those earnest student days when your father was at a place called the Staatliches Bauhaus. Some I have bequeathed to you, now that there is, for the first time in decades, the possibility that this horrible city where I live might open up to the world once again. I want you to understand the person I once was, the business I was in. But in saying this I don't expect to be forgiven. I just have this stubborn belief that telling the truth is not entirely futile, despite evidence to the contrary. With a greater understanding of who I was, you might have a greater understanding of yourself. I hope this is the most valuable gift I can give you, from all of the paintings I have in this room with me.

But I must start with a painting that is not in my possession:

John Delacourt

Seven skeletons dancing in a circle on fallow ground, with just the faintest outline of a foothill in the distance. A few shreds of diaphanous cloth, dyed in scarlet and emerald, drape across their capering figures; three of them have tied these scraps around their skulls. Dark, comic adornment, the fetching beauty of a skull with blackened, hollowed-out eye sockets. The central figure blows a bugle stolen from the angel Gabriel, with long strands of ribbon tied in a loose bow along its shaft. The ribbon traces out a figure in the air that arcs, dips and curlicues. It's a flourish of noise and maybe that's the point; a cacophony is a symphony for the damned. These figures seem content to ape its broken rhythm in their jerky movements, the disharmony of their gestures and their brandishing of a collection of remnants from some Arcadian field of battle: spade, scythe, pan flute, arrow, and a triangle that wouldn't look out of place if it were held up by a tuxedoed member of some local orchestra rather than the shade intent on banging out some note in time with the bugle's quavering blare. It's a riddle of a painting, speaking in a language of symbols that might have struck its first viewers with all the force of a revelation. What time erases... nothing's revealed now but the strangeness, the frustrating obscurity of the past.

I wrote this on June 29th, 1939. Almost fifty years ago, I realize. This was shortly after I had discovered this work of art in Lucerne, when I was out walking before dinner. It was on a triangular panel of the Chapel Bridge that crossed the Reuss. I was drawn to the river because the air was so fresh and cool. I had arrived earlier that afternoon from Berlin, fleeing the long, punishing days of a heatwave, the cramped apartment where your mother and I were raising you, still a toddler then. Things were not going well with our marriage, and during the earlier months of that year I had avoided responsibility at home by working late. But that had changed with the heatwave. In every cluttered room of the offices of Galerie Hyperion there was a rattling, humming fan that offered no relief, curtains smelling like your grandmother's old dresses in her closet. I had never felt compelled to walk along the Spree the way the Reuss lured me, there in Lucerne. No, in Berlin the river seemed a clotted artery, ancient and flowing with blackened blood, full of centuries of decay (it seems only worse to me now). The Reuss was clean, fed from a mountain spring, the water dappled, flashing shades of emerald as it pooled in the shallows and then slowed, darkening where it was deeper in the distance. From that Chapel Bridge I could make out a line of rocky peaks above a veil of cloud. Back in my hotel the clerk had told me of a route that snaked through the forest up Pilatus. I resolved to hike it before I left. No wonder the burghers felt compelled to remind the locals of their mortality with The Dance of the Dead there on that bridge; here was real life, you could feel ageless in the mountain air.

I had resolved to come back to view this work after the art auction I was covering. Take it all in once more, imprint it in my mind. The best of intentions. Nothing was quite the same after the auction.

I headed back to the Grand National Hotel the evening before the auction to see if I could get a glimpse of the work on display. As I approached, a grey Bugatti pulled up to the front entrance, and emerging from it was a couple that looked as wealthy as royalty on a newsreel. From the driver's side came a portly, dark-eyed little man in a tennis cardigan, buttons straining to pop around his belly. From the passenger side emerged a woman who could have been his daughter. Her shoulders were bare but for two spaghetti-thin straps. Her arms and shoulders were tanned and glowing, her curls cut in a bob to reveal the almost-pretty profile of that kind of woman who always married well and always averted her gaze, as if repelled, from young, clerkish men like me, back in Berlin.

What I could not deny, despite my sense of how petty such feelings were, was my jealousy and resentment. What did those people have that I was not capable of having? I had come to my art studies with a sense of piety and seriousness, the legacy of your grandfather the Protestant minister, back in Antwerp. I had failed at banking, but what foreigner wouldn't in Berlin in the thirties? And I had told myself it was God's punishment for my betrayal of my true vocation. After a year of courses at the Staatliches Bauhaus (where your mother and I discovered we had mutual friends among a rum bunch of theatre people the painters ran with), I decided architecture was not for me, that I would make my way as a gallerist by being an honest broker, scorning pretension, and Magda Petofi, who had taken me in at Galerie Hyperion, encouraged me in my rejection of a certain decadence she so willingly embraced.

I think she saw me as the son she never had. She even played matchmaker with me and your mother, whom she introduced as "a nice Jewish girl from Hamburg, working in theatre. She has a bright future, Harry." Impressionable as I was, I spent too much on silk neckties and English shoes, because they showed I was making enough money to mix with our clientele. (I wasn't.)

Pastor Maes, your Belgian grandfather, frowned on this. He said that as soon as a man tried to ape the gentry, he was lost. In his eyes I would grow old as a fraud and a dandy. Which makes me laugh now, when I think of the old tramp of a man I have become, here in this concrete parody of the Berlin I remember.

Anyway, despite such advice, looking at this couple I was stubborn enough to trust my sense of envy. A love of money and fine clothes did not tarnish the reputations of the artists who were selling out in Paris, nor their dealers and gallerists. Luxury did not seem to corrupt; there was greater evidence of poverty corroding the spirit, given the hard years we'd been living through in Berlin.

As I entered the lobby of the hotel, I remember taking in the thick perfume of orchids in midsummer. They were arranged in a crystal vase at the concierge's desk. I walked along the plush, blood red carpet that led into a lounge lit by the warm glow of gas lamps in pearl-white globes atop tall, iron lamps. This whole area had become crowded with those the Galerie Fischer invited for this auction. Many different kinds of tobacco smoke... Virginian, Turkish, the thick fug of Cuban cigar... were intermingling, thickening, so different from the cheap cigarette cloud of the cafes in Kreuzberg back home. So maybe it was true what Magda Petofi had told me before I left; they were coming from all over Europe to snap up the paintings the art dealer Theodor Fischer would be displaying and auctioning, and not many Berlin dealers would risk trying to outbid those from Paris or Rome.

Save for my boss Magda. But she was clear that my purchases for her would be "a rescue mission." What an unlikely saviour I made.

There was a long line to check in, and everyone working in the hotel was occupied with the wave of guests arriving, so I began looking for some information on the auction by the concierge's desk. It was then I heard a woman's voice behind me, asking if I spoke German.

I turned and recognized her as the same one who emerged from the Bugatti. Her German had a harsh accent I couldn't place. Maybe Silesian? She fixed her gaze on me, unblinking, as if my answer would be somehow more meaningful than simple directions. Up close she had the big blue eyes of a film star. She asked me if I knew where the dining room was.

As I began to apologize, explaining I was not a guest, the portly, older man in tennis whites approached, shaking his head in exasperation. He moved on his toes with surprising grace, given his girth. He said he was frustrated with the porter he had tipped, he could not understand his German. We shook hands, and when I told him my name was Harry, he switched to English.

"You're American?"

"No, sir. Harry Maes. I'm from Antwerp originally but now I'm working in Berlin. I'm here for the auction tomorrow."

"Ah. A Belgian. You have that American look about you though. Doesn't he, Dagmara? You look so much like Lindbergh."

She studied me carefully, looking so deeply into my eyes I had to look away. Then she nodded in agreement. "Yes, you're right, Connie. I can see the resemblance."

"I'm Connie Vidler. Vidler's Auctioneers. This is my wife, Dagmara. I don't speak much German anymore. I am based in London now, though we keep an office in Zurich."

I mentioned my summer course in Dorset while working for Lloyd's, and he complimented me on my pronunciation. We agreed that English was the language of money.

"We're trying to find the dining room, Mr. Maes. Care to join us for dinner?"

And so I just fell in with them. Connie made me feel like it was an obligation. "Best find a table soon, no? So many will be coming for tomorrow. It's like the Camino. We're as grubby as all those Spanish pilgrims." He laughed to himself.

Dagmara paid him no mind. Her heels made sharp clicks on the polished floor as she walked two paces ahead of him. How quick and strong her stride was for such a fine boned slip of a woman.

"Ah! Here we are. So we will not starve after all." The corridor opened up to a long, glass box of a room filled with the late afternoon light of the mountain valley. The silverware on each empty table seemed to glow, the symmetry of their placement on each table so precise on starched white linen.

All this austere elegance seemed fit for a rite of greater significance than the act of dining. My new friend Connie moved towards the maitre d'hotel who was bent over a small trolley with a coffee urn and a collection of cups and saucers on its tray. I asked if they were open for dinner.

The maitre d'hotel looked up. He had caterpillar eyebrows, dyed black—a shade darker than his hair. My first thought was that the dye job betrayed the vanity of a thoroughly conventional man in a spotless white jacket and black bowtie. "I'm sorry sir. This is the breakfast room. We have just finished…"

Connie pressed a small wad of pinkish banknotes in his hand. "It would make a great difference to us if you would be able to serve us a late lunch here. We have been traveling for most of the day and are very hungry, sir."

The maitre d'hotel looked down at the banknotes, moved his lips as he counted them up and then stuffed them in his pocket with a furtive glance out the window—even though there seemed nothing out that window but empty blue sky. The way he counted the money in his hands said something else about his dyed hair; he was probably in danger of being let go from his work because of his age and living in fear of never finding anything again. For close to a decade since the crash there were enough tramps in Berlin who might have once been headwaiters; why would it be any different here in Lucerne?

"How many of you are there?"

"There's my wife and I and this fine young gentleman Harry Lindbergh. Yes, the very same Lindbergh, my friend."

I looked over at Dagmara. A smile was forming at the corners of her mouth.

The waiter looked at me as if he couldn't quite figure out why my name would be significant in any way. And then he turned to Connie, exhaling with the smallest of sighs. "I could only serve you omelettes or sandwiches, sir. Will that suffice for your party?"

"You have champagne? Good champagne?"

"Yes of course, sir."

"Then all will be well. Your omelettes will do."

Dagmara turned to Connie after the waiter had sat us at a table with a view of the mountain valley. She watched him walk away with a look of tenderness. "Connie, the poor man hasn't started work for the evening."

"You think we are exploiting him? My wife is our favourite Bolshevik, isn't that right, dear? This is why I end up tipping so much when I am here on the continent."

"Don't be ridiculous," she said. "You would expect a tip, also, would you not, if you were him?"

"At the very least, dear. At the very least. So come Harry Maes, you worked for Lloyd's. You're a banker?"

Perhaps I could have told him about my failure, my breakdown, my year at home back in Antwerp before becoming a student in Berlin again, when I thought I was going to enter the church. I was ashamed of all that, though. I thought all my confusion and sadness betrayed a lack of character. So I lied and said I was offered a job in Berlin and, through some friends, realized there was money to be made in art. I conveniently skipped over your mother and you back home in our stifling apartment. I put my right hand over my left, awkwardly concealing my ring finger. With the most casual air I said I was just an emissary for a small Berlin gallery, looking for some bargains.

"Ah! That's fortuitous. Here's my card." Connie dug into the front pocket of his trousers and pulled out a slim, silver case that contained a small stack of them, gilt-edged. "I deal mostly in antiquities but I have, as they say, ba-ranched out into fine art. So here we are. One has to follow the market, yes?"

"Do you believe there still is a market for the work Fischer's auctioning?"

"Oh, there's always a market. You just have to know how to buy low and sell high, my friend. As with anything else."

"Connie likes to believe he is more connoisseur than businessman," said Dagmara. She spoke with a low, smoky drawl. "Until he starts to talk money, and then the philistine comes out."

I did not want to laugh and risk insulting my host, yet I also did not want to fall out of favour with Dagmara. So I just looked to Connie, as if to ask him whether she were sincere.

He rolled his eyes, leaned over and patted her hand. "A little philistinism is good for the jewelry box though, no, my darling?"

Before she could respond I thought it best to change the subject. Out of my nervousness, all I could think to babble on about was my appetite. It was true that I ate like a bird most days back in Berlin, but now I was starving again, despite a big lunch of cutlet and potatoes on the train. I put it down to the walk in this mountain air.

"It's the magic mountain, Mr. Maes." Dagmara looked to Connie as she unfolded her white linen napkin and placed it on her lap. "Maybe you're our Hans Castorp."

"That would be inconvenient. I can't stay here for years, I have to be back in Berlin the day after tomorrow."

Dagmara nodded and allowed herself more of a smile. "I love that novel. Don't you, sir?"

"I do, yes."

I wonder, Nikolaus, if I can write to you of such intimacies? I have no idea if you ever married, or even if you prefer women to men. My contact—who Silvia advises me to conceal, to protect him in case these notes reach someone else before you—has only told me you work in the foreign service. He hasn't even spoken of where you live. Even mentioning a novel like Mann's *Magic Mountain* presumes that what once mattered from the culture that's been ground to dust and papered over with Soviet kitsch here still matters on your side. These notes might all be a form of wishful thinking, like firing Gould's recordings of Bach's *Goldberg Variations* into space (Is it true they did that? Our news service is not always to be trusted). I doubt that my notes will have anything close to that profundity but I can at least attempt to give you the most unvarnished of memoirs. The body holds memories better than the mind.

I remember I was aware of an acute hunger, one that wintered and hardly stirred within me but it found reason to come awake when I took in the long curve of her neck, her silhouette in the loose, diaphanous white linen of her dress.

"You seem quite sensitive and cultured, Mr. Maes," she said. "Aren't you a little concerned about this auction?"

"Concerned?"

"Isn't it obvious? This is an auction for the German government. Fischer, this auctioneer, he's just doing their bidding."

"I am here for Mrs. Magda Petofi. She owns Galerie Hyperion. She is my employer and a friend of many of the artists of this work. I am here out of principle, I guess you'd say."

"Principle? Many of these works were in private hands and then seized or sold for a fraction of what they're worth by those who have been forced to leave Germany. Fischer doesn't want to mention that."

Connie scoffed, took a deep swallow from the glass of water in front of him. "Dagmara, is that what the gutter press is writing, parroting the Bolsheviks? There is no evidence of this."

"Evidence by omission. I'm speaking of the register for provenance."

"That is neither international nor official."

"Connie, you know yourself. The fact is there are questions."

"Dagmara, darling…" He raised his hand as if to pet her, calm her down. He flashed a small, gold antique signet ring on the smallest of his stubby fingers. "The fact is the great majority of these paintings, from my recollection, were hanging in small provincial galleries. They were government property to begin with."

A tall blonde waiter approached, as if gliding on ice skates, with a large tray bearing the omelettes and little bowls of summer greens. "Ah, thank you," said Vidler, with a quick analytical scan of the waiter's hands and slender wrists. As he forked in his first morsel of the omelette, he nodded in approval. He was in a place of luxury and familiarity; the only inelegance to bear would be from the turn this conversation had taken. "What do you think, Mr. Maes? Surely a government has the right to decide what hangs on the walls of a government building. It is the state and not the market that is determining what is of the highest artistic value. Isn't that more democratic? I would think you'd approve, sir."

"And why would you think that? Would I strike you as so opposed to the marketplace?"

"Ha! A fair point." Vidler smiled and nodded as the waiter poured coffee. "You worked at Lloyd's. I'm sure you have no quarrel with making money."

"And no talent for it," I said, frowning at my plate with my best comic timing. It worked, Dagmara smiled and laughed.

"But I don't think Mr. Maes shares the Fuhrer's taste in art," Dagmara said, as she bit into her omelette. "Do you, sir?"

"Honestly, I do not know enough about his thoughts on art."

"Oh, you should take an interest, Mr. Maes," Vidler said. "I respect the fact that he approaches art from the perspective of a painter himself. There are many terrible things said of Mr. Hitler, you know. But his opinions are informed by an understanding of certain values that he considers timeless. I mean if one reads Vasari, Leonardo, Raphael, there is the same concern for close observation… for balance in composition, perspective… for the study of nature and the human form. Now I'm no painter, but I would think that… for any true artist, these values transcend the marketplace."

"So, Connie, you would agree that a van Gogh, a Kokoschka… that these paintings were degenerate, the work of sick minds?" Dagmara gave me a conspiratorial smile before she brought his napkin to her lips.

"I just think if you were to take someone like Mr. van Gogh…" He paused while he chewed, savouring his omelette. "We all know he was mentally ill. I have read his letters to his brother. That he was unbalanced is beyond question. You know he sliced the lobe of his own ear off and presented it to a prostitute?"

"That is the story, yes."

"And what do you think of this, then? You believe his work is that of a balanced, healthy mind?"

"I don't ask such questions of a work of art."

"No? What do you ask of it, sir?"

As I paused to slow my thoughts down, formulating my response, Vidler's stubby fingers drummed on the table.

"Well I'll tell you what I ask of it," Vidler said. "Minimum thirty percent increase in value upon resale."

I tried to laugh, and then I felt Dagmara's hand on the cuff of my shirt.

"I am also curious, Mr. Maes." Dagmara spoke softly but clearly. I felt a stillness, a sudden quiet, as if we had been paddling through shallow water on a rowboat and had drifted into a deeper pool. "What do you ask of a work of art?"

"I suppose I just ask that it makes me see things differently, Madame Vidler. The first time I looked… really looked… at a painting by Paul Cezanne, I had that feeling. The world looked new again. More vivid. Alive. It was a curious thing."

Dagmara smiled. "I think I understand what you mean, Mr. Maes."

That was all I needed to hear. I would come to remember it as the moment Vidler went out of focus, receding into the periphery. I no longer had any interest in ruminating on beauty; no, these were the kinds of conversations men who only knew money believed artists had, and so they spoke in declaratives with people they had no interest in listening to, because all they were really listening to were the sounds of their own voices. Gentlemen like this wandered into Galerie Hyperion, usually on Friday afternoons. They hoped to hear something authentic emerging in their partially-formed thoughts and notions that betrayed their enthusiasms as undergraduates, excavating the handful of epiphanies in the few weeks of their lives when they had yet to turn into what they had become, when they might have been open to an original thought. What was really worth considering were the thoughts in Dagmara's head, and how she and I could see more of each other.

The champagne continued to flow with the conversation, long after the omelettes had been cleared away, followed by small, silver bowls of vanilla ice cream, scooped into three mounds so perfectly shaped. The mystery of ideal forms, that was what Cezanne wanted to investigate, wasn't it? The sun went down and Vidler remarked on the pinkish clouds, fading into these colder, cobalt blue masses… and then into black, glittery night.

I was long since drunk by then. I looked up through the glass ceiling above me and blurted out, genuinely surprised, "So many stars. You never see this many in Berlin."

"Is it that you never see them or you never look, Mr. Maes?" Dagmara asked.

"That's a very good question, Madame Vidler."

I could fall in love with this woman without a second thought, I realized. I'm still ashamed of how little I thought about you and your mother in that moment. And the worst of it was I did not feel guilty about this.

"And yet, if you look over to the left there," Vidler said, "the stars, they disappear, yes? Just this mass of darkness. That is where Pilatus blocks out the horizon during the day."

"The shadow, the light and shade… there is an Italian word for that effect. Help me out, Harry Lindbergh."

"*Chiaroscuro*, Connie."

"*Chiaroscuro*, exactly. Thank you, Harry."

Vidler looked over at Dagmara and raised his eyebrows to amuse her. At one point in his courting her, she must have thought him comical and therefore harmless, a man worthy of measured affection. One could come to tolerate intimacy with such a man, perhaps. You can get used to anything. She gave him a look she would have given a misbehaving but harmless child.

And then she looked over to me with a different look entirely. She had decided we would be fellow conspirators. And I resolved, as we spoke of darkness and light, to make of our conspiracy the romance I had always hoped for and never experienced... until then, in Lucerne among the thieves, confidence men and murderers who would determine the path my life would take.

3.

03 / 23 / 89

Masks Confronting Death (James Ensor, c. 1888)

I sit down with these notes again, Nikolaus, pen in hand, and I am already conscious of your critical eye. I can see you reading these words and judging me not only capable of rationalizing the sale of art that was stolen property. I was also capable of rationalizing my betrayal, my infidelity. You could say I was convincing myself that I had found an ally in Dagmara, someone who would take part in such transactions with a higher purpose: the survival of not only individual works of art but the higher ideals of a culture fighting a covert war against the philistinism that was at the core of Hitler's vision of empire. I needed to believe in my own heroism. Because such a man deserved the love of Dagmara. I wish I felt more guilty about all this half a century later.

Unfortunately I don't. I still consider Dagmara the great love of my life. And this painting by Ensor, which I managed to purchase at the auction in Lucerne, summed up, in its title, what would be required of us for the years of the war: our own masks for survival, and the eventual confrontation with the inevitable.

We moved from that improvised dinner that night to this reception for all of the guests of the auction. I see her so vividly at that table in the hotel, breaking into a wide grin, holding her hand up to her ear. "Now how about that, Constant? I'm sure that is music playing somewhere here."

And yes, it was true. It was unmistakable, the sound of a saxophone behind a rhythm section that thumped and swung over the laughter and chattering voices.

"That is not music. That's the schwarze racket they love in America," Vidler said.

"I like it, Connie. It makes me want to dance."

"Darling, you know I will always waltz with you but that music? No."

Dagmara turned to me and lightly touched my wrist. "Mr. Maes, would you like to accompany me into the ballroom?"

"But I'm not dressed…"

"Just a turn on the floor. No one will mind. Besides, you look sharp enough."

I looked at Vidler for approval. See what the champagne has done?

"Please go on ahead, Mr. Maes. I will follow you both later."

"Well?" Dagmara cocked an eyebrow with her hands on her hips. I rose and followed her as she exited the breakfast room.

I would remember the way she walked just a few steps ahead of me, the gentle sway of her hips, forever. She must have sunbathed in the nude because all of her back, revealed in the plunging, V-shaped curve, was tanned to a bronze hue. A simple gold necklace that she wore caught the light just above her collar bone and glimmered under the gas lamps. Etched in my memory was the way her pace quickened as the music became louder, how she turned and giggled like a schoolgirl, grabbed my hand and led me through a cloud of tobacco smoke and brought me onto the dance floor. Begin the Beguine, the song was. She hummed the melody in my ear.

"Mr. Maes, you move well."

"Not always, Madame Vidler."

"Dagmara. Dagmara to you."

"I move well with you, Dagmara."

"And I with you… Harry. What a solid name. It is a name of character."

"You think so?"

"I do, yes. I noticed your wedding ring. Your wife… what is her name?"

"Why do you ask?"

"I can usually tell if a couple will remain together by how their names sound."

"You're serious?"

"Of course I'm serious. What is her name?"

I exhaled, said "Sa-bi-nA," drawing out each syllable.

"Sabine? Sabine and Harry? Well of course that is not going to work."

"So you think."

"So I know."

"What about you? Connie and Dagmara."

She drew me closer and whispered in my ear. "No, that will never work either."

"And yet here you are with him."

"No, no, Harry. Here I am with you."

My heart began to pound harder as I pulled her closer. As we slowly turned I took in the room beyond the dance floor. Every cocktail table had women in beaded gowns but none like her. There was a flash of pearls on pale freckled skin, the sudden quavering little flame from a platinum lighter, a waft of a perfume with such musk and spice I was compelled to turn and take in a dark eyed woman dancing with her man. I closed my eyes and the word *Levantine* was on a white page in my mind and then erased as I opened them again.

"What is your room number?"

"Pardon?"

"Your room number, Harry. I can come to you. Wouldn't that be better than you trying to come to me?"

She looked into my eyes. She was serious and here I was, at sea, trying not to look confused or indecisive.

"Yes, that would be best."

"Unless you don't want me to."

"Of course I want you to."

"Then I will later," she whispered in my ear.

I could not look at her now. I cast my gaze about the room. Now as I remember it, I first questioned myself: was there really a plump woman who looked like Theda Bara? But I swear… I can still see her there sitting near the band. At another table a tall man with a van Dyke beard was speaking English. It sounded even worse than the Swiss German. This man did not have the manners to take off his Trilby as he sat with two women who, in their pearls and fine silk dresses, were conservatively dressed but odd-looking, with their hair cut mannishly. One had the shoulders of an athlete and a large nose that made her homeliness almost exotic.

I asked Dagmara, "You think those ladies, there with that odd one in the Trilby, you think they're German?"

"Those ladies? Pardon? You don't know who they are? They're Americans! That's Gloria Morgan Vanderbilt and Peggy Guggenheim. Vanderbilt has a home here. Guggenheim is probably staying with her."

"Should I know who they are?

"Guggenheim has a gallery in London. I'm sure she is here looking for bargains."

"They were so mannish I mistook them for Berlin ladies of the evening."

"Ah no, dear. The Germans, they are not listening to the music. Did you not see?" Dagmara gestured with a nod to an arched doorway that led to a salon. Seated at a table under a crystal chandelier were a couple of bored looking mediocrities, dressed in green loden suits and with them, in white Nazi uniforms with shiny black riding boots and puffed out jodhpurs, was a trio of bloated middle aged officers, their heads like polished apples, shiny and pink from the sun. They were smoking small cigars and drinking cognac from a decanter, leering at the crowd in the other room. "For them we are like animals in a zoo. A spectacle. Connie and I... we are beneath contempt."

"You know them?"

"Just the fattest one there, with the ruby ring. Goring is his name. He considers himself a connoisseur. He bought a Roman bust from Connie at an auction in Vienna last year. That is when I slapped him."

"You slapped him?"

"He pinched my bottom in a restaurant, so he got what he deserved."

"And what did he do once you hit him?"

"He laughed, made a face like a comedian on stage for everyone looking. I suppose that is all he could do."

As a trumpet solo began, a bespectacled, muscular figure rose from their table. He was concealed behind Goring's uniformed companion, but now, as he got to his feet, I recognized him as Theodor Fischer the auctioneer; he had greying, finely-coiffed hair and the same smirk from the photograph of him in the Zeitung I read on the train. He proceeded to do an odd jig to the music. Goring and his friends began to chuckle; one of the men in loden waved Fischer off as if he was dismissing him like a waiter.

"I wish I believed they were only comedians."

From a side entrance to the room Connie finally appeared. He had changed into a smoking, with bowtie and shiny patent leather shoes. He hailed Fischer and walked over to his table.

"Connie gets on well with these men, though. At least that's what it seems."

"He is tolerated. They will deal with him because he makes them money. But that he is rich   … it fills them with contempt. If he lived in Berlin rather than London, I know they'd do everything they could to destroy him."

"How does that make you feel   … his wife?"

"I don't care either way. I make sure I'm good to myself. In that private room they will play cards and gamble all night. That is not how a woman should spend her time." She touched my lips with her finger, as if to quiet me. And once we had turned on the dance floor and she knew we were out of Constant's sight line, she kissed me. "Now tell me about you, Mr. Maes. This topic is more interesting to me."

I'll pass over the next few hours—out of a sense of my own propriety and yours—and only speak of the next morning, I was late for the auction. I could recall reaching for Dagmara in the first light of dawn but all that was there was a tangle of bed sheets. Perhaps she returned to her hotel room before Connie's last game of cards, perhaps not. I thought to myself this was probably the arrangement they had. She had singled me out as her diversion from the moment she first saw me in the hotel. And Connie indulged her, as he always did.

After a walk and some breakfast to shake off my hangover, I bathed and dressed for the auction. All I wanted to see was

Dagmara again, but I was duty bound to Magda, my boss, to spend wisely. I got to the room where the paintings were displayed, and it had all begun. Fischer himself was on the auctioneer's platform, gesturing to a work that was unmistakably a Braque. In a tired monotone he was calling out the numbers… twelve thousand, two hundred… twelve thousand, three hundred… as hands shot up from around the room. I recognized Walter Feichenfeldt from Cassirer; Pierre Matisse, based in New York and successful enough to fly over to Berlin and purchase twenty or thirty paintings at a time at these big auctions. How his father would have detested this spectacle. Fischer was displaying such thinly-veiled contempt as he gestured to the Braque. "Going once… going twice…" He smiled with delight at the fools who would pay so much for these works. I could tell he was performing for his masters, chief among them that fat man with the ruby ring, just one row behind me.

I looked around the room for Dagmara. If I spotted her with Connie, I had resolved to get through the awkwardness of the moment with the bumbling solicitude that served me so well among older men with money and power back in Berlin. Here I was, quietly fuming about Fischer's behaviour, but was I any less of an actor, putting on my usual costume of false humility? The truth was I was proud of how I had taken Dagmara in my arms the night before, stolen her away from an old philistine who preferred she amuse herself while he mixed among the Germans and advanced his business interests. It was all too easy and it seemed that Vidler knew it as well, as if he had surrendered her the moment Dagmara led me onto the dance floor. No consequences… yet was I expecting a duel with pistols? My outmoded conception of honour was evaporating as I took in this spectacle, all these cultured, wealthy socialites, people of great power and influence who all knew well enough this work was of great value, and yet they played along with Fischer, as if they were deigning to purchase these paintings out of charity. No this was not a good moment for integrity. It was all the more reason to fall in love with Dagmara that she preferred not to be present in a room like this.

Fischer put up a Picasso and then a Kokoschka behind him, drawling out the numbers. His delivery and his snide commentary were earning him titters of laughter at first, and then some of the older gentlemen openly guffawed. Once the Kokoschka was bought and taken down, Fischer shook his head and muttered one word: "foolish." Big cigars lit up, arms folded, the auction was becoming a floor show. And as with his performance of an odd little jig the night before, Fischer was emerging as a capable comedian for their purposes. Maybe it was the stubbornness of my hangover, and now the smell of these cigars, but I was feeling nauseous. I needed to get up, get out of the room, and get some air.

And I wanted to find Dagmara, if even just to say goodbye. Of course there were paintings I needed to bid on but all that could wait. The realization that I might never see her again, that she had told me nothing about herself beyond a few remarks about her once living in Berlin, set my heart pounding once more and quickened my stride.

But she was nowhere to be found. The terrace, the garden, even the breakfast room where perhaps she might have gone. I sat in the lounge by the front desk, smoking a cigarette, then another, until I was in the frame of mind when I could think of the evening for what it was, a brief escape for two people who hoped to discover a way out of the lives they were leading. Yet I had enough intuition to trust my fears. That she was nowhere to be found probably meant she was thinking the same thing.

It was only the next morning, as I ambled up to the front desk to check out, that the desk clerk behind the counter, a young man with an unfortunate case of acne, stuttered out that there was a letter for me. He handed me a small, lemon yellow envelope. There in light blue font along the seal were the words "From the desk of Mrs. Dagmara Vidler."

Harry,

I regret that I could not stay for the auction. It would have been all too much after the night we had together. I have taken the train to Berlin and then on to Calais, ahead of Constant.

Our time felt like a brief moment of light in the midst of this gathering darkness. Perhaps it is best that it remains so, and yet I just know that somehow, sometime sooner than we imagine, we will see each other again. One has to believe in something right now. This is as much as I can hope for.

Adieu, mon cher.

Dagmara

I folded the note and placed it in the inner pocket of my blazer, close to my heart. I caught the next train to Berlin and never did get a photo of the Dance of the Dead. I had resolved, in my mind, that I would never let this woman out of my life now that we had spent one night together.

Oh yes and I did purchase two paintings for Magda and Galerie Hyperion: Chagall's The Blue House and, as mentioned, the Ensor.

I know why I felt Magda's gallery must have the latter painting – and why I've kept it here for you: it was the masks in the painting. I've done a little research on the English painter, and I love how he has described his particular obsession – he painted masks many times: "the mask means to me: freshness of color, sumptuous decoration, wild unexpected gestures, very shrill expressions, exquisite turbulence."

Exquisite turbulence is all that Dagmara brought into my life.

4.

03 / 24 / 89

Portrait of Doctor Immelman (Otto Dix, 1926)

And yet, despite such turbulence, there is always obligation, yes? Nikolaus, I realize I cannot speak of this time without summoning the ghosts from my former life that you might only barely remember—and might have even tried to forget. I don't mean your mother, who I still cannot call "Sally," the name she took to shed herself of her German identity. She will always be Sabine to me. No, as I write this I'm thinking of your grandparents: Sabine's mother and father Gisela and Benjamin Ostriker, and my own parents whom you spent two Christmases with. I'm sure my father Pastor Maes must have made a lasting impression on you. Yet there are others—your uncle Anton, Magda and Lazlo Petofi—who played larger roles in our lives before the war, and before your mother left me for that Irishman Francis Cluny, whom I heard she wisely separated from as soon as it finally seemed the war was ending. All these people once were so important in our lives and then, as if a black curtain went down, they were hurried off the stage, not to return for the second and third acts. The war was fate's dramaturg, and it's made a mess with the whole production of our post-war lives.

But you should know more about those opening acts, given that I would not have anything to pass on to you without them. So I'll return to the time of that auction in Lucerne, when so much was about to change for us.

The train taking me back to Berlin arrived in the station later than expected, and I had time to reflect on my betrayal. Of your mother and the child you were then, not yet four. There was no one in my cabin for most of the trip. Out my window the lushness of the alpine fields in late summer unspools in monochrome in my memory, the forests bleached of colour, woods turned bone white. I was alone with my guilt, my hangover, the grim sense of foreboding the whole contemptible business of the auction had given me.

Well perhaps that is not entirely honest. My good self, the son of Pastor Maes, the dutiful husband and father, the dependable steward of Magda Petofi's notorious little gallery, was luxuriating in self-loathing. The raging headache and the dry mouth seemed just a taste of the penance I should have to serve. This good self, while he was waiting for a taxi, lining up to board at the station, had felt that overnight there was a coarsening in how everyone around me regarded each other…transacted, mistrusted, withheld their contempt publicly but only in order to retract further into their private selves. It was the light shifting from the mob cloud, inviolate and immunized from the darkening, like poison in the air. You could sense the virus of war-mind that was just days from surging. I had watched an old couple, a kind of parody of Connie and Dagmara, in tennis whites and gum-soled shoes, elbow their way ahead of passengers for the train and almost start a fist fight. It was as if the day before rhymed like doggerel. A new, satyr-like part of me sniggered at the episode. This goat-man I had glimpsed in the half-light of the bedroom mirror at dawn, as Dagmara had left me. He was the man who had realized he suddenly had a sense of power at a time when so many certainties were evaporating, and who knew this power was attractive to people. Like Connie and Dagmara. As the train rattled along the morning mist rose from those fields of wild sedge and alpen flowers. I wanted such colour to stop shouting at me. I had decisions to make.

Here I am at that point in my life, from these paintings still with me: the portrait of Doctor Immelmann, by Otto Dix. Starched white collar, syphilitic pale green jacket and trousers. The shocked expression, as if he was taking in the way hypocrisy had transformed his profile in the mirror. It's the shock of a determined innocence. Willed naïveté. Let me exist on the other side of the mirror, just a reflection for others to impute their own motives and notions of agency. Let me be just a hollow vessel.

The bond between your mother and I was disintegrating. We had been trying, over two years, to reconcile our differences.

There didn't seem to be anything I could do correctly. I was not making enough money, but if I worked late or showed any sign of ambition, I was ignoring her and you. Apparently I made her feel guilty about not cleaning our apartment, disregarding how busy she was, but if I tried to clean I upset her working area or used too much expensive detergent. She was becoming more erratic, temperamental, careless with you and what I viewed as her responsibilities as a mother. Just two weeks before my trip to Lucerne I had returned from the gallery to find your arms and the back of your neck blistering from a sunburn, and she admitted she had left you out on the balcony of our small apartment while she claimed one of her old theatre friends had come over for coffee.

I knew she was drinking during the day. I saw the bottles of cheap vodka in the trash bins on our floor and I knew it could only be her (like a foretelling of my own little problem with the bottle twenty years later,). The sewing work she was doing from home—alterations and costumes from the cabaret shows—had now tapered off. I presumed it was because she had become unreliable, her work shoddy.

And yet I just let it all unravel without confronting her. I didn't ask what was going on for fear of what I would discover if we argued. I saw this theatre friend of hers in the local grocers, listened to her prattle on about a holiday in Bad Harzburg that she had just returned from, which confirmed that your mother had lied to me about her afternoon guest. As she was probably lying to me about so much. I couldn't solve the puzzle of her unhappiness.

Permit me some fatherly advice for you, that probably comes too late: you should never try to love someone because you feel you can save them. It has been a mistake I have made time and again over the years. It is as if desire for someone seems too selfish, too wrapped up in the body rather than the higher ideals to be worthy of claiming for myself. Now that I've reached this age it no longer really matters, I suppose. But the wreckage.

I don't know who your mother is now, and I'm sure she's put a lot of energy into concealing her past, but the girl who came to Berlin from Hamburg when she was barely eighteen was quite a work in progress. She had shown some talent in theatricals and was convinced she could become a great actress. She was not conventionally pretty; she told me that one director said her black eyes seemed too closely-set, her profile too sharply-etched. But it was her long, swan-like neck and her angular grace, that mysterious elegance and reserve she had, that caught my eye when we first met in Galerie Hyperion. She seemed well beyond her girlish years until she laughed, and the way her elegance dissolved both charmed and intrigued me.

Magda, my employer, knew your mother's parents well. She had initially sold them some art and had become quite close to your grandmother. Yes, Magda and Gisela Ostriker were probably lovers, one of Magda's many diversions, but I was so blithely unaware in those days. I later discovered that your mother was headstrong, prone to hysteria. So said Benjamin Ostriker, your grandfather, the mild-mannered optometrist, upon my first visit to the family. It was clear they had thrown up their hands about their only daughter but saw in me the qualities of a good minder.

Your mother had spent four years trying to make her way in the theatre when I met her. At first she had worked in the cafés, living with her aunt and uncle, auditioning for shows with little success. Until she set her sights on less ambitious productions that neither the Ostrikers nor Sabine herself would talk about. Cabaret shows, burlesque… the entertainment traveling salesmen didn't tell their wives they went to when they came into the big, bruising city. At some point, perhaps to avoid any further scandal for her family, she began making costumes for these shows. It was in this craft, rather than any turn on the stage, where she showed some talent. Off the stage and off the books of most theatres, she could stay safe from the brownshirts too.

She started getting regular work, enough to quit the last of her series of café jobs. She took some delight in how terrible a waitress she was. By the time my boss Magda played matchmaker, introducing us, I remember your mother had her own greasy black warhorse of a sewing machine and was earning union wages under the table in places like the Schaubuhne theatre, with plays that Benjamin and Gisela would not have been ashamed to attend.

Provenance

It is only now that I look back on how clever Magda Petofi was—and not just as a matchmaker with your mother and I. To most of her regular customers and indeed to most of the painters and writers and theatre people she mixed with, she had an unerring ability to be in the right places, with the right people, all the time. She slept with whom she liked. More than a few of them were the wives of some prominent Berliners, but there were some men as well. I remember a burly Russian journalist with the eyes of one of El Greco's saints, who dressed like a janitor and smelled like pickled herring; she called him "my Bolshevik poet." She knew how to promote the painters she gave shows to, getting them full-page spreads in the magazines and newspapers. And most important, no matter how worrying the rise of the brownshirts were, patrolling with all their oafish, drunken menace in our neighbourhood at night, it was as if they were magnetically repelled by Galerie Hyperion, warned off by some directive from their superiors. Magda had secrets she kept about certain people and such knowledge had provided her with a diplomat's passport in the streets.

Yet she was increasingly at risk. Despite her marriage to Laszlo Petofi, whom she coldly described to me as "a respectable Catholic historian," Magda kept some dangerous secrets of her own. She came from a wealthy Jewish family—the Zeisels—in Budapest (but of course I was sworn never to mention this to anyone). She had converted for her husband but, much like her marriage, there was never any question of her being faithful—to anything or anyone but her love of 'art that was not scheisse.' Not that anyone would have blamed her; I met Laszlo Petofi once at a Christmas party and he stoked his round belly with tarts while he spent close to a half-hour telling me about his essay on church spires. There was Bavarian cream on his moustache hanging stubbornly like snot. Honestly, he would have made anyone stray. When she joined the KPD, not long after she opened her gallery, the orthodoxy of the party's Marxism would have given her an out on any obligation to church-going. It hardly mattered though; by '35, Laszlo was headed back to Budapest after his teaching position at Humboldt University was not renewed, and she refused to follow him there. Her business was thriving, yet the painters she was showing were attracting the wrong kind of attention.

It was around this time I came to work for her. I walked off the street and inquired, with nothing but a letter of reference from the Berlin branch of Bank Helvetia (rather than Lloyds where I was fired, of course), if she needed any sales staff. She asked me if I knew how to frame paintings (I did not). Then she asked about my education and I could not lie about my time before my aborted studies with the Staatliches Bauhaus, when I took a degree in economics at Mannheim, bending to my father's will. There was really little to recommend me but my desperation—I had been out of work for six months and probably looked it, with my one suit that was shining at the knees and elbows. Indeed every other gallery laughed me out the way I had come in. And yet she saw something in me. 'Imagine my good fortune at last!' I had written to my mother, the only one in my family still believing I might become a success.

That letter from the bank, I should note, was a fake. It is only now, when I remember how I cajoled Rudi, my one friend at the branch of Bank Helvetia, to get the stationery and write it with me, that I realize this was like a dress rehearsal for my later transgressions. Yet the fear of being found out was one of the reasons I did not attempt to get work at another bank after the weeks of unemployment turned into months. I just presumed no art gallery would ever inquire about my references and of course I was right. Bankers are like dentists; nobody wants to talk to them except other bankers.

What I did have, which was of value to Magda Petofi, more than I could have known upon meeting her, was my party membership. All of the Lloyds staff in Berlin had to take one out, with papers and a pin which we were advised to wear in our lapels every day. It was my luck that the pin was still in my suit jacket when I walked into Galerie Hyperion for the first time.

That first six months when I was learning from Magda, I only had a dim sense at first that I was being watched carefully by her. And shaped and moulded for her purposes. Yet it became more obtrusive when she would provide me with gifts I felt obligated to show I valued. She would come back from lunch with a Hermes necktie that she had seen in a shop window. Naturally I would wear it to work, though it made me feel foppish and, as my father would put it, like 'a trivial man.' Then there was a new Swiss fountain pen she insisted I sign our receipts with and carry with me at all times. I remember, just weeks before Sabine made her entrance in the gallery, Magda had reached up, casually changed the part in my hair, saying 'there, that's better. Keep it like that.' She just brusquely wiped the pomade from her fingers on the folds of her skirt and it seemed such a vulgar gesture, yet she had transformed it with her queenly disregard. She only cared for appearances if they were at the service of her ambitions. Counter to all the preconceptions I had inherited from my philistine upbringing, I was coming to understand the charm of Magda's abrasiveness. I considered her truly bohemian, what I secretly longed to be.

Here is my confession about that. This flirtation with how I thought artists lived was motivated by one thing only: my ambition. I needed to be recognized as unconventional. Urbane, cosmopolitan, the kind of businessman the doomed, degenerate painters and writers could mix with and not, among themselves, dismiss as a cultural tourist. I knew the best route to credibility was to sleep with the women they wanted. Be careful who you wish to become.

Over my first summer in the gallery, I began seeing your mother regularly. She was committed to her own quiet sense of anarchy and misrule with herself. In my later years, long after our estrangement, I realized there was some early, primal act of violence that marked her. I imagine a pack of sniggering boy-men at her gymnasium, the cruelty and banality of the usual rape without consequence for the criminals who carry it out. She was patiently but ruthlessly focused on a blazing path of revenge, her reclamation of her sexuality. The more lawless the better. Let me risk a little more candor, so you understand the kind of people your parents once were, earnestly rebelling from the bourgeois propriety we were both raised to respect: one night we were in a bar where men were dancing with men, women with women and she put it to me directly: 'You do like sex with women, don't you, Harry?' I said of course I did. 'Well you should take me to bed tonight; we've been talking around it long enough. And I need you to be bold.' She had two small rooms above a tobacconist's shop and in the hot July mornings she'd walk around naked. A marvel to me. I didn't know what I had done to deserve the love of such a free-spirited woman. I embraced the new trivial (but sexed) me and began dressing a little flamboyantly, to be more like 'the gypsies who play the negro jazz,' your mother's favourite musicians who played at the Haus Vaterhall. I was dipping into my savings. I remember a suit like the Duke of Windsor's. And I bought her a Chinese robe of silk in an effort to tame her immodesty, but it really didn't work. She told me she loved her naked body and she knew, by how attentive I would become, that I did too.

She introduced me to her friends. More than a few were our mutual acquaintances from the Staatliches Bauhaus. I started to understand that there was a whole other world of entertainment people who were mostly living by their wits in the city—musicians, set painters, dirt-poor playwrights and actors—and she was like a princess among them. On Sundays at her apartment they would come over for afternoon coffee and poppy cake and stay until the sun went down. I realized they all knew of Magda and considered her a woman of quiet influence and power. For them I was the useful provincial boy, the son of a pastor who had let himself be corrupted. I didn't always get their jokes. I suppose they first considered me a comical figure: sweet-natured, the rube who comes up to the stage for the magician's trick. Saw me in half and make my wallet disappear. I was naïve but ultimately a good influence on your mother—the boyfriend who ensured she kept a solid footing in the straight life. Toting the grocery bags up the back stairs, I ensured there was always enough coffee and cake to go around.

It was just past our first New Year's together when she became pregnant with you. I was distraught, far more upset than your mother was. I still wasn't making that much at the gallery and I didn't feel like I was prepared for us to live together, never mind whether I could take on the responsibility of being a father. Yes, there was a good chance at the time that you would have never been born. Your mother said she could "get the situation taken care of" but from what I knew only prostitutes did such things. Ever the pastor's son. We quarreled, and she told me there were a few of her friends—people I had met casually—who had taken money from men for more than a couple of dances. I asked her if she had ever done so as well and she became infuriated, said I could afford to take the moral high ground because my family would never let me fall that far below my station, never wipe their hands of me the way her father had of her. I mused aloud about your grandfather Benjamin, the mild-mannered little fellow who had his storefront optometrist's practice and made a little fortune for himself with his eyeglasses factory. He was busily making plans to leave the country. How had he abandoned her? She threw a plate at me and it grazed my temple before it shattered, breaking a window.

"You think giving a child up would be an easy decision for me? Have you not noticed how little I've been working since November? I haven't asked you for anything."

As she broke down in tears I took her in my arms, apologizing for being insensitive. But before I could speak she shushed me. "Just hold me. Don't say anything more." I followed directions, submitting to play my minor role in her melodrama. It was one of my few talents as a young man—how well I obeyed.

In an effort to explain how distracted I was at the gallery, how my eye on the books was not as sharp as it usually was, I told Magda what was going on. It was nearing six and we were about to close for the day, and as soon as I began to speak she locked the door, put down the window blinds she had installed to protect the paintings from smashed windows and attempted thefts—the new street life. She said she knew all about what was happening with your mother and me. Gisela, your grandmother, had told her. She pulled out a bottle of cognac from one of the drawers of her desk and poured two tumblers for us. It was time for her to offer me some advice.

"You know that Sabine is hardly working, yes?"

"I know that many theatres are struggling. These are difficult times."

"They're difficult because the Nazis have clamped down on who is working in these places. They don't want any Jewish influences on their precious culture. First it was the names in bold in the programs. Now it's everybody."

I nodded, doing my best to look like I was aware of this. But really I wasn't. I began to think about how little your mother had told me about her working life. I had put her troubles down to her own nature. Mercurial, temperamental, shiftless… these were the words I had written in anger in my diary, time and again. She had kept from me how perilous her hold on making a living and respectability was, how easily she could have slipped into destitution without sending up any kind of flare for the help of your grandparents (it was a war she was in with her mother, who had gone behind enemy lines by making of Magda a kind of auntie figure for her). Then I realized how much shame she'd feel in admitting this, how her pride was such a fundamental part of who she was. I felt something more than tenderness, something like love for her surge within me.

"Yes I understand why she would consider giving up this child, but…"

"Do you? Have you thought of what a child of hers might face, growing up here? You're a smart boy, Harry. And you have a good eye. You know a real painting when you see it. And yet you can't see what's happening right in front of you."

"I don't know what I can do."

"Yes, you do. Marry her. Give her a new name. From what you've told me of your family, she'll probably have to take your faith. Well, so be it."

"Our child…"

"Your child will have a different life. Probably a good one, Harry." She downed her glass and motioned for me to join her. "You've got a bright future. This I know."

I suppose she was appealing to my vanity, but she was also telling the truth. I did have a good eye and I could speak about, say, an Otto Dix on the wall, in a way that was comprehensible for the rich foreigners and tourists who would come in, curious about its value. I knew I was Magda's secret weapon. The effect of a young man, well-dressed and plain-spoken, one you would expect to see in a bank or law office, suggesting that George Grosz's portrait of a beggar, crudely disfigured and be-medaled, was a sound investment for a visiting Englishman, was apparent in how quickly the work on the walls sold each month. No one could move 'the unlovable work' quite like Magda's gallery, the painters said. For the first time in my life I was actually good at something. 'Effective,' my father's highest praise. Why wouldn't I have a bright future? And more to the point, if anyone could be a good husband and father to you, your mother's boy, it was me.

And I did have real feelings for your mother. Though there were many things about her that I could not abide: her love of music hall songs, cheap costume jewelry, romance novels. She never read the newspaper, just the theatre magazines. She was brassy and loud after two glasses of cheap "zekt," harshly dismissive of most of the art that was on the walls of Galerie Hyperion. But her beauty and comportment, the grace of how she moved through a crowded room… it was this contrast that held me so fast to my belief that she was the most compelling woman I would ever meet. As Max Seidel, a playwright friend of hers who spent most Sundays chain-smoking on her divan had said to me, 'She's like a golden Cleopatra you discover in a pawn shop.'

And she was about to bring you into the world if I just followed Magda's advice. It was the best thing to do. It showed I was capable of real responsibility, of caring for the welfare of others, planning for the future rather than living for the present moment. If these intentions were the foundations of our life together, how could things ever really go wrong?

Your Belgian grandparents had a different perspective. I realized that if I was going to make such a precipitous decision, it was time they really got to know your mother. At Christmas we took the train to Antwerp and stayed, in separate beds, in my boyhood home. Your uncle, my younger brother Anton, was home from Amsterdam, where he was succeeding in growing a goatee, but failing the courses he was taking toward a medical degree. He and your mother hit it off like brother and sister, smoking in the front parlour as they listened to the comedy and music shows on the radio. Your grandmother, grown stouter and more disappointed with life, did not do well at concealing her dismay, calling your mother 'that vulgar girl.' Your grandfather took it upon himself to take me for a walk along the river, just a few streets over from our house that I once thought I would inherit, (long before it was completely destroyed, of course) and he set me aright at last.

"When we visited you in Berlin and you brought her to dinner, we thought this… between you, it was not serious. Now it has gone too far, Harry. I don't know why you thought it would be a good idea to bring her here."

I strode on at a quicker pace. I would not meet his gaze. I remember patches of ice were forming on the banks of the Scheldt. The winter-burned river, flowing black as coal. Black as your grandfather's rage at life.

I stopped myself from telling him about her condition. I wanted to know why he and my mother felt so strongly about her. But as he started to speak, I felt like the air was charged magnetically, repelling me from him. So pious, so wizened and pared down to the bone, with that bent, lurching gait I have now inherited, your grandfather the pastor and hypocrite. He proceeded to tell me how 'different' the Jewish people were, that no matter what I told him about how respectable her family was, their decadence was revealed by your mother's vulgarity. A vulgarity your uncle Anton was the very embodiment of, I could have added, with his love of jazz music and theatre. But of course to your grandfather he was just young and impressionable, going through a phase. I told him more about your other grandparents, boasting that Benjamin and Gisela Ostriker's art collection had to be one of the best in Hamburg and this only exercised him further. He said these Jews, they could never be truly 'spiritual' people, and this was why they acquired the work of the 'crackpots' Magda Petofi sold at such inflated prices. It was just like the stock market, as far as he was concerned, it was when you gave people like the Ostrikers money that a crash happened.

"Your mother and I, we gave you everything of value when you were growing up. Your faith, your education. Maybe   with your love of art we indulged you too much, yes? That's what we realize. You come home dressed like a Frenchman, your Berlin German… you sound like a gangster… and you bring this Jewess into our home. You don't even realize how corrupted you are."

It was the first time in my life where I felt I could strike him. I hope you have not inherited any of that piety. I felt such rage! What a bitter, dessicated bigot of a man he was. One who had the nerve to put on his vestments on Sunday and preach compassion, the power of faith to transform lives. Because of your grandmother's inheritance from the family textile business, he was comfortable enough to pass judgment on what the struggle to make a living did to people. And worse, for all his talk of how learning was a process of refinement and living by higher ideals, he was held captive by that defining trait of intellectual and cultural mediocrity in Antwerp, a hatred of the Jewish people. He had exposed this side of himself to me now, and there was no returning to any authentic understanding between us.

I should probably tell some lies here to make myself look better. I want to write that I exploded in anger, dressed him down for his hypocrisy and defended your mother and myself with all the passion I had. But I did not. For years I told myself I was so conciliatory because that was just my presumptive role as the oldest child. Your uncle Anton was allowed to act out but it was my job to bring everyone into accord, to use a little gentle humour to keep everyone calm and rational. Yet I realize now I said nothing for another reason: I did not want to break your grandmother's heart, make her feel like the differences between their lives and mine were unbridgeable. She had defended me after I had failed so badly at the bank. It was her decision to support me in Berlin while I struggled, first at the Staatliches Bauhaus and then looking for work for all those months. I still needed to be the good son in her eyes. What a mother's boy I was!

So I bowed my head and I accepted his judgment. And I told your grandfather that it might not look like it to him, but I was doing everything I could to make the family proud. If your mother and I were truly committed to each other and made a life together, I told him, most of what he deemed foolish or trivial about us both would prove to be ephemeral, would it not?

"What would you say if I told you that she and I have spoken of marriage, and her converting? We're more capable of seriousness than perhaps you think."

He just laughed. "Let me tell you what it would take. Our religion, it is unstained by any Jewish residue that stains other faiths. If you and she were to read deeply, you'd soon understand that ours is… as it is said… (his gloved, spidery hands grasping the air) the unbridgeable religious contradiction to Judaism. Do you understand what I'm saying, Harry?"

"I think so."

"I'm saying you would be attempting to change this young woman's very nature. Or worse, changing your own. Love and marriage is not an experiment, Harry. You don't think it's serious but it becomes so. Sooner or later you'll have your souls to contend with."

I granted your grandfather his sermon and did not argue. I knew he was taking some sensual delight in the sound of his own voice, in the snippets of rhetoric—'unbridgeable religious contradiction'—that he had managed to retrieve from the yellowed pages of his memory. We would return to the house and I would focus my efforts on your grandmother.

And it was relatively easy; after two brandies with her on Christmas Eve, it was decided. Your mother and I would marry in your grandfather's church in February, and your grandmother would never tell your grandfather that she knew of your mother's condition. I was your grandmother's favourite son, doing the honourable thing. Her grey eyes watered as she pulled me close. For the rest of our time in that house I caught her giving your mother softened looks of willed affection. Yet your grandmother had a more powerful will than your grandfather, this I knew, and he was no match for her endorsement of the marriage.

On the train journey back from Antwerp I lied to your mother for the first time. I told her your grandparents were becoming very attached to her. I could tell, by her smile, that she didn't quite believe me. She told me she was beginning to like Anton very much, that he was going to be an interesting man if he maintained his courage in the midst of such conventionality.

"I should tell you I asked my parents if they would give their blessing if we were to marry."

"You're serious. Maybe your brother's courage is rubbing off on you."

"They said yes. If you were to say yes to marry in our church. With all that means."

She reached her hand over to mine and squeezed it. "Means to them and not to us, yes?"

I squeezed her hand in return. "Precisely."

"I'll marry you, Harry Maes. With all it means. To us."

That should have been the moment when I asked her to define these terms. But of course I didn't.

Let me take you to almost five years later from that moment. To that very different train journey, returning from Lucerne. Me alone, contending with my self-loathing and my self-regard, the poles of my reflection on my infidelity, getting closer by the minute as the train clacked along.

It was about an hour away from Zoo station when a young man with a wispy blonde moustache came into my cabin. He was dressed in a green loden jacket, with a swastika pin in his lapel. This was Odon Heimrath, and he introduced himself by saying he worked for the new commission, set up 'for the exploitation of degenerate art.'

"I recognized you, when you went into the dining car for a glass of beer. You were at the auction last night." Of course he recognized me. I was the quarry since I was first sighted with Dagmara.

"That is correct. I'm sorry if I can't recall your face."

He laughed, a high, flutey trill that petered out quickly. "We can't all be memorable. Like that woman you were dancing with. I thought to myself you were a lucky fellow." I was starting to like him. What a jumble of personalities he later turned out to have, confected from the usual Prussian cruelties of a boyhood in military school, but there will be time to discuss our good friend Odon. He pitched himself forward as if his back was hinged. "She is not traveling with you?"

"Unfortunately, no."

"Ah well." A quick glance down at the ring on my left hand, his lips pursed. "Maybe it's best."

"It probably is, yes."

"Your purchases last night. You are at Galerie Hyperion, yes?"

"Well… I work for the gallery."

"For Magda Petofi."

"You know her?"

"We have to. She is one of the few whom we are dealing with."

"Dealing with?"

"There are only five art dealers in all of the country we have given the license to sell such work. She did not tell you?"

I thought of all the meetings I had been kept out of in her private office in the back of the gallery. The door was always closed. On many occasions I just assumed the poker-faced men who dressed like bureaucrats were old customers who wanted to keep their purchases to themselves. Magda never introduced people to me unless I was going to deal with them. There were people I just did not need to know.

"I was not aware."

"Well, it might not matter soon enough."

"Soon enough?"

"Did you know of her family in Budapest? Before she was Magda Petofi…" Odon turned to look out the glass doors of our cabin. There was no one passing in the aisle but he was making it clear he was about to share a secret. I realized I would need to look shocked and surprised. "She was Magda Zeisel. A Jewish family."

"Ah. I see."

"My higher-ups in the ministry, they weren't so careful about this back before my time."

Or Magda knew how to strike a deal with them, I wanted to say. "But now it matters."

"Yes. It might matter quite a bit soon. But you… we were watching you. Your accent is not quite Berliner."

"I'm from Antwerp, actually." And then, reaching into my own little juju bag of costume charm, I added, "The prodigal son of a pastor." I knew exactly how that would register.

The brush-fine hairs of his moustache could not quite span the stretch of his grin. He reached into his jacket and pulled out his card. Pale vanilla, with stark, Roman cursive, above his name a black swastika encircled in a blood-red band. "You should come to my office this week. I would like to discuss how we might work together. We have so many paintings we must dispose of."

"For the highest prices possible."

"We understand each other."

"I think so, yes."

"It was a great pleasure meeting you, Mr. Maes." He rose and slid open the cabin door, pausing only to turn and curtly nod to me. "I'll see you again soon."

Let's say he exited with a whiff of sulfur for effect, shall we? But no, that costumes him in too much banality, not evil. Because Odon proved himself capable of evil, trust me. And I discovered evil has no smell, no taste—it is like a vodka you only dream of as you try to drink yourself to death.

Now let me bring these two strands of my story together for you, Nikolaus, and give you an old man's summary statement about a central theme in my life: my willed innocence about the role I play in transactional relationships. Despite all the seeds of future betrayal being planted from the very beginning, like a dutiful gardener I tend a plot and let the poisoned flowers bloom. It is my sole wish that you somehow managed to be raised inoculated from this poison... and that you were able to transcend this legacy.

Back to my return trip from Lucerne. As the train rolled into Zoo station, I had to force the window in my cabin down. The heat wave I had left had only worsened. My collar was too tight, the air felt like it was processed through the engine and I knew I would faint if I did not get on my feet soon. I could feel the sweat bead on my forehead. I needed to be home, reunited with your mother and you, draped over our small fan, imagining I had plunged into the cool, clean depths of the Reuss.

But as I heaved the paintings and my overnight bag up the stairs of our apartment building, I knew... by the hush of the third floor... your mother was not going to be home. I caught my breath as I unlocked the front door, felt the hot blanket of air in the kitchen smother me and cried out her name. Just out of a reflex, I suppose.

What usually followed in those days was the stirring of you and these slurry toddler noises you'd make. But no… silence.

What I would say to the women I became involved with over the next few years of my rise of fortune—all the stand-ins for Dagmara—was that your mother 'left me for the radio.' I would frown like a stage comedian to signal this was my punchline. The women who were cheating on their husbands would laugh. The ones who hoped for something like a real relationship with me were less sure about such a reaction. Probably because I sounded so sincere. And to a certain extent I was.

This episode does not conclude like a radio script in my memory though. In fact there was no dialogue of note. It unspools as a silent film. Here is our hapless cuckold bolting back down the stairs with the note his wife left him, that she has gone 'for a meeting. Job! Nicki is with Hilde.' Here he is briefly speaking with Hilde, the wife of Horst, the building superintendent. Hilde shrugs, unsure of where your mother has gone, she had just said when she'd return. There's you on a couch with your toy soldiers, Napoleon's front line peering over the carpeted battlefield. Close-up on our protagonist's shaky, pleading hands as he stresses he'll just be a few minutes before he picks up his son. Then out on the streets, hurrying past the pram strollers, the Hombergs and grim faces (when did we all stop wearing hats? I'd put it down to the Kruschev-Sputnik years, when we all wanted to be modern) to Sperlingsgasse, this narrow lane where the Raabe-Diele was. It was the bar that theatre people liked to frequent. Now, as he opens the door, he stops in his tracks. He doesn't have to go farther. Because he can see a bad haircut in a cheap grey suit, the man's cheeks flushed from drink. Your mother is not sitting across from him. No, she is beside him, and his hand is on her knee.

I do not remember much of the spectacle of our argument on the street, your mother pounding my chest with her balled fists. But do we really need to know any more about this moment? It was the beginning of the end between your mother and I. What I could not share with her was how her dalliance relieved me of my guilt about Dagmara, and how it solved a problem that my brief meeting with Odon presented. No, the moment required as much righteous indignation as I could muster.

The sadness and guilt I felt about what would happen to you would come later. Perhaps too much later, all things considered.

5.

03 / 30 / 89
Madonna and Child (Masaccio, c. 1426)

The night of September 1ˢᵗ, 1939 I can still remember vividly. It was the end of the week and I was in no hurry to return home. I would have to negotiate the new terms of disengagement with your mother once again. It was a nightly conversation, complete with veiled insults and recriminations that just provoked further bitterness. I had taken to a quick aperitif on Ku'damm most nights to steel myself, carefully varying my choice of café so that it did not seem as if I was turning into a regular anywhere. I was outside at a table at Café des Westens, reading the evening paper when the air raid sirens began to sound.

The sun had not yet gone down and there were still enough people on the street, including a few brownshirts on a drunken spree, patrolling for no other reason than to ensure that rumours of what was happening spread quickly. A waiter, hurriedly clearing two tables, looked as though he was ready to weep. I remember his basset hound eyes, his chin trembling under his moustache. I saw him speaking to two of these thugs. They stood, arms folded, demanding something he could not provide. They were unsteady from all the steins they had drained. I had been reading about antiquities over my drink, as if I was already preparing for my next meeting with Connie and Dagmara Vidler, and the brownshirts made me think of a photograph of thick, blockish, sandstone figures guarding a necropolis. I couldn't tell if they were hectoring the waiter to close or demanding him to seat them, but the poor man's face was turning redder, as if he was embarrassed for them. I waited until he hurried away from them to ask him what was going on.

Provenance

"It's the Poles. Their aircraft are coming. We're under attack and those idiots think it's a celebration. I told them we're not going to stay open and risk everyone's safety."

I asked him how much I owed for my pastis, gently placed the money in his hands, and then hurried out onto the street. At first I considered jumping on the tram but then decided it would be quicker if I just walked back to our apartment. It was you I was worried about; we needed to get you safely in the basement of our building, as soon as possible. I walked as briskly as I could. To run would have shown people I was afraid. Why did I care so much about complete strangers or believe anything I did mattered? I had an anxious need to be a paragon of composure. In my clipped trot, my expression frozen to suggest some unflappable, mildly-concerned model citizen, I was a joke waiting for the punchline of a falling bomb.

Which never came. How could it? We weren't being attacked at all. They were 'our' Stuka bombers up in the sky, headed for Poland. Call it a white lie told to prepare for years of darker ones.

But there had already been years of lies that everyone in my insulated little world, whose boundaries were defined by Galerie Hyperion and the few blocks I traveled each day, just laughed to ourselves about. We expected the lies to get worse. And we knew enough about the cruelties—the torture in interrogations, the stories of those in camps and the humiliations some of these thugs who were now empowered had carried out. One friend of your mother's had finally been released and spoke of having to walk on all fours, with his plate in his teeth, in order to get any food at all. We all knew there would be no limit to the bullying, the sadism, the outrages possible. Yet outrage itself had become an impossibility. Apart from myself, no one I knew—not Magda, not your mother, or any of the friends we let into our home—would give the government and its many servants and apologists we took money from anything remotely like a sincere opinion. Or a real emotional response. Of course we feared the risks of being rounded up, but we also felt they didn't deserve our honesty. A lie for a lie, that was the unspoken credo of the aesthete, the cynic's gospel.

Well now we were going to pay the ultimate price for our cynicism and inaction. Or perhaps I should condition that by saying eventually. In the meantime there was money to be made and influence to cultivate, self-interest above all.

Magda Petofi and I both knew the risks. We were making money from artwork that was officially deemed degenerate, mixing with people the government had either broken, forced into exile, or simply removed from the streets and detained in camps where all manner of enormities were being carried out. I had resolved to go through the days as the solicitous face of the gallery, yet I was secretly willing myself into a state of readiness for escape, to slip out amid the noise and spectacle of this dance of the dead.

As I burst into our apartment, the living room was in its usual state of untidiness. Your toys littered the parquet floor and furniture. Out of all of your expensive toy cars and soldiers, what you loved the most was this crudely-carved duck I had found in a junk shop, daubed in a sickly green and khaki. Do you remember that? It was perched on a chair, its bill plunged into the cushion like it dive bombed from the ceiling—perhaps to the sound of the chorus of Stukas. Everything looked suddenly abandoned. Pompeii turned to stone from a rain of ashes.

Then I heard your mother cooing in a sing-song reading voice. The sound was coming from the bathroom. I padded down the hall, shoes still on (how she hated that!) and slowly opened the door to see her, dressed in slip and bathrobe, reclining in the empty bathtub with the picture book of Grimm's fairytales in her hands. She put her finger to her lip to shush me as I approached. There, lying in her lap like a sled racer, was you, your long eyelashes closed, your chest rising and falling with your sleep-breaths.

The stillness, the tenderness, the way your little body curved so perfectly between your mother's legs as your head and shoulders rested in her lap. *Madonna Col Bambino.* There was such peace, such a cocoon of safety your mother had made for the two of you. It is how I always tried to remember you both—and still do.

But I had to spoil this moment soon enough. My harshly whispered interrogation of your mother began. Why was she in the bathtub? This was her pleasing her needlessly theatrical self, delighting in how whimsical and defiantly playful she could be with you in a moment of great seriousness and urgency. My scolding just caused her to smile wearily, as she roused you and you both clambered out of the tub.

"If you had come home early for the superintendent's meeting last week, you would know that we were advised, if we heard planes overhead, to wait in the bathroom if we couldn't get underground in time. The pipes for the plumbing serve to fortify the walls and ceiling in the case of a bombing."

"And he fell asleep."

"Yes. Before the witch could put Hansel and Gretel in the oven. And how was your afternoon, darling?"

The sound of the airplanes overhead had finally dissolved into the darkness. I followed her back into the living room where I stood on the carpet, stammering out my banalities, trying to settle into a genial, husbandly register. We communicated more in tone than in words by then, and this was my effort at humility, at almost-apology.

And yet I did blurt out, despite myself, words that had meaning.

"I think this is the end of something."

"I think so too, darling."

We both knew we weren't talking about the beginning of the war.

We should have made a clear decision to separate, but at my advanced age I'm amazed at all the days one can accumulate in some kind of transition, vacillating between living in the truth of your emotional responses and the belief that the expectations of others can define your understanding of happiness. Close to a year of these days elapsed, marked by needless deliberation, sleepwalking through obligations. Dishes washed and stacked, bills paid. Counting the marks in my wallet in line at the grocer's when suddenly an image of Dagmara, smiling blissfully, eyes closed, gently rocking in my lap… would come into focus, sending my heart racing, demanding I change my life, make an empty space in preparation for this stranger's return to fill it. And then a day or so later I would ease back into my role, clothing myself in a willed simplicity to conceal my uncertainty. I feared inflicting hurt for selfish reasons on the two vulnerable beings that depended on me.

Well, it was either fear or the belief that one looks squarely at the state of one's marriage, sees a house crumbling at its foundations, and calmly stacks the bricks one can salvage, beginning to reconstruct from memory. Where did that leave a man like me? I walled myself in, imprisoned by my own delusions.

In the end it was not I who would be decisive, it was your mother. In that first winter of the war, as business was brisk at the gallery, she was spending her days and nights productively, mixing with the actors, writers, and sundry 'cultural workers' as she formulated her own escape plan from our marriage. In many ways it was also an escape from the friends who supported her and gave her the strength to believe their world would survive.

I suspect she realized that there wasn't much of a future in the world of make-believe, given that most of the imaginative work was being done in the creation of official truths. Yet she had undergone so much change since our marriage that it feels foolish—and arrogant—for me to set down my speculations on what was motivating her, apart from a desire for some form of happiness. Her marriage and conversion to my family's faith did, as Magda had predicted, provide us both with some sense of safety for those first couple of years we were legally husband and wife. She could get by, and not only by sewing costumes, working under the table for various theatre companies, but she was finding work doing wardrobe for the films the UFA studios were churning out. These were gaudy propaganda spectacles that introduced her to a new circle of people she kept from me. Though she hated the endless days on set at Babelsburg, and we both bridled at her mother "summering" with us to look after you and spend time with her good friend Magda.

Which ended soon enough, before the first year of the war was over. With the final sales of his few pieces of art, Sabine's father had purchased over the years he had made enough to finance a trip to Palestine for him and Sabine's mother. They left the Hamburg port in a commercial trawler, some months before the deportations to Theresienstadt officially began. Your mother and I knew we might never see them again.

6.

04 / 02 / 89
Portrait of Oswald Spengler (Fritz Behn, c. 1928)

Nikolaus, I write each day now, I realize, to a stranger. Or at least that is what I tell myself. Yet I know there is, within me, the same watchful boy I once was. And I remember you had inherited that same trait. Withdrawn but intuitive. You would often startle your mother and I with how much you understood. And I'm sure you understood so much about the quiet dismantling and eventual destruction of our little family unit. And remember it well.

I was capable of seeing things from the perspective of your mother, believe me. I was all too aware that all the two of you had was me, the ex-banker who played at being bohemian and who, as your mother said (or should I say accused), sold his soul along with all the work of real artists in order for just a little more money, a little power and influence with the cranks, gangsters and mediocrities running things. Why wouldn't she start looking outside her marriage? And why not with a man who found her attractive, a foreigner who might provide her with an escape route? The suitor I first called her "Irish friend" must have provided her with the best conditions for a final transformation.

This was the foreigner I had seen her with in the Raabe-Diel, on the afternoon of my return from the auction. She introduced me to Francis Cluny that day, out of a reflexive boldness, a show of candor that was probably more for Cluny than me. "He is from a place called County Wicklow, and he will be sharp with you if you think he is a Britisher." Cluny chuckled and nodded Sabine's way, pleased by her directness. He rose from his seat to shake my hand. His German was quite good but I spoke English in my response. He could be familiar with your mother but he was not going to be familiar with me.

"I'm on contract with Irland Redaktion. It's a new radio service. They've asked me to write and read a weekly broadcast. The contract has allowed me to stay in your wonderful city, sir. With all its charms."

With the look that passed between him and your mother in that moment, I knew he had already slept with her.

"I'm sure there's much to tell your countrymen about what's happening here. I hope you're honest with them."

"Of course, Herr Maes. Would I strike you as a dishonest man?"

"You don't have to answer that, darling," your mother said. Wisely.

It still amazes me how much gall I had to argue with her about him later. In my jealousy I had completely absolved myself of any guilt about my night with Dagmara. How could my betrayal compare? It was unlikely that I would ever see Dagmara again while your mother could view her relationship with this Irishman as her means of escape. How unfair.

She had a new, sharper, ironic tone with me as she parried my accusations masterfully, once we were back home. "He's a married man with a family back in Ireland, Harry. I should think any kind of relationship with me is out of the question. Wouldn't you think so too? Or do you think that would mean nothing to him? Perhaps that is how all men carry on now."

I told her I was less interested in his family life than I was my own. She laughed, congratulated me on my new commitment to putting my family first above everything else. I'm sure my complexion betrayed how flustered I was, as I worked myself up into a state of righteous indignation.

"Do you think I'm working long hours at the gallery and then drinking with all of Magda's customers because I'm not putting my family first? I'm trying to keep us going, to pay for the milk in the ice box, the shoes on Nicki's feet." I was close to tears of self-pity. Oh, how I suffered.

What I should have said was something a little braver, something that would have admitted we had grown apart despite our best intentions. When I put my head on the pillow at night and closed my eyes, I saw Dagmara, not your mother. And I could only imagine that when she in turn closed her eyes to kiss me, she was seeing Francis Cluny. Love requires more than that feeling of self-congratulation that you're fulfilling your obligations. I hope you've also realized this—but without causing anyone pain. It requires the possibility of happiness, and your belief that the lover embodies it. I should have said something like that. At least it would have had the ring of self-awareness, despite my fondness for the platitude.

Yet I struggled with the thought that your mother was attracted to this stranger. Cluny looked like he had about a decade on me, leather-skinned and lean from some hard garret years. His hair was cut like a convict's, with the bristles at his temples shining a silvery grey. He dressed in a baggy grey tweed suit that smelled of suet and body odour, and his teeth were yellowed and stunted, stained a brownish-yellow from the steady chain of hand-rolled cigarettes he'd wet with his grey tongue and then smoked down to a little pile of ash in front of him, his baby finger meticulously shaping it in the tray. Yet even from our first conversation, the more he spoke, I could see that under his bushy eyebrows his bright blue eyes seemed lit up from within, and even his German had a musical lilt. He could make anyone feel like they were interesting, and that quality had to appeal to your mother, who required rapt attention. There was a puzzling joy he seemed to find in nothing more than indulging his curiosity, savouring what he could find out about you over a drink.

Which I ended up having with him again, some weeks after our first introduction. By then your mother and I had discussed the offer of work at the radio station that she insisted he made to her in the Raabe-Diel. It meant her first regular pay packet in years, and it was why she had to set out alone that afternoon despite my imminent arrival back home. Her version of their first meeting corroborated with what he told me, over our glasses of the last weissbier of summer at the Adlon Hotel. We were there with the team of Irland Redaktion, celebrating their first month on the air.

"I was invited by your culture minister for a literary tour of four cities in the spring—and then, because that went well, I got this offer for the radio program. An effort at Irish-German friendship. I suppose he realized that our ties might be valuable, given that we're staying neutral with this whole war business."

"You sound resigned to it now. Do you not think everyone will come to their senses and find some diplomatic solution? When Chamberlain left—   "

"Chamberlain… ha! The poor man was never going to win support back in his own parliament. No, the empire's been crumbling for quite some time. It was inevitable."

I was intrigued enough to ask him why he would say that and he did not disappoint. He took half a cigarette to give me the finer points of a perspective that he assured me was shaped by some of the keenest minds who had predicted that historical moment.

Which brings me to this painting I've kept, perhaps out of spite: the Portrait of Oswald Spengler. That day Cluny took it upon himself to educate me about the writer, specifically his
"decline of the west" thesis. Cluny said there was much to commend with Spengler's observations and prognostications. It was this author's contention that we were living through a period that would lead to about two hundred years of autocratic rule, beginning at some point around the year 2000. Cluny particularly admired Spengler's phrase 'optimism is cowardice' and shared many of the criticisms of Nazism the author espoused: the vulgar glorification of industry and technology, the 'foolish and doomed' anti-semitism. Yet Europe was in a 'pre-death cultural phase' and all of the energy of destruction, this 'fascinating emptiness' was playing out in Germany, and we were right in the center of it—its neon Rome. The Fuhrer was a genius, he said, but not in the way that he would prefer to be recognized as one. "He has too crude a mind to realize the era he will bring about will not be his own."

I had to protest, gently chide Cluny about his hypocrisy. I had listened to two of his broadcasts and heard him speak about this Third Reich of the Fuhrer's in terms that were more than complimentary—no, they were fawning.

"They're paying me well, Mr. Maes. The ends justify the means. But when I speak of those ends, I'm not simply talking about my bank account, sir."

I was trying to draw him out, taking the measure of him as an interesting crackpot who could invoke his own household gods of doom. He had more in common with the pseudo-intellectuals around the Fuhrer, the ultimate pseudo-intellectual, than he did with Oswald Spengler. I wanted to know why he couldn't earn the same kind of living back in London or Dublin. I told him he was obviously a talented speaker ("I'd prefer just a working man's thinker" he corrected me), and surely his perspective was shared by many of the more 'enlightened' and 'well-traveled' English-speaking writers.

"Oh, you'd be surprised, sir. We're not the cosmopolitans you'd quite imagine." He peered past me through the smoke from his cigarette, smiling beatifically. I glanced over my shoulder to see who might have walked in but he was only staring at his own reflection in the window.

He nimbly changed the subject to ask if I followed cycling. Yes, he truly loved this perfect marriage of man and machine, the sense of spectacle, 'like great gladiator's battles,' in the velodromes. He sensed I'd have nothing to say on that, that I was compelled to nod politely to his rhapsody. I realized he loved the sound of his own voice.

Anyway, some weeks later, one of Magda's newer clients brought in the portrait of Spengler for consignment. This was Herr Kranek, a big bull of a man who worked for Krupp, and who was going to Poland to work after separating from his wife. The portrait of Spengler is more of a study than a portrait, really. Behn was known as a sculptor rather than a painter. He was a particular favourite of the Nazis for his "realistic" renderings of African lions, panthers… even orangutans. The nobility of nature and all that. With this painting, I believe I once thought I would give it to Sabine and him as a wedding gift rather than sell it in the gallery, when they were able to finally wed.

Yes, I say finally able because Cluny was already married. It was your mother who would end up telling me more about his wife and children back in Ireland, and that was days later. This was in our talk over the first coffee of the day about what she proposed as an open marriage. She moved quite fast. No time to lose, I suppose.

"I don't see the point in lying to you. Of course Francis and I have slept together. We will no doubt continue to do so. He tells me I am beautiful and I have no reason to disagree. And he backs up his words with deeds."

"This is surprising,"

"No it isn't. It can't be."

"Not your sleeping with him. Just his initiative. You'd think your favourite radio personality would believe that talk was action enough."

"I'm serious, Harry. Your sarcasm is unbecoming."

"My concern is not for you or me, darling. It's for Nicki."

And to that she could only laugh before she launched into her summation of my failings. How would I know what's best for you? She said I took a passing interest in your welfare. When was the last time I had actually spent time with you, not just scolded you for your table manners, your untidiness? Here I was, a 'typical provincial,' pretending to be sophisticated, and yet when presented with a true, modern solution to the failings of bourgeois marriage I could not even grant her the validity of her argument. There were whole communities in Russia who were now living in more open arrangements, thriving because women were no longer property, they were equal.

"Your new lover doesn't strike me as much of a Bolshevik," I said.

"True. I suppose you'd know better about that."

It must have been entertaining to see me trying to conceal my surprise. I could feel my cheeks were hot, as I took on that flustered, stammering defense of my hypocrisy. I had never felt more like your grandfather, the secret unbeliever, in that moment. She calmly rose from her chair, opened the drawer in my desk to produce the letter Dagmara had sent to Galerie Hyperion, just days before. I had brought it home to respond over the first coffee I had in the mornings before you were both out of bed.

"Let's avoid any melodrama, shall we?" She lit up a cigarette, blew out a strong cloud of smoke and examined her nails, bitten down to the quick. "Anyway, Francis now has a more open agreement with his wife. She's an actress, she comes from a theatre family. Her mother's quite famous there. They're stuck living with her, raising their two daughters in this woman's house in Dublin. He says they're committed republicans. They want to drive the British out of their country. Francis has no interest in violence. They do."

I was quickly re-reading Dagmara's letter to see if she had been indiscreet in any way. It had arrived the week before and I was initially delighted, but I had yet to write a response I could live with. Line by line, yes… no mention of our sleeping together. Though she did make a quip about Connie calling her a Bolshevik, so your mother had evidently read it closely enough to remember that.

"I want to tell you this woman—

"Dagmara, isn't it? You can call her by her name. I'm sure it's familiar to you."

"She has an auction house in London with her husband. This was all about how we could help each other."

"Oh I'm sure it was. Now don't be tiresome. I'm trying to tell you Francis and his wife have come to an agreement which seems entirely sensible for us as well. I know you're not happy, darling. There has been a lot of change in our lives."

I could not look at her. I was fixated on Dagmara's letter in my hands, her loopy cursive. She did put a heart beside her name, along with an X and an O. "I am doing my best for you, Sabine. For you and Nicki."

"I know you are. I know you are."

It was as if by repeating herself she could soothe me, tell me all was forgiven. But she did not really care if she was forgiven in turn. She was indifferent.

"I suppose I have no choice here. You want an open marriage and I will just have to accept it."

"It is my hope that you will accept me telling the truth. As I will accept you doing the same." She stabbed out her cigarette and rose to prepare for bed. But not before she could say just one more thing at the bathroom door. "When you're ready."

I wish I had kept Dagmara's letter so I could quote it here, but I burned it. There came a time when I had to destroy all evidence of our knowing each other so I could save my life. But that was years later. You can probably imagine it anyway. Yes, there was an invitation to visit both her and Connie in London. There was flirty language about how well I danced, that I made a Bolshevik, peasant girl like her look like a woman of royalty on the ballroom floor. She said she hoped to come to Berlin soon, that she did not imagine things would get much worse. Chamberlain and Hitler were ultimately sensible men. It hadn't been a month since she posted it and already it had seemed like a letter from another time.

All these years later, I still puzzle over how your mother transformed herself with Francis Cluny. From Sabine to Sally, yes? Cluny was not one of those fellow traveler communists like her theatre friends, and his pretensions were more literary. He had told me he was one of only a handful of Irishmen who were 'truly modern writers.' Yet he wanted something different than literary fame, if his broadcasts were any indication: he fancied himself a 'visionary of destruction'—your mother's words. And I think she liked that. Perhaps she thought it more profound or in tune to her self-dramatizing pessimism. However, when I'm more reductive and cynical about their relationship, I see her as merely pragmatic. Here was a foreigner who loved her like a schoolboy, who represented the prospect of escape. He'd given her work, a new career she quite liked, and he was actively looking for someone who would provide him with grounds for escape from his own failed marriage back in Ireland. This would be your mother, who never really had an interest in any open marriage, I believe. She just wanted to slowly acquaint me with the reality of us no longer being together. Despite whatever transactional, predictable infidelities I might have committed, in her mind our separation was going to be catastrophic for me. I would be the un-betrothed, the un-father, while she was moving to the next spotlight on the bare stage where she was always the star.

Now I can honestly say that I hope that is how she lived. Because if I know anything, I am sure it was always what she wanted.

7.

04 / 03 / 89

Portrait of a Man in Oriental Costume (Follower of Rembrandt, c. 1650)

New day and new month here, grey as the last. Aside from telling you about this next painting, I'm going to try and write of disappearances and reappearances, Nicki. When I think of those next few years of the war, leading up to the destruction of Antwerp and Berlin, my fate was marked by the way those who had been so much a part of my life vanished, as if a curtain had come down on the act when they had a role, while those whom I presumed I'd never see again returned, as if they were emissaries from the future when I first encountered them. The disturbing thing about it all was that, if you were observing the direction my life was taking, you would think I was in the absolute centre of everything. Yet everything of consequence to me occurred beyond my line of sight.

I write that and ask myself if this is an attempt at escaping culpability. My Houdini act, slipping out of the chains of judgment and consequence. You'll judge for yourself, I'm sure. Your father is a poor magician.

Over the years, I have tried to understand Magda's motive for ceding so much of Galerie Hyperion's operations to me. Granted, the business was in no way independent anymore. To have come from Budapest and make a name for the gallery by nothing more than her savings and her love of the most original and innovative painting she could get her hands on, this was an accomplishment. But out of a desire to help Jewish families who needed to fund their emigration, or to keep the painters working and solvent while the government increasingly viewed them as degenerate enemies of the people, she welcomed the interest of the Reichskulturkammer. Maybe she thought she could play things to her advantage at first. I could see why having a young man with impeccable Aryan origins as the new face of the gallery made sense. It was all logical, until they asked her to find buyers for work they had pillaged, claimed as property of the state, blacking out any documentation of their provenance. At that point, why didn't she simply shut her doors? The gallery did not need to remain in business with me in charge.

I think it was the illusion of control. When I came to work with her, Magda had been in business for more than a decade. She had seen the rise of the Nazi party for six of those years, done business with some of the more vulnerable and conflicted among them like Odon Heimrath, and she had been able to survive—even flourish—while the street violence, the disappearances, the stories of the cruelties meted out on those painters and writers detained without charges in the windowless rooms of the Reich Main Security Office on Prinz-Albrecht-Strasse (yes, the street is now renamed for Kathe Niederkirchner, but I can't get used to calling it Niederkirchner-Strasse) continued, and with greater frequency. I can still see her as I remember her greeting me each morning in the gallery, sitting primly at her desk at back, clamping down on that long ebony cigarette holder, her face wreathed in silvery smoke, as she squinted and clucked in amusement at the propaganda in the morning papers. What she read was 'beneath contempt,' and she attributed her weight gain to the stress the news caused her. A few extra kilos were 'insulation from vulgarity.' And her new zaftig figure could be artfully concealed beneath dark, flowing dresses that made her look like she stepped out of a Klimt painting. She applied a touch of darker rouge to her round cheeks to give them 'shape' and wore her ginger curls up to accentuate her slender neck. Given that she could manage the way her body was 'betraying' her, perhaps it followed that she could deceive the sundry thugs and philistines who'd require her 'unparalleled access to the finest works created in the ateliers of our new, modern masters'—a quote from promotional copy I wrote myself.

However, she would deal in Old Masters as well if the price was right, and this particular painting is a case in point. She brought this in one day, saying her husband was invited to dinner by the great collector Franz Oppenheimer, who had already emigrated to

Budapest from Berlin at that point. Both Lazlo and Magda were spending a lot more time in Budapest, and I would come to find out why soon enough. Oppenheimer was hoping to emigrate even further afield, and so he gave them this portrait, that he claimed was actually a Rembrandt, and not the work of one of his followers. I was never quite convinced this was a work of the master himself. Ironically, as you'll realize soon enough, I was nervous about passing it off as one and then incurring the wrath of the Reichskulturkammer. And so I never did get around to exhibiting it.

Magda would have had no compunction, I know. She knew the way the world worked, and for years she had been rewarded for her astute understanding of motivation. I don't think she had ever read anything but newspapers and a few French novels, but she was Machiavellian to her core. She knew who to flatter, how to casually mention she possessed information on others that would be ruinous to their careers. I watched her do this so gracefully, as she strolled through the gallery with millionaires like the Krupps, remarking on Nolde's brushwork and then finding a way to insert into the conversation what she knew of the War Minister's new wife Erna Gruhn. Of course she had seen the pornographic photos Gruhn posed for. 'Not bad, but there's better work done by amateurs, and Erna was professional.' "She knows everything incriminating," your mother had said to me one morning, in our final days together, "doesn't that worry you?" If anything, I felt reassured.

That is, until Fischer's auction in Lucerne, when I was pushed out on to the stage from behind her splash of light, her protégé and creation. My innocence still amazes me. I had no idea she was slowly and carefully positioning me as the face of Galerie Hyperion. Perhaps, because of my vanity and my ambition, I believed my charisma and charm was winning over those Magda had to please, and I presumed I was far better at it than she was. "You must realize the importance of the superficial, Herr Maes," she said one afternoon, "most people never truly learn to look closely, especially in this business." My success, I believed, was living proof.

Still I was not too vain to realize I would never read the field like Magda could. She sensed what made the Nazis different. Despite their mediocrity and philistinism, she knew they were truly modern, technocrats who prized one commodity over all others, including great art: information. Perhaps, at the root of the obsessive collection and cataloguing of even the most insignificant details of the 'volk' was that drive for purification, that visceral hatred of all things Jewish, or perhaps it was just a morbid fear of losing the power they were still astonished they had. But I'm convinced she knew her only way to survive the reach of the listeners, the cataloguers, the scribes in the service of the butchers, was to slowly disappear and then wait until they destroyed themselves. Because, ultimately, as the erasure of authentic provenance affirmed, the power was in what information this new and future state, this fever dream of an empire, could cause to disappear.

I just think Magda ran out of time. Even though I really don't believe she—or I—could have won such a battle against the data keepers anyway. Despite this city being reduced to rubble, defended in its final days by children who could barely hold their rifles up to fire, the modern people, their minds a-swim with numbers, souls whitened to cinders, rose up like a phoenix. You could repurpose any ideology to be in the service of the power of information, because this Berlin is now just a parody of the one they destroyed. But I digress. The data-keepers almost got her in the end—just as they'll finally get me.

I should have seen it coming when, one quiet Wednesday afternoon, Laszlo Petofi walked into the gallery. Magda had taken a few days to visit her ageing mother in Budapest—at least that is what she told me—but the appearance of the good professor, wobbling like a wounded circus bear with each laboured step, told me something else.

"Allo, Herr Maes! Good to see you again!" *Why was it good to see me?* "I don't lecture until three, I was nearby, and I thought I'd take you for a coffee. Are you busy?"

He could see for himself the gallery was deserted. Yes, of course I could go with him, the month's receipts could wait. I turned the sign on the door to 'closed,' locked up, and put on a brave face for our stroll to the nearest café.

"Professor, what happened to your leg, if you don't mind me asking?"

"Not at all, it was my own fault! I walked out into the street without looking, had my head in my lecture notes and didn't see a cyclist. I'm sure it was comical to watch for everyone but me and him."

I could almost believe this, given it was Laszlo, but I had noticed a tremor in his grip when we shook hands. I knew enough about the frequency of 'interviews' the Gestapo were carrying out, and he would have been a prime target—foreigner teaching history, with a wife known for mixing with degenerates. Laszlo was not as practiced a liar as Magda;   the next hour was going to be a chore.

He must have felt the same way, because he got down to business quickly. "Harry, I don't know if you know this but Galerie Hyperion… the lease, the business account… it is all in my name."

"I see." I had no sense where this was going, but noticed the tremor in his hands once again as he stirred two cubes of sugar into his espresso. And then a third.

"Magda and I, we're thinking of returning to Budapest for a while. Her mother's not well, as you know. And I still have not taken my sabbatical to complete my larger study on Schinkel and the gothic revival, as you know."

As I knew, as I knew... the bad liar's tic. I knew nothing of what he spoke. "So you're closing the gallery?"

"Not at all, no. But we were thinking… if we were to transfer ownership, give you the reins…"

I could feel my chest constrict, my pulse quicken. The stress of paying the key money for your mother's new apartment and the expenses for your care were already causing me insomnia. It was only a few years before when I had been practically destitute, living off black bread and paying a few pfennigs a night for a bed in a workers' co-op out in Neukolln. I was on my own once again and even though I had a closet full of suits and was breaking in a new pair of English shoes, I felt the creeping sense of dread that I was going broke.

"Laszlo, I should tell you, I'm not in the position to invest in the gallery. I haven't told anyone, but Sabine has left me, and I am now paying for two homes, really."

"Oh that's awful, Harry." He gave me a tentative pat on the side of my arm. It was a comradely gesture he must have seen in the movies. "It might be for the best, though, my friend. My impression of Sabine is that she is a very free spirit, still hanging on to her childhood, do you know what I mean?"

"I suppose that's one way of looking at it."

"She might need some time alone. One grows up quickly these days, I would think, when one has to stand alone."

Only Laszlo could provoke me into defending your mother. "But she's not alone. She's looking after our boy. She's been a good mother."

"Please don't get me wrong. I do not mean to traduce her or you. It can be that childlike nature which brings someone that much closer to children. And that can be all to the good. All to the good. With all that's going on, we need to cherish the innocence of the child."

Traduce... Laszlo chose his words like he was finding his shiniest pennies to put in the palm of my hand. I wasn't interested in his charity. Or his veiled condescension. Yet I didn't really know how I could refuse his offer. I was duty bound to the gallery. It was the vessel that contained all my ambition. And I was terrified of being jobless once again.

"I might want to be more of a child myself, then."

"It would not be possible for you. Or I, Harry. It is this we have in common, yes? We've left childhood well behind us. I can tell you are the eldest one in your family, just like I am."

I tried to laugh this off but the Professor, damn him, was actually more perceptive than I wanted to admit. "The eldest child, yes. But not the one who's shown he is responsible with money."

"But we won't be needing your money. Just a change of title and ownership. And only until this war is over. I should think it won't be more than a year until we can return to normal."

"But what if it's longer? What if this whole mess drags on and..."

"You can say it. What if we go out of business? You should know that Magda is one of a few very special licensed agents for the sale of government-owned work."

"I've been made aware, yes."

Laszlo looked puzzled for a moment. He drained his espresso and blinked his puzzlement away. I could see his brow unfurrow once again when he decided Magda must have told me, yes. Careless of her not to mention that. "Well, your trip to Lucerne a year ago was in the service of her clientele that she is authorized to sell to, semi-privately. I mean she cannot put that work on the walls of the gallery. Not anymore."

"No, I suppose not." Just to put the professor on his heels, I decided I did not have to be quite so solicitous. "It would be a terrible decision for business, anyway. To my mind."

"You're absolutely right. You see, this is why you taking the reins would be the perfect arrangement. You'll know how to make the right decisions in the months ahead. Magda and I, we think she can keep things going and do a handsome trade through her international clientele in Budapest."

It was conceivable to me that Magda actually had greater access to buyers outside of Berlin. I was naïve enough to believe that she would always be considered Magda Petofi and not Magda Zeisel of the Budapest Jewish family who owned so much property in Hungary. If she was no longer quite so visible, why would someone like Odon Heimrath and the Reichskulturkammer even care about her life back in Hungary? She was useful—more than I could ever claim to be.

"So I just purchase this government-owned work, like I did on my trip to Lucerne, and then Magda can sell it abroad for a profit?"

"Precisely. And we can continue to sell work the government won't mind seeing on the walls of the gallery. If you do well, maybe we can think about you becoming co-owner upon our return. I proposed that we increase your commission. Magda agreed that would be a good idea."

"Increased commission even on the work from the Reichskulturkammer?"

"That's right, Harry. You're a talented salesman. You should be compensated. It's about time, yes?" He patted my shoulder again. "Do we have a deal?"

"What do I have to lose?" I said, not quite seriously.

"Wonderful!" Laszlo clapped his hands together. What a huge relief this was for him. I should have been far more interested in why.

Yet it did not really surprise me, this new arrangement. It was all so logical and clear-eyed about the turn things were taking. I knew your grandfather Pastor Maes would be delighted to hear what a success I was becoming.

The only person I really wanted to tell, as soon as I got home, was Dagmara. Or should I say the Dagmara I created when I wrote to her? The nights were so quiet, now that I was living alone, and the radio was blaring nothing but triumphant reports of the army's advances across Europe, so to put pen to paper and imagine Dagmara hanging on my every word was an escape fantasy that was sustaining me. I had written a number of letters like the one I composed that night, though that one, I promised myself, I would actually send.

I know the question: why was I so timid? Dagmara had written to me as an overture—not once but three times—and here I was, a free man, a bachelor once again. But I felt like I was stringing one word along after another like glass beads on some costume necklace I was making for her if I tried to declare my feelings. I was fashioning such cheap jewelry compared to the quality of love she deserved. I feared I was too conventional, each paragraph just a collection of clichés.

Yes, look at me now! No longer so vain. I don't give a damn about my mediocrity. These are my confessions for you. I just want you to understand who your father was as you read over this small catalogue. You can keep the catalogue information and then burn these pages if what I'm writing causes you to feel ashamed. I suppose I'm beyond any sense of propriety now.

But before you do burn them, you must at least acknowledge there are some unexpected turns in my story, with all the provocative intimations of a larger design emerging. I say this almost seriously. I have that irksome tendency to become ironic which so easily offends the earnestly contemporary among us. You can stop now if you believe this larger design will finally be revealed. I'm just a decade younger than this century. Here it is, its time coming to a close just like mine and nothing really adds up. If I believed in a God like your pious old grandfather professed he did, I'd say he couldn't craft a story to save his life. Though this whole period reminds me he was still capable of a few scenes that remain vivid.

8.

04 / 04 / 89

The Annunciation (Barnaba de Modena, c. 1383)

When I think of this painting, what flickers up from memory as I type is the Irish embassy near Tiergarten park. Now long gone, of course, reduced to rubble during the bombings. This would have been a few weeks after my conversation with Laszlo Petofi. It was where William Warnock, the Irish chargé d'affaires, organized a gathering to mark the opening of a small show of paintings from the Irish trust that "celebrated the Catholic faith and the technical advancements of the Renaissance." From the embassy the show was set to tour a few university towns to "foster stronger Irish-German relations and the rich cultural dialogue our two nations have developed over the last decade."

When I had opened up the invitation that came to the gallery, addressed to Magda, my first impulse was to throw it away rather than post my rsvp. Francis Cluny would be there with your mother, inevitably. Cluny would have to cover this event for his radio program. To arrive alone and pretend I was interested in the conversations I was obligated to have with those expecting Magda rather than me was too much like work, and I'd be trying to steal glances at your mother all night to understand the woman she had become. Why torture myself in this way? Yet in the end I couldn't resist.

Was it jealousy that had me counting the days until the opening? I don't know if it was that simple. After all, there were two Saturdays when I would see your mother before then, as I picked you up from her small apartment just off Stresemannstrasse to spend the day with you. When your mother would greet me, she was always too formal. Cold, polite, like an automaton responding to my efforts at small talk with terse, one-sentence answers. If she felt I was probing too deeply about her work or her relationship with Cluny, those sentences would dissolve into fragments, telegraphed information from a broken line.

Let me admit it—there was an erotic charge for me in imagining her transformed by her new relationship with this Irishman. To see her dressing differently, speaking differently, coquettishly posing for the gaze of another man was to feel enraged by her inauthenticity, her callous ability to shake off the identity she had been uneasily fashioning as my wife and your mother. Enraged and aroused.

Yet I had the presence of mind to ask myself if her former identity was any more authentic. It was just shaped by the obligations of motherhood and the disappointment of never being able to fulfill her ambition of perfecting her shape shifting on the stage. Everything that was true, save for you, had been stripped from her: her family, her history, her faith, and her aspirations, ever since she had fled Hamburg and come to Berlin, only to eke out a living in the margins. I'm sure I had come to personify one of the new model citizens, complicit and impervious to Berlin's sharpening cruelty. I'm still ashamed by this compulsion I had felt to fantasize about claiming her for myself once again, stripping her of her sly resistance, her vitality, her will to survive.

Silvia Stanciu, the woman who now deigns to sleep with this old man, said to me: "Harry, you've lived through so much violence, and yet for all you've told me about your life, you have never been violent yourself." She finds this ennobling. Who am I to disabuse her of this notion? I could psychologize it, I suppose, claim it is the ultimate legacy of my father's casual beatings that I found a way to shape my violent impulses to criminal purposes, transform them into tactics of survival. But there is one thing for which I'm in agreement with the vulgarians who run this government: psychology is bourgeois nonsense. It was more than simply survival. I had the power, the luxury of sublimating my jealousy and my violent impulses into cold transactions, where I could dictate value, decide the fate of works given up for sale. And there would end up being lives in the balance before I was spared a reckoning. How can I explain to Silvia that I was able to view violence as the refuge of the powerless?

What Silvia knows of me is enough. I have never mentioned Dagmara. I have given Silvia a version of what happened in the Tiergarten that night that features your mother flinging half a glass of champagne at me and storming out of the exhibition, with Francis Cluny following close behind. I have described it as what led Antony Farrell, who introduced himself as an archivist for the Vatican library, to approach me, out of some gentlemanly impulse to quell my embarrassment. He was breaking the awkward silence that Sabine's tantrum caused. Silvia would tell you it was an argument about our son that provoked Sabine. I come off quite well in all this, of course.

Yet that's not what happened. For at that exhibition, accompanying this gentleman Antony Farrell, was Dagmara. I entered the foyer of the building, gave my raincoat to the coat check girl and was about to pluck a flute glass of champagne from a young bow-tied man bearing a magnum's worth on a silver tray when I glimpsed her, under the speckled play of light from the cut-glass chandelier. My lips moved to stutter out '*meine liebe*' before I could check myself, but no one around me took notice. No one but Dagmara, there across the room, eyes a-sparkle, unsmiling, tense, and poised for an embrace we would have to deny ourselves until I could finally take her home.

Among the work on the walls was this Modena I have here. I must admit it's not a favourite of mine. It is not authentic either, so you could put it down to some Dutchman's crude efforts to give this the look of an age still fumbling to understand the rules of perspective. Gabriel the angel is awkwardly placed before the virgin in a cramped space. Indeed the whole interior seems foreshortened compared to the two figures. He kneels, bearing a scroll declaring her annunciation and she sits before a prie-dieu, rightly afraid about the momentousness of this visitation. Behold the drama, yet the drama is really not there—at least for me.

Though I'm a hardened case. I don't pretend to know what love is, nor for the life of me, what force brings people together. I can only tell you that Silvia's look of hunger, in the moments before our bodies join together, is like a rhyme from another language, echoing the look Dagmara gave me every time we were reunited over those six short, terrible years. I could say it all began in Lucerne, but really, I only understood the full implications of her effect on me that night.

I approached her as if magnetized. The clamor, the babble, the shimmering facets and angles of the grand staircase, the chandelier… it all fell away, muted and out of focus. There was just her, as inevitable as a magic trick revelation.

"Herr Maes. You owe me letters. I thought you had vanished for good."

I took her hand in mind and brought it to my lips. It smelled of dark tobacco and musky soap. The gesture was not quite serious but I knew the look in my eyes told her this was as serious as the grave. "I was trying to get the words right. You have a way of scrambling my thoughts, Mrs. Vidler."

She was looking deeply into my eyes. I was opening up again, my heart beating as if I'd sprinted into a new life. And I suppose I had.

"Where are we going after this, Harry? Where are you going to take me?"

"Anywhere and everywhere."

"You see this is why I wanted your letters. I wanted you to be specific for me. I needed details."

"I have missed you like I have never missed anyone."

She put her finger to my lips. "I know. There will be time for you to tell me. Come… I want you to meet my new friend Mr. Farrell. He's with the Vatican Library."

So many questions I had. Where was Connie, her husband? And why was she at an exhibition like this? Yet they didn't matter at the moment. She had found a way to get to me, to continue what we started beyond all the misunderstandings inherent in the letters we could post to each other (envelopes steamed open, each word read by the Gestapo, upon the recommendation of Odon Heimrath). I've come to believe that in any relationship like ours, one lover plays the director, the other becomes the central character. Dagmara was directing, she would tell me what I needed to know when the time was right.

And in that moment, she made it clear to me that meeting Antony Farrell was imperative. It was in the stern way she clasped my forearm, directing me through the crowd over to him, where Farrell was leaning against the wall, visibly bored, as a woman in an absurd feathered hat yammered on, in broken Italian, about seeing Modena's work in Bologna. Farrell turned to Dagmara with a pleading look to be saved.

"Excuse me, I hope I'm not interrupting, Antony, I just have to introduce you to my friend Harry Maes of the Galerie Hyperion. He's curated some wonderful shows over the last few years."

The woman in the feathered hat turned with a startled look. Who would be so rude? But then she took Dagmara in from head to toe and, in the unspoken competition for attention, ceded ground, made her retreat.

Antony Farrell un-propped his elbow from the wall to hold out his hand for me to shake. He moved with a kind of fluid grace, as he gestured to Dagmara and flattered her as "the woman who knows the most interesting people in every city." Or was he flattering me? I would learn that Farrell was a man who always had two motives, equally plausible, at work, leaving you both charmed and puzzled when he held court.

Within five minutes of speaking, I discovered that he was new to the Vatican library. He mentioned an Irish archbishop who had spoken for him with the pontifical council, assuring he got the job. He was "just a boy from the country, the youngest in his family who was sent to be a priest." He left the church soon after he was ordained and ended up at Cambridge and then the Courtauld Institute.

Dagmara cut in. "He was brilliant and the priests who taught him knew it. That's why they pulled him back in."

"Ah, no, now. They will never manage that. They had me once and not again."

Watching him speak and charm Dagmara and I, he reminded me of that American film actor Fred Astaire. Save for his attire, that is. No top and tails, just the threadbare tweed and corduroy of a penniless academic. There was a white rose in his lapel though, and I wasn't quite sure what it meant.

Until I saw it in the lapel of Francis Cluny too. Yes, through the crowd who had now filled this room, was Francis and Sabine (I still couldn't call her 'Sally'—Cluny named her that). As expected. But I didn't expect how distant they were to us. Francis and Sabine nodded to me and your mother sized Dagmara up as judge and jury, straining to smile. But there was no scene, no drama. I was left to speculate on what those roses meant, why they were the only two men wearing them.

The bigger mystery, of course, was why Dagmara brought us all together. How did she manage to choreograph this whole scene? And where was Connie?

I had many questions. Dagmara could see how I was trying to piece it all together and sensed my unease. As we moved through the exhibition to look at the paintings with Farrell, she squeezed my hand, nodded as if to say it's all right, Harry. "I promise, all will be understood in time."

All these years later, I can say it was the one promise Dagmara never kept.

And yet, if I'm completely honest, I must tell you it didn't really matter if she explained it all. I knew enough from Farrell's manner and from Dagmara's constant scheming, to sense that what would be required of me could get me hanged as a traitor, after the torture of the Nazis' methods of interrogation. But it didn't matter. I decided she was worth it.

9.

04 / 08 / 89

The Saint (Emil Nolde, c. 1918)

As I sit at this desk, with my view of the skyline in the morning light, where the office towers have reclaimed the rubble over the fourteen years I have had this apartment, it is almost a consolation to age as a poor man in Berlin. Consider it a legacy from your grandfather's religious vocation, Nikolaus, but poverty can feel something like virtue restored, if I can finally forget what my life was like at thirty.

And of course forgetting is impossible with those paintings, stacked away in the other room. What a thoughtful gift from that old vulture Odon Heimrath. They are more of a problem than some 'hidden treasure' that this Czech, Mr. K, speaks so fondly of, with just the right amount of effusiveness to signal he wants them for himself.

But I'm sure I'll speak more about this particular Mr. K in time. Particular, or should I say peculiar? My grasp of words is escaping me by the day, it seems.

Antony Farrell, my old friend from the Vatican Library, had a good English word for Mr. K's kind: a chancer. When I first heard the expression, in my palatial apartment just a few streets over, all those decades ago, Farrell was speaking of Francis Cluny, the con man who was sleeping with my wife. "A chancer is a fella who lives by his wits, who's got a good game going until the bank or the polis comes after him. All credit to Francis, he's done well."

It was just the three of us, drinking Dagmara's favourite Alsatian sekt, as we spoke of the Vatican exhibition, the tour he was about to go on of the southern cities to show the provincials all the masterpieces, the great cultural legacy of the Renaissance burghers who were descended from barbarian warlords, and who claimed Rome for themselves. It was a conquest narrative that aligned seamlessly with the Fuhrer's aspirations, and with Goring's crazed appetite for any and everything that could transform him into a beer hall Medici. It felt liberating to ridicule their pretensions. And to speak of those opportunists like Cluny who were so transparently in it for themselves. Dagmara laughed along too but she was mad for my secret collection of jazz recordings—the ones I never played for Odon Heimrath's friends—and was flitting back and forth from the phonograph as we talked.

"I just knew you two would hit it off! Do you have more of this wine, darling?"

I told her to help herself to what was in the kitchen, because I didn't want to interrupt my conversation with Farrell. The Hot Fives were blaring at double the volume I would risk on any other occasion but this was Dagmara, more beautiful than ever with her blonde curls grown out from the flapper's hairstyle she had when we first met. She was actually in my home, not some apparition conjured in fitful, drunken sleep. She would be in my bed that night and I felt like the luckiest man in Berlin.

Yet I still wanted to know more about Cluny. And Farrell obliged, putting his slim ankles on my Ottoman. Red sheer socks, just like the Pope's, he said. "I didn't know that woman he calls Sally was your wife. He described her to me as his 'little Jewess.' He told me that he'd gotten her a job and diplomatic immunity because his radio broadcasts were too important to Goebbels. Said she'd be lost without him, would that be true now?"

I did my best to affect an air of complete detachment, but I was enraged. It was jealousy, and it was also my own sense of failure. Your mother knew I wasn't enough to save her or you. How dare she make something heroic out of her infidelity.

If Farrell picked up on how much he was wounding me, he did not show it. Encouraged by Dagmara, who loved his stories, he began telling us all that was really going on in the Vatican.

He spoke of Pacelli, Pope Pius XII, quietly entertaining, in his private quarters, Goebbels and Goring and their 'pasty-faced sycophants.' All this was happening while Pacelli played the saintly father of the poor and the afflicted, the Vicar of Christ, for the crowds that would amass in St. Peter's Square. The Curia was busy behind the scenes trying to manage relations with the diplomatic emissaries from America and Britain, but it 'was really like the court of some dangerous prince' behind the gilt-encrusted doors.

"This Pope is vain enough to believe he can bargain with these gangsters over his art collection. But it's like mad King Ludwig installing a couple of crocodiles into his menagerie. Suddenly the gazelles will disappear."

The Curia, Antony's real employers, were worried, he said. They had managed to persuade the Pope that a tour of some of the paintings would be an appropriate gesture. It helped cement the alliance and friendship between the Vatican and the German government. And Mussolini, whom Antony described as mad as a loon, could not have been happier with the arrangement, insisting he select several works that he knew the Fuhrer would love, for his private viewing that was scheduled for the following day.

"Antony is going to be his special guide," Dagmara said boastfully, as if she was speaking of her younger brother. Farrell blushed and said he was dreading the thought.

"I hear he loves his cocaine. Maybe you can get some for your good friend Dagmara. Your little emerald island is a desert of pleasure, Mr. Farrell."

"Why do you think I left as soon as I had two pennies to rub together?"

Whether it was all the wine I was pouring or just my rusty English, I was feeling like I really couldn't keep up to their banter, with all their veiled allusions to people I had only heard about and never met. I had many questions, and there was so much I really didn't know about Dagmara.

She explained, as she toasted our small gathering, why Vidler's had relocated to Dublin soon after the war was declared. It was necessary, given the trade in antiquities and fine art that Connie relied upon, to be working from a neutral country. They had set up shop in an area called St. Stephen's Green and bought a townhouse just a few streets over so Connie could walk to work. "He hates umbrellas. He leaves them everywhere. I swear, he's keeping the umbrella trade afloat in Dublin."

For the first hour or so, I wasn't sure if she and Antony had been lovers. They had that kind of rapport where they knew each other's weaknesses and teased at every opportunity. He called her 'la Vidler' like she was an opera diva and she called him a flirt. But on our second drink I realized she was chiding him about flirting with Rainer Gurlitt, a lieutenant with the SS who was at the opening of the exhibition. I should have picked up on Antony's inclinations, given how bashful he became when Dagmara briefly left our company.

"Antony knows everyone worth knowing in Italy, Harry. Antony, tell him about Suckert and his Casa Malaparte. It's on the island of Capri. Antony, you must get us invitations."

I knew who Suckert was, had heard about his book called *Technique du Coup d'Etat*, where he'd been provocative enough to title one chapter "Hitler: A Woman". Mussolini had put him under house arrest and Suckert had built what Dagmara called 'this astonishing villa.' Just the prospect of spending time on Capri with her would be worth all the time we were apart, all the bothersome complications that defined the distance between us.

Antony spoke of Suckert, who went by Curzio Malaparte, as a man who fascinated him because you couldn't pin him down, couldn't figure out just what he was loyal to, and yet he seemed to thrive in this era when loyalties defined one's ambitions.

Now I realize he could have been speaking of himself, really.

From his line of questioning, he was figuring out my loyalties as well. He needed to know all about Magda, and I realized, as I spoke about her and Laszlo, I really only had a sketchy understanding of her life back in Budapest, and why she had opened Galerie Hyperion. I couldn't tell him much about you or your mother, apart from my exasperation that your mother had insisted on making a bit of a scene before Antony, Dagmara and I had left the exhibition. I must have come across as a passive rather than active force in my own life, someone who had things happen to him, whose good fortune was an accident of timing more than anything else.

What I realized too, as I explained my transactional relations with the government, was that my distaste for them all was really not deeply felt. I could rationalize what I heard about the deportations, the depravity and cruelties of those who'd led us into war because these were the losers doing all the dirty work, the broken men who came out of the Great War and had spent years on the margins. They were a lot like the aesthetes and the penniless bohemians your mother mixed with. They suffered, in their awkward alienation, from a kind of homesickness for what could never be home again. Even the ones I dealt with had no real talents except for advertising and propaganda, which thrived on the clichés and banality that was central to their grand theme of racial supremacy. This was the thin gruel of inspiration that had sustained them in their years as underground men. Their ultimate crime to me was their philistinism, their mediocrity.

It is outrageous, I know. These psychopaths and bullies were carrying out horrific acts of violence in the small cells that lined the basement of a building I passed every day—and of course in the camps. They were making plans to murder literally millions of people. I had heard of one cultured gentleman—who bought a couple of Noldes from me—who was stationed in Trieste and ran a concentration camp in an old rice mill. Like the witch in Hansel and Gretel, the joke was that he threw children into an oven he had made for the camp. We laughed about this, pretending we didn't think it possible. I was invested in believing their ultimate crime was that they really did not understand what great painting was, and who had true talent.

The Nolde I have kept—the woodcut called *The Saint*—always brings that murderer to mind for me. Perhaps that is why I have kept it concealed behind the Otto Dix work all these years. Old Emil had the worst luck. He got on so well with them all and was only too willing to declare his allegiance publicly. Indeed he shared so many of their repellent prejudices. And yet they turned on him. A couple of his paintings were auctioned off in Lucerne where they were openly ridiculed.

But they granted him their version of mercy. They figured out a way to kill him off more effectively by ordering that he could not paint anymore. From '41 until the end of the war, I don't know how he survived. I had heard he was still secretly painting watercolours but he would not dare visit Berlin to show me anything. They had broken him. The picture of suffering in this woodcut could have been a premonition of his own fate.

We all knew of these stories. Dagmara often had the latest gossip yet I could detect, steeped in my hypocrisy of convenience, that she and Farrell were up to something more than a little cultural tourism with this Vatican tour. If I presumed they were just cynical bystanders to all that was happening, I would be misreading Dagmara's interest in me… perhaps even her belief that I might be capable of doing some good. I just couldn't discern what her intentions were yet. But some clues had to be found with Farrell himself.

As that evening was winding down, he told me of how he ended up in the Vatican Library. He said he'd come from a small town on the seacoast called Bray, that it was a kind of 'poor man's Brighton… or an Irish Brighton, if you like.' The youngest son of a family of six, the one who showed the most promise in school, he was the natural choice among his siblings to be 'donated' to the Christian brothers, and to study for the priesthood. Of course we got on so well, we were both would-be men of the cloth, really.

I told him about my father, my failed attempt at being a banker, and he laughed, said my career with Galerie Hyperion was proof that I made the same 'category error' about painting, making the works we loved the only true articles of faith worth believing in.

This error had led him to a promising academic career before the war. He ended up leaving the priesthood after a year. He had won a scholarship to Cambridge and then did his Master's thesis on Andrea del Sarto. Fitting, perhaps, given the painter was famous during his lifetime for painting a copy of his own work, a portrait of Pope Leo X, and trying to pass it off as the original. But I get ahead of myself. On a research trip to Rome, Farrell met with one of his old mentors, an Irish bishop that he still called Father O'Rourke. "It was he that brought me in, insisted I could do some useful work in the library, cataloguing all the scholarship on the Vatican art collection. That was five years ago, and now here I am trying to save the best of it from Pacelli."

"To save it? What do you mean?"

Dagmara, who was listening closely to more than the Hot Fives while she was in the kitchen, quickly interrupted. "Now Antony, you do go on! I want to hear more about you, Harry. What the hell is happening with your gallery? Are you in charge now?"

I could tell, by the looks the two traded, that Antony knew he was being a touch too indiscrete. Chastened, he sipped his wine and re-crossed his legs as she sat close beside him on the divan. They were composed like brother and sister there, as I related all that I knew of what Magda was doing, back in Budapest.

"I should contact her," Dagmara said. "Connie has me purchasing antiquities on this junket, but this is really the best time to pick up some bargains from her. I'm sure we could sell them in Dublin for double the price."

"You can always deal with me," I said.

"I don't mix business with pleasure, darling. Though I love the work on your walls. And this apartment. If I knew you were doing this well, I would have come sooner."

I do have such fond memories of that brief period of luxury. I was able to justify all that square footage to myself because I was entertaining so much. I would have dinners and parties catered for the higher-ups in the Reichskulturkammer, including Goebbels, that vicious, grinning monkey himself, on a few occasions. I'd be lying if I said I didn't enjoy playing host, and even the gossip among all the officials Odon Heimrath introduced me to was worth the hangovers and all the cleaning I'd have to do on Sunday mornings. There were a few months, after Paris fell and I had opened up the second Galerie Maes in Antwerp, with your uncle Anton in charge, when it seemed like the war would soon be won, and with all the trade in cast-off art from the government, I would amass quite a fortune. Such a bright future ahead of me.

That whole apartment building, Erdmann Residences, was leveled in the bombing. I lost everything but a platinum lighter that your mother had given me for my thirtieth birthday. I saw it shining in the rubble, as I returned to the site from the shelter. I remember feeling so hungry, like I hadn't eaten in days. I'm still ashamed to say I scrounged for my cigarette butts because only chain smoking would quell my hunger pangs.

All this talk of the lost. It is still, after all these years, too difficult to return to the happiest times with Dagmara. I know I risk any sense of propriety by speaking about my desire—especially with you, my son who I hope remains devoted to his mother. But it is central to the direction my life took. I can't gloss it over. It is not just the heart that it is selfish. It's the whole body, don't you think?

After Farrell finally left for his hotel we did not even make it to the bedroom before I was following Dagmara's commands to strip her, take her forcefully. I remember the way she was clutching the sides of my dining room table so tightly, with her dress up around her waist... the way she cried out over the music, her breathless laughter as we heard the muffled taps on the ceiling above us from a broomstick. It had felt like years rather than months since I had made love to a woman, and I was as aroused and impatient as a teenaged boy.

"Not yet... not yet..." Her refrain was also the answer to the one question that filled my days: when would we finally be together, not just as lovers? Why couldn't she leave Vidler now and come to me?

"Connie's a good man. I owe him everything. It is not his fault I am the way I am," she said, sharing a post-coital cigarette with me. The sun was already coming up and I had a full day at the gallery ahead of me. Yet I wanted every waking hour I could possibly have with her. "But now that we're settled in Ireland, you'll see, I'll be back here often enough."

"Why doesn't he open a Berlin location? His lovely wife could run it for him. You could change the name."

"That might have been possible a few years ago, but not anymore. And there are only a few people who can get licenses to sell the work your government has appropriated. But this is why we must see each other on a regular basis, no? I'm sure you can give us wholesale prices."

"You know I'll do what I can." I meant it, but the truth was I really didn't know what amount of control I had over the sale of the work we'd get, apart from my new commission rate.

And I was determined to be a model steward of Galerie Hyperion—soon to be Galerie Maes. I couldn't remain loyal to your mother, clearly, but I was determined to be loyal to Magda. And she had definite opinions about Connie Vidler and his reputation. When I had returned from Lucerne after the auction of so-called degenerate paintings, she told me that Vidler was notorious throughout Europe. "He has a reputation for selling fake antiquities. I wouldn't be surprised if he sells fake art too. Stay away from him."

The more I asked around, Vidler's reputation was only confirmed. Odon Heimrath was my most reliable source for received opinion, and he described Connie as "a typical Jewish cosmopolitan. He was invited to Lucerne because we know he would sell to the English and Americans with deep pockets. We gave him authentic work to sell, and briefly made an honest man out of him."

Upon hearing this, I was convinced I was the best thing that ever happened to Dagmara. I could save her from such a disreputable character. But it wouldn't happen overnight. Time, and perhaps the roaring business I was doing, would eventually turn her head. As far as I was concerned we were made for each other, she'd see it eventually.

10.

04 / 10 / 89
Kurfurstendam (Martin Bloch, c. 1933)

Over the next few months, as a fragile peace shattered after the invasion of Poland, everything that would happen made me believe in destiny, that all my years of struggle and my failed marriage were necessary for the role I was going to play when Berlin was the cultural capital of the world. I seriously believed I was one of those men who owned the future. Because Magda and Galerie Hyperion would not be part of this grand vision of mine, and it was important not to look back.

Like everything else, I believed this because someone told me, rather than me doing any work to find out for myself. In this case it was Odon, who seemed invested in my new prominence as the Reichskulturkammer's favourite art dealer.

I remember it as a warm April afternoon when he just dropped by the gallery without warning, saying we had to talk. It was one of those first days of spring where everything was bathed in golden light and you could remember what the world looked like before the snow and the cold winds of obligation came in with the war clouds. I look at this work by Sabine's old friend Martin Bloch – the cloudless sky, the jumble of Ku'damm in the afternoon, and I'm transported there once again. It was a day for new beginnings, Odon said, as he insisted I close early and join him for a drink in a private officers' club that had just opened in an old dance studio, not far from where Bloch must have pitched his easel on the street for this.

Odon took some delight in the location. "There isn't much of a market for waltz lessons, right now," he said. "But there's English gin under the table at this place." He winked and I just laughed, as if I had some greater understanding of the significance of this contraband. It was indicative of our imminent victory, that was all that mattered.

Barely into our first drink, as I took in the starched white table cloths with embroidered swastikas, Odon got right to the point. "It's my understanding that Laszlo Petofi was smart enough to transfer the ownership of Galerie Hyperion to you, is this correct?"

I wanted to ask him how he knew this. But of course it was a part of his job to know everything about me. "This is correct, yes. I still telegram them both, and there are the bank transfers."

"That can end now. Laszlo will not be able to contact you. He is currently detained. As for Magda... you should forget about her."

"What are you talking about?" I felt enraged. I wanted to wipe Odon's grin and his little duck-fluff moustache off his face.

"I'm talking about what is best for you, Harry. I would send no more telegrams or transfer any money. You have a good name with us. You should use it now. You have access to markets for work we need to sell. You should think about that. And fast."

"I want to know what has happened to Magda."

"No, you don't." Odon gently tapped my hand that held my cigarette. Ash fell on the table. He brusquely wiped it away with the back of his hand. "Clean slate, my friend. You know what has a nice ring to it? Galerie Maes."

"Galerie Maes." The name sounded so vulgar in my mouth. The little man's vanity of calling a business after oneself   ... I didn't run a fruit stand, this was work of value on the walls of Galerie Hyperion. "I don't think so."

"I think it reminds one of Nicolaes Maes. He was a great northern painter. We have more than a few of his portraits in our archives now."

"We sell modern work, primarily."

"There is no we. Only you. And you will sell the work we ask you to, my friend." Odon struck the table, as if he was slapping away at a fly. It was the first forceful gesture I had ever seen from him, a flash of temper he immediately seemed ashamed to have revealed. "I think you'll realize the end of Galerie Hyperion is the best thing that has ever happened to you. Do you understand me?"

Odon looked as if he was pleading with me. It was clever, really. He made me feel as if I were relenting, so I could preserve my sense of pride. My sense of agency. All that would be required of me was silence. Silence and forgetting, looking forward, not behind me. But of course the risks were now significant: I was effectively serving two masters.

I heard later from Heimrath that Laszlo, that oaf with the Bavarian cream in his moustache, had managed to get out of Hungary and save himself (Bloch too, the painter of this work – I heard to England eventually). Odon considered this proof of how corrupt the Hungarian government was, regardless of the Occupation. But as for Magda, no word. Odon encouraged me to not look into it. No, I would not be required to rewrite the past, just live in the present with all the ruthlessness I was capable of. And as it happened, I was capable of quite a lot.

11.

04 / 11 / 89

~~**Selbstbildnis mit Vanitassymbolen**~~

Before I speak of one particular portrait, let me start with a letter. It was from Dagmara, and it had been steamed open and re-sealed. This was not surprising. I had come to expect this ritual for all the correspondence that came to Galerie Maes. As I had come to expect the presence of the amiable looking strangers, a little too well dressed, who tracked me at every public gathering. Of course they were with the Abwehr. Perhaps by Odon's request, there was never any palpable sense of menace. I admired their professionalism. No one had to explain to me the consequences of working with the enemy. Great predators high up the food chain, like crocodiles or sharks, can take in their prey whole. It is as if a door to hell briefly opens, snatches the chosen and closes again, leaving no trace but the silence afterwards. That is what happened to Magda, she who once figured so prominently in my life. Two years later, it was hard to imagine that life, when I was the dutiful employee and son-in-law. I was wise enough to realize I could be 'disappeared' at any time, along with any trace of a flourishing Galerie Maes in Berlin and Antwerp. Thankfully Dagmara knew the ways of these beasts too, and she was always careful.

Harry darling,

I'm here in Rome for the next two weeks. You should come! It will be our holiday. I have much business to attend to but the city is so beautiful this time of year. And I miss you! Who knows? Perhaps there is some business here for you too.

I'm staying at the Excelsior on the Via Veneto. This suite is too large for one person. How perfect it would be for two!

D.

Provenance

As concise and assertive as she was in person. No one could have faked Dagmara's choice of words. I retrieved the envelope which had the address of the poste restante, and made my way down to the Berlin station to check fares and times. This rail journey would not be without risk but she was worth it. I dashed off my reply with my itinerary and mailed it at the post office by the station, as excited as a schoolboy to have an extended holiday with her. Every day in Berlin was hard, grey, and cold, despite the warm spring wind in the air. I needed a little sun, some warm colours, and a little beauty in my life more than ever.

This was the first time I closed the gallery for an extended period of time. I put all the paintings in the large vault in the basement, the ones Magda had purchased in the worst days after Kristallnacht. For the first time since I had taken on the gallery myself I felt a premonition. It was not so vivid that I could foresee some cataclysmic scene of destruction. It was only like the quality of silence had changed, deepened in some way. I swear, if I had believed in ghosts, I would have identified this as proof Magda was there, where her spirit was required.

After a painfully slow journey—more than two days because of the frequent stops for 'train safety,' we finally rolled into Ostiense station just after six a.m. I had had no way to inform Dagmara of my delay and I was fretting so much about it I could not concentrate on anything, could only sleep for maybe two or three hours at most. *What if she gives up on me? What if she never received my letter in the first place?* A young diplomat was traveling back to his posting with his wife and two daughters, and the little girls would not stop screaming and giggling in their cabin for most of the night. I tried writing a letter to you, Nikolaus, but I felt strangely guilty that you were not with me. I know, why would I have wanted to risk your life, just so you could be with your fool of a father? I was irresponsible, impulsive. I was merely playing at being someone of power and influence. Out the window nothing but the dark, open fields of war. Yet in the first brassy rays of sunlight in the morning, we were rolling past the outskirts of Rome and everything was bright Panavision hopefulness again. I could smell something like magnolias in the breeze when I pulled down my cabin window. The buildings and houses appeared in clusters past the tall grasses that fringed an ancient aqueduct… then a lemon grove and a glimpse of tall Cypresses forming a corridor along an ancient road. I felt my first breath of something like happiness rise in my chest. This quickening sense of truly living, not waiting in the wings…I suppose this was what real love felt like.

To pass the time on this journey I sketched myself on the stationery I had brought along. As a young man I once did a lot of that sort of thing. For a while I would even say compulsively, before I realized I was talentless and just stopped cold. This is probably where my passion for art originated. The sketch was a cartoon, drawn for Dagmara. It was based on a self-portrait by an English artist, David Bailly, who had painted himself at a table, with symbols of vanity and transience scattered about. Spilled wine glass, extinguished candle, and curiously, a small portrait of the artist himself as he really looked, not the younger man in the painting.

I suppose there was something about this image, or two images of myself, older and younger, that caused me to keep it rather than give it to Dagmara. It was meant to be an amusement. It really was crudely done. Anyway, the end result wasn't quite so amusing. I have kept it all these years, pressed between the pages of Mann's *Magic Mountain*, one of the few gifts from Dagmara that survived the war. She said it was in memory of our first meeting in Lucerne. It is probably time to burn it.

Upon my arrival in Rome I realized I never should have doubted her. Of course she was there at the station, in a white lace dress and an odd, spindly little parasol, her bare arms golden brown, the colour of her eyes now changed to a lighter blue. She was always transforming, it seemed, some subtle change to confound the snapshot impulse of my memory to fix her in time. She would not be possessed on any terms but her own. When she held out her arms to embrace me, laughing, I felt transformed as well, made whole once again.

"You must be weary from the journey. Let's go back to our room and let me draw you a bath. They have room service, it's the latest thing. We'll have time to see the city and make it our own, don't you worry."

In that moment I could not care if we only saw the Via Veneto from our window, as long as she was in my arms.

It was at breakfast on the terrace the following morning, when she patiently explained to me the true purpose of our little holiday. "Harry, you and I must visit the Vatican while we're here."

At first I didn't quite understand. The English word 'must' always confused me. Was it an obligation? It caught me off guard but I managed to voice something like approval, even a little enthusiasm. It was easy for me to be enthusiastic, every decision she had made for us since I arrived seemed perfect.

"Have you been there before?"

"Only briefly. I was a student, traveling on my own here with my Baedeker. It was really just another place to check off on my list. And the list was long."

I looked out onto the Via Veneto. Even in the midst of war the women were like sirens in brightly patterned dresses, the men all wolfish suitors, unabashedly parading their commitment to la bella figura. There was a natural elegance to the way they moved on the street. Here I was scrubbed clean of the Berlin grit and sipping the taste of real oranges, feeling renewed but also incomplete, unable to shake off my gracelessness, my prim, northerner's formality. I babbled about the Rome I remembered, that I hoped we could get to San Pietro in Montorio, perhaps take a day trip to the Villa Aldobrandini so I could see Domenico's fresco of Judith once again. I couldn't bear listening to myself. I was an earnestly-assembled pastiche of received opinions about the architecture and the paintings in the Borghese and the Vatican museums, and I sensed Dagmara would see through me soon enough.

Some years later, when I had returned to Berlin from my re-education years, the Rome of our time together had etched itself so indelibly on my memory that I became obsessed by—for want of a better term—Rome's aesthetic history. My job at the library allowed me to indulge myself with Gibbon (translated into Russian, ridiculously), Goethe's Italian journey, Piranesi's carceri and Winckelmann's writings… all of this reading was a way to cloak my grief and my nostalgia with some notion of a continual refinement (or perhaps confinement) of my sensibility. I could call it self-preservation while I transformed myself into a ghost in this concrete gulag of a city, sustained by Polish vodka and Russian cigarettes.

Eventually, because of my reading, I began to discover a different, secret history of Rome. It had always been the capital of forgery and pillage. From street trade in relics during the dark ages to the auction of fake Titians in private salons (arguably still in the dark ages), I realized that the city had remained stubbornly pagan, manufacturing fetishes and counterfeit tokens of a divine presence. In the frantic pillaging of the public and private collections, carried out by so many of my esteemed patrons with the Reichskulturkammer, I believe they were only dimly aware of their own psychological reversion to pagan instincts. It was as if they believed that the aura of some classical ideal would bestow upon them an affirmation of their true beginnings. So of course they looked upon Rome's treasures as a kind of ultimate prize of conquest, after they had taken Paris and so many of its paintings off the walls. This impulse to pillage confirmed the crudely fashioned narrative of warrior kings that the Fuhrer and Albert Speer crafted, where a new Rome would be made out of Berlin, the ultimate fake modeled on the classical original.

For a while, in the worst of my alcoholic years, I was researching and writing this as a long essay that included my own conjectures on works faked, others lost forever to the sack of Rome. But I was prone to so much ekphrasis, as I could not resist trying to paint these works in words, one finger stab at a time, on my junky Lubava typewriter. I realized this attempt at a book was a form of therapy full of subconscious confessions. It would fail as a thesis, be questionable as history and tenable only as an eccentric's memoir. I burned all six hundred pages on my last birthday (seventy-eight—how did this happen?), out there on my small, concrete balcony, much to Silvia's horror.

I resolved that I had to have the courage to tell it all straight, no matter how painful it was. And look at me, just as I get close to telling of my ultimate crimes, veering away from the confessional once again. I need to feel that rough pull on my collar from the ghost of your grandfather, hauling me back towards the truth, returning me to the scene of my deepest shame. And I have only the ghost of my former self to count on, as unreliable as he may be.

They tell me that even to this day, no matter how open the Vatican city is, the library remains closed to the public. Too many priceless ancient texts, many of which would disintegrate if they were handled and brought out for display. And of course it is a place of secrets, transactions that must remain unspoken about because of what they would reveal about the Church and who held power within it.

So perhaps it was inevitable that I would end up there, sitting at a spare, crudely fashioned oak table, across from Antony Farrell. Dagmara had accomplished what she needed to do. She had delivered me to the people who could offer me redemption.

12.

04 / 12 / 89

The Card Cheat (Georges de la Tour, c. 1637)

Nikolaus, if you take an interest in this painting, you would have to credit Hermann Voss with a revival of interest in the French painter Georges de la Tour. I had had some dealings with Voss before '43, when he was named the Director of the Dresden Gallery and Special Commissioner for the new art museum in Linz, the Fuhrer's pet project. A mild-mannered fellow, bespectacled, a little stooped. A creature of the library, not the battlefield. Voss had a sharp eye and he had done some pioneering scholarship on the Dutch Caravaggisti, the painters who were influenced heavily by Caravaggio. And he saw in la Tour's work the same compositional compression, the same flair for the dramatic moment.

It was my understanding that Voss's career also suffered because of his anti-Nazi sympathies. Odon Heimrath told me Voss had written a poem decrying the government that he once read at a dinner that Odon attended. It was embarrassing, he said. The poem was terrible and Odon himself told Voss he would be lucky if no one reported him.

So it was a surprise to see, in March of '43, that the Neue Wiener Tageblatt ran a notice about him. I still have it among my old papers. It is a directive to the Occupation authorities of Norway, the Netherlands, Alsace, Lorraine, and Luxembourg, effectively saying that if they found any work of true artistic value, they should seize it, so Voss 'might wish to exercise the Fuhrer's right to disposition of works of art.' Voss was given quite a promotion, and I took note: here was a potential client for Galerie Maes that would keep the lights on for me.

As for this painting, la Tour had made a few attempts at the familiar theme of the card cheat. Caravaggio himself, among others, had a fondness for this street scene as a subject. Consider it a meditation on the seductive power of games of chance, when the mark's vulnerability is so palpably revealed.

Here the mark is a young nobleman. His pale skin and fair hair, the lush colours and richly patterned silk, and lace of his tunic suggest a young man about town who can pay well for his many pleasures. He holds his cards close to his chest, as if he were fiercely protecting his innocence.

But he has no chance against the card sharps. The dirty fingernails and the swarthier complexions of the cheat and his accomplice tell us these are men to watch out for, outsiders and rough types who personify the criminal element. Yet our gaze is drawn to them, the interplay of the accomplice's expression, and the mild-mannered, innocent look of the sharp the mark is playing. The composition, the play of light… like fortune, they favour them.

If you were a painter like la Tour, you could sell this to a patron like the young nobleman as a cautionary scene. But the pleasures of the work are invested in the moment of the deception and its subversive power. Because cheating this young nobleman is portrayed as an act of playful liberty—and perhaps a higher form of justice.

So let me take you back to that meeting in Rome, which might illustrate how seductive such deception can be when one can wager their very life on subverting the powers that be. There I was, brought to this room in the Vatican Library by Dagmara. And sitting across from me, this mysterious ally of hers, Antony Farrell.

"Thank you for coming, Mr. Maes," he said. "I know this couldn't have been an easy journey. I hear things are only worsening, that Mussolini probably won't stay in power for much longer."

"Though what I could make out on the radio this morning, they are close to victory in Tunisia, yes?"

"Darling, that's a lie," Dagmara said. She was seated at the table right under yet another lovingly-rendered *Madonna col Bambino*. She bore no resemblance at all.

"Yes, I'm told it's actually a disaster," Antony said. "They're my clients, not my friends."

"We're probably weeks away from your friends taking over the whole of the country, Harry." 93

"Is there a difference for you?" Farrell asked this in the most solicitous tone he could muster, which made it sting all the more. "They've been so good to you, haven't they? I'm sure they've made you a very rich man."

"Most of the work in my gallery that is not on display is sold to foreigners, Mr. Farrell. The alternative would be to let these paintings be destroyed."

"Just as they've destroyed the families who owned them originally. Exterminated after being rounded up like cattle for the slaughter. You know that's what happened to Magda Petofi, don't you?"

"There was nothing I could have done—"

"No. Nothing at all but claim her assets for yourself and become their favourite boy. You launder the provenance of all this work and wipe the blood from your hands each working day. It's a living, I suppose. We all have to get by, yes?"

"Antony, for God's sake, have some manners!" I had never seen Dagmara angry. She practically hissed at him.

"It's all right, Dagmara. I'm happy to defend my hypocrisy," I said. "As I'm sure you must be too, Mr. Farrell, working for the Pope that's openly complicit, carrying out such important work for cultural education. What did the publicity for your 'Treasures of the Vatican' tour of the provinces call it, a 'marriage of two great cultures'?"

Farrell looked to Dagmara and nodded, with just the faintest of smiles, as if he was conceding the argument. Only to her, though.

"I've been quietly working on making up for my sins, Mr. Maes. I'd like to ask you   ... if you were given the chance to make up for your own, would you take it?"

I could feel Dagmara's eyes on me. And I could sense my answer would be just as important to her as it might be for Farrell. She was the only one I hoped to please, however.

"What are you talking about, Mr. Farrell?"

"There are those within the Curia... those I am quite close to... they are very worried about Pacelli. He seems prepared to sacrifice a great deal for the Germans. He says he'll do everything he can to preserve the sanctity of the Vatican, ensure that we're not swallowed up by the Reich, yet the line between a pragmatic, transactional approach and complicity… it's getting very blurry. I'm sure you know what I mean, Mr. Maes."

"Not completely, no."

"Antony, you don't have to talk around things," Dagmara said. "We are all friends here." I couldn't tell whether she was prodding him for more information or coaching him. When I look back on it now, it was probably a little of both.

"His Holiness came to the Curia with a request to make an offering to your friends."

"What kind of an offering?"

"A selection of paintings. Speer is creating this museum for the Fuhrer in Linz, apparently. The Pope would like to make a significant donation to foster trust and signify the state of accord he said he's worked so hard to establish. He claims it would be done in an effort to save our independence. Much like our silence… our ability to look the other way when the tanks roll in."

"Look the other way with the Jewish—"

"That's already happening. Don't believe otherwise." Farrell folded his hands with his elbows firmly on the table, giving me a hard look, as if he was daring me to argue.

"This donation… it would be a public gesture?"

"Pacelli knows the implications if that were the case. No, the conversation has progressed where they're discussing a third party. Consignment… some creative work with provenance. Your areas of expertise, Mr. Maes."

"Harry, no one could manage this like you," Dagmara said.

"So a private donation."

"Those who need to know will know the truth, it is said. It's become a familiar phrase here over the last few months."

It was only the sound of my chair on the stone floor that made me realize I had instinctively retracted, trying to distance myself from the direction Farrell was taking with this proposal.

"It sounds like this is going to happen with or without me."

"Yes. So as a businessman you might as well make some money from it, yes?"

"A lot of money," Dagmara said. She looked at me as if I was suddenly the most attractive man she'd ever seen.

"And a lot of work that will be lost forever from the Church. You're quite comfortable with that, Mr. Farrell?"

He exhaled sharply, his gaze darting to Dagmara, who nodded in assent. "Not exactly. We don't intend to provide your friends and clients with the authentic paintings. Our mutual acquaintance Mr. Vidler will be of great help."

"Connie's been selling fakes for twenty years, Harry," Dagmara said. "He has a few trusted sources we can depend on. There's a gentleman who works at Cinecitta. Set design. He's done paintings for opera sets."

"Theatre! You think you can pass such work off as the real thing?"

"We have for years, my love. You remember, in Lucerne, the work we purchased? Connie turned eight paintings into thirty and sold most of them in Milan. He provides generous commissions. It's amazing, the quality of work you can get when you pay for it."

"You both know what would happen if just one of these works would be called into question."

"Harry, last night we were speaking of the Reichmarschall's new Vermeer. He traded more than a hundred paintings for that work, yes?"

Farrell began to laugh like a schoolboy. He leaned back, plucked a cigarette from his platinum case on the table and lit it up to compose himself once again.

"You're telling me that's fake, Dagmara?"

"I know it is. It's the work of a Dutch artist we've worked with many times. I'll introduce you. I think you'll quite like him."

"All you need to do, Mr. Maes, is be the go-between and fictionalize the provenance. Your hands are practically clean."

"Practically is a capacious term," I said. "Receipts and papers from Galerie Maes, I'm presuming."

"If it goes badly, you're at one remove from all of this," Dagmara said. "Harry, we're not going to put you in harm's way."

The look Farrell gave Dagmara was stern, like a schoolmaster silently admonishing his favourite pupil. Yet she answered it with a fixed, tight smile of defiance.

"So." Farrell leaned forward, placing his hands flatly on the table. "Will you do it?"

In my head I was back in that hotel in Lucerne. Was it just four years before? It seemed at least a decade had passed. I recalled Dagmara's hand in mine, small and warm, gently pulling me forward onto the dance floor. When she turned to look at me she tilted her head, like she was adjusting a canvas on the wall before her. She was deciding something about me then, which clearly led to this moment.

I had so many questions for her. Who was she doing this for? What had brought her and Antony Farrell together? Was she actually married or still together with Vidler? Had the three of us—Connie, Antony, and I—been seduced and charmed by her, only to find that we had been conscripted to carry out some crucial act of betrayal? This seduction had already cost me my marriage. Now it could easily cost me my life.

I pulled up straight in my chair, cleared my throat. I fumbled at the knot of my tie to loosen it. "Yes. Yes, I'll do what you ask, if I must."

And in that moment I felt like I had crossed over to the world of the card cheats. Some months later, when I had seen the la Tour among a selection of paintings that Farrell had photographed, I knew it would be perfect for our little project. I had done my homework, read enough about Voss's scholarship to know the painting would be of interest. But if I had been honest with both Dagmara and Farrell, I would have confessed that the painting was of great interest to me as well.

13.

04 / 13 / 89

"The Manor" (various artists)

I'm sitting here at this small table in this apartment, Nikolaus, fidgeting with a rubber band. I have an aversion to metaphors and similes, any tarting up of the facts, yet I can't resist thinking of the elastic quality of time as I remember. Whole years can stretch and then events can create an effect of time snapping back, a concentration of all that led up to some decisive point.

It all started to fall apart quickly, faster than I ever would have imagined. And by 'it,' I mean virtually everything: my business, my relationship with Dagmara, and of course, the faith I had stubbornly held on to regarding the victory of my most dedicated clientele over the Allied effort. Over the last forty years, on this side of the Wall, the story is told that Stalingrad was the great patriotic battle that decided the course of the war. And perhaps that's true. But I felt the unraveling from the west, not the east, with what happened to my gallery in Antwerp.

It was my friend Odon Heimrath's 'suggestion' that I open up another location in my hometown. This was about a year into the occupation there, which your grandparents, it must be said, welcomed as the best thing that could have happened to our city. Your uncle Anton's interest in theatre and his decadent group of friends was indicative of the poisonous cosmopolitan influences that were taking hold, save for the civilizing purge the occupation would provide. Well, cosmopolitan was the word your grandfather used in my company, given my relationship with your mother, but he really meant Jewish influences, whom he casually told me had too much power and money.

Too much power and money. Too much influence. I wanted to ask your grandfather what would be just enough? Who crossed the line? But I had lost any interest in confronting him.

His presumptions were shared by the Reichskulturkammer. They believed some of the most degenerate examples of modern art they had pillaged could be sold to the locals before harsher measures could be enforced. And then, boldly enough, they might be confiscated once again and resold, given the ties they allowed me to maintain with the grey and black market. I was such a useful man to them, the more they thought about it, Heimrath told me over cigars and contraband whisky.

And I suppose that was true, but I believed I could also do our family proud. The opening up of a second gallery with the family name, signifying a kind of prodigal's return, impressed your grandmother and earned me your grandfather's respect. Begrudged, of course. But I was doing more than expanding the business; I was giving your uncle Anton a chance to remake himself, prove that he too had talents that could be put to good use.

All these years later, it still fills me with regret that I couldn't have done more for him. In some ways, our paths were so similar. He too had failed in his first attempt at a respectable career. He had convinced himself, after acting in a few amateur productions, that continuing to study medicine in Brussels was a waste of both time and our family's money. He and a group of friends had toured a rather lurid version of Goethe's *Faust* through some university towns in the south of Germany and collected clippings of their strong reviews (though our family never saw the bad ones). He had come home broke, with a guitar and new Spanish boots he insisted on wearing everywhere, even to church. He grew a goatee and initially I thought he had met a woman like your mother whom he was trying to impress. But no, it was she who told me Anton preferred men, and that he was terrified of telling your grandfather. After trying and failing, over the course of fourteen months, to make a go of it with his own theatre company in Brussels, I knew that offering him a position with my gallery was a way of giving him a fresh start. I should have predicted he'd come to resent my generosity.

Like everything else Anton did though, he never showed me or told me what was really going on. He would open the gallery two hours late most weekdays, was careless about the books, (and predictably, he was dipping into them) and seemed to take some pleasure in offending the customers who had the deepest pockets. He didn't realize that his behaviour was being reported back to me from Odon's friends based in Antwerp, the result of Anton's drunken rambling in the gentlemen's clubs he'd frequent, looking for companionship.

Even more frustrating, he did not realize the expectations for Galerie Maes as a distinctly German business during the occupation. Antwerp never fully recovered economically after the Great War, and that it fell so quickly was a source of shame, especially for the Communist organizers, journalists, and artists—those whom Anton once counted among his friends (until he borrowed money from most of them and reportedly never paid it back). What was on the walls of the gallery represented wealth and sophistication, and a reverence for the aesthetic traditions of Europe the Reich was going to save for posterity. We were an instrument of propaganda and that, he told me, offended his commitment to living authentically.

We quarreled and he threatened to walk out, leaving me with no one to run things. But the truth was he had nowhere to go, and his drinking had gotten so bad we both knew he would have been fired soon enough from any other work he could get. Once I had confronted him about his dipping into the till, and he offered to take on the gallery single handed, letting go of Wilma Duesberg, a young, responsible, hard-working Flemish girl to make up 'the blood from the stone.' The gallery became a complete liability, one that by '44 I was pouring money into from Berlin in order to keep afloat. It was some small blessing that the threat of the Allies taking back the city had made Anton's behaviour the least of my concerns.

It had become apparent, with the nightly bombing raids over the city, that keeping the gallery open in Berlin would be foolhardy. I was needlessly endangering the work in the hopes that those still flush with hard currency would want to hoard what they could before they fled the city. Meanwhile the number of break-ins and street muggings had risen dramatically, despite what the newspapers reported. The neighbouring shopkeepers and I shared our stories as we swept our doorways to keep busy. Every morning I'd put on a suit and tie, open up and spend hours alone, watching the angle of sunlight travel across the floorboards. An end felt near, but I was too scorched from my years of destitution only a decade before to have the courage to imagine what might follow, or to prepare myself for how bad it might get.

The little project that Dagmara and I launched in Rome with Farrell continued, however. It was a distraction that kept me engaged, making me feel like I had some agency. Being involved in fraud of this scale created considerable risks, but it also felt like I was taking revenge on those who had used me, and who had debased the very notion of cultural preservation in the midst of all this destruction.

The rage I felt wasn't directed at people like Odon Heimrath or his flunkies. They were just bureaucrats whose timidity and conformity were their means of survival. In the empty hours in the gallery my memories would take me back to those few days in Lucerne, when I first met Dagmara. I could still see, so vividly, Theodor Fischer doing his ridiculous jig to the jazz music playing, the table of card players who were laughing along with his antics. They personified whom I hoped we would deceive, the focus of my revenge.

Dagmara would write me every week. We had agreed on a code before I left Rome that the work would be referred to as "the manor," a house in the Wicklow hills that she and Connie were fixing up. Who knows, maybe such a place actually exists.

Of the ten paintings selected from the Vatican, each was given a feature or room that they were working on. I still have that list we devised on a napkin from our hotel:

1. The Masaccio: the kitchen
2. The Modena: the master bedroom
3. The first Romano (Luna): the attic
4. The second Romano (Bacchus): the wine cellar
5. The Dossi: the library
6. The Jordaens: the landing
7. The van der Weyden: the attic
8. The la Tour: the pantry
9. The Caravaggio: the parlour
10. The Rubens: the nursery

The work was contracted out to those who did not know of the larger project, or who else was working on a fake. This was a necessary precaution, given their discretion could not be counted on. We were dealing with talented criminals for the most part. Vidler, Dagmara said, had a lot of people he kept busy over the years, but six of the forgeries were the work of just two men: Wim Hertmans, working out of his studio in St. Jean Cap Ferrat, and Ferruccio Raspi, a set painter and designer in Rome. They were paid well, Dagmara reassured me. Farrell was flush with American dollars the Vatican bank could convert, and not even Connie knew where he got it all.

I still wonder if this whole operation was just a trial run for a larger effort. Over the last forty years there has been so much mythologizing by the victors, clearly. The generation that has come after mine, the pale, timid men running the library that finally retired me, will convince their children that it was inevitable that the Fuhrer's dreams of empire would crumble, that his regime was rotting from the inside, virtually from the beginning. To this I can only laugh. These are the same people who seem to believe nothing will change in the Kremlin. At the time of my trip to Rome, there was every reason to believe that Hitler could triumph in Europe, and that the last front for the Allied effort would be on the shores of America. After years of war it was conceivable, at least to me, that the spoils of this victory would include so much of what defined any claim to civilization. To create whole museums of simulacra while spiriting the real work off the battlefields and into safe hands would have been an effort brilliant in conception, and it made sense to serialize such a massive operation of fraud incrementally.

The grand project of an empire, how quickly it collapses. Oh, I know this is banal, but it is what I genuinely felt at the time. To live through those final months in full knowledge of Speer's conception of Germania was to be aware that such grand designs are actually far more fragile than the art they inspire—or reclaim as their own. I'm seeing the same process happening now here in Berlin. It's all dying quickly. The art and architecture made in the spirit of the revolution, the victorious arrival of a new era? Crumbling like the concrete foundations of this monstrously ugly apartment block. Not much left to reclaim, though.

Silvia, my companion who still tolerates me, she just laughs, says such a perspective is proof of my solipsism. I'm projecting the sense of my physical decline onto the larger world. Maybe, but the ceiling still leaks and stains the walls with rust-coloured streaks like old tears, and the elevators groan and lurch from floor to floor. Your father's an old solipsist who's kept his eyes open.

But perhaps it is good not to take too stern an approach in my response to her teasing. To be so declaratively realistic. A certain lightness is necessary. Not so long ago—or perhaps a decade is long, really—there was something about her that made me believe I could conquer what time was doing to me and still be capable of something more than the transactional dealings that corrode the soul.

I still have such a strong capacity to deny my intuition and better judgment. I'll admit to being afraid of being alone in my final days.

What I cannot say to her is this: "I know about the reports you write, the meetings you'll have with our friend…"—who, for my safety and and even Silvia's—I'll still just refer to as Mr. K. Silvia and I both know what will really survive us, if it's true that this 'glasnost' from Moscow is an indication it's finally falling apart. It will be the information, the reams and reams of data we have on each other, which would probably fill the walls of every library in this country. To see it all lining miles of shelves would be the perfect artistic project, truly avant garde in its conception and execution. It would confirm that this is the real legacy of the war years… we've been ceaselessly documenting how our private selves are betraying the ideals of our public identities. When everyone is Stasi, no one has to be Stasi.

Yet I simply can't be that interesting a subject, if Silvia is indeed reporting on me. At least not anymore. All of this is my only testimony of interest. A confession, if you like. And I'm still not sure if I will burn it, that it's served its purpose as a kind of therapeutic attempt to resist self-deception. Even within such meagre expectations for this process, I wrestle with why it's so hard to be truthful. I'm undoubtedly less interesting because I'm still holding on to some belief that I tried, in my way, to be on the side of light rather than darkness.

As I know Dagmara believed she was too, but the darkness managed to swallow her up.

That was inevitable, given how much freedom she was granted. Her Irish citizenship and her usefulness in being Connie's agent throughout Europe, finding buyers for the degenerate work the government wanted to profit from, did not mean they weren't watching her, and closely.

She had become friendly with a certain officer stationed in Nice and allegedly took close to fifty paintings off his hands, work that had been confiscated in the small towns and villages in the south of France. This former Austrian Gauletier, Udo Morike, barely tolerated that fraud, the painter Wim Hertmans, who flaunted his wealth and his connections with Petain's inner circle to project an air of diplomatic immunity. When Dagmara had spoken openly to Morike of visiting Hertmans she could tell, by the way Morike's mood darkened so quickly, that she had made a wrong move, and that she would have to be extremely cautious on her next visit to pick up the work Hertmans completed.

She told me all this on her last visit to Berlin. Hertmans had completed the fakes of the Jordaens and the Hals. Now it was up to me to store the authentic paintings, at least for the time being, and find willing buyers for the fakes from my regular clientele.

Hertmans was especially good with the work of his own countrymen, she said. "He tells me it is because he has lived with them for so long in his head." She rolled her eyes.

"Maybe so. But his Venus looks a bit too much like a Parisian whore."

"How would you know, love?"

"Touché."

"I just wish he'd work faster. He has two more to complete and there is the officer down there, Udo Morike, who's a bit of a madman."

"Any madder than the rest of them?"

"The more ground the English and the Americans claim back right now, the more desperate he seems. He invited me to this manor he's taken over, a huge pile along the cape where he hosted a dinner, celebrating the victors of the municipal elections. A sham, of course. He'd packed the rooms with local government people, a good number of Nazis as well. At one point in the night we were all led out into the courtyard for cocktails and speeches. There was a propaganda unit filming the members of the local guard… it was bizarre. Then he and his wife open a back gate and his men bring in a cart full of paintings. He tells us that they were taken from homes in the area, the work of sick artists from a sick culture, proof that 'a new way of governing' was necessary. If the Americans and the Brits were as close as the reports said, he was going to ensure they didn't claim these 'Jew-boy smears of paint' for themselves. One after the other, he throws them on the fire. Everyone around me, they started clapping and cheering."

"What did you do?"

"I couldn't give a damn. I wasn't going to join in. But this bastard, he was watching me, eyeing me up all night."

"Maybe he's interested in you that way."

She raised one eyebrow as if my motive was suspect, mentioning this over our small candlelight dinner of one small piece of sausage made of horse meat and a few green beans I had grown myself in the courtyard. This was what our romance was reduced to.

"I know when men are looking at me like that. Or when they're thinking they'd like to look at me… I mean, you were more the latter."

"Oh, probably." I took her hand and squeezed it. Even thinking of it now, it still fills me with an ache for all I lost. More than forty years… but it could have been yesterday.

"This was the look of a different kind of wolf. I won't return to his house to enjoy his company ever again."

We spoke of Hertmans, how odd he was. He thought of himself as quite a dandy, wearing one of seven identical orange cravats tied like a gypsy around his neck, and these bespoke white silk shirts with their oversized collars. The cravat showed his fealty to his homeland, he said, when asked about it, but he had been living in France for more than half his life. For a while in the twenties, Dagmara said he was considered "one of the best of the worst painters in Paris." He got by doing portraits and still lifes for the old money clients who recoiled from any painting that betrayed the influence of, as one old dear put it to Dagmara, "any work after Cezanne." Many of these patrons were military families, the anti-Dreyfusards who were stubbornly hanging on to power and prestige, and they ensured an Aryan painter like Hertmans would keep working. He was unabashedly anti-Semitic, the ideal artist for the Vichy regime, yet he knew he would never be considered truly French. Too unfashionable to show in the good galleries, even during the war years, and too much the eccentric foreigner to ever be more than a lapdog in the salons of the old aristocrats; he was completely cynical and mercenary. That he could paint so thoroughly like the old masters he proudly considered the proof of his talent. The fakes he created were like his acts of resistance against an age too debased to recognize his authentic genius.

"He knows who is buying these fakes, yes?"

"Of course! He said he's hated the Germans ever since the great war, when he was serving in the Royal Netherlands Army. That's when he realized they were still barbarians, these Boches. He's happy to take their money. His sole consideration, when he signed this contract from Vidler's, was that no work of his would be sold to a French family."

"And he knows Connie's Jewish?"

"You think he's interested in you?" I tried to sound nonchalant about this but there was a quaver in my voice that she picked up on. My jealousy… I was seeing betrayal with every man she mentioned. She put her hand on my knee.

"He looks happily married to me. He has a shrewish little sow from Nice that has given him a couple of children. Calls her his little grisette. But I wouldn't go near him, darling. I think he's got the clap… the serious kind… from the whores who work the harbour. That's what Connie heard."

"At least I know you're safe in his house then."

"Well… as safe as possible, anyway."

Dagmara was with me for two more days. During that brief stay, her last, she also paid a visit to Francis Cluny and Sabine, who was now openly announcing herself as Sally to her old friends (the ones that weren't killed or in camps, that is) and dying her hair platinum. She had finally found a role she could play to perfection. She and Francis had rented that cottage in Rathenow, the last home in Germany you probably remember, so far out of the city to be safe from the worst of the bombing but close enough that Cluny could take the train in each week for his broadcasts. I should have gone with Dagmara, at least to see you. The city was no place for children, given all the bombing raids. But Dagmara assured me she was only carrying out an errand for Antony Farrell, ensuring a message was delivered.

When she returned from Rathenow, she did have a letter for me, however. Your mother had written a note on Cluny's monogrammed stationery. Brief, but composed for maximum impact:

Harry,

It is three months since I have received any support payments from you, and more

than one month since Nikolaus has seen you. I suppose it is understandable.

Business must be terrible, and it is not safe for any child to be in the city. And yet

this Polish woman, who seems to be your lover, is able to make the effort to come to

Rathenow and do business with Francis. As it has always been throughout this

war, despite your excuses, where there is a will, there is a way.

It is now I realize it has always been a question of will with you, Harry.

My father has written to me from Palestine. He knew, from my correspondence with my mother, that I was living with Francis, and so he sent his letter to the Irish consulate. I was surprised, because he and I, as you know, have barely spoken in years. However, he had an important message for me: the reason I have not heard from my mother is that she left him and had gone through a rough time in Hungary. But he gave me her new mailing address in Palestine—she moved in with someone else upon returning from

Budapest, where she just barely missed being detained and sent to a camp.

Surely you were aware of this, given what you might know of Magda? And yet you did not have the decency to inform me as soon as you knew. Were you ashamed that you had done nothing? This government sees you as an asset. For once, you could have used your influence to save someone other than yourself. Yet you were incapable. I'm sure your first and only thought about this was what it might mean for you and your business.

I think of Nikolaus. How quickly he is growing up, how he looks to the men in his life for

support and guidance, examples to follow. And I am glad he has seen so little of you, the

famous Herr Maes.

Francis and I are making plans to leave this country at last. Or at least to try. Francis

knows of a route through the Ore mountains that should take us to Prague. And from there to Geneva through a network of friends. Two Irishmen he knows did it, and they ended up safe in London. I'm sure this strikes you as odd, even foolhardy, but I'm not thinking of my safety or my welfare. I'm thinking about Nicki, the boy who was once your son.

We will probably be leaving Rathenow in a matter of days, not weeks. I don't expect to see you, don't expect any farewells for either Nikolaus or me. Please take this note as I'm

sure you took the news of what happened to Magda and my mother: with a sense of relief. Another weight has been lifted off your shoulders—you, who have to carry so much.

Goodbye, Harry.

I waited until Dagmara left to make my way out to Rathenow. To this day I still hate myself for this. Yet here is my most painful admission, Nicki. To see you for the last time was less important to me than spending what I thought would be my final days with Dagmara. But in my defence, if I can credibly claim any, I also thought that your mother's letter was a touch too dramatic. I believed that she and Cluny would probably come to their senses, realize the risk they would be taking, especially with you, and stay where they were. I wasn't factoring in Cluny's cowardice, however, nor how eager he was to save his own skin.

When I got to the address I had for the cottage, it was deserted. The curtains were shut and there were two rolled-up newspapers at the doorway. I was so enraged, I scaled the stone fence around the backyard, wrapped my hand in my jacket, and punched through a window, like a burglar, to get in the back entrance.

I still remember the silence, in that abandoned bungalow, as I walked from room to room. The walls were bare and grey in the half-light. In the kitchen there was nothing but the scrap of an onion skin on a cutting board. Perhaps it was some final attempt to transform what could be salvaged from the garden into a meal. There was a dining table, colourless living room furniture … in the main closet nothing but three wire hangers. A train went by, rattling the windows and one solitary clay mug on a shelf above the sink.

I entered the room that must have been yours, given the size of the cot and chest of drawers. On an end table under a bedside lamp was a small toy car, a replica of a Daimler, painted pale green. Do you remember this toy? Such detail… its doors were hinged and it had little rubber tires. On the undercarriage it read, 'this car is fitted with independent suspension.' Such an odd inscription…I kept repeating the sentence in my head as if I was softening the harder edges of this absurdity.

I had to sit down on that cot and weep. I then put it in the pocket of my blazer. It was a little piece of you I'd never know. It still fills me with such sadness and regret. But it's a heaviness, like a millstone placed on my chest.

The tears no longer flow when I hold the toy car now, perhaps that's some consolation. I too have independent suspension—of my grief.

Upon my return to Berlin, the weeks turned into one month, then two without me hearing from Dagmara. Initially I just put it down to the crisis we were living through, the fact that the postal service was barely functioning, if at all. But as the days became shorter and it was virtually impossible to heat the gallery, closing its doors meant this little project of ours was all but abandoned, and I didn't want to acknowledge it.

Just days before I had resolved to close though, this old boat of a Mercedes 770 pulled up in front of the gallery. The swarthy, dark-eyed man who emerged from the driver's side looked like a chauffeur with his cap and gloves. He opened the passenger door and Antony Farrell, in a rakish new greatcoat and white silk scarf, stepped out, squinted in the daylight and then nodded to the driver, who opened up the trunk and heaved onto his shoulders a large canvas bag. I had watched enough of this pantomime to realize what was happening and bolted from my desk to meet them at the door. Farrell was here from Rome, playing courier.

I embraced him in the street like an old friend, and he introduced me to this fellow Dario, who was indeed a driver for the Italian ambassador. The embassy was, as always, very helpful with Farrell. Dario gently deposited the canvas bag in the gallery, to Farrell's gentle, sing-song chant, "lente... lente..." He then instructed him to return in an hour with a lordly, imperious tone that seemed new to Farrell. I felt his hand at the small of my back as he gently directed me into the gallery before anyone on the street was taking notice of us.

I locked the door, put down the blinds, and led him into Magda's old office. I so rarely went in there; it would have felt like I was desecrating my memories of her. Yet I wanted to show Farrell this was my little empire, in all its desolation. I switched on the desk lamp and gestured to a chair on the other side of the desk. He shrugged off his greatcoat and then laid it across this lap, with his scarf still draped loosely around his neck.

"I have all the paintings. The originals and the ones that have been completed. There are still four fakes we are waiting on but that will be my concern, not yours. We're calling an end to the project."

"An end? What do you mean?"

"Dagmara. She was arrested six days ago in Hertmans' home outside Nice. Both of them, we've been told, were interrogated. Soon they'll be deported. We don't know where— likely to a camp still in operation."

I took pride in my ability to give so little away of myself, a necessary skill in my line of work, yet I could not carry it off with Farrell. It was probably because I felt so comfortable in his company. I rose from the desk, turned from him, pantomiming looking out the window. As if there could be an answer to what would happen to Dagmara out there. It was at that moment that I realized so much of what I hoped for, coming out of the war, revolved around her. In my head I imagined she was going to leave Vidler, and we were going to settle in England or America, our new lives the reward we'd earn for the completion of this project. Now that was all shown up for the ridiculous fantasy it probably always was. I had never felt so alone. I began to weep.

I don't know how long I stood there, perhaps less than a minute, but it seemed so much longer. I had heard, when one is electrocuted or struck by lightning, the moment is experienced in the subconscious like the longest dream. My inner world was collapsing, and the moment carried all the voltage of such an ordeal. Until I felt, on my shoulder, the comradely grip of Farrell.

"I know, I know, my friend. Listen, my advice to you is to close up shop, take the whole lot of what you have left and store it away for now. Let's leave no trace in case Dagmara does talk."

"That won't be so easy. My brother Anton, he runs my other gallery in Antwerp. He has the fake of the la Tour. He needs all the money he can get, I told him he could keep the commission..."

"That's the Hertmans."

"It is, yes."

Farrell bit his lower lip, looked down at the floor as if he could find a solution to this quandary in the pattern of the tiles.

"That's the only one?"

"That's it."

"I'm sorry, my friend. All we can do is hope. I'll do what I can and speak to my American friends once I get back to my work at the library. If all goes well in the weeks ahead, there may be someone who can contact you. In the meantime, keep your faith. We both know Dagmara. She is tougher than all of us. And probably braver."

"Probably, yes."

I was back in Lucerne, walking onto the dance floor, my gaze fixed on the back of this woman who had claimed my heart as soon as our eyes first met. *Todentanz*... yes, that was the fresco I had seen that afternoon. I blinked the last tears out of my eyes.

14.

04 / 15 / 89
Red Scarecrow (Paul Klee, 1935)

Nikolaus, so much that I have written within these pages I am now questioning. *Was it really that way?* Everything from the last dress I saw Dagmara wearing to the taste of orange juice in Rome. When the Russians questioned me for days, (weeks? I went in and out of consciousness from the beatings so it could have been longer) I had begun to doubt my own memories and believe I must have known more about the Reichskulturkammer than I could recall. When I was finally sent to Sachsenhausen, the most vivid memories were like all my open wounds. As those abrasions healed and left scars, my acts of reconstruction in my mind took on the same blurry texture as my scar tissue.

And yet I kept a secret. I'm still amazed by my nerve. I quickly sensed that no one had a clue that I was largely responsible for the disappearance of so much priceless artwork. I was still capable of a coward's rationalization; if they weren't going to ask, why would I tell?

But the secret wore away at me. To ease my conscience and maintain my sanity, perhaps I should have written it all down over those two years in prison. But where would I have kept those pages? My cell made a tramp's hovel look like a luxury hotel suite. Each Saturday, as I walked the perimeter of the yard, they would blast the concrete floor of the cell with a hydraulic hose, mop everything down with harsh disinfectant soap, change the sheets on my cot, and perform a strip search of every crevice and fold of my personal space. Property is theft, as my interrogators reminded me, with just a touch of sarcasm, during one of my initial 'interviews' with them. And I wasn't going to make my memories into a commodity they could confiscate.

I told them everything they asked anyway. I even reminded them that I had voted for the Communists when a vote still mattered. As did Magda, the one person who established relations with the government long before I did. Registered party members, the both of us, check the records. If we were 'typical bourgeoisie' who were complicit with the Nazis, at least she and I tried to get rid of them, which was the strongest indication of our true sympathies. For 'Rudi,' the one officer who spent the most time with me, such an argument was, as he put it, 'specious.' We personified a Berlin strain of intellectual decadence, and as such 'Koba'—Comrade Stalin— had spoken plainly about how it was worthy of nothing but contempt from those who were 'clean.' Aside from how 'dirty' I was, I believe Rudi and his colleagues with the truncheons and bullwhips hated me more for my candor about not hating them.

There was a trial, they granted me that. I sat at a table with a lawyer provided by the state. She was a woman named Frau Konig—pock-marked and sour, her mousy brown hair pulled up severely in a bun. She was repelled by my very presence as she sat beside me over two short days, speaking for me, confirming my guilt as she made niggling points of correction to the record. She would not make eye contact with me until the judge read out my sentence: five years as a willing vendor for the Nazi government's art procurement activities.

I wanted to laugh. Hadn't I told them about all I had done with Dagmara to save priceless work from the government's voracious appetite? Hadn't I been responsible for spiriting so many paintings out of the country? I would have added that these were painted by those the party counted as members and actively championed before the Russians implemented their edicts against such decadent formalism. You could say my efforts were hardly heroic, but then you would have to say Magda died for nothing. What was five years in prison going to prove, and what kind of reform and re-education would make me worthy of freedom and citizenship once again?

The only person permitted to laugh at my absurd predicament was Frau Konig, who could not quite keep a straight face as I was led away. I believe I was weeping. I must have really put the 'show' in 'show trial' for her.

Yet I should have taken some consolation in the very theatricality of all this. These servants of the state were only replicating, in a farcical way, what was occurring to the whole country: they were governing by signals and gestures, displaying the power of their new laws to discipline, punish, and crush the souls of those who could never attain the ideological purity my interrogators claimed for themselves. As part of my sentence, I had to pay for the porcelain dentures they provided after knocking most of my teeth out during our 'conversations.' I had a fake smile for fake justice.

It ended up that I only served twenty-three months. Maybe they just got bored with the very idea of keeping me around. They had real enemies of the people they needed to put behind bars—pimps and rapists and even a few genuine psychopath murderers in my block near the end of my stay—and they couldn't quite justify doing away with me, as they executed so many other dubious 'collaborators.'

The conditions were as good as could be expected to commit suicide. I knew of four cellmates over my time who managed with shoelaces, torn sheets—even a rusted nail snatched from planks left by the fence line. If I had been just a little creative and enterprising, I could have managed it. But the amazing thing about depression, which I've been told I've had throughout my life, is that one can't even summon the energy to do one self-harm.

Unless one has alcohol, but I get ahead of myself.

And I realize I've left out how I was arrested once the Russians took the city. But truthfully, there is not much of interest to tell.

It was not as though an escape from the city was possible. I stayed in my apartment—no longer quite so luxurious, given all that I had pawned for the rent—and I spent the last week eating canned meat and dry sausages I had managed to pay a month's salary for. In the early hours each day, I would listen to the reports on the wireless until the Russians and Americans took those programs over. By then I knew it was every man for himself. I could hear the tanks two streets over on the morning I walked out of my apartment building with a small suitcase, containing all that was left of my belongings. In a matter of minutes I had my hands in the air, as I pleaded with three Russians on foot patrol not to shoot me.

I remember it was a Monday morning, April twenty-third. I took off my gold watch and handed it over to one Russian soldier who smelled of vodka and piss stains. He already had four watches on his wrist. The time on mine was 8:36. I still think of it as the day my real life ended and my fake life began.

Let me explain what I mean. There was an older gentleman two cells from me on my floor, a history professor at one point, apparently. One Sunday evening he had gotten news that his son was executed in Siberia. I could hear his wailing for hours. The next day, as we walked the perimeter of the yard, I told him that I too had a son, and that I knew how he felt—I doubted whether I would ever see you again. As I spoke these words, I actually surprised myself: his tears became my tears.

There is all the proof you need of your father feeling things from the outside in. I'm told it is the only way a certain species of narcissist can experience emotions. Now I know my kind. And I know it's no consolation, but I'm sorry, Nikolaus. What separated us is the strange inevitable distance I seem to need from anyone who can claim some part of me.

But enough. I'm still amazed by my capacity for self-pity. How easily I slip into my elegiac, mawkish tone to relate what anyone with a little foresight would say was inevitable. As Silvia said to me, early on in our relationship, in an effort to console me after I had relapsed with my drinking, "you go up high, you fall down low. That's what I know of physics." I could have benefited with some basic understanding of science with my mood swings.

Yet even when the end was clear to everyone, and it seemed likely that Galerie Maes would no longer be standing if the shelling continued, I was still making plans for how business might continue for me after the surrender.

Of course it was delusional, but I was listening to those who told me what I wanted to hear. Those like Odon Heimrath.

Right up until March of that year, just weeks before the end, he was still going to his office every day in the Ordenspalais—

among all those buildings around the Wilhelmplatz that were eventually flattened. We had seen each other on the street. He was another familiar face glimpsed under an umbrella, waiting for one of the trams that were still running.

As we parted he invited me up to see him. "We must discuss business," he said. Whatever business might mean.

Once in his office, he began to quiz me about the work I had, still in the old bankers' vault in the gallery's basement. His eyebrows raised at a few I mentioned and he jotted down the names of painters in a notebook splayed open before him. He assured me that any paintings in my possession would become the property of the state "once things settled down." It wouldn't even matter if he were personally involved, such dealings were normal in transitions of government like this. He'd seen it occur in Poland, "a most recent example, I believe indicative." It was all very straightforward.

I didn't believe a word. I knew what I saw of how the Russians operated. A young woman in my building, who was in Halbe visiting her mother one weekend, had been raped for a flashlight by a Mongolian conscript, out on patrol. He had left her for dead, and she crawled out of the occupied sector and made it back home. There would be no orderly transition of government and Odon knew it. I presumed he would wait for my arrest and sell my property via whatever black market dealings he might have access to, as he bargained for his escape from prosecution.

"I'll provide you with the paintings that remain with me, but you must do one thing for me," I said.

"Of course, my friend. You look out for me, I look out for you. That's how it works."

"It's just a small favour. Please find out what happened to my son and my ex-wife, Sabine Ostriker."

"Sally?"

"Yes, that's her. She and my son were living with an Irishman, Francis Cluny. He did broadcasts…"

Odon raised his pale white hand and made a sweeping gesture, which I initially thought was an indication that you both had been disposed of quickly and handily.

"Yes, yes, I know of Cluny. Of course I do. Unfortunate that your ex-wife ended up with him."

"Why?"

"You know we get all the memos from Propaganda and Public Enlightenment, yes? I have to read them. I can recall one on Mr. Cluny from a few months ago. We knew he was talking to Russians through code in his letters from Ireland. He was making overtures, claiming he could spy for them."

"And did he?"

"We heard they didn't want him. He likes young boys and his information was frequently unreliable."

In that moment I felt the closest thing to a murderous impulse that I have ever experienced. If Cluny had ever, even casually and obtusely, made an overture to you, I felt in that moment that I was ready to hunt him down and kill him with my bare hands. But there was no way of knowing.

I still pray this did not happen. If I think of how this may have broken you, how you could be carrying this pain through the rest of your life. If we could actually speak, all I would hope for is your confirmation that your innocence was not taken from you this way.

Anyway, when I asked if you were both in the enemy's hands, Odon shrugged and primly shut his notebook. "My understanding is they ended up in Munich. Everyone has given up on getting out through France. But in Munich the English were accepting refugees, so… rats leaping from the battleship, yes? Quite a mob scene of the so-called stateless, I heard."

"I just want my son to be okay," I said. I swear I did. It was all I asked.

"Please take this in the best way when I tell you to forget about your son, my friend. You can't do anything for him. No one can, among us here. You're not an old man quite yet."

"I feel like an old man."

"Maybe you can find yourself another wife. Start a family once this is all over."

I shook my head, still ruminating on how repellent Cluny was. I didn't want another family. How could anyone replicate you?

"Odon, if I give you all the work I have left from the gallery, all I ask is this one thing for me. Can you find out as much as you can about them? I believe their official names would be Sally and Nicholas Cluny now."

Heimrath visibly brightened, flashed his yellowing teeth. "I can get a truck to come 'round if you've taken them out of the gallery now. It's not conspicuous. They've done many repossessions, as we've called them. Same address from that dinner party you had, yes? It seems so long ago now."

I knew that the paintings would be useless to him without the papers detailing their provenance. There was only one person I was absolutely sure would never have a case to reclaim the art that Farrell didn't give me, should the government be obligated to return it all at some point: Gisela Ostriker, Sabine's mother. I had arranged the consignment of some work that was in her name for tax purposes. I even had some old stationery where she had a seal made with her name. You could say it was a cold, bloodless decision, but I was simmering with rage directed at Sabine for how she had jeopardized your innocence. I watched each painting be carried out of my building by boys in mismatched uniforms and oversized boots—this was what the great forces of the Reich were reduced to—and I felt nothing but a wish that I might never see all that work again.

Except for one. Klee's *Red Scarecrow*, this gold square, topped by a blue circle and pegged like a tent by four pinkish rectangles, all against a scarlet background. It was, he said, more of a study for a later painting. It is a work that is notionally representational. There is a figure disappearing into abstraction, into the freedom of deeper compositional considerations: the balance of colour, the play of 'pure forms.' Klee painted this just a few months after the Nuremberg laws were passed. He was safe in Switzerland by then, and there is a palpable gesture towards freedom in this work, a willed escape from the spiritual ugliness that had spread like a blood-red stain from a spilled vessel. Maybe I wanted to be that scarecrow who might disappear as well. I held the painting one last time, let my eyes drink it in, then blinked them shut, as if I were capturing this image in the vault of my memory. And then I let it go.

Now that it is here, along with these few others back in my possession; there is no question in my mind about who should inherit this work. It seems like it has never been more possible that you could claim these, if it's true this government might be in its final days. But as my high blood pressure and diabetes have affirmed for me, on a daily basis, it is unwise to wager on me living to see the Wall coming down.

I have come to terms with how much I'll never know. I had waited a few days and then went back out to the Ordenpalais because I hadn't heard from Heimrath, but the building was closed and no one among the scarecrow teenagers guarding the building could tell me his home address. One laughed when I wrote down Heimrath on a playing card I picked up from the security desk. I was too tired and weak to be enraged. I had a good idea about what Heimrath had done. He had seen in me an opportunity to get something of value, a cache of paintings he might be able to bargain with to ensure his own survival. He probably felt that he had a clear conscience because he did, in actual fact, tell me all he could about the fate of you and your mother. Question of survival—we all did what was necessary for ourselves.

But permit me this coda: back in the early seventies, when Honecker first came to power, there was an interesting bit of history about him I read in a magazine story on his 'heroic journey.' Apparently he, too, spent some time in Sachsenhausen, though his detainment was under the Reich. Safe to say he managed a better second act in his life than I did.

When they took me into one of the old tribunal rooms to tell me I had been paroled, the official—young, as handsome as a young movie actor from the old days of the Aryan code—instructed me on the importance of finding my footing back in society as soon as I could. I had an appointment at another government office for a job placement, the address of a halfway house that was expecting me. He shook his head as he glanced down at my records, moving his lips as he read. He said it was up to me to decide my fate, that rehabilitation required an acceptance of responsibility. I told him my father had been a man of the cloth; I was raised with an understanding of sin and atonement. He slowly blinked those long blonde lashes and said, in a droll monotone, that I would do well to forget 'all that old church nonsense.'

And yet so much about my life over the next decade made me feel like a monk returning to the land of the faithless. There was a churchlike hush in the library where they found employment for me, an unwavering Spartan routine to my days. Calisthenics, instant coffee, a small closet in my first apartment that I gradually filled with an overcoat, two woolen suits, and three shirts. Two plates, one fork, and one knife left to dry on the rack by the sink each night. One year I vacationed for a week on the North Sea, in another I joined a table tennis club. I was considered a good sport. At one retirement party for a colleague working in government archives, I discovered there was a nickname for me: 'the ghost man.'

My gradual dependence on alcohol is still mysterious to me. Yet most nights, what gave me a feeling of the old luxury was a tumbler of vodka with a library book, while the radio played the music still in favour of the government: Beethoven more than Mozart, Shostakovich more than Prokofiev. There are some symphonies and concertos that still bring back the harsh taste of some of the worst vodka on the shelves from back in those days— and I haven't had a drop in eight years. But when I closed my eyes after my first couple of drinks each night, it felt like I was floating, benumbed, able to glide along the corridors of my memory theatre, as I waited for the lights to go down on my consciousness and the old films from my past to play as dreams. A walking ghost with a magic lantern show to haunt me every night, once he had my elixir vitae.

Of course there were still faces from the past I'd glimpse most days. I would be on the street or one of the new buses and I'd recognize a former customer, or one of Sabine's old friends. These were people for whom I really had nothing to say; just a simple nod of recognition seemed appropriate and respectful. *Ah, I see you too have survived and are now faking a new life for yourself.* I suppose I wished them all well in my heart.

Except for Heimrath.

On the afternoon I saw him, there was probably no more fitting an occasion: we were both in the Alexanderplatz for the observance of Stalin's funeral. There were loudspeakers broadcasting the ceremony, a small wooden stage erected for a series of speeches that all of us in the crowd, shivering in our flimsy overcoats in the freezing rain, knew would be unendurable but compulsory. Any tittering at the stilted, wooden rhetoric or visible displays of boredom or irritation would be noted and put into the file on you. There was only one way to get through it; I was already drunk before I found a place in the crowd.

And as the service ended and the crowd began to file out of the square, we spotted each other. Over the eight years since we had last met, it looked like he, too, had not had an easy time of it. His mouth looked shrunken, his hair had turned ash grey. But those milky blue eyes were the same, and I could see a kind of feral growl form on his lips, a shiver of fear go through him. He knew I would want to ask about the paintings and that was a conversation he was determined not to have.

So he began to run. First it was just a hurried walk, as if he was late for a bus. And because he was clearly a stickler for veracity, he pulled out of his pocket a number of bus tickets, folded into a small packet. I had no choice but to follow and broke into a trot myself. It was embarrassing.

He looked back and picked up the pace, and when that didn't seem to open up some distance between us, he made a sudden turn down a side street by the university. It was a smart move; the university was shut down for the day so no one was on the sidewalks. There was a sign that read 'service entrance,' pointing to a small alley. I had gained on him and felt sure of myself. After all that time, all I really wanted to know was what happened to the work, what he had done with it.

The alley was a dead end. There was just a loading ramp and a rusted steel door. I called his name and he turned. He grinned and showed me the wreckage of his teeth. Clearly he didn't get the deal on dentures that I did in prison. With his hands in his pockets, he made as if he was opening his overcoat to show me he was carrying no weapon. As I approached, I didn't see the piece of brick in his hand until it was too late.

When I awoke I was in a hospital bed. The nurse attending to me said the x-rays revealed the contusion was serious, and that I was lucky to be alive. From my jaw to my right temple, I felt a dull, heavy throbbing, made bearable by the pin prick of the needle and the sudden pillowy cloud of morphine she had just administered.

"The police will be coming in shortly. They just have some questions before you drift off to sleep again."

"What kind of questions?"

"Do you know who the person who assaulted you was? If not, do you think you might be able to describe him?"

I just shook my head, mumbled something about being attacked from behind. I was drunk at the time. I had gotten lost on my way home. I would try my best to help them, but really, I didn't remember much.

The police came to their own conclusions. A forty-three year old bachelor, led into an alley by another man. Some transaction for a dalliance that suddenly went badly. Berlin was a city that hadn't changed that much. The stories they could have told, I'm sure.

I never did see Heimrath again. The whole attack felt like the inevitable conclusion to the period in my life when I felt freest. And yes, even once in love.

15.

04 / 28 / 89
Self-Portrait (Egon Schiele, c. 1912)

Nicki, some days I say to myself what does it matter if the government reads this before you do? It is probably inevitable. At one point… this had to be more than twenty years ago now… I had a conversation with a library colleague in archives who was quite open about working for the Stasi. He was a rather horse-faced Prussian with a foppish thatch of red hair. He would have been perfectly cast as Judas in some Berliner Ensemble play. He told me had spent some years working in Hungary and in the Far East— though he would not tell me where or what he was doing. Yet he did say this to me, over a stein of beer one May Day: "it is easier to turn a western agent than you think. Most people, they don't really have a good sense of who they are, or what their value is to others. It is so difficult to truly see oneself." He told me he had been watching me carefully.

"Does anybody seriously believe I'd be spying for America? I would be terrible. I couldn't keep a secret."

"There we are. You've just proven my point," he said.

It was the perfect, puzzling response. Because I knew I couldn't keep a secret, did that mean I knew myself and therefore could have made a good spy for the Americans? Or did me saying this prove I didn't know myself, and therefore…the same conclusion obtains, and either way he was correct.

I pondered over these questions for years. If I truly knew myself, why would I contemplate betraying anyone? Perhaps this central fact provides me with my answer. And his.

I can say that my drinking proved that something about me had changed. For years, while I was still courting and then married to your mother, I prided myself on how unsentimental I was about love and what I meant to her. What I meant to any woman, really. It allowed me to tell myself I was realistic about her infidelities. After you were born, it was pragmatic to tolerate her behaviour for your sake. Later, with Dagmara, I thought I was clear-eyed about the prospect of her ever leaving Connie Vidler. I never would have asked her to do such a thing. Yet when I came out of Sachsenhausen, the self-pity I had, the sentimentality about how I was fated to be alone and unloved, was undeniable.

There was only one thing that soothed the soul: vodka in the evenings. I would come home with a library book and gradually get inebriated enough to sleep through the sounds of the street. Farewell to the old sirens. I will say this about the Communists; they managed to scare off those who were once indifferent to spending one or a few nights in jail, and in the first decade that they were in power, the petty crimes and misdemeanors seemed to disappear. One of my favourite American writers when I was young and still believed in some notion of the sublime was Thoreau, and he had this phrase about men living lives of quiet desperation. Now I think we all knew what he meant, nothing was lost in the translation. There was no cure, only the palliative care the bottle provided.

I also told myself that I needed the alcohol to sleep through the nightmares I had most nights. And perhaps that was true. I could rarely call them back into consciousness in the morning, but there was one that recurred where I was locked in the central station in Antwerp, with that cathedral-like dome, the grey and white granite walls so stately and cold. I was waiting for your grandparents to arrive and take me home. Yet I was not me; I was your uncle Anton. It was like I was dreaming up a narcopolis. I would speak Flemish and English as I would roam the corridors, looking for a porter who would take the large trunks I had traveled with. Only once did I open one of these – and yes, it was full of emaciated corpses: my Sachsenhausen friends.

I spent twenty years as an alcoholic. I still find this hard to believe. The years went so quickly! One develops strategies to manage it, of course. I told myself that if I was able to read one, sometimes two books a week, I was still functioning as well as ever. Aside from that failed Roman project of mine I was taking notes for a monograph I would one day complete on the underappreciated painters of the Neue Sachlichkeit, with a special focus on Dix and Beckmann. 750 millilitres of vodka, 250 words a day was my motto, and though I held fast to the vodka total, the word counts dropped dramatically the more I wrote truthfully, and I ended up burning the pages I managed to complete.

When the drinking got bad enough that I lost my position at the library, the state decided that part of my rehabilitation, apart from weekly counseling, would be an assignment on the social committee in the neighbourhood sports club. I spent the good part of another decade officiating volleyball, umpiring tennis, an absurd advertisement for the positive benefits of exercise, while I abstained from engaging in any activity that required a change of clothing.

Yet I could not stay so detached forever. Soon after I turned sixty Drago, the young Yugoslavian president of the club, informed me there were not enough men to fill out the ballroom dancing classes, and that my attendance would set a strong example for other senior members. The only woman I wanted to remember dancing with was Dagmara. Just the thought of waltzing with, say, my neighbour Eva Borschmann, the nurse who smells of cabbage and is nearly twice my size, repulsed me. However, I feared the implications of another negative report from the Stasi (possible exile in some prison-like home for seniors out in the country), and everyone knew Drago was capable of writing it.

About three weeks in to these Wednesday evening classes, a young woman from Timisoara approached me. She said she had just come from Moscow, where 'it didn't work out,' and that she had come to Berlin and recently got a job in the local bakery. She mentioned staying with a friend in the first few weeks, but I have never probed further. A younger, attractive woman like her, I just presumed it was her lover.

Yet I was the one she wanted to dance with, week in, week out. Strauss waltzes weren't exactly sanctioned music, as far as the Russians were concerned, but Drago and his friends were tolerant of a little ideological slippage. When Silvia and I spun around the club floor I imagined we were in the ballroom of one of the baroque palaces the revolution had claimed for itself. We were stubbornly keeping some kitsch notion of romance alive for our friends in the class, as I teased and flirted with her.

There was no way I thought any of this was serious, so imagine my surprise, as the romance cliché goes, when I found her waiting for me outside the sports club one night. She asked if I might like to have a drink with her somewhere some time. It pains me to say I invited her home for herbal tea.

She told me about her life back in Romania as cook in an officers' canteen, the difficult decision she had made to give him up and go to Moscow for work. After five years in a hotel kitchen, her boyfriend found work in Berlin and they claimed common law marriage and got an apartment together. Yet he was unfaithful to her. She felt alone in a strange city, and I was the one man who showed her some warmth and affection.

Within a month she was living with me. I know she has other men in her life, and you might say maybe I was just gullible enough to give her a roof over her head when she needed it. But I know that when we are together, the intimacy is real. As real as it was with Dagmara, the love of my life.

And we are good to each other. When the cache of paintings Heimrath had were, secretly and quite miraculously, returned to me, she was sincerely interested in learning more about each one of them. She listened so intently as I spoke of the provenance of each. This Schiele, the self-portrait from around 1912, she particularly likes. I've always found his work a touch too mannered, but in the stark, contorted image of this slender young aesthete, she said this was how she imagined me as a young man. I laughed and she seemed to be a little hurt by this. She was paying me a compliment.

I want to be good to her. I suppose, reluctantly enough, we all have to be good to someone, don't we? I started to inquire (through Mr. K, who returned these to me) about who might be interested in having one or more of these works from this cache in their possession, so I could barter for a trip back home for Silvia, and she could be reunited with her son. It is all so oddly ennobling.

I told Silvia almost everything about me. And this included my marriage and my years as a father, all about my family in Antwerp, all that I had lost. I suppose it was therapeutic, and Silvia seemed genuinely touched that I would share this with her. It was she who urged me to write it all down for you, in the faint hope that you might someday read it and find out just who I was, and what pulled us apart.

And in so doing, maybe I have started to discover myself at last.

The one crucial episode I did not tell Silvia, and which I will put down here, is something you might appreciate. It is about the last time I saw Francis Cluny. I want you to know how I left things with this man.

The year was '72 or '73, and the library was sponsoring an international symposium on 'writing for the workers.' There was a conscious attempt, with the graphic design work chosen for the publicity, to imitate the kind of bold colours and thick, child-like font we had seen on TV during the Munich Olympics. The mustard and chocolate coloured graphics in the signage attained an inspired degree of ugliness. And it would soon be replicated on paperbacks, because the government had made a commitment to publish a new series of fiction titles from countries as far afield as Cuba, Angola— and interestingly, from 'the Republican movement' in Ireland. The celebration of this laudable cross-cultural initiative would culminate in a series of readings, over two weeknights in the main library hall, with the works of these international voices that we would all now be able to enjoy. There, in an iris-like cameo photograph on the brochure was Francis, 'poet, novelist, playwright, actor, and revolutionary socialist.'

He had not aged well, if the photograph did him any justice at all, I thought. He wore his grey hair in a Beatle-like shag, with his fringe of bangs hanging over his eyes, and his monkey-like grin revealed those small, yellow teeth I remembered. He was representing the United Kingdom with this bearded poet-miner from the North of England, but his bio stated he had 'spent over four decades writing of the effects of English imperialism on the people of Eire.' 'A striking septuagenarian full of revolutionary fire,' the Zeitung reported, after his first night of reading.

I spotted him prior to his second night of reading. He was drinking coffee in the library cafeteria, thumbing through the pages of a Cuban novel.

"Your German is still good enough to read such literature?"

I startled him, and his frightened glare told me he had recognized me immediately. Yet he pretended otherwise. "Excuse me. Did I meet you before?"

It was a tactic of distancing himself from the man he once was. He could affect a convenient amnesia about his years in Berlin. I was impatient, and probably rude in my directness.

"What do you know of what happened to Sabine—"

"Sally, you mean."

"Yes. I suppose that is who she was to you."

"We soon split up after we left Berlin. I realized she was using me. All she ever wanted was an escape route out of the country."

"Do you know where she went?"

"I imagine London, wouldn't you? She always liked the English, didn't she?"

"My boy Nikolaus. I'm an old man now. You're an old man. Maybe you understand."

"I have no children, sir."

He could see how his formality was causing me discomfort. And I will admit to playing it up, in an effort to tap the shallow reserve of compassion he had. And it worked.

"Look, you seem to have had a rough time over the years, my friend. There is a gentleman I know who helped organize this little junket. We speak regularly, if you know what I mean. He will know. If he doesn't, he will have the resources to help you."

He took his plastic pen from the breast pocket of his tweed blazer, tore a page from the book, and wrote down the contact information for Mr. L. I swore I would not disclose this to anyone and thanked him, left him to whatever peace of mind he could manage.

That was more than fifteen years ago now. Mr. L. and I have kept in touch and he has proven to be helpful—as I believe I have proven myself to be for him. He told me to stay away from Mr.

K. a few months ago, and though he wouldn't elaborate, I trust him, and have always found it prudent to follow his advice. Whatever Mr. K. might be able to promise for me, with the secret transactions he says he can carry out for what I tactfully elided, "will only create problems for you, old friend."

More promising, he believes, is the direction things are taking within the government. It is finally crumbling. The rot from the centre has been exposed with Gorbachev, and no matter what they try and do to rein him back in, there is little that Honecker, the old bastard, can do to put his finger in the dyke. Or the wall.

So I may have something like a legacy for you—or at the very least an inheritance that might give you a sense of what your father's life was like after we were separated. These notes, along with what I can draft as a final will and testament, can be read and validated in courts of law where justice might be possible. From this decaying world where all is simulacra rather than real, and fakery and fraud have been scrupulously documented, if only to empower the fakes and frauds in charge, a great collapse could be imminent.

This would be all I could ask for: the answer to an old man's prayers. Because I have still prayed and believed over the years. A pastor's son right to the end, it seems. If what I have written finally gets to you, this is what you will discover. As Odon, my Judas friend, might have admitted if he were still alive to read this, here is a portrait of a man who finally might know himself.

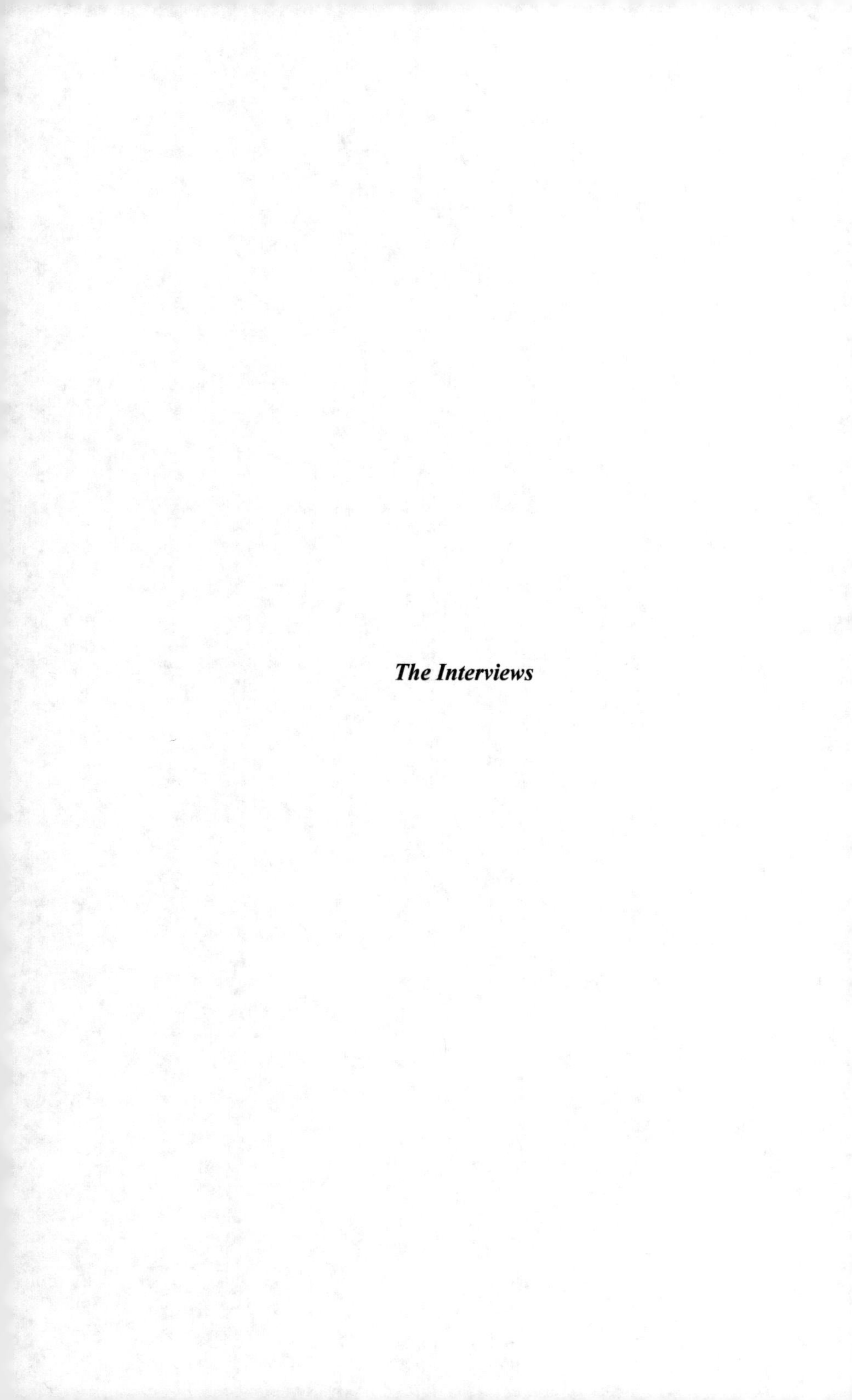

The Interviews

16.

Mr. Lorenzo Verzaro,
Director, Art Crimes Unit (Milan)
INTERPOL NCB
November 13th, 1993

Dear Lorenzo,

As you can see from Maes' notes, they could hardly be considered a record of the provenance of some works that were in his possession. However, the Schiele was clearly referred to, so as it followed, the others had to be somewhere as well. And to add to the challenges, the issue of these fakes released into the market from a series of clandestine Vatican sales was a whole other, provocative development that would require investigation.

Yet Maes was frustratingly secretive about who also knew about the paintings in his possession. He feared the reach of the Stasi. Who wouldn't? Especially someone like him who had already spent five years in prison. All I had to go on was mention of a 'Mr. K.' and a 'Mr. L.' But the German government remains, as you know, frustratingly slow about providing information of the Stasi's activities. They say it's a question of volume. Virtually everyone was spying on each other, it seems. We could be waiting months, and if these other stolen paintings were on the market, they could be lost forever. I was losing precious time.

Maybe Vidler's auction house—if it still existed in Dublin—could be of help? No. You probably know this, but Connie Vidler was jailed for selling fake antiquities soon after the war, and Connie himself died in 1952, just a few months after his release from prison.

But what about this mention of the original owner of the *Schiele*, Benjamin Ostriker, yes? This was once Harry's father-in-law. Maybe I would find Doctor Benjamin Ostriker in, say,

Ramallah or Jerusalem, and he would fly to Berlin to be reunited with this painting after more than fifty years. Think of the photo: the grateful old man with the painting in his hands and me beside him. Our unit couldn't pay for better press.

Except there was no Benjamin Ostriker in the region anymore. He had left the country in 1951. It took me a few months, but with the help of an organization called the Weissman foundation (more on this below) he was finally tracked down in Montreal, Canada. There was an Ostriker's Optical shop there. He sold eyeglasses for more than three decades. He passed away in his sleep two days before the first day of Hanukkah in 1985.

Still, there were others that still might be alive, you'd presume. What about Antony Farrell? If the Vatican had any record of his time of employment in the Library, they were not going to share it. It seems he had vanished like the young Nikolaus Maes and Harry's wife Sabine (Sally) Cluny. The painter Wim Hertmans had a wife and son after he was rescued from a camp, I discovered, but his eventual trial for painting fakes during the war had brought him and the Hertmans name such ignominy they, too, had been redacted from any historical record. As one of our American colleagues said to me in New York, "it's like everybody who knew Harry Maes went into the witness protection program."

There was a breakthrough, however. I continued to pore over Maes' notes for days until finally I found something of a lead. It came from this episode that Dagmara Vidler mentioned from her time in the south of France: that bonfire of the paintings. I knew it sounded familiar.

But to explain why this would become the key that finally opened the door into this case, I will have to tell you about Rifka Solomon and my trip to Jerusalem four years ago. This is already a long note. I will send you a complete memorandum on Solomon and the Weissman Foundation over the next two days.

I could provide this and my subsequent interviews to you as a dry report, I suppose. But I have the tapes, their voices themselves. I was openly recording these conversations. With a case like this, where authenticity became so central to the questions Maes' notes have raised, I think it best for me to give these interviews to you as they happened. Maybe you will draw different conclusions than mine about who was speaking the truth. As always, I look forward to our own conversations.

    Sincerely,
    Lt. Christina Perretti
    Art Crimes Unit (Rome)
    Interpol NCB

17.

Mr. Lorenzo Verzaro,
Director, Art Crimes Unit (Milan)
INTERPOL NCB
November 17th, 1993

Dear Lorenzo,

My first exposure to the Weissman foundation occurred before you were with the unit, when you still had your university position, I believe. An invitation came to the Milan office regarding a seminar, convened as part of a conference on Jewish modernism at the Hebrew University in Jerusalem. There would be a short talk and presentation by Dr. Baruch Weissman. I still remember the date because I wrote it down in my diary: May 3rd, 1989. I suppose, out of all of us, because of my faith, I was chosen to go. Inside on stiff, ivory-coloured card paper, the title was italicized: "Of Provenance and Erasure: Art Recovery and Jewish Heritage." A short biographical note overleaf stated that Weissman held a research position at the University of Geneva, but I had never heard of him before. Seating was limited; I was told this was one of the smallest lecture rooms the conference was provided, and so I had to RSVP as soon as possible.

I was flattered. There was an air of exclusivity about the whole event, something I was not used to, given how marginalized our work in the unit seemed in those days. And I had never been to Jerusalem. This would be an adventure.

I arrived on the day of the seminar. I hurried to the conference and when I finally found the venue there were twelve people in the lecture room. Most of them looked like they had come off a cruise ship for the afternoon. They were older, well-dressed, and well-preserved, carrying themselves proudly. If you've ever wondered, as I sometimes do, who really cares about the work our unit does, that first day would have provided you with something of an answer.

It was ten minutes after the appointed hour when Baruch Weissman finally shuffled in. He was short, squarish and beetle-browed, with a crown of thick grey curls that seemed a bit too artfully unkempt. He was like a Talmudic scholar draped in ill-fitting Irish tweed, all wrong for Jerusalem in May. It seemed a costume of humility and anonymity, but his signet ring and Rolex watch, both gold, revealed the touch of vanity that offset his solemnity. Vanity and wealth.

As soon as the attendees were seated and quiet, a woman about my age rose from the back of the room. This was Rifka Solomon, from Columbia University, who said she was a director with the Weissman Foundation. She was dressed all in black, a bit too dramatically, I remember thinking. She turned off the lights and a square of white light filled a screen on the wall behind me. Everyone turned at once as the roll of film whirred through a projector.

"What you are about to see is not supposed to exist," Baruch Weissman said, peering over his glasses at notes placed on a lectern, traced by penlight. "The French government denies it. They say it's a propaganda film. The Dutch government denies it. The German government denies it. They say the paintings were fakes. And yet here it is: a bonfire."

The film was grainy black and white, the shots poorly lit, yet I could make out the familiar Nazi helmets, soldiers carrying framed canvases in their arms, moving in quickened, stutter-step motion towards an open fire. It looked like a courtyard of some manor, given the shadowy outline of cobblestones, a wrought iron fence, high windows squared in panes that glowed like polished chrome.

"This occurred in a home near Nice. We know the Nazis took this residence over as they worked with Petain's troops to quell the Resistance. What you see are masterpieces the troops had looted which the Nazis decided they did not want for themselves. Paintings by Cezanne, Otto Dix, Franz Marc… all lost forever. Now why would they destroy these? I would answer that if the words of

Goebbels and Hitler himself were to be taken seriously, these paintings were degenerate. They were the product of defected humanity, the decadence of Jewish cosmopolitanism. And so they had to go the way of all defective products in a civilized, industrial state."

The screen bled into white once more. The film could not have been more than two minutes long. Weissman turned the projector off and Rifka Solomon flicked the fluorescent lights back on.

Weissman continued reading from his lecture notes, often peering up to take his audience in, to see if what he was saying was creating the desired effect: a slowly-building, transformative rage about all that had been stolen or destroyed. "Before you scoff at any description of a Cezanne as Jewish or decadent, you must think about where these paintings came from. Who owned them? What we know is that many were originally the property of Jewish families. It did not take a Kristallnacht for, say, a man like Bruno Spiro, a Berlin arms merchant, to realize his possessions might be seized, and that emigration had to be seriously considered. Yet there was the capital flight tax and later the Jewish wealth levy to pay. What is a Cezanne or two in comparison to safe passage to London or New York for you, your wife, your children? Spiro, by the way, had quite a lot of art in his Berlin villa. He also committed suicide in Sachsenhausen in 1936."

As I listened to Weissman, I felt my heart beating faster. The lecture was a summoning, a sharpening of my senses. I just knew that our work with the unit could play an important role in the work of this foundation. Afterwards, I took Rifka Solomon's card, spoke to her briefly. She suggested we meet for a drink after the conference concluded the following afternoon.

And then I was called back to Milan. There was a breakthrough in a case we were working on, with two arrests in Napoli. I had to catch the next flight back and never did see Rifka Solomon.

But I had kept her card. There it was, yellowing in my Rolodex here in Rome. I just knew, given all we had from Harry Maes, that she might be of help. I made a quick calculation of the time difference and waited until late in the afternoon to call the number on the card. And she answered. It had been four years, but yes, she still remembered me.

I began to tell her about the case of Silvia Stanciu and the Schiele, and how it had led to us recovering these notes on provenance from Maes. There was silence on the phone. For so long I thought the line had gone dead. And then she finally spoke.

"Lieutenant Perretti, I don't think you realize that your call couldn't have come at a better time."

The New York police had just recovered a stolen painting that had been considered lost, thought to be destroyed during the war. It was *The Card Cheat*, by Georges de la Tour. One Malcolm Wylie, who was with the troops liberating Antwerp, had purchased it. He had gone back to the US and made a lot of money in mining— or resource development, as it is called now, so we don't think too much about the miners, I guess. He had a mansion in Connecticut, about two hours from Manhattan, where the la Tour hung in his office on the second floor. Records from the Weissman foundation confirmed that it was originally exhibited and up for sale in a small gallery in wartime Antwerp. Galerie Maes. Yet there was some question of it actually being authentic.

Everything Maes had written about the work of Antony Farrell's within the Vatican accorded with what Solomon had to say. Because I knew, from Maes's notes, that Wim Hertmans faked this work, there could be another version of la Tour's painting out in the black market. For a man who traded in fakes, there seemed much that was authentic in the notes Maes had written.

I explained what we might potentially uncover to Roberto Calzetta (who I can't believe is now my boss here in Rome, but I know you can't either). I'm sure he told you… or should I say complained to you about that. Begrudgingly, he approved my request to travel to New York.

And then I called Rifka Solomon once again, told her we would finally meet to have that drink together. The feeling I had, it was like that old footage of the paintings set ablaze had gone from black and white to colour. I'll write soon again, with more on this.

Sincerely,
Lt. Christina Perretti
Art Crimes Unit (Rome)
Interpol NCB

18.

Mr. Lorenzo Verzaro,
Director, Art Crimes Unit (Milan)
INTERPOL NCB
November 19th, 1993

Dear Lorenzo,

As you can imagine, I am used to the resistance to our work from the organization. We come in as academics, with our idealism about research, presumptions that the legal system is founded on strong principles, that more light is like a disinfectant. To the career police officers and detectives, I know it seems we're the ultimate bureaucrats, putting all our faith in inductive rather than the more intuitive, deductive reasoning they rely upon. Because they have a better understanding of human nature, apparently. And because they know that evil exists. I'm a 'sociologist,' they say, because I look for broader, schematic explanations as to why people break the law.

This is just a small sample of what I've heard over the years. I'm sure you've heard the same, if not worse. I think, at the root of it, there is a belief that we're too innocent. Experience consists of a greater understanding of how powerful the attraction to the irrational can be. Evil has its own charisma—its power—and cannot nor will not be eradicated. And justice could almost be considered a happy accident once we've filed a final report. It is just one of the many advantages of your mentorship that I have had the fortitude not to accept such received ideas.

But I've expected such arguments from many quarters over the years. From the police who are often the first ones to find stolen paintings and make arrests, from the culture-crats within government, local politicians. But I did not expect it from those who worked with Baruch Weissman and his foundation.

The day I arrived in New York, Rifka Solomon agreed to meet me in the West Village, a couple of blocks from her apartment, for dinner. She told me, without any explanation, that we had much to discuss.

She had chosen a bistro run by two old Parisians. Over the phone she said she liked it for its wine cellar and Gauloises for sale behind the bar. She said the couple who owned it, Yves and Tibor, had come to New York just after the war and turned the place into a "shoebox for all their memories of the city they never wanted to leave." Tibor's old cycling photos and jerseys lined the walls. She considered this place her neighbourhood spot, she said. "I gravitate to exiles with long memories."

"War child," she said, as we sat down. "I was a DP, orphaned by the war. I grew up with my adopted family out in Greenport, Rhode Island. I tell you this because I find I inevitably get the questions. Why would someone like you get involved in the Weissman foundation?"

I told her, as politely as I could, that my questions were not of a personal nature. "I'm hoping you have read the notes I faxed you, written by Harry Maes."

"I did, yes, of course. Let me ask you, Lieutenant, do you believe every word?" She lit up her first of many cigarettes. Her long fingers kept slowly turning over her Ronson lighter, the kind I remember American GIs carried, the ones who stayed in Italy for months after the war finally ended.

"I'm not sure why he would falsify anything. He was writing to his son, it seems."

"Uh huh. And you think you might find this man? Maybe he has all of the paintings this old man mentioned?"

"All but the Schiele, yes. And perhaps this la Tour that has turned up."

"Yeah. And what did you get from the thief who broke into the Wylie mansion and stashed this painting in the back of his rented car?"

"Mirzoev?" I smiled but I'm sure I looked exasperated. Solomon was beginning to irritate me. We both had read everything about this thief Vladimir Mirzoev who, from all reports, was just a low-ranking member of the Vory, the Russian mafia. Career criminal, working under the table in a restaurant in the Brooklyn neighbourhood known as Little Odessa. Yes, he had booked a flight to Moscow, and yes, he seemed to be working for someone who had tipped him off about the Wylie estate in Connecticut and the painting he attempted to steal. But Mirzoev was extradited back to the motherland and was not going to disclose anything. A closed book.

"You see what I mean? There's probably nothing you can do," she said. "The Russian government is not that different from the others Baruch and… we at the foundation… have been dealing with over the years."

"We're trying to change that," I said.

"Yes, I'm sure you are," Rifka said. She smiled and for a moment her dark eyes shone above the candle light between us. But it was a smile of consolation. She seemed to pity my innocence. "I'll tell you what I've discovered working with Baruch. It doesn't seem to be in anyone's interest to look closer at provenance and restitution. Anyone with money and power, I mean. Or anyone who's been dealing in art over the last fifty years."

"Yet Baruch seems like he's making progress. Baruch and the foundation. Your work…"

"Baruch believes he can get enough money and support to get a museum built in Jerusalem." Rifka shrugged, sipped from her glass of the Morgon she selected for us.

"You don't think it's possible?"

"I think if I wanted to break the spirit of a whole nation, I'd wait until that museum is built. I'd patiently observe as hundreds of paintings and pieces of sculpture, stolen from families that were murdered, whole histories lost forever… that all of that work fills a building as big as the Louvre. And then I'd find a way to destroy it."

"That would be evil. An atrocity," I said.

She gently waved the smoke from her cigarette away from my wine glass, as if she didn't want to spoil the bouquet of the Morgon. It was like a Beaujolais, she had said. Like spring. "Baruch, you know he's a bit of a rabbi. My first trip to Geneva, we walked through this small gallery he's got on the campus. They gave him an old rectory for these paintings. I was just getting started with him, just discovering all that was lost. Baruch's a complex man; he's far from perfect, believe me. But I remember he turned to me… we were talking about an image from a panel of an Uccello triptych. A man of deep faith, Uccello… how he so lovingly rendered the Jewish figure in this painting as the deviant, the outcast. Anyway, Baruch, he turned to me and he said, 'you must remember, this hatred, there is nothing like it, nothing compares. What they did in this war was not new. Thousands of years, thousands of lives.' That has the ring of truth, don't you think?"

"Yes," I said. And in the silence between us, as the tape ran, I said it again. And again. It was the only word I had.

After Rifka had stabbed another cigarette into the ashtray between us, she finally spoke. "Here's the interesting thing. You know of the Tapp-Waldenstein gallery here?"

"I've heard of it."

"Very interesting, the Waldenstein family. The transactions over the years to ensure so much of their collection got out of Paris and over here to New York. You should look into them."

"I would think Baruch has spoken to them. Surely they would be interested in the foundation's work and your plans for a museum."

"I'd say more concerned than interested. Concerned about what we might discover."

"But the Waldensteins—   "

"Yes, an old Jewish family from Paris. This is what I'm saying. It's complicated, this work."

I may have been too impatient to turn to the matter of the la Tour, how it ended up. But Rifka warmed to the topic of Malcolm Wylie and his estate in Connecticut.

"This guy, he made his fortune in mining and horses. Married an English baroness named Deirdre Glynn. That ended in tears soon enough. Over the last ten years before his death, Wylie was a bit of a regular client at Sotheby's. He had come to them with a number of paintings he wanted to sell."

"Off-loading his estate?"

"Financial troubles. You can always tell the type, those in the business tell me. They're chatty. A bit frantic. And very practiced at glossing over questions of provenance."

"He had documentation?"

"He gave Sotheby's a faxed copy, taken from a letter, of a list of five paintings. This was in correspondence from a Galerie Maes to Vidler's in Dublin. This is why your fax with all these notes on paintings from Harry Maes were of interest. Thank you once again."

"We found them hidden in the back of the Schiele. But from everything you know, you think what he wrote down is true?"

"You should go to Sotheby's. See the note I'm talking about for yourself. The letter was to Sir Constant Vidler. Who was just Connie then, it seemed. Letter was signed by Harry Maes from a gallery of the same name. I'm saying those notes you sent me, that you said Harry actually wrote? I'm saying yes. Maybe there's something to it all."

"When was the note sent?"

"It was dated March 15th, 1945. From Antwerp. According to the accounts I read, Antwerp was liberated in February. Maes must have been trying to sell some work quickly. Writing to an old friend to help."

"Connie Vidler had a lot of friends, I guess."

"And some enemies. He made a lot of money for a few people during the war."

"It is no wonder the Irish government had watched him so closely and finally arrested him. They were probably doing Scotland Yard a favour."

Rifka looked past my shoulder and out into the street, steepling her fingers over the ashtray. "You should go to Christies while you're here. Just to look around one of these auction houses. Everybody looks so buttoned down, so staid and British. They've even got the goddamn Laura Ashley pot pourri. Christ."

"But you Americans like that, no? All that Princess Di business."

"Not this American," she said. "My point is, places like Christie's, they're no different than Vidler's really. Believe me."

"I'm glad you're doing your work with Baruch," I said. And I meant it.

"Yeah, well… some days I wish it paid, for all the time it's stolen from me. But I've got the resources at Columbia. And they leave me alone, nobody asks about it."

Maybe it was the Morgon, but I was warming to Rifka Solomon, and I could sense she was letting her guard down a little. I realized she probably had good reason to question my motives. My commitment. She was impatient with those who were not serious. Perhaps I had passed a test with her as well. She poured us both another glass and ordered for us both. Apparently I was obligated to have the roast capon.

"Let me tell you what I know of Vidler's. Connie Vidler put the con in Sir Constant, believe me. He got his start as a travel agent in London after the first World War, and he goes on this junket, sponsored by a German rail company, to Turkey. Turkey made a deal with the German government: you build our railway, you get our antiquities. You ever been to Turkey?"

Well, who hadn't among us hippie university kids in Milan? I'm sure you must have memories of traveling there too, Lorenzo. Istanbul… I was stoned for most of it.

"You go along the coast and there are more antiquities than in Greece. And that's after all the pillaging of guys like Connie Vidler. He set up his own auction house and made a mint. Offices in London, Zurich, and Berlin. Then in the thirties, he diversified into paintings and jewelry. A rush of consignments after the crash."

"Of course."

"But this is the thing. There are two different stories about why he moved the business to Dublin. One is that he became embroiled in a scandal over art he'd sold to Seton Waring."

"That name sounds familiar."

"Waring would have been pleased to hear that. He was actually quite forgettable. He spent his family fortune and wrote this weird monograph on British cathedrals. He did run for the BUF though."

"The BUF?"

"Oswald Mosley's British Union of Fascists. It was probably why Waring's wife, Moira Coe, divorced him. She had most of the money in the family anyway but she got two Armenian icons in the settlement. Those icons, she discovered, were fakes. Among more than a few auctioned off by Connie Vidler."

"I think I would have liked Connie Vidler. A fascist aristocrat like Waring comes into my shop. I'd be selling him a fake too. I'd pawn off a brass pot and tell him Mussolini pissed in it."

To my surprise Rifka actually laughed. "Anyway, that's one story. Vidler had to get out of London before the whole antiquities business would get investigated. The other story though, that's the one I believe was the real motivation for the move. He was operating like a fence for stolen art. In his best years he had an office in Venice, got to know Peggy Guggenheim. I'm sure she gave him a lot of business."

"Was he actually married to this Dagmara, the one Harry fell in love with?"

"He told people he was. Dagmara Skarbek. She was a Polish refugee who let it be known she came from a grand family… related to Chopin. It's hard to know when she was recruited but she was actually MI6."

"A spy?"

"That's right. And I think I know why you couldn't find any mention of an Antony Farrell at the Vatican."

"He was lying to Maes?"

"Let's just say protecting himself and this whole project of theirs, with the fakes. Two years ago I'm at a show at Tapp-Waldenstein up the street. And there's this older Irish gentleman, charming old guy… squiring one of the old millionaires' wives around the room. He knew I was at Columbia, said he heard of the foundation too, but a lot of people say that, believe me. Gives them an air of nobility, maybe. Anyway he was among a bunch of people that ended up at Minetta's after the show. We were in the same booth for the rest of the night. This old guy was the first who ever mentioned Connie Vidler to me."

"He knew about him?"

"Oh he knew him all right. Called him Connie. He knew him down to the fact that he said he wore a girdle. Vidler and this Dagmara Skarbek, they were buying up all this stolen art during the war. He said he was sure that the Waldensteins worked with him. Now when I think of him, he's got to be who Harry mentions."

"So you think he's actually Farrell."

"Declan Stuart, he told me. I looked him up after that night and couldn't find any mention of him in all the foundation files I have. But he gave me his number on the chit from the bill that night."

"Would you know where I could find him?"

"As a matter of fact I do." Rifka leaned forward and took out a pair of glasses from her purse and put them on as she read from this chit.

"He lives downtown?"

"He volunteers at a hospice down by Cooper Union most days. You have to talk to him."

"You talked with him recently?"

"I called him after I read your fax. I told him about Mirzoev's theft of the la Tour out in Connecticut. You know what he says? He told me, as if to confirm what Maes wrote about Hertmans, that the la Tour is probably a fake. That I should look into it. And so I did. I asked my colleagues in our offices in London and Paris to see if it had gone on the market anywhere over the last year. It's difficult, because there are so many new paintings being found, now that there's no more Iron Curtain."

"This has been my challenge. I've contacted as many houses as I could. I need more resources."

"Baruch has his sources and his contacts. You should just come to us first. Anyway, eureka. There was word in Prague of all places. A private sale of this same painting."

"No one knows who bought it?"

"No. But because I know it was probably stolen by the Nazis originally, I figured you'd want to check this out for your work. Declan Stuart or Antony Farrell was pretty cryptic with me about what else he knew about this. I think he enjoys keeping his secrets. If he knows you're with Interpol, maybe he'll see good reason to be a little more forthcoming."

"You think so?"

"What have you got to lose?"

She had a point. As you can see, Lorenzo, this trip to New York was turning into something that was well worth the expense. I was glad I got it all on tape.

Sincerely,
Lt. Christina Perretti
Art Crimes Unit (Rome)
Interpol NCB

19.

Mr. Lorenzo Verzaro,
Director, Art Crimes Unit (Milan)
INTERPOL NCB
November 22nd, 1993

Dear Lorenzo,

Perhaps I should not have been surprised that Declan Stuart would meet me and immediately speak of himself as "a bit of a wanderer. Like an old gypsy that's me." He spoke of India.

"This city doesn't really remind me of any other place on this side of the world. If it's similar to anywhere, it's Bombay."

"Why Bombay?"

"It's screaming. It just needs the bloody monkeys in the trees."

He looked up, regarded the upper branches of this fragile little Japanese maple as we walked towards a part of New York called Cooper Square. What a relic he was. I remember the sunlight caught his silver-framed glasses, causing him to squint, the lines on his face appearing like the creases on an ancient map. We had left the hospice where he was volunteering. It seemed the last refuge of the city's forgotten, and to 'lighten the mood' he thought he'd take me to his favourite place to lunch in the neighbourhood, a Tibetan tea house that served good chai and dumplings, he promised. He moved quickly and gracefully for a man of his advanced years. I found myself hurrying along to keep up.

I suggested that New York still must be an interesting place to live. "This is where the art is… where artists are working."

"That's over, dear. This war on the poor, the jailing of the crack addicts every weekend so the tourists don't see them… the money's moved in now. It's just cheap nostalgia or internal exile. These are the only options if one is going to stay."

"And which option have you chosen?"

Stuart laughed. He was going to keep his answer to himself. "I don't meet many Italians who fancy a cup of tea in the afternoon. You're not indulging me, are you now?"

"Maybe a little."

"Well you'll like this, I promise you."

I could detect the Irish lilt to his voice, though he'd told me he hadn't been back to Ireland for anything more than funerals over the last fifty years. He said he was useful enough to be granted American citizenship but he had remained "virtually stateless" after he left the Vatican Library soon after the war. He had spent some time in Los Angeles, then Cuba, "parts east" for two decades, and then down in Managua working for a Catholic charity. New York had all the best art collections, and he wanted to return, in his last years, to spend more time with the paintings he loved. Then he gently touched the back of my hand and leaned in to whisper, "the life of a spook, I've lived."

"As in officially so?"

"James Jesus Angleton. When you meet a man like that, you're intrigued. Even the man's name… wouldn't you have been?"

"He was CIA, was he not?"

"OSS when I met him in Italy. But mind you, he was also a poet. A good one. One of our first conversations was about Empson's *Seven Types of Ambiguity*. Have you heard of that? I wonder if Empson's still read in Italy. Or anywhere now… anyway, I realized I could work with these people. There was a lot to attend to after the war."

Stuart led me into the small, storefront teahouse. He greeted the owner, a round little woman who was bustling between the tables. He held his hands clasped in front of him and gave her a quick bow. Then he spoke to her quickly, in a language I couldn't recognize, and she nodded, heading off into the kitchen.

"You know Tibetan?"

"Burmese. And not enough to get by. Mya humours me. It's been more than a decade since I was over there."

"In any official capacity?"

"Good heavens no. I was just a Catholic volunteer." There was a hint of boyish mischief in his smile. "I'm officially retired now so I suppose I don't have to give a damn anymore. I can be a little indiscreet. But I must tell you, I didn't think that what I shared with Rifka would have been so broadcasted."

"I believe Rifka to be discreet, Mr. Stuart. It's just that she is helping me investigate the theft of a work—"

"That la Tour she called me about."

"You know of it?"

"I heard there might have been another one found, yes. Did she tell you that?"

"That squares with what I know. We're working on finding the auction house. You see I have these notes of Harry Maes. He mentions a son. I'm trying to find him. I believe he'll know of the other work that's lost."

As the little woman served us chai he poured out two cups then composed himself before he spoke. He straightened his thick woolen necktie, told me he wore one every day, and conceded he lived like it was still 1945. "I know enough about why two la Tours should exist. There was so much we were trying to save back then. Hundreds, probably thousands of paintings lost forever, as I'm sure you know. Stolen, ripped off the walls. And to address this now, not one bloody government has the courage to take this on, now that we're all just Americans by degrees. Nobody was interested in real justice and retribution when the war was over. Too many useful criminals. Transactional accords, we called them, transactional accords. Memoranda of misunderstanding, as far as I was concerned." He cackled and sipped again, swallowing noisily, his long, turkey-like neck reddened.

"My unit with Interpol, we believe there are many paintings that can still be reclaimed, given back to the families who survived. And for those works that cannot find a home, maybe Rifka and this Weissman foundation, they can hang them on the walls of a new museum."

Stuart smiled at this, and then he did a very forward thing. He took my hands in his. Normally I would have retracted, pulled away from such a gesture. But there was tenderness, something simple and direct about his touch that compelled me to relent.

"I'm going to tell you what I know. I'm going to tell you what I've seen. And I'm going to tell you what I've done. Because I think you want to do good and that you care about art. And I'm too old to care about anyone who has other motives. I'm still vain enough to want to be good. But not vain enough to care about being judged."

"I understand."

"I'm not sure you do yet but maybe you will after I tell you everything."

Stuart seemed to luxuriate in how he was adding dramatic weight to what he knew. Over the course of that first cup of chai, he spoke of his boyhood years in the Christian Brothers, escaping the priesthood and then ending up at Cambridge with Burgess, Philby and Anthony Blunt, names that sounded vaguely familiar from the pages of *L'Unita*, the communist paper my parents read in the seventies. Farrell said he and Blunt had gotten on well. They had the same passion for art, felt the same attraction to "secret societies," the duplicity that just came naturally to young gay men raised in an environment where orthodoxy and tradition were to be revered. So of course he was an ideal recruit for MI6. He was brought in by another ex-priest who wangled him a position at the Vatican.

"We were all working together at that point. The OSS, the NKVD... the enemy of my enemy and all that. It really wasn't until after the war that lines were drawn and you felt one had to choose. Either work with the Americans or the Russians. But during the war, when I was undercover in the Vatican, the Americans gave me a new name to protect me—my middle name and my mother's name... I became Antony Farrell."

"Why did you choose the Americans to work with? I mean there was your friend Mr. Blunt, the Keeper of the Queen's Pictures, right? He'd gone over to the Russians."

"I learned early on what was happening over there. I had a friend, Dagmara Skarbek. Quite a brilliant, beautiful woman. What she went through when they retook Poland from the Nazis told me all I needed to know."

"Yes. I had heard about her. Quite a woman of influence."

"Well it wasn't just her influence. I genuinely liked the Americans I was working with. Many were old lefties themselves, you know. Mugged by reality, as they say. A lot of writers and critics who weren't quite in the top tier… but many of them were brilliant. And they knew people. I mean, I liked a bit of glamour. You don't work in the Vatican for as long as I did without a love of theatre."

"But you stayed off-stage."

"Of course. Off in the wings. That's where all the real drama was."

The Americans had learned from the Germans and the Russians after the war, he said, and they realized that the culture business was the way to sell America to themselves first and then around the world. "Soft power, as they say. The new empire building."

I told him what I knew of this, that it wasn't just the movies. I probably went on a bit too much about all that I had read, as I studied for my thesis, about Ab-Ex with Pollock and de Kooning showing in London and West Berlin, and a whole platoon of critics and writers from Iowa to Paris peddling a kind of formalism that was slyly apolitical. Whether it was a focus on bold brush strokes and abstraction with painting or literature's ambition contracted to focus on interior lives, domestic settings, this conservatism aligned so subtly and effectively with the new conservative sensibility that found purchase in an era of Thatcher and Reagan and the 'end of history.' What can I tell you, it's so rare to find a moment when your academic work actually has some bearing on the real world.

He was smiling as I spoke. "Exactly, my dear. A lot of style, a lot of irony, but packaged so it wasn't threatening to the philistines out in the suburbs. All that crew were finally making it new, Europe could have all the old kitsch. Although we'd be sure to put the best of it in the galleries and museums over here. We were pillaging just as much as the Germans."

"But you weren't murdering who you stole from."

"No. In many cases we didn't have to, did we?"

I reached into my purse and pulled out the papers on the Card Cheat. "Rifka said you both spoke about this painting."

"Yes. But why, of all the paintings your unit should investigate, have you focused on this one?"

"Because it's on this list of ten paintings sold by a name you'll know: the Maes Gallery. And that was a red flag. The foundation has found many paintings that were sold out of Antwerp and Berlin. And they were, as they called it, raubkunst."

"Yes, no question. I'm sure that's the case." Stuart picked up the sheet I had put on the table between us and made a cursory effort at reading the names of paintings on the list—the ones I had hurriedly put down from the notes from Harry Maes—what he and Dagmara called 'the manor' as they corresponded in code. "I knew this Maes fellow. His ex-wife ended up with bloody Francis Cluny."

"I saw that name in the notes I received. Before then I had never heard of him."

"As you shouldn't. He was an awful poet, one of these Celtic Twilight ninnies that Yeats had taken under his wing. Cluny was broadcasting for the Nazis out of Berlin. Spying for us initially but then went over to the Russians. I don't think they wanted him in the end. More trouble than he was worth."

"Was he spying on Maes?"

"He didn't have to. My Polish friend Dagmara Skarbek, she had Maes wrapped around her finger."

"These ten paintings. It says they were once the property of Benjamin Ostriker, but that was a lie, yes?"

"That's right. Harry forged those documents because he presumed Benjamin Ostriker would never lay claim to the work. He'd be dead or exiled. You see this Ostriker fellow was once his father-in-law. Harry had every reason to believe he and his wife were no longer able to claim ownership. And he had the express permission to use their names."

"From who?"

"Their daughter Sabine Ostriker was his wife. She had converted for him but she was smart enough to know that wasn't going to save her. That's why she ended up with Cluny for a while, until she realized what she was in for with him."

"So she allowed him to fake the provenance?"

"At least that is what he told us."

"Where were they really from?"

"The Vatican, my dear. But we had no intention of getting rid of the real ones. We were working on getting about ten forged. Call it a pilot project. The idea was we could sell the fakes to some high-ranking friends of the Fuhrer. We knew Goring had a fake Vermeer. Pacelli, that little snake, he was wining and dining these bastards, and all of us in our right minds feared he was going to give away the family silver. So the plan, launched by MI6, was to give him an offering for his new friends that would buy us some time. Because we sensed, correctly I might add, that it would only be a matter of weeks until there would be American tanks rolling through the Roman streets. The ten paintings were a kind of promissory note of co-operation. Or collaboration, actually."

"Why did their provenance have to be faked?"

"The Vatican's neutrality was sacrosanct. And Pacelli knew he had to make all the right noises about the Jews. But of course he was a vicious anti-Semite, a lot of those bastards around him were. Even after the war, he and his acolytes were ensuring that some of the worst Nazis could get out of Europe safely through Italy. We called it the Ratline. It was knowing that all that was going on… well, it gnawed at me. It was an easy decision to leave the Vatican library after this little project with the Americans and MI6 ended. I could provide my services to Mr. James Jesus Angleton and his friends. They'd ensure I'd get American citizenship. The company, we called it."

"You know I'm of the generation that looks at the messes you've made with the same kind of anger you had for Pacelli. I should think no one would want to ask about your adventures in Central America, Mr. Stuart."

"You're entitled to your anger. And the luxury of not knowing. But you know, your generation, you haven't really saved anything of value, have you? You didn't have to get involved in the big dramas, did you?"

"Or committed any crimes like acts of fraud and forgery."

"No. But now that you and your colleagues in Interpol are on the case, all will be well, won't it? Just a matter of time before everyone that did so well from the underground trade starts to take restitution seriously."

"I can't afford your cynicism, Mr. Stuart." My hand was gripped tightly around my cup of chai. This old man had hit a nerve.

"I'm sorry. I didn't mean to disparage your efforts. I'm just telling you what I know because it might be of some help. Maybe even for your friend Rifka and that foundation she's mixed up with. And I'm sworn off talking politics. That's why I came to settle in this city. To finally live without the ghosts of those days running my life."

"Well somebody still needs to chase those ghosts, yes? If one of these old paintings that Harry Maes was trying to sell have surfaced, my sense is that there might be many more. There are literally hundreds of paintings and sculptures that Rifka's foundation has on record from old files of insurance companies, auction records. It's helpful for us, you know what I mean?"

"I can imagine. Resources you don't have. You'll need to make the case, my dear. The one trait I came to admire about my employers… and I'm talking about the old guard like Donovan and Angleton… it was their persistence. They could be political, deal with Washington. You have to have a stomach for that. I didn't after the war. I was too close to that kind of power at the Vatican. Scorched me."

"Well it must be good to be done with all that now."

"As much as one can ever be done. I mean, here I am, talking to you."

In the silence between us, I could tell he was anticipating my question: about the forged la Tour, and who might have more information on the paintings Harry Maes had mentioned, the list I had hurriedly scribbled down and presented to him. He knew it was ultimately why I had met with him. Yet he wasn't going to offer any more information unless he heard the request from my lips. He was acutely aware I was taping our conversation, I realize now. An old spy to the end, he'd only speak if he was compelled to.

"Rifka said you might know more about this forger who worked on a la Tour, Wim Hertmans. That he had a family and they would know some things."

Farrell looked to his friend Mya, mouthed some words of Burmese as he mimed writing the check. "There is this fellow in

Amsterdam who fancies himself quite a painter, carrying on the family tradition. Robby Martien. And you are correct: his father, Wim Hertmans, faked *The Card Cheat*. Dagmara Skarbek commissioned it and then got it to Harry. Anyway, this Robby Martien, I bet he'd help you out."

"A trip to Amsterdam. I didn't plan on going any further afield."

"Well. I can only tell you this. His father painted so many fakes, there is only one authority who the auction houses trust. And that's him, Robby Martien. He'll know of any other version of the la Tour."

"And you think this might lead me to Harry Maes' son and the rest of the paintings I've written down?"

"I don't want to tell you how to do your job, darling, but I would think he'd be the only chance you got. It's a funny business, this, believe me. Happy to be well shot of it."

As I put the money down he rose from the table and thanked me with a courtly bow. We went opposite ways on the street and as I walked, I was still processing all he said, still trying to take the measure of all his secrets. For some reason I turned to see if I could glimpse him once again, etch his image in my mind. But he had vanished, of course. Like a ghost.

More to come. I'll write again soon.

Sincerely,
Lt. Christina Perretti
Art Crimes Unit (Rome)
Interpol NCB

20.

Mr. Lorenzo Verzaro,
Director, Art Crimes Unit (Milan)
INTERPOL NCB
November 24th, 1993

Dear Lorenzo,

It was, as usual, not easy to get my trip to Amsterdam cleared by Calzetta. Maybe you'll never say, but I think you helped, yes? If so, I'm grateful to you, as always.

With Robby Martien in Amsterdam, I don't know what I was expecting, but it certainly wasn't his whole performance as a man of consequence. I think he hoped I'd be younger and more impressionable, and he had to suddenly retract, take on a solemn air that had him leaking out nervous energy in fidgets and coughed-out laughter.

I knew his type. There were many Robby Martiens in the seventies and eighties, when I spent some time in London and Amsterdam researching for my thesis. I had met a number of versions of him who survived on the margins, semi-famous. They were reconstructed hippies for the most part, boy-men with hard-to-place accents, who had put in a requisite few years in Goa or Chiang Mai. I think of a boyfriend who still carried the faint smell of patchouli in his second-hand tuxedo jacket. Men like this would introduce themselves as agents, film producers—any kind of middle-man role that allowed them access to someone of legitimate talent—and often enough, they made their living just dealing drugs.

But Martien's wilderness years were firmly behind him, the tony address in the Museumkwartier affirmed. His studio is above a modish jewelry designer's shop, with glistening parquet floors and those Wassily chairs of chrome and black leather every gallery outside of Rome seems to think so modish. I blame it on your crowd in Milan. On an easel there was a vanilla-coloured poster announcing, in a loopy font, a series of portraits track-lit along a wall of exposed brick: 'onze parlementariers.' These were headshots of politicians, presumably Dutch, rendered in thick daubs of pinkish flesh tones, as if a student of Lucien Freud had painted over some Old Masters sketches. Which is to say they were interesting, far better than I thought the son of a forger would be capable of painting.

To put him at ease I told him so, and that set him off on a rambling story about a Dutch Minister of International Trade who went to school with him. He was the one who initially commissioned a portrait, and "it all got out of hand" with more requests. Martien said he'd needed the money, he had gambling debts from a trip to Macau. "My best painting comes from necessity and needless complications, I realize. I blame myself."

He scooted out his assistant from a drab, broom closet of a back office, muttering to her in Indonesian. Lithe and scowling, with an angular, pretty face, she breezed past me with an imperious disregard. He then gathered two cheap plastic chairs under his arms from a room down a dimly-lit hallway. He angled his bulk around a little red desk, brusquely dropping each chair in position with a clatter. He nodded to one for me, breathing heavily, then slumped down into the other like a man who's just caught the last bus. Then he poked his little cloth pillbox cap further up his wide brow and lit up a Café Crème cigarillo, drumming its first ash into a Styrofoam cup that looked like it had been on the desk for months, maybe years, given the dank little pool of black coffee at its base.

"Everybody told me… you need someone to run the gallery but don't hire your wife. Keep your business and pleasure separate. I never, never listen." He rolled his eyes. This seemed like an old routine he'd kept in his repertoire.

"Can I say something? I find it interesting, given your father's reputation, that you ended up a painter, too."

"Why? Because he was a forger? He was also one of the best technical painters of his era. Of any era, as far as I'm concerned."

"It's funny that you say that."

"Funny?"

"As in funny, peculiar… because I had hunted down an old catalogue raisonné of his from one of my friends at Sotheby's."

"Sotheby's. Yes. We like them."

"His original work is quite good, to my eyes. Reminds me of Hammershoi."

"Ha! Better than Hammershoi, believe me."

"With your painting, did he teach you?"

"Much later, after I had made a mess of my life, thinking I was some kind of situationist. More like an unholy fool. I didn't know my father as a boy. I grew up with my uncle's family in Jakarta. My father didn't come out of prison until '59. You should see the work he never showed. Hammershoi   … ha!"

"You inherited all this work?"

"Some. My father's other paintings re-emerge from time to time, yes. The auction houses—I'll get calls to look at work they're not sure about. I hear of others out there but only a few are as accomplished as his best forgeries. I would make it easier for these connoisseurs if I just denied their existence, I suppose. Then they could be reassured they have originals and sell them for what the market will bear. But I'm proud of his work. I'm proud of what he taught me."

I told him I could understand that; his father was a legitimate artist. But that just gave him an opportunity to rant about how little his contemporaries understood 'the fundamentals.' He conceded there were some exceptions. Odd Nerdrum, and this Scottish painter… (inaudible) Conway… in their understanding of colour, they went back to basic components. This was admirable. But both he and his father would not be granted the same critical reception as these artists because of the 'fake scandal' of the forgeries his father was tried and imprisoned for.

"They wanted to give him the Nuremberg treatment. If he had sold his work to the English or the French rather than the Nazis, it never would have happened. My father was not a Nazi. His real motivation was simple. He was disgusted that there were painters with no understanding of history or tradition who were being treated like minor saints. So he showed how easy it was to fool the critics. The market was full of pretenders and fake connoisseurs. It still is."

"But if he was only motivated by this, surely one forgery revealed would prove his point. Yet he painted many fakes."

"Look, he just painted for who paid him, that was all. He left politics to the moralists and the politicians."

Including the Vatican, I wanted to add. But I realized it was not in my interest to let Martien know all that I already knew. It would give him further license to continue his tirade. He and his father, the great unappreciated masters of our time.

"I wanted to ask about one particular painting. Here's a photo." It was a plate of the la Tour, taken from the original documents I had at work.

"Oh, yes… all too well I know this. They caught the thief in America, yes?"

"I believe it might be your father's work. Not a la Tour at all."

"Look, you don't want to talk to me. Months ago, I had a Czech fellow who wrote me. Masny. I have his card. He's the one you want to talk to. Maybe you'll get him to really do some detective work."

I nodded, kept a poker face. *The Card Cheat,* indeed. "You must know its provenance, then. We have it listed as once belonging to an estate in Hamburg. Did he ever…"

"My father never told me about this work, but what I told Masny is what I will tell you. If there was a reported sale of this work in Prague, and then some months later, they have this theft in America… chances are…" He exhaled a small cloud of smoke from his cigarillo, stubbed it into the cup. It softly fizzed, as if it was dissolving in acid.

"In Prague?"

"You have some dubious dealers, with the wonders of the new free market. Not just there but in Budapest, in Moscow. I would think a lot of this is stolen work. Mr. Antonin Masny, he knows my circle of friends. He paid for my trip to Prague because he knows I do not make any judgments until I see the work myself. He showed me this la Tour. And he had a tip my father actually painted it.

"And what did you think, when you finally saw it up close?"

"If it was fake, it was someone else's work. Not my father's. You see, I can tell from his palette, what he used to mix colours. I know the composition. And if you must know, I'll scrape a little off and rub it in my fingers. Anyway, I told Masny what I still believe: those paintings were authentic."

"You know the la Tour in America; it had been there for more than forty years."

Martien did nothing but slowly blink as he looked at me like I'd offended him in some way.

"So it must be a fake. Maybe your father's work. And the real one..."

"Exactly. Now wouldn't you be curious about where the real one was? If I were you, I'd go talk to Masny. No doubt he shared his information with one of his Russian clients and then you have this Mirzoev idiot, doing their dirty work for them. Probably for more money than he'd ever seen working in America." Martien leaned forward, softly patted the back of my hand as if he was speaking to a child. "There you are then. You can stop the tape."

He stared at me for what seemed a minute, deciding how trustworthy I was, I imagine. Then he reached into one of the drawers of this little red desk, and produced two yellowed pages.

"You mentioned that la Tour, so I know you're looking for this. It's a list of paintings my father produced for the British and the Americans during the war. This work was supposed to guarantee his immunity from the charges he was tried for."

I leaned forward and took the papers in my hands, which were shaking. I couldn't conceal it, no matter how deeply I breathed. This confirmed everything Declan Stuart had told me. And what was in Maes' notes.

"Did you show these to your friend Mr. Masny? I'm sure he must have been interested."

"He looked the names over as if this document was mildly interesting, but ultimately irrelevant to him. Pearls before pigs, I suppose. I asked him if he wanted a Xerox of this."

"He refused?"

"Politely, though. Let no one say I am not a helpful man."

His eyes were on the pages as if they were testament to his father's genius. And I suppose they were, really.

"Maybe next time you come, you can take a look at more of my work. You'll see some continuity. The orange not far from the tree and all that."

I told him I'd like that. And no, I did not tell him that I think he meant an apple, not an orange. He was not a man of trivial distinctions; he'd take offence.

I thanked him but my voice was high in my throat as I followed him to the exit. I felt scattered, unsure how to respond initially, but then, like some reflex caused by muscle memory, the simplest, most truthful words I could manage came out. "I don't know what I know anymore, Mr. Martien, but this has been very helpful."

And then I hurriedly made my exit. So much was coming together, Lorenzo. I almost say regretfully. I should have time to continue this over the next few days.

Sincerely,
Lt. Christina Perretti
Art Crimes Unit (Rome)
Interpol NCB

21.
Mr. Lorenzo Verzaro,
Director, Art Crimes Unit (Milan)
INTERPOL NCB
December 14th, 1993

Dear Lorenzo,

I feel like I do not have to explain much about what happened in Prague, given that you know so much already about where we are now with this case. Calzetta has apologized to me, and said the recovery of all this work is better than he ever would have imagined. I told him I never would have brought him more travel expenses if they weren't absolutely justified, that I was aware of our budgetary constraints. Maybe I was a bit churlish, but for all the work I have put into this Maes case, I think I've earned some authority.

Especially because, just moments after I had entered this shop in Prague called Atelier Masny, I thought all was lost. I was met with just this sullen young woman, dressed like a frumpy old librarian, who told me she knew nothing about what I was asking and that she had already talked to the police.

I had no idea why she would respond this way. I blame our colleagues in Prague now, of course. Radio silence about this. Anyway, I prodded: "could I speak to Mr. Antonin Masny, please? My understanding is he is the proprietor."

"My father is dead. And you and your friends have done nothing to find the men who did it. And I told you who they were. I'm sure of this."

I told her I was sorry. I had no idea. I asked her, insensitively, I know, "your father was killed? A homicide?"

She nodded. "We get Russian tourists all the time, but I knew these ones... these men... they were different. I gave you people my description. The both of them, the one with the thick rimmed glasses, the other with the limp. And nothing. It's been more than a month now. No word."

I could not help but think of Silvia Stanciu. Her going to Moscow, then the death of Gennady Popov, which led to the discovery of all of Harry Maes' notes. The last thing I wanted to do was put this woman through another interview about her father's death, but there had to be some connection. I asked her, as delicately as possible, if we could talk. She came out from behind the counter, went to the doors at the front of the shop, and locked them. "Come," she said, as she directed me to a divan and a coffee table near the back of the place, "we'll talk of this."

"Your father had never met these men."

"No. Antique dealers, they said. Two shops, one in Moscow, the other in St. Petersburg, they said. They had these materials like brochures, with all their merchandise. I thought it was strange, these marketing products. We would never do this for the atelier."

"Antiques. They did not deal in art?"

"Some paintings, I think. But not their main line of business. I will tell you, the way they dressed, it was like they owned casinos. I thought, why is my father giving these men so much time? They sat right here. Drank our espresso."

"They weren't trying to sell your father anything?"

She shook her head. "When they finally left, he told me they were talking with him about purchasing this business. I argued with him when he told me he agreed to go out to dinner with them. Now I wish I would have gone, too. The next morning he did not come in. I called my husband, told him he's not answering his phone, we must go to his apartment. My father has stayed in the small place near the old Jewish cemetery… that's where I grew up. He was not there. Two days later they discovered his body in the Vltava. I told the police everything about those men. I wished I had kept their brochures. Every trace of them disappeared."

It was then that I told her the nature of my visit. About what Robby Martien had told me. I had a couple of plates of *The Card Cheat* from an old catalogue raisonné (the Weissman foundation's work once again—I owe them so much). When I saw her flash of recognition, I had to ask, "do you know where your father got this work for consignment? I believe this might be related to what happened to your father."

"I do, yes. But there is no relation. The man who owned this work was a nice English gentleman. Inheritance from his German father."

"Do you remember his name?"

"Of course. I am the one who took all his information. This is from Mr. Nicholas Hepworth. He lives in London."

And as she rose to retrieve her book with all of his contact details, I felt butterflies in my chest. Nothing was going to stop me from going to London and finding this man. I would have paid for the flight myself.

Which led to that trip to those storage spaces, out near the part of London they call the docklands, with Mr. Nicholas Hepworth. Son of Harry Maes, found at last. You'd think that might be the end of all this, given all the paintings we found. But I have something of a confession from Mr. Hepworth. And I think it may not be the end at all.

Because there is more than just the recovery of these paintings at issue, yes? Two homicides. And maybe more.

Sincerely,

Lt. Christina Perretti

Art Crimes Unit (Rome)

Interpol NCB

Nicholas Hepworth

22.

12 / 30 / 93

"If you can, to the best of your ability, explain how you were first made aware of your father's estate, and how you came to know Ladislav Komarek and Antonin Masny, whom you dealt with over the years; this would help us greatly in our investigation." This was Christina Perretti from Interpol, earlier this month at my kitchen table, explaining to me that I was not a "person of interest."

To which I couldn't help responding that I doubted I was even an interesting person. She gave me one of those smiles of calm beneficence that made me imagine her as a nun rather than a police investigator.

Yes, there was something of a person of faith about her. But not like any nun I can remember, from my stepfather Basil Hepworth's brief attempt at making my mother and I Catholic churchgoers, when I was still a boy. The nuns always seemed too stern, their defences up when encountering the potential for disorder a young boy possessed. No, it was Perretti's sense of calm, a melancholy acceptance of the weakness of humanity that was familiar from some Father Francis-or-Something. My ailing memory. Anyway, maybe I was expecting someone more glamorous, given that she told me she was based in Rome. But there was nothing ostentatious about her business attire or her pearl earrings. She seemed the model of sobriety and, yes, empathy, prepared to hear my confession.

But there is so much I know I left out. I have kept this journal for more than twenty bloody years, out of some compulsion to record, to fix my identity more firmly as a kind of dispassionate recorder of the world that has entered and exited from my line of sight. Time to get this story, the one that has defined where I am now, down at last, and then I can make of it something like a confessional report for Perretti.

This whole misadventure that has overturned my life began back in May of '89, when Dickie Knifton, my mother's longtime friend (who I'm sure was once much more than a friend) gave me a call at work, in my old office at the British Embassy in Tokyo. Back then Dickie was still one of the old guards among the spooks in MI6. I could immediately tell, from his solemn tone, that he had news for me. He had heard, from a contact he had in East Berlin (or shall we simply say a spy), a Herr Lange in the DDR's Ministry of Culture, that my 'real' father had sadly passed away. Lange said that my father left me something that might be of value in the west. "Nicky, if you like, I can get you a diplomatic visa to slip over for a day or two to the other side. Tour planning for the London Symphony, we'll call it, given your exemplary work helping to co-ordinate their tour in Asia. You may have to drop in to see Lange while you're there. But it will allow you to attend to matters."

Well, what could I say but of course I'd go. Dickie ever-so-tactfully asked if I could just let him know if there might be anything, among what my father had left for me, that might be of interest to the government. "We have records of your father once being very helpful, Nicky, near the end of the war."

He didn't have to say any more. My mother had told me that whatever Harry had done to spirit some art out of Germany hardly made up for all the stolen work from Jewish families that he had put on the market. "I'm sorry to tell you, your father was a criminal," she had flatly stated to me, when I was first leaving home for Harrow. "Best forget him." Well, if there might be some information about paintings lost to the Nazis, Dickie was of the view that what my father had might be worth retrieving.

And so, after a brief layover back in London, where I visited my GP, drove out to see my mother in Surrey (she did not approve of my going to Germany) and met with Dickie, I flew into Berlin, jet-lagged, my head in a fog of confusion and apprehension, and got a cheap hotel room by the Zoo station. I couldn't sleep, I had such deep-seated anxiety about this trip.

But why? Here I was, a middle-aged, well-traveled man of the foreign service, faithful husband to Eri Hasegawa. Model citizen and expatriate. So worldly, yes? My life a testament to the success of the British settlement and integration of those that many right-wing politicians thought would be a lost generation of post-war refugees. And yet I knew a trip behind the wall was really a trip into the past where so much was unresolved. I knew I was an innocent who feared what experience, a deeper understanding of my origins and of myself, might mean.

The next morning I shuffled out into the gloom of a cold spring morning and headed for a small border station near the old Checkpoint Charlie. I knew it was necessary, when going over to the other side, to exchange enough currency to equal fifty East German marks. I approached the counter of the hut that housed a border guard. Through the small frame of fortified glass, a sign of life: a squat, thick-lipped man whose scowl could have modeled for a gargoyle's on a cathedral—if that creaking empire still let people worship in such places.

"Purpose for your journey?"

"Tourism."

"And?"

"Shopping and entertainment."

The gargoyle nodded, his scowl evaporating. He seemed pleased that I had remembered my lines from the script. I could play the role of an innocent traveler, just like he played his role of border guard. Two natural actors unnaturally brought together. I wasn't just Harry's boy, I was Sabine 'Sally' Hepworth's son, such a talent was one of the few gifts my mother passed on. The guard stamped my British passport and waved me forward to get back on the train.

As the train lurched and then eased into gear, I could feel the guard's eyes still on me. He turned, and sure enough. But the look was not one of suspicion; it was curiosity. The guard seemed to be imagining what this foreigner's life might be like, if only for a moment. Then he quickly looked away, got back in character.

I thought of my visit with my GP, Dr. Christiansen, just two days before. Christiansen is a pale, Danish insomniac. Call it his bedside manner, but he'll often speak of many things with me save for his years in Copenhagen during the war. He says he reads Cioran because the Romanian's books are full of wisdom without consolation, perfect for being awake at three   am and walking the quiet, blank streets of Shepperton like a ghost. Christiansen said to me, while I was dressing after the checkup, "you have to choose your habits well because eventually we become who we pretend we are." I know him well enough to realize he was being glumly ironic with an old patient who got his sense of humour, sure… but I wanted to reply: what happens after we discover the role we have been playing has been cut, erased from the next draft?

Perhaps everything is eventually revised. The train crossed over to the other side at last. I stared out the window over the horizon and I could see four, then five construction cranes, stark and skeletal against the pewter coloured clouds. Reconstruction everywhere, it seemed. What they were saying in the foreign service was probably true, that if you were working over here you could feel it was the beginning of the end. My forgotten father's timing for his passing was impeccable.

A younger East German border official came down the aisle, asking each passenger to produce their ticket. The lenses on this man's spectacles were so thick, it was like his eyes were floating in jelly.

"Day pass, yes? You bring nothing but yourself and you leave with nothing besides the quality merchandise you are permitted to purchase, but must declare. Understood?"

That feeling where you are not guilty but you somehow feel you should be: do you call that Kafkaesque? It was strange, disorienting. But not necessarily in a bad way, perhaps because it shook me out of the safe conception of myself. As the officer moved past me, I felt an impulse to catch his eye and thank him.

The train's wheels made a low, screeching sound as it braked. And then it lurched forward, like a last gasp before it finally halted. The officer reappeared, buttoned up in a thick, petrol green greatcoat and motioned for the passengers to rise and exit. I nodded and got to my feet, feeling my heart thump in my chest, and then a brief cloud of dizziness evaporated.

Just too much coffee, that's all… what did I have to fear? Did I think I could not return to the west, that I would be walled off from freedom forever, just like Harry? Of course that was nonsense. And yet the feeling was real.

As the train rattled along, my thoughts went back to my last meeting with my mother's 'dear friend,' Dickie Knifton.

"Lange said your father had been living like a monk for ages and then he surprised everyone in his building. Got himself a girlfriend," Dickie had said. He was staring at the little screen under the ribbon of this humming word processor, big as an anvil, that occupied most of the workable area of his desk. Dickie hadn't aged, save for the way his weedy little beard had gone completely white. He peered over the square steel frames of his glasses to see whether the word 'girlfriend' had caused any kind of reaction with me. A little moue of disappointment.

"This is your Mathias Lange friend?"

"The same. High up in the Honecker government now, over at the Culture ministry. More effective than ever, actually. In your father's final days, Lange had gotten word, through a new friend of his at the Czech embassy, that Harry had something for his long lost boy, the one he hadn't seen in more than forty years. A woman's influence, there you are. Softened your old man's heart."

"Such as it was."

"Apparently this woman was very good to him, all the way up to the end."

"The man had his charming qualities, I'm sure," I said, shifting in my chair that croaked on its spindly aluminum legs. Dickie clearly didn't get many visitors in his corner of the fourth floor in Century House.

"Well. Good of you to make the effort. And the journey. I suppose I could have just rung over to the foreign office and found out where you are these days, but it's been ages since I looked in on Sally, so I called her. I hope you didn't mind."

"Not at all. I'll be visiting her out in Surrey while I'm here. She's getting on."

"We all are."

"She insists she can manage that house."

"Her coronation roses, I remember. At the wake for Basil."

"Oh she's still at it. Big vase of them on the kitchenette table."

"You'll say I said hello."

"Of course, Dickie."

"It may be hard to believe, but I still like to know how she's doing."

"You've always been very good to us, Dickie. She appreciates it. As do I."

I knew that, like the old spy Dickie was, he had planted the lines he intended for me to repeat, verbatim, to Sally, my mother. The terms of Dickie's relationship with her and the history they had together were always curious. Ostensibly Dickie was my stepfather Basil's 'old chum,' the one who had been so helpful when my mother and I had managed to get out of the refugee camp in Weiden and over to England. But back in London it was Basil, not Dickie, who pursued her, courted her, gave her the diamond ring that neither Harry, nor that chancer Francis Cluny were ever, as my mother said, "man enough to put their money on the table for." Yet Dickie, ever the covert operator, had maybe done more than simply carry a torch for her all these years?

Like so much of 'the life before,' as my mother called it, she was never going to speak of it. She had just done nothing more than her duty, fulfilling her responsibilities in calling me in Tokyo, tersely and condescendingly inquiring about Eri, my 'lovely little wife,' and informing me of Harry's death and the details that Dickie could provide for me. Wasn't she curious about anything Dickie said of Harry? Of course not. Washed his hands of him four decades ago. "There may be something the old con man has managed to save for the son he abandoned," she said drily, letting the pause drag out over the line, as if the thousands of miles between us had slowed its passage.

Maybe so, maybe so. But even Dickie wasn't quite sure what the hell it could be.

I found Harry's address easily… a quick cross-referencing of the street names from my childhood with the map Dickie gave me. Much was still the same from those years even with all these construction cranes looming, the squads of workers that looked Mongolian or North Korean… I couldn't tell, couldn't pick up the sound of their conversation on the street over the jackhammers. But I should have known nothing was going to be quite so simple on the other side. For the next two hours, I would be forced to wait until Silvia, the woman who was living in the apartment with Harry before he had passed away, returned.

The superintendent, a weedy looking old gent in a flat cap and three-day stubble, shuffled out to meet me and inform me of this: Silvia worked mornings in a bakery, he said. He wasn't sure where, but it was close by. He always knew when she was home because she'd water the geraniums on her balcony. The pots leaked and dripped onto his balcony one floor below. Maybe it was my old Berlin German or perhaps it was his suit and tie, but this man seemed to take me for a government official, one who might be able to mention this annoying trait to her. "Good tenant otherwise. It's a shame about that old man of hers."

"Did you know him?"

"Harry Maes? Ha!" He tapped a gnarled finger against his temple. "He lived in his head, that guy. It's a mystery to me why she… anyway, she'll be back soon enough."

I thanked him and decided to try and spend my East German marks, reacquaint myself with the city I had escaped from when I was eight years old.

In Tokyo, I had begun to dream vividly of these streets over the past few months. I wasn't a child in these episodes, but a man. In one, I had no legs, but made my way around on an old board with wheels. Halfway through, the dream got all mixed up though, and I was scuttling through the side streets near Waterloo station. I was being chased by a menacing child, a girl in pigtails who might or might not have existed—I couldn't really recall upon waking. But now in these streets that smelled of diesel, the patched-up old buildings with peeling mortar, open lots where you could still see where the bullets had pockmarked the brick that didn't tumble down in the bombing and the fires… all was still so recognizable. Dickie said there were some districts where there could be old land mines still in the ground; you had to be careful where the grass had grown through the cracks in the unpaved streets. Yes, what a Paris of the Eastern Bloc it all had turned out to be.

I went into the Centrum department store in Alexanderplatz and there seemed to be nothing I could purchase. I picked through sweaters made of some scratchy acrylic, misshapen as soon as I had put one on. Then I tried on clunky, ill-fitting Derby shoes with odd, rubberized soles. I felt like I was costuming myself in the disguise of the good socialist citizen I could have been. After a half hour of browsing, all I could manage were flimsy tennis shoes for Eri. She had taken the game up again and we were playing three times a week among the exiles at the Tokyo Lawn Tennis Club. What a million miles from Tokyo's shopping theme parks this place seemed to be.

I resolved to call Eri as soon as I got back on the western side that night. I was feeling guilty that I had hardly been thinking about her, from the moment I had gotten on the plane to London. But I would have been surprised if she had been thinking of me as well. I realize now that it was only when we were together, focused on the present tense, that our relationship fell into a natural rhythm that transformed fondness into a feeling approximating love.

Leaving Centrum, I still had a little time, so I wandered into a bookstore near Humboldt University. But there was nothing but hardcover volumes of Gorky, Tolstoy, and Dostoevsky. The woman behind the counter, in a blue tunic and dowdy floral apron, watched me carefully until I exited. She seemed incapable of smiling.

As I walked out in the street, furtively taking in those on the broad sidewalk, I looked in vain for someone who did not completely inhabit some Cold War cliché. There were miserable-looking office drones in boxy overcoats, their eyes fixed on the pavement in front of them. Many of the strolling older people looked pale and broken, squinting in the daylight. One of these ghosts could have been my father just days before.

When I finally returned to the apartment building, Silvia Stanciu was in the lobby, seated on a plastic bench with two bags of groceries. She was not what I expected. I was imagining a woman my mother's age, but Silvia looked barely fifty. There was no grey in her jet-black hair, which was pulled back from her oval face in a tight bun. She was still very attractive, reminding me of an Italian actress, one of those buxom neo-realist madonnas in a film I had seen as a student.

"You are Nicholas, the son."

"That's right. Very pleased to meet you. You're Silvia."

"Thank you for coming. I think it was not easy."

"I know this is important."

Before I could say anymore she rose from the bench and led me to the elevator. She pressed the button and it lit up with a dull, ghostly-silver glow. Once we stepped in and the doors closed, she spoke in a hurried whisper.

"Your German is good. Very natural-sounding. Better than mine, and I have been here for a decade now!"

"You came from where?"

"Timisoara. You know of it?"

"Romania, yes?"

"That's right. Your father was a good man to me."

"I'm sure he thought you were good to him as well."

"He asked for you in his last days. He told me a man to call but not from our phone. He knows people in the government, I think. You know of this?"

I just nodded. That might have been Lange she was talking about, but I felt there was no point in causing her to doubt who I was. Given the intensity of her gaze, it seemed she still wasn't sure if I wasn't from the Stasi.

"There are so many questions I have about my father. I knew nothing of his life here."

"I will tell you what I can. We will have a few hours, yes?"

As the elevator opened she motioned for me to follow. The hall was painted in a hospital blue. I took her in as she walked ahead, but not out of any other impulse than curiosity. I could smell a flowery perfume and wondered if she was wearing it just for me. Perhaps she felt it was what women in the west did all the time.

She reached into the pocket of her cheap-looking spring raincoat and pulled out a set of keys when we reached the last door along the hall. I could smell cabbage boiling, hear a mother scolding children behind the door on his left.

"I will stay as long as I can before I have to take the train."

"I can make some coffee. You like coffee? It's not like anything in England or Japan, I'm sure, but I make it strong. Your father liked it that way."

"I like it that way too. Thank you." England and Japan… so she knew a bit about my life, my time in the foreign service.

She led me into a room with higher ceilings and more space than I imagined. Bigger than our apartment in Tokyo, that was for sure. I could see the row of geraniums on the balcony through the screen door. She obviously watered them regularly; they seemed very healthy. There was a long couch upholstered in orange corduroy, a blonde wood coffee table. Harry was doing all right for a man in his seventies with a measly state pension. Perhaps this was all Silvia's doing.

"They are not much, but these were ours, these rooms. I hope I can keep them."

"It feels like a home."

"Thank you for saying that." She stood, stock-still, on the blurry old Persian carpet, staring into the scarlet-coloured pattern as if she was trying to remember something. "Before we sit, I should show you. Then we can talk."

"Show me?"

She cocked her head and smiled. She had one silver tooth. "Why you are here, of course. Please follow me."

She led me down the hall. There were three doors. She turned and opened the one on her right and gestured for me to enter first. "Please. Go in."

There, covering every inch of wall space, were paintings that, even with a cursory scan, I realized were serious works of art. I could recognize the work of Schiele, Dix and, above me, a painting of Madonna and child that would not have looked out of place hanging in the Louvre.

"These are real?"

She nodded. "He had more, once. Many he used to sell. That is all I know."

"You know what these are worth?"

"I have some idea. But they are not mine. I have some papers… his will… he wanted you to have them."

"I… they will never let me, your government… how can I take them anywhere?"

"Come. I'll show you the papers I have. Harry thought of this. He has the name and address of a man. It is in the Czech embassy."

"He told you this?"

"He gave me clear instructions when I saw him for the last time in hospital. He knew he would not return home again." She looked away from me, at the drab grey curtains on the window. She was tearing up. "Shall I make that coffee?"

"Of course."

I followed her out into the hall and gently closed the door behind me. A treasure. Each painting was worth a fortune. Nothing was ever going to be the same again.

23.

01 / 03 / 94

I knew enough about why my father might have had these paintings to assume I would have to be very careful about whom I told. After I had coffee with Silvia Stanciu, I realized there weren't many questions regarding their provenance that she could answer. She did not know where Harry got these few treasures, but she reassured me it was a secret only shared with her, a certain Herr Lange, and this gentleman named Ladislav Komarek, who was working for the Czech Embassy.

"How did this Czech gentleman come into this?"

She walked over to a drawer in a small cherrywood game table, pulled it open, and retrieved a business card. "You would be best to ask him yourself."

She handed it to me, and then her gaze went to the Persian rug. I knew her silence was for the paintings themselves; she could not say how long Harry had them hidden. It couldn't have been since the war; Dickie Knifton told me Harry had spent four years 'away re-educating' before he was allowed to return to Berlin.

Yet Silvia did say that she had tried to find out but Harry would never tell. There were limits to how much he trusted her. Maybe that was a legacy of those punishing years of exile, but I imagined that Harry was always that way, given what my mother had told me over the years. There was only so much he was going to reveal to anyone about his life before he died, it seemed.

Yet before I left Silvia, I returned to that room to mentally catalogue the paintings that were there. At first I was hesitant, because it felt like I was trespassing and grave-robbing, taking what was valuable from the woman who had to deserve something for her years of devotion to Harry. There was also a terrible thought that entered my head, one that surprised me by its sudden appearance: *this woman really has no idea what these paintings are worth.* The greed that whispered to me, in a voice of the person within who no longer had to deny that money matters, who was no longer young. I was that despised foreigner who comes to seize treasure because no one will ask him to account for it. *Raubkunst.* And I was surprised, but not necessarily dismissive of what greed was urging me to do.

In that room I also discovered there were one or two paintings that actually looked familiar. Chiefly because they were so much older—centuries older than the recognizably modern paintings I'd first glimpsed, preening for each other like beauties still circling the ballroom. *Who's the fairest of them all?* There was a portrait of the virgin with the baby Jesus. It struck me as conventional, unremarkable in relation to the many paintings with the same figures, the same palette, that I had seen over the years. But then there was the one I almost swooned for—and probably would have, if Silvia wasn't looking on, chewing her nails, and taking me in with the inquisitiveness of a feral cat. I wasn't sure who the artist was, but it was the quality of light in the painting, the interplay of the figures, the drama of deception and risk caught in one fatal moment of a card game. I knew this painting had to be worth a fortune. If I had only been allowed one to take as my own... there it was.

As I stood there, reflecting on what I should do, an old mantra from my childhood came to me once again: *look forward, Nicki... not behind.*

As a boy, just days before my mother and I received word that we were able to leave the refugee camp in Weiden, Sabine— now Sally—came to meet me at the makeshift soccer pitch where I was playing with my classmates. Of course she had known we were leaving before she held the papers in her hand. Those nice men, Mr. Knifton, who interviewed us both about 'Uncle' Francis Cluny, and Mr. Hepworth, who was good enough to get us second-hand sweaters and rubberized raincoats, I could tell these Britishers were going to do all they could. "Most people are very good, Nicholas," she said. "It is hard for you to understand this right now but it's true."

It was important to look to the future, and try to forget about people I would probably never see again. Like my grandparents, like Uncle Francis, who had decided to leave us for 'possible work in

Moscow,' and most importantly, I had to forget about my daddy, who had done some very bad things.

"He didn't hurt anybody, did he?"

"No. But he helped other people steal things. Important, valuable things that were in their families for generations."

"Why would he do that?"

"Because some people get scared. They know what's right but they become afraid of the power others have. They're not strong enough to fight their fear. But you and I are not scared, are we?"

No, of course not. I was never going to be too scared to do what was right. As she held me close I could smell the new rosewater soap in her hair, just the faintest wisp of old perfume on her scarf. She pulled away from me and straightened the collar on my jacket. There, I could see it, a tear, evidence of the soft sound in her throat when we embraced. She quickly and brusquely wiped it away, leaving a small darker line through the powder on her cheek. It was the last time I had seen my mother cry.

Really, what did she have to be sad about? Of course it would all work out, once we got to London.

And it did. In a matter of months, Basil Hepworth was courting my mother. In less than a year, I did not have to worry about anyone pronouncing my last name wrong. *Myes not Mays, please.* I was now Nicky Hepworth, third form, top of his class in maths, picking up English quicker than anyone expected.

It seemed I didn't inherit any of Harry's interest in art, either. Yet it wasn't as though I was exposed to it over the next few years. Basil and Sally Hepworth became solidly middle-class, but in that English way after the war where there was no flash, nothing unconventional about them that would cause the neighbours concern in our quiet Leyton neighbourhood. The culture that Basil approved of, which made some kind of impression on me anyway, was perceived as enriching but in no respect 'bohemian,' as Basil would say, with as much hauteur and dismissiveness as he could muster. He loved listening to Benjamin Britten's latest works on the radio on Sunday. And I could remember my mother being thrilled by the film *The Red Shoes*, in all its startling colour, which was on at the Rivoli Cinema on the high street in Leyton. It filled her with memories of her mysterious life in the theatre she would allude to every now and then, usually after too much sherry. It was a life which might not have ever really existed. But that's as high art as we got, this invented family.

And there was something political involved in all this. Basil was suspicious of those in the foreign service with him who mixed with the bohemians and jazzers, called them 'the posh boys.' They were likely to be duplicitous, closet reds. Even before Guy Burgess got to Russia, so many of his Cambridge set like Philby and Blunt were not to be trusted. And Sally had put all her dabbling in the lively arts far behind her when she got her desk job at the BBC.

How much did I unconsciously erase memories that did not align with the broad strokes of that new self of the immigrant boy, the one I was so dutifully etching in Leyton over those years? Now, in this Berlin of ghosts and the vaguely familiar streets coloured like old iron, I felt some vividness coming back. As if I was projecting myself, rediscovering the last months when Harry and Sabine were still together.

Somewhere behind the facades of these stately ruins in Friedrichstadt, that old grand apartment of Harry's moneyed years still had to exist. Such luxury! The high ceilings and two crystal chandeliers, the long mahogany dining table, under which I raced my little wooden cars. They were curvy, bug-like sedans I had to stretch my fingers to hold in one hand. The little boy I was then knew there was something special about my father. It was as if Harry was suddenly a lottery winner, after Frau Petofi, my father's boss, suddenly left the country.

I was tucked into bed early on Saturday nights by the dour Frau Schorba with the long grey skirts. God, what happened to her afterwards, when the bombs were falling? In those days I always had to be whisked away before the guests would arrive for the late dinner. The men in uniform, their wives in chic evening dresses. I can still smell the cigar smoke that would waft into my bedroom where I lay, determinedly awake, listening so closely through the laughter and the tinkling glasses for the secrets of the adult world.

Like a tripwire, these recollections inevitably called up the first years of my parents' separation. There was the move to the far humbler apartment in Kreuzberg of Uncle Francis—Francis Cluny, the Irish writer working for Redaktion Irland. By then we were all living on maybe a thousand calories a day. Those hunger pangs that were never quelled, the shivers of those nights in the shelter as the bombs whistled and then boomed. I can still smell the cheap soap on my skin, the rubber of the gas mask I wore.

All the violence that followed came with a randomness then. It was all that much stranger because it was so casual. I remembered seeing Heike, my best pal Florian's mongrel dog, breathing her last in the courtyard, her black and tawny fur smeared with blood. Florian and I both wept as he carried Heike upstairs. It was a bullet wound from a shot that neither of us saw or heard. A mystery, like so much else in those days.

As I got back on the train that day in East Berlin, beating my retreat from the past, my good fortune in surviving suddenly overwhelmed me. Forty years of borrowed time that Florian and his mother and father never got. I sat down, peered out the window impassively, and proceeded to do something I hadn't done since I was a teenager. I wept. Uncontrollably too, as if I was dredging up deep, long-forgotten reserves of grief. Reserves I did not know I had in me.

I had to decide what to do about this inheritance, but the only decision I could firmly come to was that I needed more time to process what I had discovered. *Don't tell a soul.* Yes, not even Eri, she who I had built a life with, thousands of miles away.

When I returned to my hotel I had a Japanese whiskey in the bar. Suntory, my favourite in Tokyo. That it was on the menu gave me a small moment of surprise and delight. A little bit of the one place in the world where I was truly happy. I took that first sip and closed my eyes. I could picture my wife Eri embracing me in the six tatami apartment she had before we married. I had to call her soon, but how to explain all I had just seen without speaking of my father's secret? My words, like my next moves, had to be chosen carefully.

The bar was all but deserted except for a middle-aged couple sitting glumly by the window, drinking large steins of beer. Maybe it was the sight of their doughy bodies in bright sports shirts and sweaters, or the outsized look of those beer steins, but there seemed something child-like about them both.

What would they have been like, during the years of their own childhood? Maybe they had been a couple of street urchins I would have seen playing in the rubble. I imagined that after the war they'd moved far from Berlin, had something of a normal life in, say, Stuttgart. And now here they were, like me, survivors drawn back to this city. They could look out at the garish neon lights on Ku' Damm, tap their feet to the pop music playing over the stereo system in the bar, and try to place themselves as complete beings again. Scars healed, made whole by the numbing forces of change and forgetting. A pop star crooned, 'everybody wants to rule the world.'

In the morning, after sleeping for nine hours, the longest I had in years, I went out for a walk to get breakfast and realized my mind was made up. I would call Eri and tell her that my plans had changed. I would be taking another week off, staying in Berlin for a few more days. It was just me tying up some loose ends with my father, everything was fine.

"I got you a gift at a communist department store."

"Nicholas, you didn't have to do that!"

"Oh it's not much, believe me."

"I didn't know they had such stores. Isn't everyone so poor? They line up for food from shops, don't they?"

"I didn't see that but you could certainly imagine."

"Your father must have had such a difficult life."

She said he sounded so happy, that this trip was good for me. I realized there might be something to that.

Throughout the day I tried to remember all that I could of the painting I fell in love with, among that jumble in the back room of the apartment. There was a precision to the work: the one piercing candle flame that illuminated, through the dim shadowy outlines of the folds of a cloak, a smirking toothless crone. There was the young man of wealth, the mark, so proud and impassive, and the card cheat's accomplice whose grin was betraying the moment. Something about the shape of the faces that seemed faintly Japanese as well… I was making all those subtle justifications for why this painting could only be for me.

It was mine by rights for all of the damage of dislocation, trauma, assimilation… therapy words I never allowed myself to speak. Well, now I would, but only to myself. I was entitled to them! I would suspend my cynicism and silence the voice of Sally in my head, cackling about the weakness of self-pity, that nobody wanted to hear from a little boy about how hard English was to learn, or why cricket could not be mastered on a few Sunday afternoons. You get on with it, you learn to win. 'Only little boys cry, Nicky (with a y now… the only why I was allowed). You let your classmates see you're weak and they'll bully you. I will not have that.' For all I had lived through there was a treasure that awaited me, this was his new story that I was writing in my head: the lost, forgotten, real father, the sudden revelation. I had my own fairy tale at last.

After two days of languishing in Berlin and playing tourist I had arranged my next visit across to East Berlin. I had little to go on but Silvia Stanciu's assurance that the address and phone number she had provided me would get me to Ladislav Komarek at the Czech embassy on Wilhelmstrasse. Anything could happen— Komarek could ignore my call or entrap me if I spoke with him about claiming what was rightfully the property of the government. But I had a plan and my own reserves of determination. This was about my father's legacy, I told myself. Whoever this man was, I would find a way to do business with him.

I knew that even if I used Silvia's line to call him, it was most likely tapped. So I decided to simply walk into the embassy, claim in my Berlin German that, as Silvia instructed me, that I was Komarek's 'neighbour,' that we had a lunch date so I could get some information on traveling to Prague. The worst that could happen was that I would be escorted out of the building and have to revert to a plan B—whatever that was.

The embassy itself was not far from the Wall. It looked like a concrete spaceship that had landed amid some of the older government buildings that were haphazardly reconstructed. There was a construction crane that loomed over the street, like a giant dinosaur sculpted from iron. The Fuhrer's bunker was not too far from there, if memory served. I felt paranoid and self-conscious enough, but I swear, everyone on the street carefully looked me over, as if they would be called to identify me and did not want to get any detail wrong.

And yet, when I entered the embassy and inquired about Komarek, they were surprisingly hospitable. A heavyset blonde woman was at the front desk, wearing a tight, broadly-striped turtleneck that did her no favours. She looked me over as if she quickly enumerated my secrets and found them wanting. The exchange reminded me of how I'd once been sized up walking through the Reeperbahn in Hamburg. Then she called up to her colleague as if it were just a matter of course. I think about it now and realize that the disintegration, the loss of the old regime's control must have already been happening. Though it was still months before the Wall would come down, even the loyalists heard the clock ticking.

Ladislav Komarek emerged out of an elevator and walked towards me, chuckling as if we were old friends. He was younger than I had imagined and had the sharp features of a bird of prey. He wore a nylon raincoat of an indeterminate greyish-green or greenish-grey. It seemed a kind of camouflage for the streets, and I would discover he had much to conceal. He spoke quickly, with a hushed, clipped German I had to lean into to pick up, as he led me out into the street.

"I thought we could go for a walk, yes? Up towards the Brandenberger Tor. Easier for you to find your way back from there."

"I'm recognizing more than I thought I would, actually. I lived here as a child."

His head swiveled and he fixed his gaze on me with the most polite smile he could manage. "Ah… tzo. Harry never told me this."

"You knew him well?"

As we walked I could tell, by the lack of eye contact Ladislav gave me, that our street theatre required strictly defined roles. To anyone we passed we were off to lunch in the neighbourhood to talk about our weekends, the football match on Saturday. A couple of boring working stiffs. It was not a difficult part for me to play.

"I came to know him as well as anyone, I think. Anyone apart from Silvia. He really did love her. And she, him."

"I got that feeling too."

"You must be kind to her, Mr. Hepworth. I think she is still wondering why Harry did not leave her these paintings."

"I might just give them to her. More trouble than they're worth."

"Really? I think most people would disagree with you, sir. Including me."

"Honestly, I don't know what to think yet. I'm hoping you can help me."

Of course he could, he said. There was much to explain. It all began for him when he moved into an apartment just a couple of kilometres from where we were walking. The Czech government had placed him there; he had little choice in the matter. It was small but well-maintained, with a good view of the Spree. He knew virtually everything he did and said was likely to get back to the Stasi from his neighbours in the building, but things were no different in Prague—not for him, anyway.

This is why he didn't know what to make of his encounter with an older gentleman, who simply went by the name of Heinrich—no surname. He was leaving work late and this new friend of his had approached him, not far from where we were currently walking. Heinrich said he needed to tell him a little about the apartment he was living in.

Oh but he was an interesting character. He walked with a quite pronounced limp and was wearing rubber boots with his suit as if it was the most natural thing. Ladislav shook his head. "You soon discover everyone is a little crazy in this city, no?" Sure, present company excepted.

Heinrich said the man who lived in the apartment before Ladislav was once a prominent Nazi, but he had been spared the fate of many of his colleagues. "Odon Heimrath. He was not supposed to be alive. He had been working in the canteen at Humboldt University before he retired. A good cook, apparently… if that is even possible in such a place." There was a shared cellar in the basement of his building. It was once a bomb shelter. At the very back of this structure was a false wall. Behind it, the cache of paintings that were now in Harry's apartment.

"My father must have known this man," I said. "Did he ever say anything about him to you?"

Ladislav shook his head, his gaze straight ahead of us. "When I told him his name and said he was dead, all your father said was 'good.' He would not tell me anymore."

"What about this Heinrich? Why didn't he just find my father?"

"This man wept when he spoke of Odon Heimrath. Like a man would weep for his wife, you take my meaning?"

"Ah. Yes."

"So it was left to me to follow out the last dying request of Odon Heimrath—to return these paintings to their rightful owner. I had to find your father. And when I did, it was a comedy. For six weeks I spirited that work out of that cellar, a few at a time, put them in the trunk of my car. I would pick up Silvia Stanciu from her bakery job late at night. If there were too many people awake or on the street we would drive around until it was all clear. A ridiculous ordeal. But it was the only way I could return them all."

We turned a corner and I could glimpse the Brandenburger Tor, looming like the stone entrance of a prison. Sorry, I know the metaphor is a little bald, but it obtained, believe me. In the glass doors of a government building I could make out our figures in reflection. This was what war children grew up and became: a couple of grey-faced bureaucrats finally selling off their secrets to each other.

"You skipped over something, Mr. Komarek. I'm sorry but it's an important detail for me. My father… what happened when you met? What was his reaction when you told him of the paintings?"

"You listen well, Mr. Hepworth!"

"So I'm told."

"Of course your father thought I was Stasi. He denied everything and shooed me away. So I visited him a second time, asked him out for a walk much like ours, sir. I presented him with a rather logical argument, I think. If the government had wanted to arrest him over these paintings, they would have already. And questioned him. They would have got what they needed from him."

"And what did he say in response?"

"We must have walked the length of a football pitch in silence. And then he turned to me, looked me straight in the eye as I'm looking at you now. I'll always remember what he said. "I wish I could burn them all.""

"That would be understandable for him. I know he paid some price for his work during the war."

"Silvia told you. She was good to him. She was also helpful in bringing him around to some sense. With paintings like these, there will always be people who want them. People with money, yes? And they will always pay."

We were less than a block away from the Wall. There were Volkspolizei guards by the gate. One in a sentry box who eyed us momentarily and then looked away, as if disappointed by how unthreatening we were. "Not over here."

"Yes, Mr. Hepworth. Over here. And one can find ways of getting over there if there's a good enough reason. You have now, in your possession, ten or eleven good reasons."

"You counted them."

"And catalogued each one." He pulled out, from the pocket of his raincoat, a few stapled pages, folded in four. "There you are, sir. Your inheritance."

I gave him a courtly bow as I put the folded pages in the pocket of my raincoat. "So you can help me get these paintings to England."

"I believe I can, yes."

"For a price."

"For a price or just a percentage of what they might sell for, should you be thinking about parting with a few. Or all."

"I would have to get the work appraised. I don't even know if they're…"

"Real? Yes, you do. You must. You saw them for yourself."

He chuckled, and I was irritated that I seemed so amusing to him. But I did not say anything further. I had his card and knew how to contact him. We just exchanged the last pleasantries of two strangers and parted ways.

I had much to think on but felt no rush about making a decision. Silvia would ensure those paintings were in safe hands. Maybe I was sentimentalizing her but I could not imagine her doing anything with them until she heard from me again.

And as I walked towards the first tourist bar I could find on Unter den Linden, I had no idea when that would be. I just had this intuition that if I didn't think very carefully about my next decision and take as much time as I needed before I returned to East Berlin, I would probably make a grave mistake.

As I put this down I realize that at one point I once trusted my intuition. I miss that state of innocence.

24.

1 / 6 / 94

During the time of my posting in Tokyo, Eri and I took one Sunday to brave the shopping crowds in Shinjuku in order to line up to see the most expensive van Gogh ever purchased: *Sunflowers*. The Yasuda Fire and Marine Insurance company had put it on display, after spending almost forty million on it in a private auction. There it was, on the twenty-second floor of an office tower, in a meeting room, on a plinth behind a screen of thick Plexiglas. The plinth was draped in mauve velveteen to conceal how cheaply the work had been mounted. And yet it didn't matter; the work conquered the ugliness with its rich colours. Such bright, strange beauty, the extravagance of the brush strokes. Eri put her hand to her mouth and gasped when she took it in. She still had her long hair and bangs then, and in her striped turtleneck and black jeans she was dressed like some actress in a French movie from the sixties. All those months of my infatuation with her. Afterwards we had tea and scones with real Devon cream in some department store café and she told me it might be love she was feeling for me.

A year later, there I was in this Berlin hotel room, scanning the pages that Ladislav Komarek gave me, listing all of the paintings my father had in that back room of his apartment. I realized that these works might not be worth all those millions, but they still had to be worth a great deal. 'Attributed to Masaccio'… 'Modena'… and these were in addition to his favourite, *The Card Cheat*, attributed to la Tour. The paintings represented a world of trouble that had to be managed very, very carefully.

There was a story I had heard, early on in my training with the foreign service, of a charge d'affaires known as Middleton the meddler, posted in China, who won a seaside villa off a weapons trader while playing poker in Macau. The only problem? The villa was near Balchik in Bulgaria; good luck getting there. Well that's how this all felt: a fortune out of reach.

With one additional wrinkle: all of these paintings had the same former owner listed in the catalogue pages: property of the Reichkulturkammer, the former Ministry of Culture. If any of these works had further documentation, it seemed that neither Ladislav Komarek nor Silvia Stanciu had uncovered it. Or perhaps they just presumed I would be returning soon, and as the dutiful son I would deal with such questions of provenance through my own means of inquiry over in the west. Truth resided on the other side of the Wall, didn't it? Apart from my own cynicism about this notion, I knew enough about my father's trade to fear what I would discover.

Because Benjamin Ostriker was my grandfather. And I really can't explain my reticence to return to East Berlin, in order to deal with my inheritance, without speaking of him.

For more than forty years, I did not know he was alive. I had thought that, like my Belgian grandparents, both he and Gisela Ostriker did not survive the war. My mother would not tolerate any line of questioning, however innocuous it might be, about our 'last difficult years' in Berlin. "You're a Hepworth, Nicholas. Not many people get a chance for a fresh start. We have one! And now we make the most of it, yes?" I remember she said this to me on the tube, the afternoon we were getting our British passports. The last German words she ever said to me in public. Because I wanted to be the most excellent English child I could possibly be, I did not mention anything about our former life again to her. That is, until she spoke of it, compelled to because my grandfather had found her. He'd tried and failed to reconcile with her, and I suppose I was his last hope.

This occurred when I was back home in London, between postings after four years in Beirut. It was a particularly miserable time to be back. The country was broke, and there was a clapped-out dinginess that the crayon-coloured extravagance of the sixties had only papered over—and that paper was peeling off the walls. The bachelor's bedsit I had found in Clapham came with a kettle, an ironing board, and a black suit wrapped in plastic in the closet. Mavis, my Irish landlady, admonished herself for forgetting about the suit and then told me the previous tenant was an engineer from Calcutta who had died in a fire at a plastics plant nearby. Pauper's funeral, they didn't even need the suit. I had just turned forty and it was testament to my particular state of mind that I tried the suit on, and of course, it fit perfectly. Of course.

Basil, my stepfather, was still working at the Privy Council Office; my mother had gone to part-time hours at the BBC. They were winding things down, contemplating a move far from the city and a garden with coronation roses. After a few dinners over the first months of my return, I think we had come to a mutual agreement we had little to speak about, apart from their garden and the hung parliament that was sealing Heath's fate. I had become too foreign and they were far too English, my mother passionately so. Her contempt for the 'mimsy old radicals' she worked with was one of the few topics that animated her by the time the plates were cleared and I was contemplating another Sunday bus ride home. I made a solemn promise to myself never to become as cynical and reactionary as they were, clinging to a conception of England they both knew damned well had never existed.

All these years later, I realize there was never any point in arguing with my mother if we did veer into speaking of the past. Basil for his part never argued with me—he just made his judgments in silence, with a thin smile to mask the disappointment that I would always be the alien boy he had to pretend to father. With my mother, nothing I could say would possibly alter the story of plucky self-reliance and stiff upper lip that assured her ascendance through the ranks of the BBC, past the time servers and the talentless. I shouldn't have ever provoked her. One should trust in events to cause their own points of rupture along the brittle surface of remembering. Or mis-remembering, as the case may be.

Such was the case of Benjamin Ostriker's appearance in London. On a Saturday morning he had called me, speaking English with a heavy Plattdeutsch accent that I recognized immediately. It wasn't exactly the taste of a madeleine, though I did get a flashing image of a summer day, a toy schooner with a pale blue hull, my grandfather's thick hands, like a boxer's, pushing it along the shore of a carp pond in one of those long gone parkettes that Berlin once had before the bombs and the tanks. Then the schooner flickered out as I stammered my hello. He was staying at a hotel in Mayfair and was wondering if we might meet for lunch. With an apologetic tone he said that my mother had given him my number.

But what did he have to apologize for? Apparently quite a lot with my mother. And apologies were not accepted.

We met at Nardini's bistro, a small Italian place with red checkered tablecloths and film posters on the walls. It was one of the few restaurants I knew in Mayfair, run by Mauro Nardini, a sullen Glasgwegian-Italian who peered out from the back counter like he was piloting a ship through rough seas. Where have all the Londoners like Mauro gone? Some mass migration of hard-bitten survivors like him occurred during my years in Tokyo. Anyway, Nardini's was cheap, the espresso was strong and good, and I had become something of a weekend regular because the taste of the grind made me think of Beirut, and I was already eager to leave England again, reading my three foreign papers over Mauro's Napoli omelette. I came in before Benjamin, and Mauro and I nodded our curt hellos. He had a begrudging respect for lone patrons, if only for their loyalty to him.

The brass bell on the door rang, and a small, frail-looking old man, swimming in a trench coat, shuffled in. This had to be Benjamin, but in my memories he was as stocky as a middleweight boxer, and he did not wear owlish spectacles; they would not have had that quality of refinement he insisted upon for everything in his optometrist's shop. And he no longer had the pencil-thin moustache I remembered. It was as if he was in disguise to thwart any faint recognition from me.

He approached with his two hands outstretched, poised to clasp mine. He was still thick-fingered, still had patches of fine black hair that inched past his wrists. These I remembered, this was him all right.

"Little Nicki… you still look the same! I'd recognize you in a crowd."

I bypassed his outstretched hands and embraced him instead. It was all I could do to conceal the fact that my eyes had welled up with tears. It was like hugging a sickly child, he was so fine-boned.

Over our first glasses of cheap Chianti, he said he had come to London to visit some old friends from Tel Aviv. Meyer 'the husband' had passed away, after spending half a decade in a rest home his daughter found for him, conveniently just a few miles from her. "He could hardly remember he was in England by the time he died." But this friend had had an almost perfect recollection of his childhood, right up to the end.

We both agreed that memory was a strange thing, like a muscle you can't train anymore, once you pass 'a certain point.' Who really knew what that point was, though? Then he patted my hand and said "I'm glad that you and I, we don't forget each other."

But of course we wouldn't! Why would he even say such a thing?

He proceeded to tell me what my mother had kept from me for so long. She was his only daughter, and he constantly fretted and argued about her with my grandmother from the time 'Bin-a' had left home to make her way in Berlin. When she had told them that she was going to marry my father and convert, this was unforgivable to Benjamin. And yet Gisela, my grandmother, not only defended but ultimately championed the decision. "This broke up our family. We did not recover."

This was puzzling to me. I had seen photographs of my christening with him in attendance. He said he had tried, for my sake, to see things as my grandmother insisted they must be. It was a matter of survival. But after all the years of humiliation in the thirties, the bullying, the gradual destruction of his eyeglasses factory, his business, and then his basic rights in Hamburg, he had tolerated far too much. He and Gisela had resolved to sell everything, including their small but significant collection of paintings, in order to raise the money to leave and start a new life in Palestine. And it was this decision that ultimately led to the state of estrangement he could not finally resolve with my mother. "Too much change, too many deceptions," he said, shaking his head concentrating on the checkered pattern of the tablecloth, "we're a funny family, don't you think?"

Provenance

There was something about his use of the pronoun 'we' that rattled me. Yet I did not show it. I just asked him what happened at my mother's when he taxied out to see her just two days before.

She could not forgive him, he said. He blamed himself: he had all but cut her out of the family when he and my grandmother moved to Palestine, this was true. But with good reason, he said. Harry, his own son-in-law, had promised that when he took his paintings to sell on consignment, he would not show them to anyone associated with the Nazis. It was all that he asked! He could not bear the thought. But my grandmother had discovered, through her correspondence with Magda Petofi, the original owner of the gallery, that selling those paintings was precisely what Harry had done—on my mother's urging. And so he did not answer my mother's letters during those first few months of exile. As far as he was concerned, she had become the enemy. He could understand why, all these years later, that she in turn refused to let him back into her life.

I just had one question for him: how did he find her? She was, after all, no longer Sabine Ostriker. She was Sally Hepworth. All traces of our former lives in Germany had been erased. He poured himself another glass of chianti from the carafe and patted my hand. "Let me tell you about Laszlo Petofi."

For close to forty years Benjamin had been living in Montreal, after he and Gisela had separated in Palestine. He had a small optometrist's practice and shop in a neighbourhood the Canadians called Mile-End. That very April, a man who looked quite well off—"well-fed, and I can tell when a man gets his suit at a tailor's"—had come in, browsing for new eyeglasses. As Benjamin tested his eyes, the man introduced himself, said he had been married to Magda, the original owner of my father's gallery in Berlin. He had just retired, after teaching at a place called Loyola College since the fifties. When he saw the sign on Benjamin's shop with the name Ostriker, he just had to go in. It was this Laszlo Petofi who knew our names, knew my mother married Basil Hepworth.

"How did he know?"

"Letters. Magda had passed away that very winter. Fifty years of correspondence. Your grandmother, she had a good life in

Israel without me. I don't know who she remarried there but he wasn't the love of her life. Nor was I. It was Magda."

"All the secrets," I said, shaking my head.

"Not a secret to your mother. She knew. In these letters Gisela wrote about her own correspondence with her daughter, that she had a new life, a new name. Sally. I wonder why she took this."

I could finally tell him something he didn't know. "It was given to her by an Irishman. We ended up living with him for a while. He said he didn't like Sabine. I suppose she wanted to please him."

"Your mother wanted to be an actress, did she ever tell you that?"

"Wanted? She's been an actress for most of her life."

I had meant to add a little levity to our conversation by saying this. But it only caused him to frown as he took off his glasses, polishing them with a small cloth he produced from his trouser pocket. "I just remembered her on a little stage in Hamburg, dressed as… you know the word *waldgeist*?"

"I think so," I said. "Wood sprite."

"Yes. Wood sprite, that's it."

I reached over to him, gave his bicep an awkward, comradely squeeze. I've always been a disaster at affection. "I'm so glad you found us, Benjamin. You and I, we will stay in touch. You will always have your grandson in your life now."

When I think of that train ride back to the other Berlin, the one scrubbed of memories, I realize now why I suddenly broke into tears. I knew what those paintings had done to my family. At a deeper level than I was prepared to examine. But the reckoning would come in time, of course—reckoning more than reconciliation.

25.

1 / 8 / 94

I watched history end in the members' bar of the Tokyo Lawn Tennis Club. At the precise moment, NHK was televising the chanting crowds amassed along the Berlin Wall, I was ordering two gin and tonics as my wife Eri and I were doing our own celebrating: we'd made it to the quarter-finals in the mixed doubles round robin. Eri hurried over to me as the first images of the revelers came on the screen.

"Nicholas, you must see this! Your father's city."

I quickly paid up and we took our places at a table near the television. We weren't the only ones enthralled with what we were watching. The Thursday night crowd on the courts started to stream into the lounge. Sundry gaijins like me among middle-aged hackers in garish, fluorescent shell suits, their wives in sensible cardigans and tennis skirts... everyone was puzzling this out, watching the Cold War evaporate before our blinking eyes. It was bewildering. We were muted and reverent as parishioners at a wake, and then some American near the back of the lounge let out a cheer, and a ripple of laughter turned into a larger cheer in response.

"Oh Nicholas... your father, he died too early. If he just hung on a little longer."

"Yes, he'd be free."

I took a sip of my drink to punctuate the thought. Eri and I could now use English to complete each other's sentences and this was a pleasing affirmation of our love for each other. Yet just because I could complete the thought didn't mean I believed it.

Silvia Stanciu. The problem of all those stolen paintings Harry left behind. In my thoughts I was back in Berlin, walking down the corridor to that apartment. I could smell that boiling cabbage once again. What was I going to do about all this unfinished business now?

The news camera focused on a large steel claw of a crane, painted rubbish can green. It swung in the air for a moment and then clamped on to a stretch of cement pipe that ran atop the wall. A crowd chanted and clapped below. A small group of revelers held up sparklers in their hands. They sent off little shards of white light as fine as broken crystal. No city seemed to celebrate destruction quite like those in Berlin.

"We knew after Kristallnacht that eventually we'd have to leave," my grandfather Benjamin Ostriker had said to me in Mauro Nardini's place, in the London that was just a dingy memory. "But leaving broke us apart. I wish I could put the family back together."

I had assured him he had my support. But just a few months later, Benjamin passed away in Montreal, thousands of miles away, my promise to visit him in Canada never fulfilled.

Like everything else Benjamin told me, I was still troubled by the story of my family's disintegration more than a decade later, wondering whether it was just too tidy a narrative for the truth. Because my mother and grandmother clearly kept in touch for long enough during the war that Laszlo Petofi could speak of how my grandmother made a fatal decision to leave Palestine and travel to Budapest. It broke up her marriage (though she did return to Palestine, remarried). She had needed to be with this woman who exerted such influence on her life—Magda, Harry's mentor. Like my father, Petofi must have been powerless to hold his own marriage together because of the force of this bond the two women had. In the desperate, final days before both Gisela and Magda were almost snared in the net that trapped so many Hungarian Jews, my grandmother was still writing to the daughter she refused to call Sally. Laszlo pulled some strings and managed to get Magda and Gisela free from the clutches of the police ready to deport them both. With Magda and Gisela, here was a tragedy, a love story with my grandmother prepared to sacrifice herself, yet no one could—or would—speak of it in any great detail, least of all my mother, for whom the past was not to be revisited.

Provenance

"Your grandmother was just hoping to retrieve the paintings your grandfather sold to that woman's gallery. They were on consignment and she needed to fund her life apart from your grandfather. That's all. I wouldn't believe everything Benjamin said about Laszlo Petofi. Your grandfather did a lot of revising with our family history. He conveniently glossed over how he disowned both you and me, Nicholas. He cared about his own survival more than anything else, believe me."

This was my mother's curt dismissal of Benjamin's efforts at piecing together a story that with a fine thread of forgiveness, would sew our family together again. She couldn't call Benjamin her father anymore. He had travelled all that way to London in the hope he would change this, but, despite my stepfather Basil's hospitality ("he seemed a decent, honourable man"), Sally was not going to give Benjamin the serenity that would come with her forgiveness. In her mind he had cast her out when she was too young and vulnerable to make something of herself. It was only her grandmother's efforts at ensuring her survival that provided my mother some direction—and some protection—when she needed it most.

I was far more interested in forgiveness, and in the opportunity for some healing to take place. My memories of their years in Berlin and my mother's determined efforts to survive did not align with how she spoke of the assured, heroic steps she took to secure our eventual escape to a new life in England. If anything, I presumed that time in her life was marked by misdirection, efforts at establishing a new identity once she had finally given up her aspirations to be an actress. The Sally Hepworth who had aged into a stern but sentimental little Englander was not in any way sentimental about who Sabine Ostriker was—or interested in reflecting upon her transformation.

I wanted to admire the force of will it must have taken her to make this transformation. I had never felt completely whole once we'd immigrated. For years I still dreamed in German. Which was why I, like her, had to excel at being more English than the English, it seemed. Yet my aspirations were defined by the word almost. I couldn't quite make it to the top of the class at Harrow. Then, with the civil service exam, goaded on by Basil, my fate as one of the almost-best was sealed. I never sensed my mother was disappointed in me though. Perhaps she had put it down to me being 'Harry's boy,' the one remnant of her former life she couldn't quite disavow or disown.

It was unsurprising that I finally found some sense of belonging among the eccentrics and misfits who made up the foreign service. They all carried their sense of separateness, of being exiles no matter where we were posted. Almost as a fraying badge of pride.

But then, at some point after my marriage to Eri, just before Harry died, that sense of exile no longer seemed tenable. I needed to come home, in the fullest sense of the word.

At first I attributed it to the effects of living in Tokyo for a decade. Because of all the postings in which I had served, there was no place where the familiar became quite so strange. I had arrived as the deputy head of the mission, settled into my small apartment in Shinagawa, and began, as I had done in Beirut and Singapore, to try to get my bearings, walk the streets, explore the neighbourhoods on the weekends. And I had discovered, soon enough, that the city was, through a labyrinth of flimsy, post-war rebuilds, a theme park of amusements and escapes into variations of elsewhere, full of free-floating reference points from other cultures, restaurants, and shops creating a jumble of discordant architectural quotations and facades. All was pastiche, and nothing seemed quite real. Authenticity suddenly mattered to me in a new, deeper way.

So was it any surprise I finally needed to be married, to define myself as one who loves and is loved? And with who else but Eri, who was as much in love with the idea of becoming English as she was with me.

But I want to honour our separation and not speak ill of her. Why dwell on our relationship? I still believe it is not central to what occurred, despite my brief return to Japan. But more on that later.

The larger point is me coming to an end of my years of expatriate escape from myself. When I had first been posted abroad in Bangkok more than two decades before, I wanted to shake off virtually everything English about me. It was easy to self-dramatize and imagine I was in some spy thriller among quiet Americans, many of whom, as functionaries posted during the last violent throes of what was happening in Vietnam, were playing to type themselves. Then Singapore, then Lebanon… I cultivated a rootlessness and detachment that was only possible for boy-men coddled and then groomed for power by the last, fumbling protectors of empires. There were adventures, regrettably, early on, with sex traders on Patpong Road, but by the time I had moved to Singapore, the unlovable hybrid of duty-free shopping mall and surveillance state, I was becoming that particular kind of Englishman who is less ascetic than simply asexual. A mandarin's mandarin, a solid chap.

The closest I got to marrying anyone was with Hilary Trabert. This was before she had gone to America and traded on her British unflappability for cable news. After we had split up amicably, when we were still writing the odd letter to each other, she would appear on TV screens in the bars or cheap restaurants I'd frequent in Tokyo. This was when she was still covering the Middle East for the BBC. I would stop everything and watch these clips as sternly reported postcards from her life without me, and I knew she was becoming more conservative by her jewelry and that blonde dye job. In Beirut she and I had been functional alcoholics who had come together through a small group of expats who haunted the Hamra district at night. But I quit drinking and lost interest in the heroic narrative of her daily struggles for truth and justice, and she found my sobriety to be confirmation I was ageing as a colourless bureaucrat. I realized our eventual breakup was simply caused by how tedious the routines of the exile can become unless you have an elsewhere, a shared dream of belonging—and I finally settled into that with Eri.

What better time to finally return home?

It was convenient to be patriotic from a distance as Mrs. Thatcher came to power. The Tokyo office was emboldened to be bullish on trade expositions, conferences on Pan-Pacific resource development. I had felt useful. I would speak on how the United Kingdom was 'turning a corner' and attracting investment. I had slides of North Sea oil rigs, Austin Maestros coming off the line in some Soviet-looking plant in Cowley. And on the weekends I would hone my backhand into something less of a liability, because I knew that stretch of million-dollar real estate where Eri and I played, wind-screened and as charmless as a prison yard, brought back her summer student memories of the Cambridge Lawn Tennis club. I was consenting to be English at last.

Yes, I was well-aware of the dangers of such patriotism. The last refuge for a scoundrel. It's what my colleagues and I used to say in Bangkok about our superiors. But I wasn't quite making patriotism my refuge... at least not until I finally returned to a position in the Home Office.

Credit the persistence of childhood within me. Even before my visit to Berlin, I was developing an interest in just who Harry was and his particular line of work. Those days when he had become a rich man. I still had vivid memories of where we lived before Harry and my mother had separated... before Cluny 'the Irishman.' When I thought of 'the Harry time,' I could still see the huge crystal chandelier, taste the marzipan strawberries.

I could recall a painting that hung on the wall above the divan, a river scene that Harry had said was of the Charles Bridge in Prague, by that nice gentleman Oskar Kokoschka. "I always hated that painting. It was messy," my mother had said. When I discovered a small show of Kokoschka's work on the top floor of the Seibu department store in Ikebukoro, I stayed for two hours, poring over each of his paintings, entranced.

At first it struck me as odd that most department stores would have these art exhibitions on their top floors. As a boy growing up in stark, colourless Leyton after the war, my experience of art was something church-like. You put on your Sunday clothes and you took your place in line at a gallery for a solemn pilgrimage from room to room, silent and reverent. In Tokyo, looking at paintings was what the wives of salarymen did as part of the shopping experience, an affirmation of their refinement and sharp-eyed understanding of value. In the basements of these department stores, one sampled foreign food, bought French wine, Swiss chocolate, and German sausages, while on the top floor the eye consumed exotic delicacies, and one's ticketed presence was consumption enough.

It became clear to me what these palaces of shopping were really doing. It was almost cinematic, the visual narrative of the exotic that was created as you went from floor to floor. Enter these doors, and see everything foreign, packaged, and priced, so elegantly commodified. What was once a hostile threat was now subsumed, as you ascended on the escalator, into fantasies of other places, other possibilities of living never fulfilled. As I spent my working days subjected to the triumphalist rhetoric of 'global economic superpower' and win-win mergers and acquisitions from my reserved but quietly confident interlocutors, I realized that Japan's new love of art defined these aspirations.

And there I was, my father's son after all, creating the terms for such transactions every working day. As the Wall crumbled, so did my resistance to home and remembering.

That night in the Tokyo Lawn Tennis Club, as Eri and I watched the crowd of young men hoist each other up on top of a stretch of the Wall, she turned to me and asked, "don't you wish your father could have seen this?"

I just smiled and said, "how would you feel about returning to England with me?"

"You mean, live together there?"

"I have served my term here. I'd like to go home. And maybe we can make it our home."

She put her hand in mine and squeezed it. "I would like that very much, Nicholas."

In this moment that marked the beginning of our life together and the end of my time in Tokyo, I just stared up at the screen as if the images of the revelers on the Wall would provide all the celebration necessary. There was now a secret about my father's life and the legacy left to me that I needed to tell. I just didn't know how yet.

26.

01 / 11 / 94

Silvia Stanciu had dyed her hair. It had a tint of yellow but was mostly bleached white. And her dark roots were not only showing, but winning the battle over this transformation. She was pale and thinner than I remembered her, under-slept and fidgety as she sipped tea in the Rotherhithe café that she informed me was just a few doors down from where she was staying. Whatever happened to her over the three years since we first met, it was clearly stressful. Her tight, mustard-coloured sweater looked new, still creased from a display rack. She said she had pooled all her resources to look young.

"Oh don't be silly, you are still young. It is so great to see you here. I had no idea… you should have told us you were coming!" I stopped myself from saying Eri and I would have invited her to stay with us. I was determined to be as clear as possible about personal boundaries for Eri's sake—she was already unhappy about this meeting on a Saturday, the day that was meant for our doubles game.

We had been living in London for almost two years. We had settled into a three-story townhouse out in Maida Vale. A quiet street, lace curtains snapped shut in many of the front windows. Neighbours who minded their own business. I told Eri I liked this house because it was quaint and unpretentious. I might have added it was more affordable than expected, important now that I had taken a pay cut at the Home Office.

Eri didn't seem to mind a modest home. Compared to the square footage of her Tokyo apartments this was palatial.

She had honed an exile's routine. For the first year the city still overwhelmed her at times, but the transit lines weren't nearly as complicated as in Tokyo's, and she had gotten a part-time job at the Japan Cultural Centre which kept her connected to all that was happening at home. On Sundays she would prepare five days' worth of bento lunches for us both so we could save a little more. She would take back issues of the Japanese magazines home from the centre and nobody seemed to take notice, and she'd read them to herself on the tube.

We had settled into a frugal, quiet existence, our only luxuries being our membership at the local tennis club and Eri's twice-monthly calls to her mother and father. For the first year such conversations were quite brief, just a chance to share her impressions that were a bit too much for a postcard and to get all the news from home, hear how her parents were doing.

But over the second year the conversations ran a bit longer, as her mother's health had suddenly deteriorated. She just had "iron-poor" blood, Eri said, and it was making the old woman too frail to take her morning walks some days. I wondered how much wasn't being said—her mother was hibakusha after all: a woman who had survived Nagasaki as a child. Eri was far more stoic. These things were inevitable for them, she said; nobody was getting any younger.

Such were the events I was getting used to hearing about, so it was almost expected to see how much Silvia had aged.

"Nicholas, seeing you again makes me happy. I'm happy to be here!" Silvia declared this with a look of surprise, as if she was suddenly aware of a change in her mood. I gathered she was speaking of England, not this café with its odd red and blue chevron painted on the brick wall opposite our table. An attempt at optimism for the new decade, perhaps... but the colours were already fading badly.

"I can show you around. I mean, it's London..." I really wasn't sure what I meant but it sounded appropriately cheerful. I was making an assertion which required enthusiastic agreement. And it was an opening that allowed her to say what she hoped to do in the city. Behind her smile it seemed a thin wire of anxiety had begun to vibrate inside her though. I knew she needed something from me, and I feared how much she might ask for.

"It is all so beautiful. I even like the rain."

"You'll see a lot of it."

"Yes. It's free to everyone." Silvia's gaze went to the window streaked in silvery rivulets that descended as slowly as mercury. She seemed self-conscious about how our conversation in Berlinerisch veered off into something almost childlike. She took in the people sitting beside us and looked consoled by the thought she and I couldn't be understood.

I steered the conversation back into the realm of basic information. I was good at this, the line of questioning that was not too intrusive yet also not too cold and transactional. My diplomat's skills.

She said she felt comfortable enough with me to disclose something she could not in Berlin—nor could she have ever told Harry: she had a son from a first marriage, and he had made it out of Timisoara through Germany first and then Holland. 'George' was working under the table for a plumber out here in the suburbs and was determined to stay, start his own company. Her daughter-in-law Ileana, though she was 'a difficult person,' had been hospitable, and had given Silvia the room in their small apartment they were decorating as a nursery for their first child, due in three months. "An English grandchild! I could never imagine." Yes, she said, the world was changing so fast.

"I have to change too."

"What do you mean?"

"I lost my bakery job. It closed soon after the government disintegrated."

Disintegrated, yes. Like the metal in those Trabant cars that a hard rain would perforate. It was the word that was not quite right but appropriate enough the more you thought about it. This was the curious effect of talking with Silvia; there was a fractured poetry in how she put sentences together. The rain was free.

"What will you do?"

"I don't know yet. But a gentleman in our building, widowed like me, Herr Borschmann, said he had heard that a Swedish company might buy our building and the one beside it. At least in that one they had a tenants' meeting. They got bad news. The rents will go way up if they don't rezone it for office space. Both outcomes are possible. Maybe inevitable."

"But you might be able to move to the suburbs, perhaps find other work?"

She smiled for me, showing her silver tooth. How naive, how innocent I knew I was sounding. Me with my years in the civil service, a pension. Raised on the victors' side of the world, an agent of an empire winding down to irrelevance, sure, but with all the privileges and opportunities of a certain class I was bullied into preserving and defending from my first years as an English boy. My tennis sweater felt itchy. Here in Rotherhithe, I was actually the new foreigner in the world, not her.

"Nicholas, this might be uncomfortable to discuss, but it's about the paintings. Harry did speak of one day, maybe they would come to you. I know there are lawyers for this in the west… many cases now, my son says."

"Yes. I realize they are a responsibility. One that you've shouldered all this time."

"I must tell you I sold one. Small. The dealer believes it is an Egon Schiele."

"Is the dealer someone Ladislav Komarek found?"

"No." She raised her hand as if to stop me and then she looked down at her chipped red fingernails, composing herself again. "Ladislav does not know. I have told only you. It was Russian business friends of his. But I introduced them! I know they can keep my secret."

"I see."

"I realize for you this must be the same as theft. I have the bill of sale. I can pay it back over time for you. It is just… I have few resources. I told myself this was a loan. I'm telling you now."

I could see tears welling up in her eyes. She was still so attractive, made all the more so by her strength, her determination to remake herself, start a new life.

"You do not have to pay me back, Silvia. Harry could not have known the way the world would change. It made sense to give all of those paintings to me, I'm sure. He could presume you would be taken care of, that there would be no one you would want to deal with about them. God knows, I'm sure he'd seen enough disreputable characters in that trade."

"Like Ladislav."

I laughed but she didn't even smile in return. "Oh much worse than him, at least according to my old mother."

"Your mother is still alive? Harry's wife?"

"Very much so."

"He told me something different. Maybe he really didn't know."

"Or maybe he thought it better that you believed that."

"Yes. That is probably the case."

For a moment I entertained the thought of bringing my mother and her together. But why? They had nothing in common apart from Harry. And since my stepfather Basil had passed away a week before the previous Christmas, Sally's mourning period had passed, but she hadn't really come back to the world. She refused to come to dinner in Maida Vale, even when I had offered to drive out to Surrey to bring her in. More churlish than ever, she hadn't warmed to Eri in any way.

"Listen, Silvia, I have a proposition. I will come to Berlin. Fifty-fifty."

"Pardon?"

"The paintings. I have no interest in dealing with a lawyer, do you?"

"I'm sorry. I'm not understanding."

"The document that Ladislav Komarek gave me confirmed there are eleven paintings… now ten, I suppose, in your possession. Let us each claim five. You deserve them. At the very least."

She looked at me as if I was suddenly lit up with goodness. I realized this was not the time to tell her of his conversation years before with Benjamin my grandfather, about the questions of provenance these paintings raised. These were the concerns I had thought I could delay grappling with, given my ability to compartmentalize. I was Harry's son after all.

"I couldn't imagine such kindness."

"Your son and his wife… if you think they wouldn't mind, we should all have dinner together before you travel back."

"That would be very nice, Nicholas. You know I wish Harry had gotten to know you again. I am so glad we met."

I was feeling increasingly uncomfortable, eager to leave the café. She sensed it and we soon parted, with her insisting, perhaps out of pride, that she did not need a lift back to her son's apartment.

I did not know how I was going to explain all this to Eri. She firmly believed my mother's version of who Harry was: unfaithful to her with other women, openly supportive of the Nazi efforts to loot and plunder the art of countless Jewish families like the Ostrikers. It was like a money laundering operation, my mother had said, over one of our family dinners over that first year 'back home.' She said that Harry took his cut and ensured the Gestapo— who took these paintings off the walls in the homes of the murdered—got theirs. What was worse, Harry must have known what happened to those families and all that was occurring in the camps. He deserved to be forgotten, and anyone associated with him was likely deserving of the same.

All of this was no doubt true, but from what I could remember of Francis Cluny, who took us in after she left Harry, it was never clear that my mother was always on the side of the Allies. She maintained that Francis, broadcasting Nazi propaganda, was providing intelligence to MI6 all along. Indeed, that's how she and my stepfather Basil had met, it was true. Basil's silence on all this over the years spoke volumes to me. Yet I let it be. Eri wanted Sally to like her, and that required her to see nothing but noble intentions and wisdom in all my mother said about our complicated past.

Before I headed home from Rotherhithe I needed to think, wander a little. I got into the Renault 5, the tin can of a car I had purchased second-hand for tennis and shopping excursions, and motored over to the bleak port lands of Canary Wharf. I told myself it was out of curiosity, to see how this area was transforming. I needed a little optimism, a reason to believe grimy old London was becoming a place where Eri and I could age comfortably as successful citizens of this new Europe. Yet the gleaming office towers looked closed, as artificial as plastic hotels on an abandoned Monopoly board. A bearded old man that looked like some painter's version of John the Baptist was curled up on a concrete bench, wrapped in a tweed overcoat, sleeping soundly; his tennis shoes were the same make and model as mine. I felt like I had come to the point where the city just ended elliptically. Dot, dot, dot.

And maybe that was indicative of where I was in life now. Over drinks with Dickie Knifton, about a month before, I had spoken of how I felt I was being slowly pushed out of the civil service, given pencil-pushing work to do in the Home Office so I'd get the point.

"It's Maggie's time that's done it to us, I'm afraid. She got her people in. Management experts." Dickie sipped his glass of stout and winced at its bitterness. "They think of our kind as old lefties. Doesn't matter that I've spent the last forty bloody years getting the best actionable intelligence for them from over there."

"You think I should cash in?"

Dickie tilted his head as if he had long been considering it himself. He had to be past sixty-five anyway. "If you can afford it, I'd give it some serious thought. I mean you could consult for a decade or so. I hear that's profitable."

"Consult for who? Americans?"

"Point well taken. Quite. I mean, I never could."

As we parted that afternoon, I had stopped myself from disclosing what I had discovered in Harry's apartment. Maybe Dickie knew anyway. After my return from East Berlin he seemed strangely taciturn, smiling glibly as I lied to him, claiming that Harry left me nothing but a Kokoschka painting I decided to leave behind. All Dickie said in response was that he felt 'duty-bound' to tell me of this 'inheritance,' as a favour to his valuable contact Herr Lange, and that no one could make me accept the painting. "It's a free country." He laughed at his own quip.

But lying and keeping this a secret no longer seemed tenable—not least between me, Silvia and this Ladislav Komarek. If I were to go back to the new Berlin and actually settle matters, I would be compelled to finally tell Eri. How else could I explain the trip? And I knew that any real attempt at investigating the provenance of each work would mean that some of these paintings should—and could—be returned to the families who could claim rightful ownership. Yet there would inevitably be other paintings where no families still existed to make a legally-sound case to reclaim them. Even if it were only two or three among what we had together, Silvia and I might be able to grow old as the wealthy beneficiaries of Harry's legacy.

I stepped into an old newsagent's stand, picked over the newspapers, and then bought a chocolate bar. I was hungry, I should have ordered something in the café, but all that Silvia had to say had required my full attention. The old guy behind the counter, with his flat cap and his ratty old woolen vest, looked like an extra for some film featuring plucky, cockney Blitz survivors. He called me 'sire' as he slid my change in pence across the counter. He couldn't have been that much older than me, but why did he seem like he was from another era? Between us, who was the stranger in London now?

I found another concrete bench some distance from the sleeping vagrant to eat the chocolate bar and puzzle out what I would do. The sky was still clouded over from the rain and the Thames was the colour and texture of old iron, melted down for scrap. I could not shake the feeling that going to Berlin and taking all the right steps with the paintings would bring shame upon me. The chocolate tasted waxy and as fake as I felt. I was the son of a thief who worked for those who murdered and erased a whole part of my own family's history. Was this really what I wanted to discuss with Eri and disclose to the world?

Before Silvia returned to Berlin, Eri and I both saw her again, though—along with a bearish-looking George and a fragile, pretty, and bird-like Ileana. There were a few Polaroids that Ileana took that night, in a Turkish restaurant George had found in Hackney. Silvia had mentioned she loved Turkish food and George wanted to show his mother all that was available in 'this magic city.' He had his mother's dark eyes, the same aquiline nose. In the photos we are raising glasses of beer, posing closely and stiffly beside each other in these rickety bistro chairs. Eri and I had ghostly red devil's eyes in one where I pulled her close. Behind us was a beach scene from a travel poster of the Turkish Mediterranean, like a fake backdrop on our invented life. What an odd collection of people brought together. Each with secrets from our broken families, all of us marked by a restlessness to be elsewhere. We all drank too much, split the bill despite my protests, and swore we would do it all once again when Silvia returned, as George proudly announced, to stay.

I did not think much of this announcement at the moment. To me, Silvia's son was just being sentimental, and doing his best to make up for their years apart. But in the days, then weeks, that passed, I took this resolve of hers to emigrate as reason enough not to think about the paintings. And put off, once again, mentioning them to Eri. Why even think about going to Berlin if Silvia would eventually be in the same city as us, with some precious cargo she'd lie about through customs, no doubt? There was work and our daily lives, with our regular rhythms, our routine commutes to shops, to the tennis club, the garden centre... the quiet life as brittle and breakable as the 'Hepworth china' Sally had given to Eri after Basil died.

Yet there was one observation from our evening out that did linger. I had left the Polaroids on the breakfast table, and a few days later, over tea, Eri pointed to Silvia's jewelry.

"You see that, with the panther clasp? That's Cartier."

"The necklace?"

"Nicholas, you don't notice anything. But women do... a necklace like that."

"Maybe it's just a fake."

"Maybe. Maybe not. She was a very interesting woman, I think, your father's Silvia."

It was a Sunday night, the first weekend in June, when I got the call from George. It had been more than two months since our dinner together and I felt a pang of guilt with the sound of his voice. It was partly because I had done nothing about the question of Harry's estate, but it ran deeper. On nights like this in front of the TV, watching the news, I'd find myself thinking about how easy it was for me to let all my personal relationships fade like those Polaroids taken that night, how coldly transactional I really was, despite my impeccable manners, the way I could play the cardiganed and middle-aged bureaucrat. Why did I not stay in touch with George and Ileana, see how they were making out? I just didn't care enough.

"Mr. Nicholas, I'm sorry to call you so late. I hope you're not disturbed."

"Not at all. How are you? How are you both keeping?"

I had immediately heard something worrying, a little tremor of grief in George's voice.

"It's about my mother, Silvia. Mr. Nicholas, she died."

"What? What do you mean?"

"I got a call from a hospital in Berlin. She came into emergency with a stab wound. Robbed on the street by the gypsies. They took her jewelry. I'm sure she fought them, that's how she was. She made it to her building. They found her unconscious in the elevator. They tried to save her. That city… she told me it was no longer safe. She should have been here with us. I never should have let her go back."

"My God, George… I'm so sorry."

"Now, if I leave to settle things, I may not get back here. I know you work for the government. Can you help ensure I can return if I were to go, Mr. Nicholas?"

Of course I could. I would do all I could, I said. And I knew exactly what it would mean to return to Berlin. The reckoning at last.

27.

1 / 15 / 94

A memorial service for Silvia Stanciu was to be held in a Russian Orthodox Church in Berlin-Wilmersdorf. Her son George had insisted on this. Over the final years of her life, it was some consolation that she could 'return to faith' without fear of such subversive activity making it into a Stasi file on her.

"She lived with fear so much of her life. We all did," said George, gesturing with his unlit cigarette to himself and Ileana, who sat, silent and doleful beside him, with a new Lady Diana hairstyle that did not really flatter her. They had taken me to this pokey little luncheonette a block away from the church. George had been there once before and recommended the currywurst on a bun and the Pilsen beer. "You know, we never visited her here. I never saw how she lived. I wish now we did. I realize it was never good for her. She did not tell me in her letters."

"She wrote to you a lot?"

George patted an old leather briefcase that looked like someone's castoff. This couple was still building their life back in England from second-hand pickings. "I keep every one. And the photos. I brought them for the memory table at the wake." He pulled out two large folders, one had 'RECETES' scrawled across it in red ink. "She never missed a birthday. I have the cards too."

Silvia, from all George and Ileana knew, never wanted to leave him with his grandparents. But she was too young and would have cared for him alone, living in "dishonour." She had to move away from Timisoara during the pregnancy. George's grandfather came from a small village in the Trascau mountains where she had stayed. 'His people' could manage the situation. After George was born, there was no question of him going into one of the orphanages run by the Ceausescu government; everyone knew what they were like. "Like a house of horrors," Ileana whispered, as if it still needed to be kept secret.

"Your father…"

"A mystery man. My mother would not speak of him. She said he was a policeman but more like a criminal. We lived in an upside-down world. Now I wonder if he ever did move away from Timisoara, as she said. He could have been there all the time, I never knew. My whole country… it was like one big orphanage, I think."

Ileana nodded in agreement, her porcelain white, child-sized hands wrapped around the beer stein in front of her.

"Do you think many people will come to the memorial?"

"The superintendent, he told me she had many friends at the bakery where she worked. A few will come. And she was retraining. She wanted to be working in a jewelry store. Some people from her class might come also… she made friends easily."

"She had to," Ileana said. "Your mother was a survivor, George."

I nodded in agreement, out of respect for both of them, survivors too. But I couldn't help thinking, *what did that mean?* What were the virtues that we were retroactively bestowing upon people like my father and Silvia, apart from a certain knack for good timing and a form of situational ethics unique to the darkness of the war scarred years? I could tell, with George's silence and his aversion to eye contact at the table, that Silvia's son was processing similar thoughts. And wondering, as much as I was, about the gaping silence, the mysteries that would remain unsolved when the person who once called you their son couldn't find a way to be there for you when they were needed most.

George and I were united by our grappling with this silence now—but also united by the secret 'treasure' I had revealed to him, prior to him and Ileana arriving in Berlin. I had taken him out for a stiff drink at his favourite pub in Rotherhithe, a grim, greasy little spot with electronic slot machines and a big jar of pickled eggs that looked older than the barmaid. I shared with him the papers detailing the provenance of the work and could tell, by George's puzzled look, his lips moving as he read, that he did not fully grasp the significance of this information. His mother had said nothing about this, he said, and it was clear, once I told him what all the paintings could be worth, that he was telling the truth. George's hands were trembling as he raised his beer to drink.

And for a moment, I thought to myself, I had missed an opportunity. I could have lied to him, said that Silvia inherited them all, and that now they were in his hands. I might have congratulated him on his newfound wealth, washed my own hands of what would happen to him, if he took the paintings he'd inherited to get them appraised.

After all, perhaps nothing would happen, except the work would go up for sale and then be sold to sundry anonymous bidders. Then George and Ileana would become, however briefly, tabloid celebrities, like all the lottery winners in the back pages of the Mirror, the Dereks and Maeves who bought themselves bed-and-breakfasts in Marbella and matching Jags. This was the scenario I had imagined for Eri and me in my worst moments—minus Marbella and the fancy cars, of course.

That such a quandary seemed so inconceivable, despite my having held the work in my own hands, was due, I felt, to my own lack of imagination—and my lack of courage with Eri. For I had still not found a way to tell her of what Harry had left me.

But I had the courage to tell George. I explained to him the deal I had made with Silvia, and what I suspected of many of the paintings, that they were the property of families where there could be sons, daughters who could rightfully claim the work. Now those were survivors, in the truest sense of the word.

"This is why your father did not try to sell them?"

"Perhaps. Or it could have simply been that there was really no market for them. At least none he had access to."

"How can we really know?"

"We have no choice but to take them to those who make a living selling such work."

George looked sullen, staring into his beer. "They will take a large percentage, I'm sure."

I heard a faint tapping and looked down. I glimpsed a scuffed construction boot under their table, George's nervousness exposed. I wanted to tell him that I felt the same. The last thing I wanted to do was compel anyone to secrecy, I had had enough of such concealment in my life.

"That's true, I'm sure. But I don't know what else we can do. In the meantime, this is just between you and me, yes?"

I shook his hand and I could feel the ridges of his callouses. Testament to my mother's aspirations for me, my hands could never be taken for a workman's.

Yet to live with the secret George and I had shared, even temporarily, was to put too much faith in our ability to act as if nothing were amiss with those closest to us. I had discovered this the hard way. Ever since the dinner we had had with Silvia, George, and Ileana, I could detect a simmering unease from Eri. As soon as I had begun to make plans to return to Berlin, she took this opportunity to broach it with me one night as we were going to bed.

"You fell in love with her, didn't you? And she clearly felt the same."

"Who, Silvia?"

"I could see it. The way she was looking at you over that dinner."

"Eri, she lived with my father."

"But you're practically her age."

"Don't be ridiculous. I was trying to help her. It was the decent thing to do."

"You haven't been the same since you first went to Berlin. Something happened there. It's like only half of you returned."

I had tried to protest but of course she was on to something. I could feel it. She was right about this for the wrong reason.

"Now you need to return. Why? I thought you settled everything when you were there the first time, that there was nothing of your father that you wanted."

This would have been the perfect time to tell her everything. What did I have to lose? I wasn't guilty of anything Harry might have done in the course of his life. And disclosure would have clarified so much about the secret I shared with Silvia, one that she was transparently grateful about when Eri finally met her.

It also explained quite a bit about my mother's talent for rewriting their past, and how it created such a distance between us, a divide that Eri could not fathom. For her Sally was a perfect model of the English pluck and elegance she tried to emulate—like the mother figure she'd prefer to have, in contrast to the divide she always felt with her own. No one can commemorate the empire quite like those hoping to remake themselves as British.

And more than any other reason, there was the prospect of sudden riches that should have been compelling enough. If at least some of the work in Berlin was authentic, and no further documentation on provenance could be found, Eri and I could move out to one of those old Georgian manors out in Somerset that she coveted in the real estate section of the *Sunday Times* each week. Really, it was such a perfectly fin-de-siecle way to grow old, a couple of foreign nouveaux riches, buying up the property and carrying on like landed gentry.

I knew I was a curious war orphan, no matter how self-aware I might be. Because my shame was too large a feeling inside me. It dwelled there as evidence of another possible version of myself, one I could remember as young Nikolaus Maes. And that feeling paralyzed me, rendered me speechless in the worst moments. Finally, all I could offer was an attempt at reassurance. "Trust me. I need to be there to settle what remains of his estate. Then it's over. Promise."

And I meant it, too. There was the matter of what finally belonged to Silvia in that apartment, and what else Harry had left her to deal with before this 'terrible tragedy,' as I now referred to Silvia's murder. It was my intention to close the file on Harry and his legacy as soon as possible.

And yet, there were the 'recetes,' clearly. And some photographs.

As George went through the photos Silvia had mailed to him over the years, I was not really attentive. The memory table for the funeral and this whole exercise of thumbing through some clumsily-taken snapshots from celebrations, looking for some resonant images, left me cold. Taken together, it seemed nothing more than a catalogue of Eastern bloc fashion and hairstyle choices, which could not quite make Silvia unattractive. Her dark eyed intensity, her cryptic half-smile… she inevitably became the focus of every shot.

Except for one.

"Whoa. George… that one. Could I see that again?"

It was taken on a bridge I could not recognize from anywhere in Berlin. There was a stone statue of some soldier figure and a dog that looked like a greyhound. Silvia had her hand on the dog, as if she were petting it, as did the man with her. Her companion was Ladislav Komarek.

"This? That is from a vacation some years ago."

"Where is she?"

"Prague. The dog… it was like one on my grandfather's farm, she said. She always wanted one like that, she wrote."

"You know this man with her?"

George shook his head. "No. Before Harry. She had a few boyfriends. She never really wrote about them. Only your father."

Ileana was giving me a puzzled look. She knew I had recognized the man but I was not about to disclose it. I pretended my sole focus was on the bridge, the lovely scenic view of the Vltava river, and the old city in the distance behind.

"Really? Only Harry?"

"She said he was the most interesting man she ever met. So many stories."

"Yes. Maybe even a few of them were true," I said.

Everything about my encounter with Ladislav Komarek was now in question. I wondered if there was anything he had told me about his discovery of the paintings that I could trust now.

Worse than this, it seemed Silvia had deceived me. With my father, there were sins of omission: she clearly never told him about George and Ileana, and she certainly did not tell him about her relationship with Komarek. Yet with what she revealed to me, she wagered that I would be generous, and that I would find the necessary financial support as she plotted the third act of her life.

As George continued to pick through the photos, my speculation, a kind of whirring tabulation inside my head, wound down to its ultimate question. "George, the attack on Silvia in the street… there were no witnesses?"

He shook his head. "There are always Romany begging near the station where she would get off the train. She hated them. She wrote to me about how they infested the city since the Wall came down. They are not really our people, you know. My mother, she could be a fighter when she needed to be. I believe it was probably an argument that escalated. They robbed her as the final dishonour."

I did not want to argue with George. Or Ileana, who had moved closer to him as I spoke, perhaps out of some intuitive sense my questions would feel like an intrusion, and she needed to defend George. "This is why you think she was attacked?"

"The police decided, not me. They said there were a few robberies over the last few months in the station. But none with such signs of struggle."

"They took her purse?"

George nodded. "And worse than that, there was a mark on her neck, right near her collarbone, where they ripped the necklace right off her. I think she believed she could survive the stabbing, if only she got to her phone. But she collapsed just outside her apartment building. Nobody was around to save her."

"Just horrible," I said. And I thought to myself, how English of me not to ask these questions when I had first heard of her death. Such a tribute and testament to what Sally called my 'breeding.' And how curious, upon reflection, that an altercation with a beggar in the station would lead to Silvia's new Cartier necklace being ripped from her open neck before she was stabbed.

The memorial service for her was indeed surprisingly well-attended. All women, presumably from Silvia's bakery days, dressed in shades of black polyester under flimsy, candy-coloured ski jackets. Two women who had to be twins sat side by side in one of the front pews. One was weeping. Her sister was like the public version, composed and appropriately serious. My gaze kept returning to them, as if there was some truth about Silvia this doubling revealed. George's voice quavered while he stood at the lectern, reading his tribute, but he ultimately held it together, and

Ileana whispered to me that he had drunk half a bottle of vodka that very morning.

I signed the guestbook and then quickly and brusquely made the necessary arrangements with George to meet at Silvia's apartment the next day. The whole atmosphere, with these grieving women milling about the memory table, had the feel of a larger ritual, as if everyone was in mourning for something other than Silvia. And it made me feel nervous because it was so publicly emotional. A service like this for Harry would have been unthinkable, thankfully. I hurried out into the street, grateful for the faint smell of diesel in the air, the bustle and traffic of forgetting.

I briefly returned to my hotel. It was far grander and tackier than the first I had stayed in in Berlin, much like the rest of the city now. I changed and then dined out in an Indian restaurant by myself. I tried to write a postcard to Eri at my table. My intention was to be whimsical and ironic, qualities I could summon with her in our better days. But I couldn't get the tone right. I ripped the postcard in two, left it on my plate after I paid the bill. Nothing could quell the feeling that something was amiss.

As I got back to my hotel, deep down I knew who would be waiting for me, strategically positioned at a small table to take in everyone who came in the main entrance. Ladislav Komarek was wearing the same raincoat from two years before, but he looked like he had gained some weight. Now a fat raven rather than a crow. He rose and walked towards me, grinning as if we were old friends, his hand outstretched to shake.

"Mr. Hepworth!"

"Mr. Komarek. How did you know I was here?"

"Where else would you stay but the Maritim? I remember this as the old Grand Hotel from the days before the Wall came down, you know. I took a chance and asked the desk. It's good to see you again."

He must have followed me from the memorial service. Employing his skills of stalking and surveillance from the good old days.

"Just thought you'd come into town for a few days, maybe catch a funeral?"

Komarek let out an odd little sigh of resignation. He held out his hands as if I was checking him for a concealed weapon. "You know, Silvia and I, we became involved. It was those paintings that brought us together. I wanted to go to the funeral. I took a taxi to the church but… I suppose I lost my courage. I didn't know if I would be welcome. Then when I saw you leave, I wanted to approach you but again… now that I've had a couple of drinks, I can be brave."

"Brave about what? To speak to me? I'm nobody, Ladislav. If you want to give anyone your condolences, speak to her son."

"She spoke of him to me, you know. She kept a strong connection, she said."

"Yes. With letters and photos. There's one of you and her in Prague. Tell me, when was that taken?"

"After Harry died."

"Ah, I see."

"I am back there now. No place like home, yes?"

"It must be very different for you."

He shrugged. "We have a man of the theatre in the castle. Joker trumping king. It's going as well as could be expected."

Ladislav provided me with a summary of his 'transition,' as he called it, that seemed mostly credible. With the change in government, he was deemed low enough on the org chart that he could retain a position as a 'humble civil servant' upon his return. He worked for all of five months in the Ministry of Transport, preparing files on transit projects for Brno and Prague. His superior was a woman a decade younger than him, with a PhD in philology, who knew nothing about how government worked. They quarreled and he could tell he wouldn't be long for his position. As luck would have it, however, a couple of his former colleagues had found positions in a new broadcasting company, flush with Moscow money. Things were going well now, he was a sales director who was seeing a lot of opportunity developing with the rise of a new Opposition party.

"Opposition. As in a return to how things were?"

"The past is past. Nothing could be the same. No. We need the right kind of entrepreneurs. Not artists playing at economic development."

"Your new clientele."

He made the universal gesture of money, his hand cupped as he rubbed three fingers together. "Builders. Job-makers, my friend. That's what I'm talking about."

"I see."

"You know why I came to meet you, don't you?"

"I have a feeling it might have something to do with economic development, yes."

"The paintings. You know I meant what I said all those years ago. I could find you buyers for the work you have. Now more than ever. There are lots of people starting to make some money. They're looking for safe investments."

"Yes, well there have been a couple of complications since we last spoke, unfortunately."

For a brief moment, in the way he knit his brow, I could sense how frustrating my reserve was. I had become a problem Ladislav needed to solve. But he composed himself quickly and gave me a gentle look. As if he was sure he could help me through any challenges.

"I would be surprised if there weren't complications, my friend. But I'm sure they could be solved."

"I've given half of what I inherited to George."

"What? That son of hers?" He laughed in falsetto. What a silly Englishman he was drinking with. "He has no culture. I don't know if he can even read."

"Nevertheless, it was an agreement I made with his mother. And to be honest, I feel quite guilty about it."

"Guilty. You? You would never have anything to be guilty about, my friend, trust me."

It struck me as an odd thing to say. How would Ladislav know about my intentions with anything? This gentleman had a particular gift for attempting compliments that didn't feel like them at all. But I wasn't going to show him I had thought anything about his quip.

"I feel guilty about it because you should know... my mother and I, back in England, we knew more about my father's business during the war than perhaps you do. The provenance of these paintings—"

"No, this is my point. It will not matter. Not with those who might be interested… the people I know. This has been my point all along. Maybe I never made myself clear."

"This would make us complicit in fraud."

"How can you know that? For all we both know, the provenance might be real for some, maybe not for others. Maybe there are some rightful owners, but that would have to go to court of law. That will not happen in Prague, my friend."

"I don't know how you could ensure such a thing."

"No?" He drained his glass, focused on some spot high on the wall behind him, as if he was suddenly making a complex calculation in his head. "Look, what's done is done with this son of Silvia's. I would be happy to invite him also, but I know, the people I could meet you with… sorry, meet with you… they would want to talk to you. An Englishman of culture."

"Invite him… invite us where?"

"Look, you have to take these paintings home. Before you do, before you have to pay the customs on them, explain why you have all these… come to Prague. If you meet who I bring you to and you don't want to sell, that's fine. Nothing lost. Except maybe you have a few good nights in my city as my guest. You see it like no foreigner can see it, you understand me?"

"I think I understand you, yes."

"Then you go back home. Maybe you forget I ever offered. Forget we ever met."

"I don't know if that would be possible, Mr. Komarek."

"No?" He signaled to the waiter, making a circle in the air with his stubby index finger to indicate another round. "I think that's where you're wrong. Anything is possible."

And as you can imagine, I wanted to believe him. Looking back on this all now, I'd prefer to call it willed naïveté. Not complicity.

28.

1/18/94

The only explanation I have for what occurred once I began selling those paintings is... well... freedom, and my inability to manage it wisely. I was a man well into middle age, with a good but not stellar career with Her Majesty's Diplomatic Service. I had seen the world—as much as what was available to me, anyway. I was not rich but I could look forward to a reasonable pension when I retired. And if it was not deep, passionate love that kept Eri and I together, there was still devotion, affection, and fondness, which were all sensible alternatives to the tailspins that more than a few of my former colleagues and boyhood friends had gone into   once they were past fifty. When I had heard of the former prefect who ended up a haunted, destitute regular at a 'singles bar' off Patpong Road in Bangkok, or of the poet, son of a viscount, who had been bankrupted by his love of Moroccan boys, I would chuckle along with whoever was sharing the gossip, shake my head, intone the there-but-for-the-grace-of-gods with all the self-assurance required on such occasions. But the prospect of sudden riches, with no accountability required for how it was obtained or spent, felt more like divine grace than the orderly life of propriety and rule-following, with no access to authentic feeling, that the last quarter of my life promised.

Yes, this sudden need for authenticity. I should have reflected on that, really, asked myself what it was about. I was motivated either by the price or the promise of freedom, I am still not sure which.

Dirty money. Behind every fortune, a crime. The sensible and wise version of me still sent me alerts with these phrases that would pop into my head as I contemplated what Ladislav Komarek had dangled in front of me, with the offer of him playing middleman with this black market inheritance. It was all fairly simple, he said: if I were to meet him in Prague with the paintings, he would introduce me to an art dealer friend, Antonin Masny, who had opened up his shop in the old Jewish quarter of the city. Komarek encouraged me to bring all the documentation I had on the provenance of the work. "Much could be validated easily," he assured me, and "high market prices" were possible through his network of "entrepreneurs and connoisseurs" who had the resources and ambition to amass collections that would soon rival what one would find in private collections in New York or Paris.

"You must understand, a lot of art came back to Moscow when the Red Army retreated. And many families had treasures they could not sell. Now they can, and there are people I know who are very interested... very interested." My timing, he said, could not be better. "Just come for two or three days. See for yourself!"

"I wonder... should I contact George and let him know about this?"

"Silvia's son?" Komarek looked like he had bitten into a lemon. "The labourer? He would not have a clue. You're a man of culture, Mr. Hepworth. Mr. Antonin Masny and you will get along well."

Perhaps because I had nothing to lose, I was bold enough to be direct with him. "And what would you gain from this?"

"Nothing, my friend. Just a finder's fee for each sale. All I would ask."

"Five percent?"

He recrossed his legs, gave his wine glass a pensive look. "Let's say ten. But you will see my value. With the money you make, you hardly notice, believe me."

"I don't know..."

"Give me three days in Prague. Have you ever been to my city?"

"It was not a posting made available to me."

"You see? There is so much you do not know." He leaned forward, put a hand on my shoulder. "I'm going to tell you something. From the first time I met you, here when the Wall was still up, I said to myself, here is a good man. Whatever his father might have done, he is without guilt."

"I'm not sure what your point is."

"This is what I say to friends who want to hunt down the files the government kept on them: you will never know everything about the past. But you can live in the present the best you can. You know what I'm saying?"

"I think you're telling me to relax, accept this invitation, and make some money."

"Just three days. Give my city a weekend. Then you decide."

We had another drink together, and Komarek spoke of Prague, how it was still for him "a magical place." There was really only one bombing raid of significance during the war, and because so much of the city was still standing when the Communists took it over, they couldn't do much to make it as ugly as any other massive reconstruction project in the Soviet bloc. The castle, the Charles bridge, the old town square... all still as beautiful as they were centuries ago. "You're a man who observes, who understands beauty, I can tell." It would be a shame if I missed seeing it now because who knew what would happen, now that McDonalds and Benetton and all the other western crap they warned everyone about was opening up.

"You think it's going to change?"

"Of course. I wouldn't want to go back to the old days but we're losing our innocence fast. This is a moment when the people with money still have a bit of taste, you understand? There is a good market for what you have."

He spoke of his family as a typical example. His father was a structural engineer and a serious musician, a pianist who studied the work of Janacek closely, along with Schoenberg and Bartok. "Behind closed doors. We all knew the Soviets were vulgar. You kept your head down... the culture was like samizdat. But now, if my father was still alive, the first thing I would take him to would be a Janacek opera, at the old Smetana Theatre he loved. My father didn't step inside that building for thirty years."

Such talk of fathers and cultural treasures did its work on me, along with the wine. The next morning my mind was made up, a point of clarity amid the fog of my hangover. I was going to take Komarek up on his offer.

After calling into work and telling them I'd need another week of my banked holidays, I called Eri. I just figured she would understand there was more business with my father's estate to attend to, but I wanted to dangle the opportunity of us seeing Prague together for a few days as some consolation for my remoteness. And so I broached the topic by speaking of "a couple of paintings I didn't know my father had," and of Komarek's "kind offer" to connect me with a dealer in Prague.

"I don't know this Komarek person, Nicholas. You have all these strange friends now."

"He was a friend of Silvia Stanciu, not me."

"Ah. Of course."

Silence on the phone. Which I shouldn't have gotten so peevish about, I suppose.

"You're not still on about that."

"Actually, I don't really think about it. You know, for a month I have told you about my mother's situation. You call me but you don't even ask."

"I'm so sorry. You're right. How is she?"

"She is not better. She is getting worse."

"How much worse?"

"The doctor mentioned chemotherapy. There are still many tests. She just has my father. And he is not managing this well."

"You should be with her."

"How will that be possible? You're the one traveling and spending all our money."

"We'll make this a priority."

"Meaning we put another trip on credit and go into debt?"

"Let's talk about it when I get home."

I realized that there was no way I could speak of her coming to join me in Prague without sounding like I was trivializing what she was going through. And perhaps this says everything about my own blind spot, but my first thought was that this trip to Prague was only that much more important. The sale of just one of these paintings would ensure she could go back to Japan and stay for as long as she liked without worrying about money.

"You should be careful with these people, Nicholas. I didn't trust that Silvia Stanciu. The people she knew… I wouldn't trust her friends either if I were you."

"I'll be back on Monday night. We'll be playing back at the club on Tuesday. It will take your mind off things."

"Why would I want to do that?"

I had no answer for her. Soon after I hung up and put my thoughts to what I could sell to give her the opportunity to go home. I left Berlin convincing myself I was doing the right thing. At one point during our drunken evening in Berlin, Komarek spoke of Prague's shady history as a European capital for charlatans, and that alchemists would set up shop "with thriving business." Well, I was going to transform the stolen treasures of my father's trade into real gold, carrying on the tradition.

Over the next few days I was at the mercy of Ladislav's hospitality. He picked me up in my hotel near the Vltava, a former nurse's college that still had a colourless, institutional feel to it, despite the sleek new furnishings of zinc and blonde wood. I was eager to get out walking, see the sights he promised over our drinks in Berlin.

As he drove us into the old Jewish quarter of the city, I thought he might have been taking me to see Antonin Masny. But no, that was for the next day. "First, you need to see the real city, get some perspective."

I know, you can probably already predict what that meant for Ladislav and I. He did this same kind of tour for visiting Russian "investors" of the broadcasting company he was working for, and I suppose he presumed I'd have the same interests. An American-style steakhouse had just opened up, so we started there, and then we got into a taxi and went to a series of clubs over a labyrinthine few blocks near the Mala Strana district. I could imagine the ghost of Harry over my shoulder, telling me that now I was seeing something like the Berlin that turned his head as a young man, before the Nazis cracked down on all the vice they practiced among friends at private parties. The first two places we went to were much like bad singles bars for business travelers, and I just took it on face value that the women Ladislav introduced me to really were in 'computer school' or studying fashion design. As the night progressed though, the transactional nature of the conversations was far more explicit.

I remember a woman in a fluorescent green lycra bikini, dancing in a cage that seemed in no way a playful, nostalgic nod to the sixties—no, the cage was brand new, made of old iron. Where would one get a human cage made in Prague? It was not a question for which I really wanted to find out the answer.

I made it back to my hotel with my head spinning, as soon as my head hit the pillow. But the nausea and the wave of sweat on my brow, after I vomited into the toilet, filled me with an oceanic sense of calm I hadn't felt in years. All the loud music that was thumping in my eardrums was gone, and there was this inner peace, this silence. I had survived the night, there was no woman that I paid for in my bed, my credit cards were in my wallet, and the paintings were still safely in the large vault of the hotel on the main floor. I felt confident I could handle Komarek's world and whatever I would face in the morning when we would finally meet Masny.

Atelier Masny occupied half a block on an old city square, across from a humble looking church that was back in the God business. Pre-loved faith and estate merchandise. This was the cultural renaissance, I suppose. From the display windows I could see Masny was selling antiques, family heirlooms, virtually anything of value families had hidden away during the years of Occupation.

There was something elfin about Masny, even though he was as broad and thick-limbed as a bouncer in one of Komarek's favourite clubs. His greying blonde hair was swept boyishly over his brow and he had pure white sideburns that must have given him a rakish air in the seventies. He greeted us in a three-piece suit of oatmeal-coloured tweed, his eyes pinching to focus on me through his small, wire-rimmed glasses. "Ah! Mr. Hepworth. Come in, come in! All the things I heard about you and your famous treasures."

"Well thank you! Famous?"

"Famous to Ladislav and I, yes?" He winked at Komarek, who seemed to wince in reply.

Masny led us into a backroom, sternly directing a sullen young woman behind the counter in Czech while gesturing to his wristwatch. He opened the door of an office that had a coffee table and a small tray with little discs of blood sausage and mayonnaise on crackers. I ate one and I wanted to gag but I just slowly masticated it into submission and washed it down with the espresso the young woman behind the counter hurriedly brought in.

Komarek and Masny sounded like they were already bartering about the work, all I had to contribute to the conversations was the stapled copy of the papers that provided the details about the provenance of each painting. Komarek brusquely gestured for me to produce it for Masny.

"Thank you, we are very happy you have come to us," Masny said.

"He says he's very happy you're here," Komarek said, as if he'd spoken in Czech rather than English. "And he's sure there are many buyers. International clientele. Germany, Poland."

"Saudi Arabia," Masny added, with a sage nod. "The world is coming here now."

"He says there are so many paintings people have from the war. Maybe they were bought, maybe they weren't, but it doesn't matter. There are buyers now. The market is growing. Have another piece of this sausage from a local farm. Good for your stomach after last night, eh?"

I choked down another, and by the end of our meeting, I had consigned one painting we were all sure was a Modena and another that was attributed to Otto Dix. Masny shook hands with me like I married his daughter. Yes, it was she who was working behind the counter.

A few days later, I had enough money from a wired sale in my new private account that Eri and I could have commuted to Japan every weekend for a year. The anonymity I had throughout the process, along with the mystery about who was dealing with Masny, only made all of this more compelling.

And yes, addictive. I loved the rush I felt with the sudden fortune a sale promised. Which should have been a warning sign for me.

What I had more difficulty admitting to myself was my attraction to the women in Prague. They seemed so frank and direct, with none of the reserve and shyness that once charmed me about Eri. Maybe it was just their cynicism about how everything was transactional, or how wryly they would banter with Ladislav and I that first night of my visit, but I suddenly wanted to appear more sophisticated in their presence, and to artfully gloss over any of the details of my twee existence back in Maida Vale.

And I realized some of this attraction did indeed stem from my first meeting with Silvia Stanciu. Eri was far more intuitive than I gave her credit for being. I'm not saying I ever would have done anything about that initial attraction; I was repelled by how strange and almost incestuous that would be. Yet I realize now that Komarek had sensed it as well. The tour of Mala Strana he took me on was his way of getting a better understanding of my vulnerability.

With the opening of my private account, I suppose I gave myself license to have a secret life. It was my intention, once I retrieved my share of the paintings Harry left in my name, to finally tell Eri all about them, to speak of the past with a candor not even my mother, with her avowed contempt for Harry, could manage. I'd explain the complicated issues of provenance, why it would not be so easy to put this work on the market. But with that first sale of the Modena, and the sale of the Dix likely in a matter of days, I was now implicated in a scheme I felt guilty about—but not enough to back out of it.

I flew back to London a half a day earlier with the paintings—undeclared—in a trunk I bought in Masny's shop, and then I locked them away in a storage space in Bermondsey. All Eri needed to know about was the money, and I would lie and say it was from savings no one knew Harry had.

Eri hardly asked about it, anyway. She was sullen and distracted through our first dinner together, providing me with terse, one-sentence answers to my efforts at conversation. I had taken her to her favourite sushi restaurant, the one she said was as good as those 'back home,' as a way to position my gift of a trip to be with her mother, but it was hard to break through this icy layer of detachment that had formed since my return.

"Any change in your mother's condition?"

She shook her head as her chopsticks hovered over the last piece of kappamaki. "There is a Reiki specialist in the north... up in Hokkaido prefecture. He has treated other people with cancers from Nagasaki. It is energy healing, you know? It's not a treatment government covers."

"No, it sounds experimental."

"But with good results. My father says he can take her there. He might sell the car to pay for her therapy. He rarely uses it anyway."

"He doesn't have to do that."

"What do you mean?"

"We could pay."

"How? With that money from your father?"

This was the moment when I could have explained it all to her. And yet, all I said was something vague like, "he had many things from the war years that were of considerable value." I was determined to conceal the fortune that was available to us with a few discreet phone calls and meetings among my new friends.

"I don't know what to make of your secrets, Nicholas."

"I just thought it would be a pleasant surprise. I have no need to hide anything from you."

It was an answer that she seemed to accept. As I took her hand in mine across the table, she allowed herself a smile, but she could not look into my eyes. "So tell me about this castle in Prague that you mentioned on the phone. It sounds like something from Disneyland."

Over the next few days, her concern over her mother's condition had worn away at her reserves of pride and disaffection. There was a compelling argument I was making with my offer: if my head was turned by all that I discovered with that first, fateful trip to Berlin, why would I be so focused on what she was going through? Even I believed in my best intentions. She finally consented to accepting the plane fare, and began to make her travel arrangements.

I suppose I thought this would also bring us together, but since my return we hadn't even had sex. We were living like a couple of ageing war orphans brought together in our quaint little foreign home, with our dress-up life of clubby English propriety, our childhood photos safely stored away in biscuit tins. Upon my return, our daily routines took on the same, slightly absurd decorum of our doubles court play. The world had forced a change in us, from that moment we had watched the Wall coming down, and the two of us really didn't know how to change with it. Even if the sad ordeal that was unfolding for her back at home hadn't happened, I doubt we could have managed any final understanding of freedom—freedom from the conception of ourselves as exiles, finally even distanced from each other.

My final understanding of how much our relationship was on a precipice came when we began speaking of her work. I had asked her if she had any problem getting the time off with the Cultural Centre to fly home.

"I didn't ask for time off. I quit. It is not a real job. It is for a person half in one place and half in another. Or someone whose future has passed, you know?"

"But I thought you got on well with them all there."

"Of course I did. I'm easy to get along with, aren't I?"

I laughed nervously. She sounded resigned, weary of papering over her solitude.

"Well you can get something else when you return."

"Yes. We can see when that happens."

I squeezed her hand but she gently pulled it away. I knew in that moment her 'when' really meant 'if'.

And an odd memory of time in Prague came to me, like a sudden flash. Under the glass counter in Masny's shop, there was a display of estate jewelry. And among old rings and watches was a necklace with a familiar pendant: a Cartier panther, just like Silvia's from the photos of her stay with George and Ileana.

It was just a few weeks later, and the phone calls from Eri, back in Tokyo, were not encouraging. She and her father were doing all they could to manage the situation with her mother, but they both feared the cancer's return was now untreatable.

"More than anything right now, my mother and I worry about my father."

"Your father? I don't understand."

"Without her... he is lost."

"Did the therapist in Hokkaido help at all?"

"My mother is still there in Noboribetsu, a village on the island. She believes the therapy is working and that Matusumoto-san might be a healer but she doesn't know... my father is taking out a loan. You see, it's not covered by health insurance."

"No, no, no. That's not right."

"It will be fine. He'll manage. There is no choice."

I didn't want to argue with her but I was determined to prove that I could fix or somehow alter the terms of loss, all those thousands of miles away. And of course I wanted us to be together again. Yet everything she was saying told me she wanted to be the one who took full responsibility for managing this family 'issue' that was slowly moving towards tragedy. I think she liked the closure; she was the only child who ran away from her family but had now returned. To prove her loyalty and her love. And here I was, determined to insert myself in her story, unaware that I was not welcome in it.

"Do you have a sense of when you might come back?"

"You mean, to England?"

What else could I have meant? But she interpreted this as a question about her return to me. As if our relationship only existed within the borders of this bloody island. Out of sight, out of mind.

"It is so hard to say, Nicholas."

"Yes. I suppose it must be impossible to know right now."

"We need a dog."

"Pardon?"

"You remember the junk shop in Bath? We went in and there was a mug I liked on a shelf near the door. A Winston."

"Ah, you mean that old porcelain one. The English bulldog."

"Can we get one like that? A real one, I mean."

"The mug might be easier to manage."

"We can call him Winston."

"Well… they're a lot of work."

I was providing her with my voice of experience, and maybe she was reassuring me we would be together again. I had never had a dog. My mother was partial to cats and my stepfather Basil put up no resistance when she wanted one. I remember two sleek little Egyptians over the years. Watchful, fiercely independent night predators. They spooked me.

"I want something to care for. I'm realizing this is important to me."

"We can look into it when you're back. Of course."

"You're a kind man, Nicholas. You have always been kind."

She hung up with those last words. It felt like she had put me, like an old photograph, into a gilt-edged frame on a shelf. The memory of the nice man she lived with, her tennis partner with no second serve, right there beside a 'Winston.'

Once I received the okay for more time off, my director-general clearly exasperated, I slept-walked through the next few days at work. It was clear to everyone in my section that my mind was elsewhere. I filed briefing notes for a conference on refugees with a memorandum draft on an international cricket tournament, much to my embarrassment. I felt my marriage, my whole future back in this imagined home was at risk. As much as the situation with Eri's mother was serious, it felt like it wasn't the precipitating event that had caused our separation. It was this mysterious secret life that Eri associated with Silvia Stanciu. That I had gone to Silvia's funeral, ostensibly to settle my father's estate, was evidence of a greater bond, a secret life.

On a Sunday night I traveled out to the storage facility in Bermondsey. I stopped at a news agent's and picked up a pack of Player's cigarettes. I hadn't smoked in at least twenty years—since my posting in Bangkok. Yet there was something about this trip that required the feeling that smoking gave me: a sharpening of reflection.

The locker where I had kept the paintings was like an old railcar. The same boxy construction, the thin sheets of aluminum riveted on a frame and then spray painted a matte green. I'm talking about the flimsiest materials possible, identikit cubes snapped together on land that had to be among the cheapest spots in London. Triple the price per square foot, calculate the monthly rental fees you charge from that. Then be prepared to do a roaring business from those who've come down in the world and don't want to lose everything just yet, or those who have goods and possessions they'd prefer to conceal from the world. I was beginning to feel more like the former rather than the latter kind of customer, given how much I could sense my marriage disintegrating.

My sole precaution regarding the value of what I was concealing was to put two locks on the door: a combination and a padlock. Both a sign of guilt and a cry for help. There was a brief, flustering moment when I wasn't sure I had written the right numbers down on the scrap of paper in my wallet, but no, in my nervousness, I had spun the dial one round too many between them. What was I so jittery about?

It was because of the decision I was about to make. I snapped on the switch for the one naked light bulb, my breath was already smoke before I lit up and felt my heart-beat accelerate. This was a terrible place to store paintings, despite me wrapping each one in old blankets I had scrounged from a Salvation Army in Rotherhithe. It was all a shoddy bit of business, like the work of some criminal. Which is how the ownership of all this work made me feel. Questionable provenance, questionable sales. Dirty money.

How could I tell anyone about all this? I examined the paintings carefully, one by one. I was keeping peacocks in a chicken coop. The next one that I was going to sell had to be special, had to represent a sacrifice. This would be proof of the authenticity of my love.

When I got back home I called Ladislav Komarek, despite how late it was in Prague. I was making an impulsive decision, and I knew I would sound desperate. The pathetic Englishman.

"Ladislav, your friend Mr. Masny. I think I might have another to sell for him. But I need to do it fast. And to get top-dollar. This is why I need your help."

I heard him exhale, the faint sound of a string section evoking the first light of day in a forest, a gentle stirring to life. He was either watching television or playing his old Deutsche Grammophon records too late at night for his neighbours. My insomniac finder for his ten percent fees.

"Yes. Okay. And what are you thinking?"

This was the first time I had ever detected irritation in his voice. I was a source of revenue who had not turned out to be quite so promising.

"The Card Cheat. That painting attributed to la Tour."

"I don't understand. When we last spoke I thought you were keeping that one for yourself."

"I need to get rid of it. I'm going to Japan and I could be there for some time."

"Okay, okay. Yes, I ribbed to you about your Madama Butterfly. So you're bringing the painting to Prague?"

"I will if you think you can find me a buyer quickly."

"I can talk to Masny. Can you give me two days? It will be hard for me to confirm anything until after the weekend."

"Please be as quick as you can. I'd like to make my travel arrangements by Wednesday of next week."

"It is the end of tourist season. There was ice on the river."

"Pardon?"

"Sorry. I mean a buyer might not be that easy. But I'll try."

"Let's speak on Monday again. Thank you, Mr. Komarek."

After I hung up, I threw away the cigarette package, angry with myself, and went to bed. This whole business… I had a faintly nauseous feeling and kept dreaming about being back at Harrow, unable to speak English. I wanted to call Eri but I would just sound unhinged as I tried to explain another flight to Prague without disclosing anything about these transactions.

I had my reservations about Komarek too, of course. Why didn't I just deal with Masny, cut out this middle-man entirely? Because Masny was cautious. I sensed he had already had a scrape or two with Interpol, given how he had scowled at the mention of police. There was no way that anything I could consign would be displayed openly, that was made plain in our initial meeting. And there appeared to be some working relationship he had with Komarek, some debt he owed the man or information that Komarek had on him, that kept him deferential, compliant, and assured that any risks would be managed. Me showing up alone would raise some questions; inevitably Komarek would be involved one way or another.

Besides, Komarek did bring value. He brought people with real money to the table, those looking to buy discreetly, even anonymously if possible. For the few who had found some mysterious bargains in the art market, going through Masny kept it all above board for getting the work out of the country again. The man had cultivated this persona as a simple shopkeeper even though, as it turned out, he was really running a kind of laundromat for ill-gotten gains that no one was inclined to ask questions about—least of all me. A shop like his really couldn't prosper so spectacularly without the Komareks of the new economy.

So it was this reasoning that had me back among Komarek's circle of instant friends and boon companions. It had not even been a week since my phone call to him before we were reunited, drinking Johnny Walker Black in the lounge of the Grand Mark, a former baroque palace. The two grey faced Russians in our company seemed to know it well from what they were already calling "the old days." Komarek introduced them as Mr. Kuzina and Mr. Mirzoev.

"I understand you work in real estate," I said. Komarek had briefed me before we sat down so I wasn't completely at a loss among these two, dressed like they had spent the day golfing rather than perusing the art in the back of Masny's shop.

"Real estate and other investments," Kuzina said. He shot furtive looks at Mirzoev. Mirzoev, who had a tattooed hexagram on the knuckle of his index finger. He could not conceal a smirk. Then he shifted in his chair, deciding I was worth interrogating.

"Uh huh. So it's Hepworth, yes?" Mirzoev asked.

"That's right."

"You said your father was going to sell this la Tour when he was working in Berlin. What's a guy named Hepworth doing in Berlin during the war?"

"His name was Maes, actually."

"German?"

"Belgian. It's a long story."

"We need to know this is authentic, I hope you understand," Kuzina was striking a conciliatory tone, as if he was apologizing for Mirzoev's bluntness. Drinking black coffee at seven in the evening, his doughy thigh was bobbing under the table. He had yet to look directly at me; he was addressing Komarek.

"I see. I think that's understandable," I said.

"Do you?" Mirzoev leaned forward, rounding his thick shoulders. "Your old man prob'ly picked this up for a song if he paid anything at all."

"The provenance states it was a fair price."

"You can ask my friend here about that." Kuzina gestured with a nod to Mirzoev. "We were at a private sale in Moscow. I don't think there was one painting we looked at that actually had real papers."

"And yet you bought a lot, Ladislav tells me." I looked over at Komarek but he would not meet my gaze. He was stabbing a maraschino cherry with the little plastic sword in his drink.

"We got other sources we can cross-reference."

"So did you check this one with your... other sources?"

"No." Mirzoev reclined again, exhaling sharply through his nose like an old horse. "Because I'm trusting you. Because Ladislav says you're a good man, and Ladislav, he has my trust. He has our trust. He proved it in Moscow."

Kuzina raised his coffee cup with a doleful look as if he was toasting Komarek, and Mirzoev started to laugh. Quite a comedy team.

"Look…" I was about to speak about my mother, the grandparents I never got a chance to know, the valuables that I was told they too had to sacrifice. But it felt beneath my dignity… my family's dignity. I had nothing to prove. "If you have reservations, I can understand that. But I'm not about to sell for less just because you have doubts about the provenance. I didn't get on a plane and come all the way here with this painting to fuck about."

I will probably never forget the way Mirzoev glared at me. He wanted to see right into my soul. I was ready for it, and met his gaze directly. Then he leaned forward once again, composed himself like the solicitor I was assured he was. "The Card Cheat. I like the name. That's what la Tour called it originally?"

And so we had a deal.

I made a significant amount of money. As did Komarek, incidentally. By the time I was on my flight back to London, my portion was safely in my Swiss account, the one Eri had no idea I had opened. When I looked at our joint account I realized she had withdrawn quite a bit over the last four weeks she was in Japan. We were both soon going to need what the sale provided, despite the infusion of my vacation pay.

30.

01 / 24 / 94

On our phone calls, Eri sounded resigned and hollowed-out by her efforts to make her mother feel better again. She had returned to Noboribetsu for 'intensive treatment.' And Eri had accompanied her. She was apologetic, stating that she did not know what else she could do. Of course she argued about me traveling to see her, but after about fifteen minutes of bickering about it, she finally relented. She was so forcefully against my trip initially that I began to wonder whether she had met another man, or rekindled the romance she once had with her boyfriend in university—Kenji the schoolteacher, who still sent her a birthday card each year. I resisted my urge to tell her about how I was about to solve this problem of her mother's care that was consuming her and her father, but only because I wanted to see her face and hold her when I would reassure her that she had the means to care for her mother.

I know, throughout this whole episode, I have yet to refer to her parents, Masa and Kyoko, as my in-laws. The simple truth of it is that they never made me feel remotely like a family member. I was the 'gaijin'—read foreigner—whose motives were suspect in dating their daughter initially. Eri explained their coldness to me as a result of their feeling ashamed that their English was so bad. Yet when I tried to speak Japanese to them, they would answer with the little English they had, smiling solicitously, while they relied on Eri to translate anything more important than small talk and niceties. Eri explained it away that they were both 'country people' from Nagasaki—yet they had lived in their small apartment in the middle of Tokyo for more than forty years. I did not have high hopes that my visit and my 'surprise' were going to change much. As always, my focus was on Eri herself.

After an evening with Masa, where we dined on sushi in Ginza and spoke of his retirement plans and his golf game, I felt that he, too, only reluctantly gave me his blessing to travel and reunite with Eri. He said that Kyoko had lost so much weight that she would be embarrassed in my presence. I don't think Masa really believed me when I said I would never be so superficial as to make her feel uncomfortable about her illness. That allowed him to revert to what I recalled as his stock phrase to close off all further conversation with me: "you don't understand, we Japanese have shame about sickness. We see such things differently." I could only accept this, of course. He shook my hand and wished me good luck as we went in different directions in Ginza station at the end of the evening.

Even though I was taking the bullet train in the morning, I had a two-day journey ahead of me. The route would take me to Aomori, where I would then ferry over to Hakodate, an old port city in Hokkaido, and then travel another three hours to the spa town where this 'Matsumoto-san,' the Reiki therapist, had his own private compound for his patients. As soon as I got on for my first leg, where each car was packed like a London bus on New Year's Eve, I felt peevish and resentful about how, given all the money I had and was willing to spend, I was subjected to such discomfort. And so I began to drink. Hours of paddy fields, used car lots, prefab office buildings clumped around train stations like jumbles of building blocks… they flickered past like objects captured on an unspooled film, held up to the hazy light of my fading sobriety. I slumped into a fitful sleep at last, trying to dream away my intimations that this was all a bad idea.

Because it was a journey to the end of my marriage.

I remember staring out into the dark choppy waters, a stretch of ocean cold as winter, and squinting to see the outline of Hakodate, like a jagged zipper splayed open on a dusky blue horizon. I looked down into the churning waves below the deck, closed my eyes as I felt a swoon of vertigo. What was happening to my nerve?

Once I arrived and exited the port, there were black trucks, festooned with the banners of the right wing nationalists in the city square, loudspeakers blaring wartime music, as old veterans croaked out their rants about the sovereignty of the Kuril Islands. I could make out, through my faulty attempt at translation, words that I was sure meant *beware the foreigner*. It was easy to think some old man at the bullhorn was talking about me.

I was filled with a sense of dread that I couldn't attribute to anything but how the landscape had been made strange. I remember getting to Noboribetsu, taking a walk up a mountain path, and the air smelling of sulfur from the volcano. Virtually every tree had a copper plaque at its base, as if this was all a theme park maintained by some watchful keepers artfully hidden from view. I followed schoolchildren down a narrow path through a canopy of pines to emerge in an alpine village where whole families, dressed in blue and white yukata robes and wooden clogs, were wandering from hot spring house to hot spring house. They regarded me as nothing but a puzzling interloper, unwashed and skulking like an old wolf that had come down from the forest to scavenge for his breakfast.

I found the bus that took me out to Matsumoto-san's little village—a scattering of little cabins shrouded in pines and bordered by a chain-link fence. The smell of sulfur in the air seemed even stronger. I got off at the nearest stop to the entrance and approached, unsure if I would be allowed in, despite Eri's reassurance that she had cleared it with Matsumoto-san's 'people.' A chubby woman in a powder blue tracksuit met me at the front gate, smiling like Buddha.

"You have come at a good time. I know she and her mother are both at the ikebana class, in the main cabin. Come with me."

I followed her along a wood-chipped path, passing a small group of senior citizens, all smiling serenely, as they marched along in sensible hiking gear. A few nodded to me, welcoming the stranger.

Near the back of this little phalanx was a woman with a shaved head, whose chamois shirt and tweed trousers looked a couple of sizes too big for her. My host sensed my gaze lingering on this woman.

"We have many guests from Nagasaki, like Araki-san, your…"

"My mother-in-law, yes."

"They showed no symptoms when they were children, after the war. But now it appears. The cancer."

"Everyone looks well cared-for and happy. All you are doing must help, I'm sure." I have a talent for this kind of diplomacy. I didn't really believe this could be helping at all.

"The treatment is a way to unblock the natural healing properties in the body. We all have this power within us, you know. The power to transform ourselves."

"We just have to find the right way," I said. I was thinking *we just have to find the money.*

"Hai… yes… see, you understand already!"

I first saw Eri and her mother through the window. They were mooning over some long-   stemmed irises and a frond of pine. 'A creation with a northern theme' was written on a chalkboard behind them in kanji. As I entered, Eri came to me, embraced me stiffly, and whispered in my ear that I should not speak too loudly.

I approached Kyoko-san, her mother, who gently took my hand. Her hair was so white it looked bleached, and it was just starting to soften from bristles, finally growing out after it was shaved down to her scalp. With a mischievous look she guided my hand to feel the texture, acknowledging where my look of concern had found a point of focus. See? I'm not ashamed of such change, she seemed to be telling me. We did not speak.

I looked over at Eri, but she would not meet my gaze. She was staring down at her hands, as if she was frustrated by their uselessness, her inability to fix any of this.

Well here I am, ready to take all your cares away. I projected confidence. This was a triumphant entrance after all. A victory over the force of obligation she was bending to, as if the weight of tragedy had finally tethered her to the identity that fulfilled her.

I waited until we were alone on a walk of the grounds after dinner before I shared with her the news about the money, the transfer I had made from my secret account before I got on the bullet train. No matter how much time her mother still had, she could stay up here as long as she liked. She let go of my hand, turned from me and shook her head.

"No, Nicholas. This is not right. You can't do this."

"What do you mean? Of course I can. This is our money and this is how it can best be spent."

"No. It's not our money. It's your money. Your inheritance. It is what is left of your father."

"A father I never really knew."

"That is why it is important that you keep it. Keep it for yourself. You might need it. If this trip has made me think about anything, it is how change can come so quickly. You have no way to prepare."

That she said 'you' rather than 'we' was not some imprecision, a result of her not speaking much English for a while. No, she was using her words with a surgeon's knife.

"But this is how I want to spend it. For us."

"Well, it is us that we should talk about. Nicholas, I feel like I am needed here. And despite what is happening, I feel a happiness inside me. One I haven't felt for years."

"What are you telling me?"

"I'm telling you that I must stay here in Japan for a while. To make sure my father is all right, after this. He has no one else."

"You feel obligated."

"No. It's more than that. I want to. I'm saying I don't know when I will return to England. Or if."

"I can't just up stakes and come back here, Eri. My work, our home..."

"I would not ask you to. I won't. It is your home, Nicholas. Not mine. I had hoped to put this all in a letter, when my thoughts were clear. But here you are."

I felt a rage inside me, a desire to fight and save what was slipping away from me. How could she be so self-involved that she could not appreciate my generosity, all that I was doing to bring us together? Maybe a younger me would have acted on that impulse and let his temper get the best of him. Put it down to wisdom, or just a weariness I could finally allow myself, but I said nothing more in response than "I understand."

These words were all she needed to embrace me one last time. We held each other, in that stretch of artificial forest, until the full weight of our separation pulled us apart. In little more than forty-eight hours I was on a plane, returning to London, to make of my new solitude something like a real home at last.

I still cannot regret how the money from that painting was eventually spent. I like to think Harry would have approved. Once I had transferred the funds into our joint account, it was only a matter of weeks before we closed it and she kept that money. With our separation, neither of us could be brave enough to say it was permanent. You could say it was like a tribute paid to keep that possibility open.

At the time I did not really have the luxury of such reflection though. For when I returned to our little house, the little red light on our answering machine was flashing angrily. This was strange—nobody ever called us! I hurried to it, thinking it must be Eri, ready to tell me she had made a terrible mistake and that she was getting on the next plane.

As I clumsily stabbed at the numbers on the touch-pad, my more jaded self considered another possibility. Maybe she was just calling to say her mother's condition had worsened, and she had left the compound run by the quack doctor and returned to Tokyo. I was preparing myself to be the soul of empathy.

But it was not Eri at all. It was George, Silvia Stanciu's son.

"Mr. Nicholas, I'm calling for your help. Neighbours are here but I can tell them little. The paintings that Ileana kept in the back garage, they've been stolen. All of them. All that fortune. It's eleven and I'm sorry it's late. Please call when you can, as soon as you can."

I listened to the time log again. The call was from three days ago. I know I audibly groaned, feeling a mix of disappointment with myself and… yes… a very real sense of fear. Someone had to know of George's paintings, and it was likely they knew of mine, and where they were concealed.

I dialed the numbers he'd recited and Ileana answered. She heard my apologies and with her soft, soothing voice, told me it was all right. "We figured you must be away. Otherwise you would call. We know you're a good person. A friend."

"I can help. I'll come right over if you like."

"Thank you, Nicholas, that would be good of you."

I left my bags unpacked and hurried out the door. Unsure what I could do, of course, but there had to be something… anything.

252

31.

1 / 29 / 94

Answers. There was so much about my father's life that I preferred not to know about, it seems. This was partly my mother's doing. If she could have erased the first six or seven years of my life from my stubborn memory, I know she would have. From her insistence that we speak English in the house, and that I become her schoolboy instructor, to her refusal to cook anything but bland English recipes from the magazines, our assimilation was like a performance that had to be memorized. She could not understand why I couldn't take to it like the obsessive she was, as if she was constantly afraid of breaking character. I knew her love and affection was conditional upon how well I lived my part. To ask her of what became of the man named Harry Maes, or to remark how, say, the rubber of my rain boots smelled like the rubber of the gas mask I remembered wearing, was to risk a sharp turn in her mood, a stern rebuke that ensured that everything I said or did was subject to harsh scrutiny until her mood passed once again. My learned incuriousness had exacted its own, considerable costs, and I felt in some ways responsible for the theft of the paintings and the trauma of its violation that George and Ileana Stanciu were feeling. Within five minutes of my visiting them, George had broken down, with his head in his hands, asking-not-asking why he was so cursed. I needed to take responsibility, find out what I could for their sake and my own.

"I never should have stored them outside the house. Garage was temporary but I should not have put them there, either. They should have stayed close to our bedroom. Then the coward who comes in the night would have to face me."

"Did you sense anyone watching you over the last few weeks… since your return from Berlin, I mean."

"I had a man watch me in the supermarket," Ileana said, standing at the doorway to the kitchen. George looked at her first with surprise that dissolved into acceptance, as if he was reminded of some distance between them he couldn't bridge.

"What kind of man?" He asked this as if he had no interest in the answer, staring into the polished wood veneer of the coffee table. Second hand. All their chances for new things, now taken from them.

"Not dangerous looking. That's why I did not think to say anything. A grey leather jacket, but fashionable… a flat cap like a taxi driver. But he did not look English."

"If English looks like anything," I said, as if it were a question. I was thinking aloud, really, but Ileana frowned, sure that I was discrediting her. I had caused this tragic situation to occur, not her impressionable mother-in-law, God rest her soul. I never should have entered their lives.

"I mean the shape of his mouth. Different coloured eyes. A mouth that speaks a different language."

"She is trying to remember," George said, as if he was apologizing for her. "It's like violence on you, this feeling."

I could only agree. The conversation dissolved soon after. I sensed Ileana would prefer it if I did not overstay my welcome.

This violence on them required that I approach my mother. Ever since my return from Japan with Eri, who she was to her had become who Sally was to me, the old woman who possessed ambassadorial functions for the imagined England we'd work so intently to realize, now that I was finally 'home.' Of course Sally was going to ask about Eri, wonder why she hadn't returned with me, and I was grateful for the lie we told each other about our separation being temporary, because I could tell it to others now and somehow will it to be a statement closer to the truth.

"Yes, that's very eastern, the duty to the parents," Sally said. She had a small collection of cultural observations he'd bring out when the occasion required, like the duty-free Napoleon brandy after dinner. "I worry that your trips abroad and all this business about your father have been needless distractions, Nicholas." She was wearing the string of pearls Eri and I bought for her in Tokyo, subtly declaring her preferred allegiance, given the news of our separation.

There was so much I could tell her about Silvia's version of Harry, and all that occurred over the last few years since my first trip to Berlin. At one point I even debated presenting her with one of the paintings I had, but such a gesture could have touched a nerve. I knew she considered everything about my grandfather Benjamin Ostriker and what he shared to be off-   limits. The temper that she worked so hard to control—that Dickie Knifton told me she was notorious for at the BBC—would be on full display, and we were at that stage of our relations where a rift could mean we never spoke again.

"You're probably right. I hope to settle the matters of his estate very soon. But I'm having trouble getting some straight answers from a few people."

"I heard that when they tore down the Wall, there were still buildings on the other side that hadn't been touched, streets with craters from the bombs," She sniffed, shaking his head. "It's a travesty. Their whole Paris of the Eastern Bloc was nothing but a…"

"Potemkin. Potemkin's village."

"I was going to say sham, but yes, Potemkin's village. No wonder you can't get any final will and testament."

"Indeed," I said. And then inquired about her garden, the climbing roses she was entering into competition, her trip to the Cotswolds coming up. I knew she would spend much of her time reflecting about how I probably destroyed my marriage once I had left, so there was no need to dwell on it while I was in the room. It was not like I could muster any credible defense.

Until I chose my moment to get the information I needed. I had offered to help her move a few boxes of old dinnerware into the boot of her car for the St. Crispin's church sale. I worked away and left Sally to her glass of sherry and her remote to change the channels on her TV. Maybe it was all her time at the BBC that did it, but she glared at the screen, as if each attempt at entertainment or information from the box was fated for extermination at her fingertips. I walked out to their carport. And I suddenly heard chaffinches in the trees, smelled old wood and wet earth, the first autumn chill in the air. It was now or never to ask her.

"I'm going to see Dickie this week. You know he has an East German contact, the one who got us the news of Harry's death."

"Dickie is not retired?"

"He might be. They're sending us all out to pasture these days."

"Well… you tell him he should take care of himself. None of us are getting any younger and he's probably working too hard."

That was all she was going to reveal about her and Dickie, that was clear. She had her chance and simply chose not to. What was past was past.

Just prior to leaving, we were sitting in the sun room with its screen door to the garden, and Sally was providing me with her counsel on how to save my marriage. It involved gifts, naturally enough, and a discussion with her investment advisor. She was not looking at me though. Her point of focus was somewhere out past the garden, past what she was comfortable discussing and remembering.

32.

01 / 31 / 94

I knew there was no sense putting it off. I'd have to speak to Dickie Knifton once more. I called him first.

"Yes, it's the old Stasi files that have been a help," he said. "Quite an archive, I must say. Bloody Mexican standoff. Horst telling on Klaus telling on Rudi."

"Zugzwang."

"That's it. Your German's still quite good, isn't it?"

"Never leaves you, fortunately or unfortunately."

"It's old Maes we're talking about, yes?"

"And his network, if there's anything."

"I will speak to Herr Lange, my old friend. I get faxes. Berlin area code. Every bloody week, it seems."

"This is so very much appreciated."

"I remember Basil said you were quite a tennis player when you were younger. Out in Maida Vale, aren't you?"

"My club's the Paddington, yes."

"Oh! I've played there. Men's C league."

I sensed an overture, so I invited Dickie out for a couple of sets and a pint afterwards. It would be better this way, I thought; he would not want to tell me anything among his esteemed colleagues at 54 Broadway. I expected he'd want to shred the faxes as soon as he could. I had told him enough in the call for him to realize this required him to do a little digging. Always willing to help, of course.

Dickie arrived early, in his rusting Vauxhall Cavalier. He sprung out lean as a whippet, in his pressed, ancient whites. He had shaved off his beard and looked younger. I gave him a wave from the clubhouse as I headed out to court five. There was a quick wave back with his Dunlop Maxply, two knee bends, and then he was ready. I heard that familiar punch of breath as he opened the can of tennis balls in his hand. "Hallo!" I liked the music in his voice and regretted not meeting him in person earlier when he first got the message about my father from his good friend Herr Lange.

And he turned out to be a fierce competitor on the court. He was one of those old vets who had mysterious reserves of vitality, whacking away at everything I could send over the net until I wearied and sent balls wide or long. Yet he hardly seemed winded at each change of side. He reduced my game to shreds, nimbly strode off to the clubhouse and then lit up his first of many hand-rolled cigarettes from a pouch in his racquet bag before his post-game Carlsberg was served.

"I must tell you, before Lange sent his tranche of files, he called me. Quite a lot with Herr Maes, he said. Many, many questions."

"That's exactly what I have, Dickie. I thank you for this."

"Not at all. Your stepfather Basil was very good to me. He never told you we were in Dunkirk together?"

"Ah. No, I had no idea."

"Hm. Well I could see that. It's hard to put all that in any kind of recognizable box, you know what I mean? As a memory."

Dickie took a pensive sip of his pint, swallowed noisily. He was looking out at a point past the wind-screened fence. A blank beyond. At last he turned his head and regarded me once more.

"This Silvia Stanciu. The Romanian woman he was living with. She was reporting on him, but of course there's a file on her too. She was on the game in Moscow and had a lot of clients in the Politburo. And diplomats. That's when she got on the KGB's radar. Imagine her black book and the stories she could have told. I mean my God."

"Silvia?"

"You met her, I take it."

"Yes. She was trying to emigrate. She had family here."

"Hard lines. She got mixed up with a bad lot. This Ladislav Komarek who was KGB. Feathering his nest for years with black market dealing. Even the rotten crew around Husak, they knew he was a liability in Moscow and packed him off to Berlin. I guess they thought that would keep him out of trouble. And this Silvia, it seems she followed him soon after."

"All of this in the Stasi files?"

Dickie nodded, tapping his cigarette against the edge of the ceramic ashtray in front of him. "From a chap who was tasked with watching Komarek. Fuhrmann. That may or may not be his real name. Anyway, there are reams of Komarek's meetings with Silvia, once he finds this stash of art. Did she tell you about that?"

There was a brief moment where I thought about disclosing what I had to Dickie. I could swear him to secrecy, sure. The man had built his life up after the war on his reputation for discretion. But whatever pact of secrecy I could attempt, it wouldn't hold with him and his old pals. Their secrets trumped everything.

"She might have mentioned. To be honest, I was more interested in her relationship with my father."

"You should have been. I mean she and Komarek plotted it all out, clearly. They were going to make him the source of all the paintings Komarek could fence. Then their world blew up when the Wall came down."

"You mean they were still seeing each other? Like, romantically?"

"From what Lange provided it was all pretty transactional. He was pressuring her into getting the old man to give up the paintings but he never would. And she was getting cold feet about pushing things any further. I think she had actually become sweet on your father. There's a tape from a conversation in Komarek's car late at night that…"

"That what?"

He stabbed out his cigarette. What he was about to say was like a bad toss for his serve. He thought better of following through. "The cause of death for your father. What did they say?"

"Silvia said cardiac arrest. You got the same report from Lange your contact, didn't you?"

"Yes. Until I saw these Stasi files, anyway. I'm not so sure anymore, given the rage in Komarek's voice. You can see the tape transcripts. I've got the whole load in my car. It's like a phonebook."

I finally realized the implications of what Dickie was telling me. I had a memory that I kept in my mind like a photo in a locket. It was of my last real day with my father, a late Saturday afternoon when he met me after my football game, walked me home, and told me that I would be moving away with my mother. Mr. Cluny was a decent fellow, we would still see each other, I was not to worry. He hugged me before the door to our apartment building, and he smelled of heavy cologne and cigarettes. He'd been drinking; this was his usual camouflage. Now I felt this deep ache of longing for him again. And there was nothing I could do.

"You think my father might have been murdered."

"My understanding is that Komarek had promised some of these paintings your father had to his Russian friends already. Then your father was a problem. Alleged suicide, wasn't it? The wrong medication, pills he never should have been given at the chemist's."

"Silvia said she missed him so much."

"I would wonder about her death too, my friend. All things considered. Of course I have nothing about it in the documents I have. But when you told me the circumstances of her attack."

"Komarek?"

"Probably his associates. These are ex-KGB. I mean they're gangsters but useful to the gangsters in charge over there. It's not like anyone is going to arrest them."

"You know I met him in Prague a little while after my father died and the Wall was down. I remember telling you there was just one Kokoschka. Well that's not quite true. I have quite a few of my father's paintings."

"You didn't deal with Komarek, did you? Are you mad?"

"I have not yet, no."

Yes, I lied. I could not tell him my relative safety was only assured because Komarek had found in me a willing source for his finder's fees. He and his good friend Masny, trading looks, knowing smiles in that first meeting we had. What a mark I was.

"You should take those paintings in. I would if I were you. You're risking your own safety. Seriously! You didn't tell anyone else?"

"I have not. Not even my mother. And I'm hoping you might not as well, Dickie."

He gave me a quick wave of his dismissal with his cigarette hand, mumbled into the collar of his tennis shirt. "Sally and Basil were always good to me. All these years."

"Yes. And I thank you for all you have provided me. Including the tennis lesson."

By the time we left the club it was dark. I sat in the passenger seat of the Vauxhall and he had all of the faxed pages in a plastic bag from Tesco. I pulled out the first page. Matthias Lange. Berlin area code indeed.

"There. With all that, I imagine you've got all you could ever want to know about Mr. Maes."

"The first pack of papers?"

"The one that Lange gave me in Berlin back in '89. All that Harry put in his hands, with a promise that he was working on a larger document. 'Paintings in his life,' he called it."

"You gave this to Basil?"

"Well, Basil and Sally. A photocopy. I mean it was my understanding they were once married, she and Harry. But they were for you, Nicholas. That's what Lange said. Instructions from Harry himself before he died."

"Ah. I see."

There was no way I could conceal my surprise. Or probably my anger as I made some babbling remarks about Basil's and Sally's carelessness. Maybe they had lost these pages, stowed them away in their garage and let them rot from neglect through all these winters since Harry's death. Or maybe she had burned them because of what he had to say about their marriage. I felt like George and Ileana. Robbed. Deprived of what was owed me from my parents' complicated story. And unable to disclose this crime to anyone.

"I'm sure they still have those pages. They'll turn up."

"You're probably right."

He patted my shoulder, called me a good lad as if I were twelve years old and not just these few years from retirement. I got out of his car and thanked him again. He tooted his horn as he drove off, playing the avuncular old pro right up to his exit.

Yet as I walked away I had this feeling. I caution myself as I write, wondering if I'm prone to revisionism right now. Still it just seemed that what happened after all this, with Christina Perretti finding me, telling me she had tracked me down from sources as far afield as Antonin Masny's shop, that it was inevitable. The whole web of connections, including Silvia's murder and the theft of this other la Tour, made sense, horribly enough. I would come to be grateful to Christina Perretti for who she introduced me to, but more on that in my next entry.

33.

02 / 07 / 94

Once I had spoken to Interpol, told Christina Perretti all that I have put down in these pages, I had gotten the call from this Ms. Rifka Solomon. I was at work, one of my last days before my retirement party. It was like a call from the police, not the foundation she said she was working for. I was sure she could sense my defensiveness. Yet even while we spoke, I was asking myself, *what do you have to feel guilty about? You've sold some paintings that you have inherited. This was your right!* I was self-conscious about what could be heard by my colleagues in the cubicles nearby so I affected a casual tone, as if this stranger and I had a straightforward transaction to discuss.

Of course I wanted to be co-operative. The work of the Weissman foundation sounded noble... even important. Yet a part of me also wondered whether I was being set up, that the foundation didn't really exist. Maybe it was her American accent, but I thought this could all be an elaborate sting operation, coming out of an investigation into Masny's death and Komarek's dealings. No matter how innocent I was of any wrongdoing, that was not how it was going to look to anyone piecing together my relationship with Komarek and Silvia now. I agreed to meet her on Saturday, on what I saw as neutral territory near the storage facility, at a small café I had found in Bermondsey.

I got there early and found us a table outside. It would be easier to talk that way, and the day was unseasonably warm. I fidgeted with my sunglasses, unsure if wearing them might make me look as if I had something to hide. I had finally put them in my breast pocket when she arrived. I knew it had to be her by the confident way she walked. It just seemed so American. And I guessed correctly.

I ordered a lager and she found an herbal tea I had never seen on the menu. I remarked on what an exotic choice that was for Bermondsey, laying it on a little thick that I was a man of simple tastes, and I think she sensed it.

She chipped away at this veneer of mine soon enough by asking me about my foreign service career: where I had served, what my roles were. I insisted I was not one for moving up the ladder, that I really should have been an ambassador years ago if I was at all ambitious.

I saw she had glanced down, looking at my hands, as I had hers. No ring on her finger, but I was still wearing my wedding band.

"My wife has returned to Tokyo. I have to decide whether I'm going to stay in London, now that I'm retiring. Where do you want to call home as you grow old—I never thought that was a question I'd be thinking about."

I thought I was going to be more truthful with this woman. Maybe it was how comfortable she seemed with silence—more than I was—but I felt my resolve evaporating.

I must tell you, Mr. Hepworth, it is likely one of those gentlemen was arrested in America trying to sell a stolen painting."

"The la Tour. Yes, I know. It was a fake."

"So how does a gentleman like you get involved in all of this?"

"I think you might know that already, yes? From your work with your foundation?"

She recrossed her legs and pulled back from the table, as if she was shuffling the cards in her hand for the cheat she was playing. "I probably know less than you think. I ask myself, do I trust what this Christina Perretti found, these alleged notes from your father? I'll be honest, there is some question about the provenance of *The Card Cheat*."

"Yes, there is, I know. One set of papers state it was probably owned by a family that was murdered during the war. Property of the Reichskulturkammer, yes? But there is another that states it was once the property of the Vatican. I would trust the latter."

"And why is that?"

"Because this nice woman Christina Perretti is correct. My father was a dealer of stolen artwork for the Nazis during the war. His name was Harry Maes. In your research for the foundation, maybe you heard of Galerie Maes?"

She just nodded and smiled. Of course she knew.

"I am sure you have a certain perspective about my father's work. About his complicity. You may look upon him as a thief and a criminal. I know I did."

"Provenance, true provenance matters, don't you think?"

"Of course. My mother had told me about all that he had done during the war when I was old enough to understand. And for years I was ashamed of him. I kept it a secret."

"I imagine it would be hard to keep such secrets," she said. Her tone had softened. If I was after something like forgiveness, perhaps I would have found a way to end our conversation, pay for our drinks, and make my exit. But I could have cared less about forgiveness.

I pulled out, from my battered old briefcase, the numbered and bound pages I had photocopied back at the office. "This is his testament that you were faxed, yes? Whether he tells the truth in those pages is another thing. But I have chosen to believe this is the truth."

"And why is that?"

"He does not try to justify his actions. But it is clear to me he did try to make things right, to work against evil, however he could. He was not without some measure of guilt, of course. I believe he quite openly admits it here. It would be going too far to say he was a victim. But I can't see him as evil and inhumane."

"This man was your father. Don't you think it's almost impossible to see him as evil, unless he had done evil to you?"

"Perhaps, but he did abandon me before I could understand any larger reason why. I never really forgave him for that, believe me. When I read these pages, it helped."

"I see," she said, softly.

I realized, as I was speaking, that I had never spoken so honestly to anyone about my family. Not even Eri. Perhaps because I had never felt so sure of what I knew about my own past. Finally.

"Do you forgive him now?"

"I do, yes."

"I'd like to thank you for being so honest with me, Mr. Hepworth."

"Yes, well… this is not all I have for you, Ms. Solomon. Did you think I brought you out to this part of the city for its… charming views of the Thames?"

"I guess I just figured you lived around here."

"I have something to show you in a storage facility I have rented, just a few blocks away. I'm surprised Ms. Perretti didn't tell you. My father left me more than his words, as that la Tour might have suggested."

"Other paintings?"

"Yes. The other works that really should not belong to me. This foundation… I think Harry would have approved if they ended up in your hands."

The look on her face… I had forgotten what it was like to do something that caused this reaction in another person. Of course I have always been capable of kindness, but this was something different, and I was surprised how much this feeling overwhelmed me too. She seemed quite beautiful to me in that moment.

Now I think of the image of her as a wide-eyed beauty only matched by the look on her face when she finally saw the paintings I had hidden from the world. And finally brought to light.

34.

Mr. Lorenzo Verzaro,
Director, Art Crimes Unit (Milan)
INTERPOL NCB
March 15th, 1994

Dear Lorenzo,

What else could I do but hunt down Komarek myself now? All that I had heard and transcribed from my interviews with Rifka Solomon and Nicholas Hepworth, all that I had read from the notes from Hepworth's father and from Richard Knifton, a former British intelligence officer, and all that had come from our investigation into a Russian art theft ring (how this Mirzoev actually had ties to Masny and had been to Prague before he stole the fake Card Cheat, determined to verify which version was authentic) … it pointed back to this man. The paintings that Nicholas Hepworth had donated to the Weissman foundation were only half of a collection that Harry Maes had at the time of his death. If George and Ileana Stanciu had told the truth to Hepworth—and there was no reason to believe they hadn't—then the paintings that disappeared from their residence were probably in the hands of someone with ties to Komarek. And I believed Komarek was at the very least an accessory to the murders of Silvia Stanciu and Antonin Masny.

I argued my case about Komarek to Calzetta. He heard me out, complimented me on my diligence and all the work I had done on this case in my own time. But the simple fact of the matter was that there was nothing on record regarding the theft of George and Ileana Stanciu's property. They didn't go to the police. And therefore, as far as he was concerned, there was no rationale (read: budget) for me to travel to Prague and question Komarek. I had an interesting theory, he said, but surely my academic training would tell me that a good theory was nothing but a plausible story, and we had to make decisions based on facts.

Well, it is time for my confession—on top of all the others here. I couldn't leave things at that. I booked my winter holidays and told everyone in my unit that I was heading to Lucca to see family. What I really did was catch a cheap flight to Prague.

I knew where Komarek was working. This broadcasting company that employed him had a suite of offices on some prime real estate overlooking the Vltava, just a couple of blocks from the Charles Bridge. The advantages of having Russian investors were all too evident with the gleaming chrome fixtures and plush leather furniture in the lounge of the reception area. When he came down to meet me, dressed a little too young for his age in jeans and a chic black blazer, he impressed me with his flawless English ("my thanks to Berlitz tapes") and his courtly charm.

He would be happy to speak about the ongoing investigation of Antonin Masny's murder, he said, but that was some time ago, and he felt he had told the Prague police everything he knew at the time. The more I looked at him, the more I realized he had dyed his eyebrows a slightly different tint than the black dye in his hair.

"Might we go somewhere else to talk, though? Let me take you to Café Slavia. Do you know it? While you're here, you must go. You can be my guest if we meet there at noon."

He was prompt to the minute. The restaurant was, like Komarek himself, a little too well- presented, a tourist's conception of an old Prague café, with its tall windows and green marble walls, its glittering art nouveau chandeliers. The tables were full of overweight Americans and locals who dressed as if they were making more money than they could have ever imagined. There are many places that attract the same kind of clientele in Rome of course, but I had spent most of my twenties and thirties avoiding them as much as I could. Komarek led me to a table by a window, and he seemed acutely aware of the looks we were getting from those dining nearby.

"I won't let you look at a menu. You must trust me to order for you. A guest of our city all the way from Italy."

And so I let him. He said there was a special tomato sauce, rajská, that was not on the menu but that he could get for us for our beef sirloin, which we simply had to have. "Don't worry, no one gains weight in Prague. You'll want to walk everywhere, yes?" He was doing everything he could to avoid why I had come to his office.

Once our dishes came and he had run through his list of places I simply had to see; I could no longer be quite so polite. He was exhausting. "You know I have some serious questions for you, Mr. Komarek."

"Of course," his tone remained cheerful, but he quickly sensed, from my expression, that it seemed a little odd, so his voice dropped an octave as he lamented how horrible it was that the same criminal element that had made a city like Rome so 'unlivable' was now 'infecting' Prague—as Masny's death all too tragically confirmed.

"You should know, Mr. Komarek, that it is not just your relationship to Mr. Masny that has piqued my interest. Silvia Stanciu. You knew her well."

His gaze drifted out into the street and he smiled as if he was recalling a pleasant dream. "I'm sorry, you must enlighten me. I see no connection to someone I had a brief relationship with in Berlin a hundred years ago to Antonin."

"I have seen the notes that the Stasi had on you, sir. I know of Silvia Stanciu's Russian connections and yours. I would wager that the bills of sale that were missing from Masny's office would connect you to a Mr. Sergei Mirzoev."

"Really? Your Interpol is improving, yes? Maybe you have some kids who know the world wide web like we have in our office. They amaze me, what they find."

"Many people are interested in you and your friends, Mr. Komarek. Friends you've cultivated carefully for years, I would bet."

He gently placed his fork and knife down neatly on the side of his plate and then dabbed the sides of his mouth with his starched white napkin. The dark red colour of the rajská was a bit too suggestive, I supposed.

"You have, it seems, some fragments of a story you have put together like… jigsaw puzzle… yes, like a jigsaw puzzle in your head. These fragments, to me, if I were doing your job, would come together as…"

"Circumstantial," I said. "Yes, we call it circumstantial evidence."

"Thank you. Circumstantial evidence. But I must ask, circumstantial of what? You think I kill people? An old girlfriend? An old friend?" He laughed. Too heartily, really.

"Old partners in the sales of paintings you'd discovered, that's what I'd call them. I'm actually wondering about what happened to old Harry Maes, also. But I suppose with these people they could not have meant anything more to you than transactional relationships."

"I don't like to mix business with friendship, Ms. Perretti. Or anything else. Either the business or the friendship ends badly then."

"So it seems, Mr. Komarek."

"Badly, but not necessarily tragically." He sounded cheerful again. He'd recovered his confidence.

"Tell me, then… how has it ended with Nicholas Hepworth?"

It was worth my trip to Prague to see how his expression darkened, the tremor of a deep, murderer's worry ripple to the surface of his affected calm.

"You have… nothing. You understand me? You have nothing because there is nothing but an Englishman's stories. An Englishman who did not have the guts to bring his paintings to market. Because of the secrets they would tell about him and his family."

"His father made some notes."

"Oh, did he? Are you sure?"

"I've seen them myself."

Provenance

"Let me tell you something about Hepworth. And his father Harry Maes. I helped these people, but I never trusted them. I don't believe any painting Harry Maes had was actually real."

"And yet you happily took your cut. Your finder's fee."

"Look around you, Ms. Perretti. You like this place? You like what money brings? I do. I'm not ashamed to say it. Maybe you think we should all go back to our happy socialist lives so people like you can say what tragic, suffering peasants we are. How noble, how virtuous in our poverty. It's like a religious hangover or something, yes? All your Catholic guilt and corruption, maybe. You want us to be the people you never could be after the war. Well... with the greatest respect, Ms. Interpol Perretti... fuck you."

"The paintings stolen from George and Iliana Stanciu... you know we will find them. And you know our conversation is not over."

"Maybe so. But for now it must be. I have given you too much time." He opened his wallet, quickly counted out a stack of bill notes in Czech crowns, and placed it on the saucer beside his empty coffee cup. "I wish you all the best for your stay in our beautiful city. There's an American phrase I have learned... just right for you."

"How charming. Just like you imagined our lunch would be, I suppose."

He leaned forward, as if to kiss me, and whispered, "don't worry, be happy." And then he laughed as he hurried out of the restaurant.

From the window, I watched him hurry along the wide boulevard towards the river, heading for his office. A man who had truly hit his stride, who had finally found his moment: our new age where the authentic really didn't matter anymore. A man who never looked back.

Sincerely,
Lt. Christina Perretti
Art Crimes Unit (Rome)
Interpol NC

John Delacourt

Acknowledgements

Provenance is a novel inspired by both official and unofficial, "secret" histories, including, most overtly, the case of Cornelius Gurlitt, who had hoarded the works acquired by his father, Nazi art dealer Hildebrand Gurlitt, for more than four decades. I am grateful to the many intrepid journalists who've taken on this story and unraveled all of its many narrative strands, both legal and biographical, since Gurlitt's trove of stolen art was first discovered in 2010.

The Gurlitt case represented a culmination rather than an entry point regarding my interest in "degenerate" art, the complexities of raubkunst and restitution, and the role such cultural properties, both real and fake, played in the legitimization of cold war narratives we once thought would lose their power with the "end of history." I am also grateful, over the years, for Frances Stonor Saunders' work *The Cultural Cold War*, Lynn H. Nicholas's *The Rape of Europa,* Edward Dolnick's *The Forger's Spell* and Jonathan Petropolous's *Goring's Man In Paris.*

But I'm most grateful for a story only half-told, of a young art history instructor, working at Queen's University in the sixties, who found a mentor in Anthony Blunt, the Surveyor of the Queen's Pictures and Director of the Courtauld Institute of Art. That young instructor was my uncle, Michael McCarthy, who may or may not have known Blunt was a Soviet spy.

Provenance is dedicated to the memory of Professor Michael McCarthy, who taught art history at the University of Toronto and University College Dublin, and to my wife Andrea Stewart, my best reader and the love of my life.